REMARKABLE
CREATURES

ALSO BY TRACY CHEVALIER

The Virgin Blue
Girl with a Pearl Earring
Falling Angels
The Lady and the Unicorn
Burning Bright

Remarkable Creatures

TRACY CHEVALIER

HarperCollins*Publishers*

HarperCollins*Publishers*
77–85 Fulham Palace Road,
Hammersmith, London W6 8JB

www.harpercollins.co.uk

Published by HarperCollins*Publishers* 2009
1

A catalogue record for this book
is available from the British Library

ISBN: 978 0 00 731117 0

This novel is entirely a work of fiction.
The names, characters and incidents portrayed in it,
while based on real historical figures, are the work of
the author's imagination.

Set in Giovanni

Printed and bound in Great Britain by
Clays Ltd, St Ives plc

Mixed Sources

Product group from well-managed
forests and other controlled sources
www.fsc.org Cert no. SW-COC-1806
© 1996 Forest Stewardship Council

FSC is a non-profit international organisation established
to promote the responsible management of the world's forests.
Products carrying the FSC label are independently certified
to assure consumers that they come from forests that are managed
to meet the social, economic and ecological needs
of present and future generations.

Find out more about HarperCollins and the environment at
www.harpercollins.co.uk/green

This is for my son, Jacob

I

Different from all the rocks on the beach

Lightning has struck me all my life. Just once was it real. I shouldn't remember it, for I was little more than a baby. But I do remember. I was in a field, where there were horses and riders performing tricks. Then a storm blew in, and a woman – not Mam – picked me up and brought me under a tree. As she held me tight I looked up and saw the pattern of black leaves against a white sky.

Then there was a noise, like all the trees falling down round me, and a bright, bright light, which was like looking at the sun. A buzz run right through me. It was as if I'd touched a hot coal, and I could smell singed flesh and sense there was pain, yet it weren't painful. I felt like a stocking turned inside out.

Others begun pulling at me and calling, but I couldn't make a sound. I was carried somewhere, then there was warmth all round, not a blanket, but wet. It was water and I knew water – our house was close to the sea, I could see it from our windows. Then I opened my eyes, and it feels like they haven't been shut since.

The lightning killed the woman holding me, and two girls standing next to her, but I survived. They say I was a quiet, sickly child before the storm, but after it I grew up lively and alert. I cannot say if they're right, but the memory of that lightning still runs through me like a shiver. It marks powerful moments of my life: seeing the first crocodile skull Joe found, and finding its body myself; discovering my other monsters on the beach; meeting Colonel Birch. Other times I'll feel the lightning strike and wonder why it's come. Sometimes I don't understand, but accept what the lightning tells me, for the lightning is me. It entered me when I was a baby and never left.

I feel an echo of the lightning each time I find a fossil, a little jolt that says, "Yes, Mary Anning, you are different from all the rocks on the beach." That is why I am a hunter: to feel that bolt of lightning, and that difference, every day.

2

An unladylike pursuit, dirty and mysterious

Mary Anning leads with her eyes. That was clear even the first time we met, when she was but a girl. Her eyes are button brown, and bright, and she has a fossil hunter's tendency always to be looking for something, even when on the street or in a house where there is no possibility of finding anything of interest. It makes her appear vigorous, even when she is still. I have been told by my sisters that I too glance about rather than hold a steady gaze, yet they do not mean it as a compliment as I do with Mary.

I have long noted that people tend to lead with one particular feature, a part of the face or body. My brother, John, for instance, leads with his eyebrows. It is not just that they form prominent tufts above his eyes, but they are the part of his face that moves the most, tracing the course of his thoughts as his brow furrows and clears. He is the second eldest of the five Philpot siblings, and the only son, which made him responsible for four sisters after our parents' death. Such circumstances will move anyone's eyebrows, though even as a boy he was serious.

My youngest sister, Margaret, leads with her hands. Though small, their fingers are proportionately long and elegant, and she plays the piano better than the rest of us. She is given to waving her hands about as she dances, and when she sleeps she throws her arms above her head, even when the room is cold.

Frances has been the only Philpot sister to marry, and leads with her bosom – which I suppose explains that. We Philpots are not known for our beauty. Our frames are bony, our features strong. Moreover, there was really only family money enough for one sister to marry with ease, and Frances won the race, leaving Red Lion Square to become the wife of an Essex merchant.

I have always admired most those who lead with their eyes, like Mary Anning, for they seem more aware of the world and its workings. That is why I get on best with my eldest sister, Louise. She has grey eyes, like all the Philpots, and says little, but when her eyes fix on you, you take notice.

I have always wanted to lead with my eyes as well, but I have not been so fortunate. I have a prominent jaw, and when I grit my teeth – more often than I ought, for the world frustrates me – it tenses and sharpens like an axe blade. At a ball once I overheard a potential suitor say he did not dare ask me to dance for fear of cutting himself on my face. I have never really recovered from that remark. It explains why I am a spinster, and why I dance so seldom.

I have longed to move from jaw to eye, but I have noticed that people do not change which feature they lead with, any more than they change in character. And so I am stuck with my strong jaw that puts people off, set in stone like the fossils I collect. Or so I have thought.

I met Mary Anning in Lyme Regis, where she has lived all her life. It was certainly not where I expected to live.

London was, of course, specifically Red Lion Square, where we Philpots grew up. Though I had heard of Lyme, as one does of seaside resorts when they become fashionable, we had never visited. We usually went to Sussex towns such as Brighton or Hastings during the summer. When she was alive our mother was keen for us to breathe the fresh air and bathe in the sea, for she subscribed to the views of Doctor Richard Russell, who had written a dissertation about the benefit of sea water, to bathe in and to drink as well. I refused to drink sea water, but I did swim sometimes. I was at home by the sea, though I never thought that would become a literal truth.

Two years after our parents' death, however, my brother announced at dinner one evening his engagement to the daughter of one of our late father's solicitor friends. We kissed and congratulated John, and Margaret played a celebratory waltz on the piano. But in bed that night I wept, as I suspected my sisters did as well, for our London lives as we knew them were over. Once our brother married there would be neither the place nor the money for us all to live at Red Lion Square. The new Mrs Philpot would of course want to be mistress of her own home, and fill the house with children. Three sisters was a surfeit, especially when we were unlikely to marry. For Louise and I both knew we were destined to remain spinsters. Because we had little money, our looks and characters were meant to attract husbands, yet ours were too irregular to help us. Though her eyes lifted and brightened her face, Louise was very tall – far taller than most men could manage – and had large hands and feet. Moreover, she was so quiet that suitors were unnerved by her, thinking she was judging them. She probably was. As for me, I was small and bony and plain, and I could not flirt, but would try to talk about serious things, and that drove the men away too.

We were to be moved on, then, like sheep shifted from one cropped field to another. And John must be our shepherd.

The next morning he laid on the breakfast table a book he had borrowed from a friend. "I thought for your summer holiday you might like to go somewhere new rather than visit our aunt and uncle in Brighton again," he suggested. "A little tour, if you like, along the south coast. With the war with France cutting off travel to the Continent, so many more coastal resorts are springing up. There may be places you will like even more than Brighton. Eastbourne, perhaps, or Worthing. Or further afield, to Lymington, or the Dorset coast: Weymouth or Lyme Regis." John was reciting these places as if going down a list in his head, placing a little tick beside each one as he named it. That was how his tidy solic-itor's mind worked. He had clearly thought through where he wanted us to go, though he would herd us there gently. "Have a look to see what you fancy." John tapped the book. Although he said nothing, we all knew we were looking not simply for a holiday destination, but for a new home, where we could live in gently diminished circumstances rather than as London paupers.

When he had gone out to his chambers, I picked up the book. "*A Guide to All the Watering and Sea-Bathing Places for 1804*," I read out, for Louise and Margaret's benefit. Flipping through it, I found entries on English towns in alphabetical order. Fashionable Bath had the longest entry, of course – forty-nine pages, along with a large map and a pull-out panoramic view of the city, with its even, elegant

16

facades cupped by surrounding hills. Our beloved Brighton had twenty-three pages and a glowing report. I looked up the towns our brother had mentioned, some of which were little more than glorified fishing villages, warranting only two pages of indifferent platitudes. John had made a dot in the margin of each. I expect he had read every entry in the book and chosen those that suited best. He had done his research.

"What's wrong with Brighton?" Margaret demanded.

I was reading about Lyme Regis then, and grimaced. "Here is your answer." I handed her the guide. "Look at what John has marked."

"'Lyme is frequented principally by persons in the middle class of life'," Margaret read aloud, "'who go there, not always in search of their lost health, but as frequently perhaps to heal their wounded fortunes, or to replenish their exhausted revenues'." She let the book drop in her lap. "Brighton is too expensive for the Philpot sisters, then, is it?"

"You could stay here with John and his wife," I suggested in a burst of generosity. "They could manage one of us, I expect. We may as well not all be banished to the coast."

"Nonsense, Elizabeth, we shan't be separated," Margaret declared with a loyalty that made me hug her.

That summer we toured the coast as John had suggested, accompanied by our aunt and uncle, our future sister-in-law and her mother, and John when he could manage it. Our companions made comments like "What glorious gardens! I envy those who live here all year round and can walk in them any time they like," or "This circulating library is so well stocked you would think you were in London," or "Isn't the air here so soft and fresh? I wish I could breathe this every day of the year." It was galling to have others judge our future so casually, especially our sister-in-law, who would be taking over the Philpot house and didn't seriously have to consider living in Worthing or Hastings. Her comments became so irritating that Louise began excusing herself from group outings, and I made more and more tetchy remarks. Only Margaret enjoyed the novelty of the new places, even if only to laugh at the mud at Lymington or the rustic theatre at Eastbourne. She liked Weymouth best, for King George's love of the town made it more popular than the others, with several coaches a day from London and Bath, and a constant influx of fashionable people.

As for myself, I was out of sorts throughout much of the tour. Knowing you may be forced to move somewhere can ruin it as a place for a holiday. It was difficult to view a resort as anything but inferior to London. Even Brighton and Hastings, places that previously I had loved to visit, seemed lacking in spirit and grace.

By the time we reached Lyme Regis, only Louise, Margaret and I were left: John had had to return to his chambers, and had taken his fiancée and her mother back with him, and our uncle's gout had caught up with him, sending him and our aunt limping back to Brighton. We were escorted to Lyme by the Durhams, a family we'd met in Weymouth, who accompanied us on the coach and helped us to get settled at lodgings in Broad Street, the town's main thoroughfare.

Of all the places we visited that summer, I found Lyme the most appealing. It was September by then, which is a lovely month anywhere. With its mildness and golden light, it will soften even the grimmest resort. We were blessed with good weather, and with freedom from the expectations of our family. At last I could form my own opinion of where we might live.

Lyme Regis is a town that has submitted to its geography rather than forced the land to submit to it. The hills into town are so steep that coaches cannot travel down them – passengers are left at the Queen's Arms at Charmouth or the crossroads at Uplyme and brought down in carts. The narrow road leads down to the shore, and then quickly turns its back on the sea and heads up hill again, as if it wants merely to glimpse the waves before fleeing. The bottom, where the tiny River Lym pours into the sea, forms the square in the centre of town. The Three Cups – the main inn – is there, across from the Customs House and from the Assembly Rooms that, while modest, boast three glass chandeliers and a fine bay window overlooking the shore. Houses spread out from the centre, along the coast and up the river, and shops and the Shambles market stalls march up Broad Street. It is not planned, like Bath or Cheltenham or Brighton, but wriggles this way and that, as if trying to escape the hills and sea, and failing.

But that is not all there is to Lyme. It is as if there are two villages side by side, connected by a small, sandy beach where the bathing machines are lined up, awaiting an influx of visitors. The other Lyme, at the west end of the beach, doesn't shun, but embraces the sea. It is dominated by the Cobb, a long grey stone wall that curves like a finger out into the water and shelters the shore, creating a tranquil harbour for the fishing boats and the trading ships that come from all over. The Cobb is several feet high, and wide enough for three to walk along arm in arm, which many visitors do, for it gives a fine view back to the town and the dramatic shoreline beyond of rolling hills and cliffs in green, grey and brown.

Bath and Brighton are beautiful despite their surroundings, the even buildings with their smooth stone creating an artifice that pleases the eye. Lyme is beautiful because of its surroundings, and despite its indifferent houses. It appealed to me immediately.

My sisters were also pleased with Lyme, for different reasons. For Margaret it was simple: she was the belle of Lyme's balls. At eighteen she was fresh and lively, and as pretty as a Philpot was ever going to be. She had lovely ringlets of dark hair and long arms she liked to hold aloft so that people could admire their graceful lines. If her face was a little long, her mouth a little thin, and the tendons in her neck a little prominent, that did not matter when she was eighteen. It would matter later. At least she didn't have my hatchet jaw, or Louise's unfortunate height. There were few to match her in Lyme that summer, and the gentlemen gave her more attention than at Weymouth or Brighton, where she had more competitors. Margaret was happy to live from ball to ball, filling the days in between with cards and tea at the Assembly Rooms, bathing in the sea, and strolling up and down the Cobb with the new friends she had made.

Louise did not care about balls and cards, but early on she discovered an area near the cliffs to the west of town with surprising flora and wild, secluded paths shaped by fallen rock and covered with ivy and moss. This pleased both her botanical interest and her retiring nature.

As for myself, I found my Lyme pursuit on a walk one morning along Monmouth Beach, to the west of the Cobb. We had joined our Weymouth friends the Durhams to search out a peculiar stone ledge along the beach called the Snakes' Graveyard, which was only uncovered at low tide. It was farther than we'd thought, and the stony beach was difficult to walk on in thin pumps. I had to keep my eyes cast down so as not to trip on the rocks. As I stepped between two stones, I noticed an odd pebble decorated with a striped pattern. I bent over and picked it up – the first of thousands of times I would do so in my life. It was spiral shaped, with ridges at even intervals around the spine, and it looked like a snake curled in on itself, the tip of the tail in the centre. Its regular pattern was so pleasing to the eye that I felt I must keep it, though I had no idea what it was. I only knew that it could not be a pebble.

I showed it to Louise and Margaret, and then to the Weymouth family. "Ah, that is a snakestone," Mr Durham declared.

I almost dropped it, despite logic telling me the snake could not be alive. It could not be just a stone, though. Then I realised. "It is a – fossil, isn't it?" I used the word hesitantly, for I wasn't sure the Weymouth family would be familiar with it. Of course I had read about fossils, and seen some displayed in a cabinet at the British Museum, but I didn't know they could be found so easily on the beach.

"I expect so," Mr Durham said. "People often find such things here. Some of the locals sell them as curiosities. They call them curies."

"Where is its head?" Margaret asked. "It looks as if it's been chopped off."

"Perhaps it has fallen off," Miss Durham suggested. "Where did you find the snakestone, Miss Philpot?"

I pointed out the spot, and we all looked but couldn't see the head of a snake lying about. Soon the others lost interest and walked on. I searched a little longer, then followed the party, opening my hand now and then to gaze at this, my first specimen of what I would learn to call an ammonite. It was odd to be holding the body of a creature, whatever it was, and yet it pleased me too. Gripping its solid form was a comfort, like holding on to a walking stick or a staircase banister.

At the end of Monmouth Beach, just before Seven Rocks Point, where the shoreline turned out of sight, we found the Snakes' Graveyard. It was a smooth ledge of limestone in which there were spiral impressions, white lines against the grey stone, of hundreds of creatures like that which I held, except that they were enormous, each the size of a dinner plate. It was such a strange, bleak sight that we all stared in silence.

"Those must be boa constrictors, don't you think?" Margaret said. "They're enormous!"

"But boa constrictors don't live in England," Miss Durham said. "How did they get here?"

"Perhaps they did live here, a few hundred years ago," Mrs Durham suggested.

"Or even a thousand years ago, or five thousand," Mr Durham ventured. "They could be that old. Perhaps the boa constrictors then migrated to other parts."

They did not look like snakes to me, or any other animal I knew of. I walked out onto the ledge, stepping with care so as not to tread on the creatures, even if they were clearly long dead and not so much corporeal bodies but sketches in the rock. It was difficult to imagine them as alive once. They looked permanent, as if they'd always been in the stone.

If we lived here, I could come and see this whenever I liked, I thought. And find smaller snakestones, and other fossils as well, on the beach. It was something. It was enough, for me.

Our brother was delighted with our choice. Apart from Lyme being economical, William Pitt the Younger had stayed in the town as a youth to recover his health; John found it comforting that a British Prime Minister would think highly of the place he was banishing his sisters to. We moved to Lyme the following spring, with John securing for us a cottage high above the shops and beach, at the top of Silver Street, which is what Broad Street becomes further up the hill leading out of town. Soon after, John and his new wife sold our Red Lion Square home and, with the help of her family's money, bought a newly built house on nearby Montague Street, next to the British Museum. We had not meant our choice to cut us off from our past, but it did. We had only the present and the future to think of in Lyme.

Morley Cottage was a shock at first, with its small rooms, low ceilings, and uneven floors so different from the London house we had grown up in. It was made of stone, with a slate roof, and had a parlour, dining room and kitchen on the ground floor, with two bedrooms above as well as a room in the eaves for our servant, Bessy. Louise and I shared one room, giving Margaret the other, for she complained when we stayed up late reading – Louise her botany books, I my works on natural history. There was not enough room in the cottage to fit our mother's piano or sofa or mahogany dining table. We had to leave them behind in London and buy smaller, plainer furniture in nearby Axminster, and a tiny piano in Exeter. The physical reduction of space and furnishings mirrored our own contraction, from a substantial family with several servants and plenty of visitors, to a reduced household with one servant to cook and clean, in a town with many fewer families whom we could socialise with.

We soon grew used to our new home, however. Indeed, after a time our old London house seemed too big. Its high ceilings and huge windows had made it hard to heat, and its dimensions had been larger than a person truly required; the grandeur false if you were not grand yourself. Morley Cottage was a lady's home, the size of a lady's character and expectations. Of course, we never had a man live there and so it is easy to think that way, but I believe a man of our position in society would have been uncomfortable. John was whenever he visited; he was always bumping his head on the beams, tripping over uneven door sills, ducking his head to look out of the low windows, wavering on the steep stairs. Only the hearth in the kitchen was bigger than the grates in Bloomsbury.

We also grew used to the smaller social circle of Lyme. It is a solitary place — the nearest city of any size is Exeter, twenty-five miles to the west. As a result its residents, while conforming to the social expectations of the time, are peculiar and unpredictable. They can be small-minded, yet tolerant as well. It is not surprising that there are several Dissenting sects in the town. Of course the main church, St Michaels, is still the Church of England, but there are other chapels too that serve those who question the traditional doctrine: Methodists, Baptists, Quakers, Congregationalists.

I found a few new friends in Lyme, but it was more the stubborn spirit of the place as a whole that appealed to me rather than specific people – until I got to know Mary Anning, that is. To the town we Philpots were for years considered London transplants, to be viewed with some suspicion and a little indulgence too. We were not well off – £150 per annum does not allow three spinsters many treats – but we were certainly better off than many in Lyme, and our background as educated Londoners from a solic-itor's family brought us a degree of respect. That we all three were without men I am sure gave people plenty of mirth, but at least they aimed their smirks at our backs rather than our faces.

Although Morley Cottage was unremarkable, it did offer stupendous views of Lyme Bay and the string of eastern hills along the coast, punctuated by the highest peak, Golden Cap, and ending, on clear days, with the Isle of Portland lurking off land like a crocodile, submerged but for its long flat head. I often rose early and sat at the window with my tea, watching the sun rise and give Golden Cap its name, and the sight softened the sting I still felt at having moved to this remote, shabby watering hole on England's southwest coast, far from the busy, vital world of London. When the sun drenched the hills I felt I could accept and even benefit from our isolation here. When it was cloudy, however, blowing a gale or simply a monotonous grey, I despaired.

We had not long been installed in Morley Cottage before I grew certain that fossils were to be my passion. For I had to find a passion: I was twenty-five years old, unlikely ever to marry, and in need of a hobby to fill my days. It is so tedious being a lady sometimes.

My sisters had already claimed their territories. Louise was on her hands and knees in the Silver Street garden, pulling up hydrangeas, which she thought vulgar. Margaret was indulging her love of cards and dancing at Lyme's Assembly Rooms. She persuaded Louise and me to go with her whenever she could, though she soon found younger accomplices. There is nothing to put off potential suitors more than old spinster sisters in the background, making dry remarks behind their gloves. Margaret had just turned nineteen, and still had great hopes for her prospects at the Assembly Rooms, though she did complain of the provincial quality of the dancing and frocks.

For myself, it took only the early discovery of a golden ammonite, glittering on the beach between Lyme and Charmouth, for me to succumb to the seductive thrill of finding unexpected treasure. I began frequenting the beaches more and more, though at the time few women took an interest in fossils. It was seen as an unladylike pursuit, dirty and mysterious. I didn't mind. There was no one I wanted to impress with my femininity.

Certainly fossils are a peculiar pleasure. They do not appeal to everyone, for they are the remains of creatures. If you think on it too much, you would wonder at holding in your hands a long dead body. Then too, they are not of this world, but from a past very difficult to imagine. That is why I am drawn to them, but also why I prefer to collect fossilised fish, with their striking patterns of scales and fins, for they resemble fish we eat every Friday, and so seem more a part of the present.

It was fossils that first brought me in contact with Mary Anning and her family. I had hardly collected a handful of specimens before I decided I needed a cabinet in which to display them properly. I have always been the organiser amongst the Philpots – the arranger of Louise's flowers in vases, the one to set out the china Margaret brought from London. This need to put things in order led me to Richard Anning's cellar workshop in Cockmoile Square at the bottom of the town. Square is far too grand a word for the tiny open space about the size of a good family's drawing room. Though just around the corner from the town's main square, where fashionable folk went, Cockmoile Square was made up of shabby houses where tradesmen lived and worked. One corner of the square held the town's tiny gaol, with stocks sitting out front.

Though Richard Anning had been recommended to me as a decent cabinet maker, I would soon have been drawn there anyway, if only to compare my fossils to those at the table young Mary Anning tended outside the workshop. She was a tall, lean child, with the hard limbs of a girl used to working rather than playing with her dollies. She had a rather plain, flat face, made interesting by bold brown eyes like pebbles. As I approached, she was sifting through a basket of specimens, picking out pieces of ammonites and tossing them into different bowls as if playing a game. Even at that early age she was able to tell apart the various types of ammonites by comparing the suture lines around their spiralled bodies. She glanced up from her sorting, her look spirited and full of curiosity. "You want to buy curies, ma'am? We got some nice ones here. Look, here's a pretty sea lily, only a crown." She held up a beautiful piece of crinoid, its long fronds spread out indeed like a lily. I do not like lilies. I find their sweet scent too cloying, and prefer sharper scents: I have Bessy dry my sheets on the rosemary bush in Morley Cottage's garden, while she hangs my sisters' over lavender. "Do you like it, ma'am – miss?" Mary persisted.

I flinched. Was it so very obvious that I was not married? Of course it was. For one thing, I had no husband with me, looking after and indulging me. But there was something else about married women that I noticed, their solid smugness at not having to worry about the course of their future. Married women were set like jelly in a mould, whereas spinsters like me were formless and unpredictable.

I patted my basket. "I have my own fossils, thank you. I am here to see your father. Is he in?" Mary nodded towards steps that led down to an open door. I ducked into a dim, filthy room crammed with wood and stone, the floor covered with shavings and gritty stone dust. It smelled so strongly of varnish that I almost backed out, but I could not, for Richard Anning was staring at me, his sharp, shapely nose pinning me to the spot like a dart. I never like people who lead with their noses: they pull everything to the centre of their faces, and I feel trapped by their concentration.

He was a lithe man of medium height, with dark, lustrous hair and a strong jaw. His eyes were the kind of dark blue that hides things. It always annoyed me how handsome he was, given his harsh, teasing nature and his sometimes rough manners. He did not pass on his looks to his daughter, who might have had more use for them.

He was perched over a small cabinet with glass doors, holding a brush coated with varnish. I took against Richard Anning from the start because he did not even set down the brush, and barely glanced at my specimens as I described what I wanted. "A guinea," he announced.

It was an outrageous figure for a specimen cabinet. Did he think he could take advantage of a London spinster? Perhaps he thought I was well off. For a moment, as I glared at his handsome face, I considered waiting for my brother to deal with him when he next came down from London. But that could be many months, and besides, I could not rely on my brother for everything. I was going to have to make my way in Lyme without the tradesmen laughing behind my back.

It was clear to me from looking around his shop that Richard Anning needed the business. I should use that to my advantage. "It is a pity that you have suggested such an exorbitant sum," I said, wrapping my fossils in muslin and placing them back in my basket. "I would have made your name prominent on each case, and everyone who looked at my collection would have seen it. Now, however, I shall have to go elsewhere, to someone more reasonable."

"You going to show *them* to others?" Richard Anning nodded at my basket, his incredulity deciding me: I would find someone in Axminster, or even Exeter if I had to, rather than give this man my business. I knew I would never like him.

"Good day to you, sir," I said, turning to sweep up the steps. I was thwarted in my dramatic departure, however, by Mary, standing square in the entrance and blocking my way. "What curies you got?" she demanded, her eyes on my basket.

"Clearly nothing that would be of interest to you," I muttered, pushing past her and out to the square. I hated being stung by Richard Anning's tone. Why should I care for a cabinet maker's opinion? In truth, I'd thought my bits and pieces rather fine, for someone new to finding fossils. I had found a complete ammonite, as well as parts of several others, and the long shaft of a belemnite, the pointed tip intact rather than broken, as they so often are. Now I could see, even as I passed the Annings' table in my anger, that their fossils far exceeded mine in both variety and beauty. They were whole, polished, varied, and abundant. There were specimens displayed on the table I hadn't even known were fossils: bivalves of sorts, a heart-shaped rock with a pattern on it, a creature with five long waving arms.

Mary had ignored my rude remark and followed me out. "You got any verteberries?"

I paused, my back to her, the table, the whole wretched workshop. "What is a verteberry?"

I heard a rustling by the table, the clinking of stones knocked together. "From a crocodile's back," Mary said. "Some say they're the teeth, but Pa and I know better. See?"

I turned to look at the stone she held out. It was about the size of a twopence coin, though thicker, and round but with squared-off sides. Its surface was concave, the centre nipped in as if someone had pressed it between two fingers while it was soft. I recalled the skeleton of a lizard I'd seen at the British Museum.

"A vertebra," I corrected, holding the stone in my hand. "That is what you mean. But there are no crocodiles in England."

Mary shrugged. "Just not seen 'em. Perhaps they've gone somewhere else. Like to Scotland."

I could not help smiling.

When I went to hand back the vertebra, Mary glanced around to see where her father was. "Keep it," she whispered.

"Thank you. What is your name?"

"Mary."

"That is very kind of you, Mary Anning. I shall treasure it."

I did treasure it. It was the first fossil I put in my cabinet.

It is funny now to think of that, our first meeting. I would never have guessed then that I would come to care about Mary more than anyone other than my sisters. How can a twenty-five-year-old middle-class lady think of friendship with a young working girl? Yet even then, there was something about her that drew me in. We shared an interest in fossils, of course, but it was more than that. Even when she was just a girl, Mary led with her eyes, and I wanted to learn how to do so myself.

Mary came to see us a few days later, having discovered where we lived. It is not hard to find anyone in Lyme Regis – there are only a few streets. She appeared at the back door as Louise and I were in the kitchen, picking the stems off the elderflowers we'd just gathered to make into a cordial.

Margaret was practising a dance step around the table while trying to convince us to make the flowers into champagne instead – though she did not offer to help, which might have made me more amenable to her suggestion. Because of her clatter and chatter we did not at first notice young Mary leaning against the door frame. It was Bessy, huffing into the kitchen with the sugar we'd sent her to get at the shops, who saw her first.

"Who's that, then? Get away from there, girl!" she cried, puffing out her doughy cheeks.

Bessy had accompanied us from London, and relished complaining about her revised situation: the steep climb from the town to Morley Cottage, the sharp sea breeze that made her chesty, the impenetrable accent of the locals she met at the Shambles, the Lyme Bay crabs that brought her out in a rash. While Bessy had been a seemingly quiet, solid girl in Bloomsbury, Lyme brought out in her a bullishness she expressed with her cheeks. Behind her back we Philpots laughed at her complaints, though at times it brought us close to giving her notice as well, when she wasn't threatening to leave.

Mary didn't budge from the door sill, Bessy's temperament having no effect. "What you making?"

"Elderflower cordial," I replied.

"Elderflower *champagne*," Margaret corrected, with an accompanying flourish of her hand.

"Never had that," Mary said, eyeing the lacy flower heads and sniffing at the muscat bloom that filled the room.

"There is such an abundance of elderflowers here in June," Margaret said. "You should be making things out of them. Isn't that what country folk do?"

I winced at my sister's patronising words. But Mary didn't seem offended. Instead her eyes followed Margaret, who was now spinning about the room in a waltz, dipping her head over one shoulder, then the other, twisting her hands in time to her humming.

Lord help her, I thought, the girl is going to admire the silliest of us. "What is it, Mary?" I did not mean to sound so short.

Mary Anning turned to me, though her eyes kept darting back to Margaret. "Pa sent me to say he'll make the cabinet for a pound."

"Will he, now?" I had gone off the idea of the cabinet if it was to be made by Richard Anning. "Tell him I will think on it."

"Who is our visitor, Elizabeth?" Louise asked, her fingers still in the elderflowers.

"This is Mary Anning, the cabinet maker's daughter."

At the name, Bessy turned from the table, where she was turning out a fruitcake she had left to cool. She gaped at Mary. "You the lightning girl?"

Mary dropped her eyes and nodded.

We all looked at her. Even Margaret stopped waltzing to stare. We had heard about the girl struck by lightning, for people still talked of it years later. It was one of those miracles small towns thrive on: children seeming drowned then spurting out water like a whale and reviving; men falling from cliffs and reappearing unscathed; boys run down by coaches and standing up with only a scratched cheek. Such everyday miracles knit communities together, giving them their legends to marvel at. It had never occurred to me when I first met her that Mary might be the lightning girl.

"Do you remember being struck?" Margaret asked.

Mary shrugged, clearly uncomfortable with our sudden interest.

Louise never liked that sort of attention either, and made an effort to break up the scrutiny. "My name is Mary too. I was named after my grandmothers. But I didn't like Grandmother Mary as much as Grandmother Louise." She paused. "Would you like to help us?"

"What do I do?" Mary stepped up to the table.

"Wash your hands first," I ordered. "Louise, look at her nails!" Mary's nails were rimmed with grey clay, her blunt fingers puckered from limestone. It was a state I would become familiar with in my own fingers.

Bessy was still staring at Mary. "Bessy, you can clean in the parlour while we're working here," I reminded her.

She grunted and picked up her mop. "I wouldn't have a girl who's been struck by lightning in my kitchen."

I tutted. "Already you're becoming as superstitious as the local people you like to look down on."

Bessy blew out her cheeks again as she banged her mop against the door jamb. I caught Louise's eye and we smiled. Then Margaret began to waltz around the table again, humming.

"For pity's sake, Margaret, do your dancing elsewhere!" I cried. "Go and dance with Bessy's mop."

Margaret laughed and pirouetted out of the door and down the hallway, to our young visitor's disappointment. By then, Louise had Mary plucking stems from the flower heads, careful to shake the pollen into the pot rather than around the kitchen. Once she understood what she was to do, Mary worked steadily, pausing only when Margaret reappeared in a lime green turban. "One feather or two?" she asked, holding up one, then another ostrich feather to the band crossing her forehead.

Mary watched Margaret with wide eyes. At that time turbans had not yet arrived in Lyme – though I can report now that Margaret pushed the fashion onto Lyme's women, and within a few years, turbans were a common sight up and down Broad Street. I am not sure they complement empire-line gowns as well as other hats, and I believe some laughed behind their hands at the sight, but isn't fashion meant to entertain?

"Thank you for helping with the elderflowers," Louise said when the flowers were soaking in hot water, sugar and lemon. "You may have a bottle of it when it's ready."

Mary Anning nodded, then turned to me. "Can I look at your curies, miss? You didn't show me the other day."

I hesitated, for I was a little shy now to reveal what I had found. She was remarkably self-possessed for a young girl. I suppose it was working from such an early age that did it, though it was tempting, too, to blame the lightning. However, I could not show my reluctance, and so I led Mary into the dining room. Most people when they enter the room remark on the impressive view of Golden Cap, but Mary did not even glance through the window. Instead she went straight to the sideboard, where I had laid out my finds, much to Bessy's disgust. "What are those?" She gestured to the slips of paper beside each fossil.

"Labels. They describe when and where I found the fossil, and in which layer of rock, as well as a guess at what they might be. That is what they do at the British Museum."

"You been there?" Mary was frowning at each label.

"Of course. We grew up near it. Do you not keep track of where you find things?"

Mary shrugged. "I don't read nor write."

"Will you go to school?"

She shrugged again. "Sunday school, maybe. They teach reading and writing there."

"At St Michael's?"

"No, we ain't Church of England. We're Congregationalists. Chapel's on Coombe Street." Mary picked up an ammonite I was especially proud of, for it was whole, not chipped or cracked, and had fine even ridges on its spiral. "You can get a shilling for this ammo, if you give it a good clean," she said.

"Oh, I'm not going to sell it. It's for my collection."

Mary gave me a funny look. It occurred to me then that the Annings never collected to keep. A good specimen to them meant a good price.

Mary set down the ammonite and picked up a brown stone about the length of her finger, but thicker, with faint spiral markings on it. "That's an odd thing," I said. "I'm not sure what it is. It could be just a stone, but it seems – different. I felt I had to pick it up."

"It's a bezoar stone."

"Bezoar?" I frowned. "What's that?"

"A hair ball like you find in the stomachs of goats. Pa told me about them." She put it down, then took up a bivalve shell called a gryphaea, which the locals likened to the Devil's toenails. "You haven't cleaned this gryphie yet, have you, miss?"

"I scrubbed the mud off."

"But did you scrape it with a blade?"

I frowned. "What kind of blade?"

"Oh, a penknife will do, though a razor's better. You scrape at the inside, to get the silt and such out, and give it a good shape. I could show you."

I sniffed. The idea of a child teaching me how to do something seemed ridiculous. And yet. . . "All right, Mary Anning. Come along tomorrow with your blades and show me. I'll pay you a penny per fossil to clean them."

Mary brightened at the suggestion of payment. "Thank you, Miss Philpot."

"Off you go, now. Ask Bessy on the way out to give you a slice of her fruitcake."

When she was gone Louise said, "She remembers the lightning. I could see it in her eyes."

"How could she? She was little more than a baby!"

"Lightning must be hard to forget."

The following day Richard Anning agreed to make me a specimen cabinet for fifteen shillings. It was the first of many cabinets I have owned, though he was only to make four for me before he died. I have had cabinets of better quality and finish, where the drawers glide without sticking and the joints don't need to be re-glued after a dry spell. But I accepted the flaws of his workmanship, for I knew that the care he neglected to put into his cabinets he put into his daughter's knowledge of fossils.

Soon Mary had found her way into our lives, cleaning fossils for me, selling me fossil fish she and her father had found once she discovered I liked them. She sometimes accompanied me to the beach when I went out hunting for fossils, and though I didn't tell her, I was more at ease when she was with me, for I worried about the tide cutting me off. Mary had no fear of that, for she had a natural feel for the tides that I never really learned. Perhaps to have that sense you must grow up with the sea so close you could leap into it from your window. While I consulted tide tables in our almanac before going out on the beach, Mary always knew what the tide was doing, coming in or going out, neap or spring, and how much of the beach was exposed at any given time. On my own I only went along the beach when the tide was receding, for I knew I had a few clear hours – though even then I often lost track of time, as is so easy to do while hunting, and would turn to find the sea creeping up on me. When I was with Mary she naturally kept track in her head of the movement of the sea.

I valued Mary's company for other reasons too, as she taught me many things: how the sea sorts stones of similar sizes into bands along the shore, and which band you might find what fossils in; how to spot vertical cracks in the cliff face that warn of a possible landslip; where to access the cliff walks we could use if the tide did cut us off.

She was also handy as a companion. In some ways Lyme was a freer place than London; for example, I could walk about town on my own, without needing to be accompanied by my sisters or Bessy, as I would in London. The beach, however, was often empty save for a few fishermen checking crab pots; or scavengers of debris whom I suspected were smugglers; or travellers walking at low tide between Charmouth and Lyme. It was not considered a place for a lady to be out on her own, not even by independent Lyme standards. Later, when I was older and better known in town, and when I was less bothered about what others thought of me, I went out alone on the beach. But in those early days I preferred company. Sometimes I could convince Margaret or Louise to come with me, and occasionally they even found fossils. Though Margaret hated to get her hands dirty, she did enjoy finding chunks of iron pyrites, for she liked the glitter of fool's gold. Louise complained of the deadness of rock compared to the plants she preferred, though she did sometimes scramble up the cliffs and study blades of sea grass with her magnifying glass.

We spent much of our time on the mile-long beach between Lyme and Charmouth. East past the Annings' house, at the end of Gun Cliff, the shore bends sharply to the left so that the beach is out of sight of the town. The shore is flanked for several hundred yards by Church Cliffs, which are made up of what is called Blue Lias – layers of limestone and shale with a blue-grey tint forming a striped pattern. The beach then curves gently around to the right before straightening out towards Charmouth. High above the beach past that curve hangs Black Ven, an enormous landslip that has created a slanted layer of mudstone from the cliffs down to the shore. Both Church Cliffs and Black Ven hold many fossils, gradually releasing them over time onto the shoreline below. That was where Mary found many of her finest specimens. It was also where we experienced some of our greatest dramas.

By our second summer in Lyme, Margaret had settled well into her new life. She was young, the sea air gave her a fresh complexion, and she was new, and therefore the object of much attention amongst the entertaining set. She soon had her favourite partners for whist, her preferred bathing companions, and families who would parade with her along the Cobb. During the season there was a ball at the Assembly Rooms every Tuesday, and Margaret did not miss a dance, becoming a favourite for being so light on her feet. Louise and I sometimes accompanied her, but she soon found more interesting friends to go with: London or Bristol or Exeter families in Lyme for part of the summer, as well as a few select Lyme residents. Louise and I were relieved not to have to go each time. Ever since the cutting remark I had overheard about my jaw years before, I had not been comfortable dancing, preferring to sit and watch or, better, read at home. One hundred and fifty pounds per annum between three sisters does not leave money for the purchase of many books, and Lyme's circulating library contained mostly novels, but I requested that any gifts at Christmas or birthdays should be of books on natural history. I went without a new shawl so that I might buy a book instead. And friends from London lent books to me.

My sisters did not complain of missing London life. Being the centre of attention in a modest place suited Margaret better than fighting to be noticed amongst thousands in London society. Louise also seemed more content, for the quiet suited her nature. She loved the garden at Morley Cottage, with its view of Lyme Bay and a huge hundred-year-old tulip tree in one corner. The garden was much bigger than we'd had in Red Lion Square. There, of course, we'd had gardeners, whereas now Louise did most of the work herself, and preferred it that way. The climate challenged her as well, for the salty wind demanded hardier plants than those that thrived in soft London rain: hebe and sedum and juniper, salvia and thrift and sea holly. She created rose beds more beautiful than any I had seen in Bloomsbury.

Of the three it was I who thought of London most. I missed the currency of ideas. In London we had been part of a wide circle of solicitors' families, and social occasions had been mentally stimulating as well as entertaining. Often I had sat with my brother and his friends at dinner as they discussed Napoleon's prospects, or whether Pitt ought to have become Prime Minister again, or what should be done about the slave trade. I even occasionally contributed to the conversation.

In Lyme, however, I heard no such talk. Though I had my fossils to keep me occupied, there were few people I could discuss them with. When I read Hutton or Cuvier or Werner or Lamarck or other natural philosophers, I could not go around to friends to ask what they made of these men's radical ideas. The Lyme middle classes were surrounded by noteworthy natural phenomena, but they did not show much curiosity about them. Instead they talked about the weather and the tides, the fishing and the crops, the visitors and the season. You might think they would be concerned about Napoleon and the war with France, if only because of its effect on the small shipbuilding industry in Lyme. But local families discussed repairs to the sea wall that was taking a battering, or the bath house not long opened that was doing so well others were sure to copy it, or whether the town mill was grinding flour fine enough. Summer visitors we met at the Assembly Rooms or at church or over cups of tea at others' houses could sometimes be encouraged to discuss topics of more substance, but often they were travelling to get away from such talk, and relished local news and gossip.

I was particularly frustrated, as the fossils I was finding were so very puzzling, and filled me with questions I wanted to air. Ammonites, for instance, the most visible and striking of the fossils found at Lyme: what exactly were they? I could not believe they were snakes, as so many unquestioningly did. Why would they curl up into balls? I had never heard of snakes doing such a thing. And where were their heads? I looked carefully each time I found an ammonite, but could discover no trace of a head. It was very peculiar that I could find so many fossils of them on the beach, and yet not see them alive.

This did not seem to bother others, however. I hoped someone might suggest to me over a cup of tea in our parlour, "Do you know, Miss Philpot, ammonites remind me rather of snails. Do you think they might be a sort of snail we haven't seen before?" Instead they talked about the mud on the road from Charmouth; or what they were going to wear to the next ball; or the travelling circus they were going to Bridport to see. If they did say something about fossils, it was to question my interest. "How can you be so fond of mere stones?" a new friend Margaret brought back from the Assembly Rooms once asked.

"They're not just stones," I tried to explain. "They are bodies that have become stone, of creatures that lived long ago. When one finds them, that is the first time they have been seen for thousands of years."

"How horrible!" she cried, and turned to listen to Margaret play. Visitors often turned to Margaret when they found Louise too quiet and me too peculiar. Margaret could always entertain them.

Only Mary Anning shared my enthusiasm and curiosity, but she was too young to engage in such conversations. I sometimes felt in those early years that I was waiting for her to grow up so that I could have the companionship I craved. In that, I was right.

At first I thought I might talk about fossils with Henry Hoste Henley, Lord of Colway Manor and Member of Parliament for Lyme Regis. He lived in a large house set back at the end of an avenue of trees on the outskirts of Lyme, about a mile from Morley Cottage. Lord Henley had a large extended family; apart from his wife and many children, there were also Henleys in Chard, several miles inland, and Colway Manor brimmed with guests. We were occasionally invited too – to a dinner, to their Christmas ball, to watch the start of the hunt, where Lord Henley handed out port and whisky before the hunters rode out.

The Henleys were the closest to gentry that Lyme had, but Lord Henley still had mud on his boots and dirt under his nails. He had a collection of fossils too, and when he found out I was interested, he sat me at his side at dinner so that we could talk about them. Thrilled at first, I discovered after a few minutes that Lord Henley knew nothing about fossils other than that they were collectible and made him appear worldly and intelligent. He was the kind of man who led with his feet rather than his head. I tried to draw him out by asking what he thought an ammonite was. Lord Henley chuckled and sucked in a great slug of wine. "Has no one told you, Miss Philpot? They are worms!" He banged his glass onto the table, a signal for a servant to refill it.

I considered his reply. "Why, then, are they always coiled? I have never seen a live worm take such a shape. Or a snake, which some suggest is what they are."

Lord Henley shuffled his feet under his chair. "I expect you haven't seen many people lying on their backs with their hands crossed on their chests, have you, now Miss Philpot? Yet that is how we bury them. The worms are coiled in death."

I held back a snort, for I had a vision of worms gathered around to roll one of their dead into a coil, as we prepare our own in death. It was clearly a ridiculous idea, and yet Lord Henley did not think to question it. I did not probe further, however, for down the table Margaret was shaking her head at me, and the man sitting across from me had raised his eyebrows at our indelicate talk.

Now I know that ammonites were sea creatures rather like our modern nautilus, with protective shells and squid-like tentacles. I wish I could have told Lord Henley so at that dinner, with his assured talk of coiled worms. But at that time I had neither the knowledge nor the confidence to correct him.

Later, when he showed me his collection, Lord Henley revealed more ignorance, not being able to distinguish one ammonite from another. When I pointed out one marked with straight, even suture lines crossing its spiral while on another each line had two knobs picking out the spiral shape, he patted my hand. "What a clever little lady you are," he said, shaking his head at the same time and under-cutting the compliment. I sensed then that he and I would not puzzle over fossils together. I had the patience and eye for detail needed to study them, where Lord Henley painted with a much broader brush, and did not like to be reminded of it.

James Foot was a friend of the Henleys, and our paths must have crossed at Colway Manor, certainly at the Christmas ball, when half of West Dorset came. But Louise and I first heard of him over breakfast after one of the summer dances at the Assembly Rooms.

"I can eat nothing," Margaret declared on sitting down at the table and waving away a plate of smoked fish. "I am too agitated!"

Louise rolled her eyes and I smiled into my tea. Margaret often made such pronouncements after balls, and though we laughed at them, we would not have her stop, for these remarks formed our primary entertainment.

"What is his name this time?" I asked.

"James Foot."

"Indeed? And are his feet all you could hope for?"

Margaret made a face at me and took a slice of toast from the rack. "He is a gentleman," she declared, crumbling her toast into bits that Bessy would later have to throw onto the lawn for the birds. "He is a friend of Lord Henley's, he has a farm near Beaminster, and he is a fine dancer. He has already asked me for the first dance on Tuesday!"

I watched her fiddling with her toast. Although I had heard similar words often enough before, something about Margaret herself was different. She seemed more clearly defined, and more self-contained. She kept her chin down, as if holding back extra words, and tucked into herself to listen to new feelings she was trying to comprehend. And though her hands were still busy, their movements were more controlled.

She is ready for a husband, I thought. I gazed at the tablecloth – pale yellow linen embroidered at the corners by our late mother and now sprinkled with crumbs – and said a short prayer, asking God to favour Margaret as He had Frances. When I lifted my eyes I met Louise's, and they must have reflected mine, both sad and hopeful. It was likely mine were more sad than hopeful, however. I had sent many prayers to God that had gone unanswered, and wondered sometimes whether or not my prayers had been received and heard at all.

Margaret continued to dance with James Foot, and we continued to hear of him over breakfast, dinner, tea and supper, out on walks, while trying to read at night. At last Louise and I accompanied Margaret to the Assembly Rooms so that we might see him for ourselves.

I found him very agreeable to look at, more than I'd expected – though why shouldn't Dorset produce men as fine-looking as any you'll meet in London? He was tall and slim, and everything about him was tidy and elegant, from his newly cut curly hair to his pale, slim hands. He wore a beautiful chocolate brown tail-coat the same colour as his eyes. It looked glorious against the pale green gown Margaret wore – which must have been why she wore it, and had taken the trouble to get me to sew on a new dark green ribbon at its waist, as well as fashion a new turban with feathers dyed to match. Indeed, since James Foot's arrival in Lyme, she had begun to fuss even more over her clothes, buying new gloves and ribbons, bleaching her slippers to remove scuffs, writing to ask our sister-in-law to send cloth from London. Louise and I did not bother much about our own clothes, wearing muted shades – Louise dark blues and greens, I mauve and grey – but we were happy

46

enough to allow Margaret to indulge in pastels and flowered patterns. And if there was money enough for only one new gown, we insisted she get it. Now I was glad, for she looked lovely dancing with James Foot in her green gown, with feathers in her hair. I sat and watched them, and was content.

Louise was less so. She said nothing at the Assembly Rooms, but when we were preparing for bed later – having left Margaret still dancing, with an assurance from friends that they would see her home – Louise declared, "He cares very much about appearances."

I secured my sleeping cap over my indifferent hair and got into bed. "So does Margaret."

Though it was too late to read, I did not blow out the candle, but watched the cobwebs flutter on the ceiling in the draught of heat from the flame.

"It is not his clothes, though they are a reflection of his inclinations," Louise said. "He wants things to be proper."

"We are proper," I protested.

Louise blew out her candle.

I knew what she meant. I had felt it when James Foot was introduced to me. He was polite and straightforward – and conventional. I found myself trying to respond as blandly as possible. As we talked, his eyes flickered over the slight fraying on the neckline of my violet gown, and I felt a judgement clicked into a place in his head, a bit of information tucked away to be brought out and considered later. "Elizabeth Philpot does not attend to her gowns," I could imagine him saying to his own sister.

For Margaret's sake I tried to be proper when James Foot visited us at Morley Cottage one day. James Foot himself was obliging too. He asked Louise to show him the garden, and offered to send her cuttings of his hydrangeas when he found she had none. She did not tell him she detested them. He was keen to examine my fossil collection, and knew more about fossils than Henry Hoste Henley. When he suggested that I go to Eype, farther east along the coast near Bridport, to look for brittle stars, he added that I was welcome to visit his nearby farm. For myself, I did not quiz him about fossils as I wanted to, but let him lead the conversation, and it was pleasant enough.

After he left Margaret was in such a daze that we took her to bathe in the sea, hoping the cold shock would sharpen her. Louise and I stood on the shore while she paddled. The bathing machine, a little closet on a cart, had been pulled far out into the water to give her privacy, and Margaret swam with it between her and the shore, preserving her modesty. Once or twice we caught a glimpse of an arm or a plume of water as she kicked.

My eyes scanned the pebbles, though I did not expect to find any fossils amongst the chunks of flint. "I thought his visit was very successful," I announced, aware of how uninspired I sounded.

"He won't marry her," Louise said.

"Why not? She's as good as anyone, and much better than many."

"Margaret would bring little money to a marriage. That may not matter to him, but if there is no money, then the character of the family he marries into becomes important."

"But we did well today, didn't we? Talking about the sorts of things he'd prefer, being agreeable but not too clever. And he was interested in us – he spent long enough with you in the garden!"

"We did not flirt with him."

"Of course not – thankfully we could leave that to Margaret!" Even as I protested, I knew what she meant. Sisters are expected to engage in sparkling conversation with their sister's suitor, to assume a slight intimacy that anticipates a familial link. However I was meant to act with James Foot, I had been awkward and leaden rather than a naturally welcoming family member. He would dread each occasion, as I already did, when we must repeat such conversations. For it had been tiresome being careful in order to please a gentleman for an afternoon. After little more than a year in Lyme I'd come to appreciate the freedom a spinster with no male relatives about could have there. It already seemed more normal to me than twenty-five years of conventional life in London had.

Of course Margaret felt differently. I watched her now as she floated into view for a moment on her back, her hands wafting about her like seaweed. She would be gazing up at the reddening afternoon sky and thinking of James Foot. I winced for her.

Perhaps for Margaret's sake I would have managed to temper my behaviour, and grown used to spending time with James Foot without it always feeling like a burden. A few weeks later, however, I had an encounter with him on the beach that undid all my previous efforts to be a benign sister.

Richard Anning had just given his daughter a special hammer he'd made, its wooden points covered with metal. Mary was keen to show me how to use it to slice open lozenge-shaped stones, called nodules, to reveal crystallised ammonites, and sometimes fish. I did not tell her I'd never handled a hammer before, though she must have realised it when she saw my first feeble attempts to swing it. She made no comment, simply corrected me until I improved, a surprisingly patient young teacher.

Although it was a fair September day, there was a chilling breeze that reminded me autumn had chased away the summer. I was on my knees, aiming sharp taps along the edge of a nodule, which I held against a flat rock. Mary was leaning over, watching and guiding. "There, Miss Elizabeth. Not too hard or it'll split the wrong way. Now, cut that bit off the end so you can prop it and hold steady. Oh! Are you all right, ma'am?"

The hammer had slipped and knocked the tip of my index finger. I popped it in my mouth to suck on it and remove the sting.

At that moment I heard stones rattle behind me, and made the mistake of turning towards the sound with my finger still in my mouth. James Foot was a few feet away, gazing down at me with a peculiar look on his face of distaste overlaid with a mask of civility. I pulled my finger out of my mouth with a squelching pop that made me blush with shame.

James Foot held out a hand to help me to my feet. As I scrambled up Mary backed away, instinctively knowing how much respectful distance to give us and yet remain my guide and chaperone.

"I was just opening that stone to see if it held any ammonites," I explained.

James Foot's eyes were not on the nodule, however. He was staring at my gloves. To protect my hands from the cold and from drying clay, I often wore gloves, as in any case would be expected of a lady outdoors, whatever the weather. While first out fossil hunting I had ruined several pairs, stained with Blue Lias clay and sea water. Now I had a pair set aside to use on the beach, ivory kid leather that was soiled and hardened from the water, with the fingers cut off to the knuckle so that I could handle things more easily. They looked odd and ugly but they were useful. I also kept a more respectable pair with me that I could slip on when visitors approached, but James Foot had not given me the time to do so.

He himself was well turned out in a double-breasted burgundy tail-coat with polished silver buttons and a brown velvet collar. His own gloves were in matching brown. His riding boots shone, as if mud didn't dare to come near.

At that moment I acknowledged to myself that I did not like James Foot, with his clean boots, and his collar and gloves matching, and his judging eye. I could never trust a man whose dominant feature was his clothes. I did not like him, and I suspected he did not like me – though he was far too polite to show it.

I clasped my hands behind my back so that he would not have to continue to stare at the offending gloves. "Where is your horse, sir?" I could think of nothing better to say.

"At Charmouth. A boy is taking him over to Colway Manor. I decided to walk the last stretch along the beach, as it is so fine."

Mary was waving at me behind James Foot's back. When she caught my eye she vigorously rubbed her cheek. I frowned at her.

"What have you found today?" James Foot asked.

I hesitated. To show him what I had would mean bringing out my gloved hands again for him to inspect. "Mary, fetch the basket and show Mr Foot what we have found. Mary knows a great deal about fossils," I added as she brought the basket to James Foot and pulled out a heart-shaped grey stone impressed with a delicate five-petal pattern.

"This is a sea urchin, sir," she said. "And here's a Devil's toenail." She held out a bivalve in the shape of a claw. "Best, though, is the biggest belemnite I ever seen." Mary held up a beautifully preserved belemnite at least four inches long and an inch wide, its tip perfectly tapered.

James Foot looked at it and went bright red. I could not think why until Mary giggled. "It looks like my brother's—"

"That's enough, Mary," I managed to interrupt in time. "Put it away, please." I too turned red. I wanted to say something, but to apologise would only make things worse. I am sure James Foot thought I had deliberately set out to embarrass him. "Will you be at the Assembly Rooms tonight?" I asked, trying to put the belemnite out of mind.

"I expect so – unless Lord Henley has other plans for me."

James Foot normally spoke very definitely about what he was and wasn't doing, but now I had the feeling he was giving himself a little room to get away. I thought I knew why, but to be sure I said, "I will tell Margaret to look out for you."

Though James Foot did not move, he gave the impression of stepping away from my statement. "If I can, I will come. Please give my regards to your sisters." He bowed, and moved away down the shore towards Lyme.

I watched him skirt a rock pool and murmured, "He will never marry her."

"Ma'am?" Mary Anning looked puzzled. And she was calling me "ma'am" now. Spinster or not, I had outgrown "miss." Ladies were called "miss" while they still had a chance of marrying.

"Nothing, Mary." I turned to her. "What was it you wanted before? You were dancing about and rubbing your face as if you'd been stung."

"You got mud on your cheek, is all, Miss Elizabeth. I thought you'd want to wipe if off so the gentleman wouldn't stare so."

I felt my cheek. "Oh dear, that as well?" I took out a handkerchief and spat on it, then began to laugh, so that I would not cry instead.

James Foot did not come to the Assembly Rooms that night. Margaret was disappointed, but did not become alarmed until the next day, when he sent word – without delivering it himself – that he had been called to Suffolk to tend to family business and would be gone some weeks. "What family?" Margaret demanded of the hapless messenger – one of Lord Henley's many cousins. "He said nothing to me about family in Suffolk!"

She wept and moped and found excuses to visit the Henleys, who could not or would not help her. I doubted James Foot had told them why he'd gone off Margaret – or at least, he would not be specific about my gloves or the belemnite. He was enough of a gentleman not to mention such a thing. But it would have been clear enough to the Henleys that we were not an appropriate family for him to marry into.

Margaret continued to attend Assembly Rooms balls and cards evenings, but she had lost her glow, and the times I went with her I sensed she had slipped from the top rung of the social ladder she had been climbing. A snub from a gentleman, whether or not it is justified, does a subtle damage to a young lady. Margaret was not asked to dance every set, and compliments on her gown and hair and complexion were less frequent. By the time the season ended she looked weary and dull. Louise and I took her to London for a few weeks to try to cheer her, but Margaret herself knew something had shifted. She had lost her best opportunity to marry, and she didn't know why.

I never told her about meeting James Foot on the beach. It might have brought some comfort to Margaret to know that my eccentricity had contributed to his decision not to continue to court her. But she would have sensed too that even if I had given up my fossils and bought new gloves, it would not have been enough. A man chooses a wife by taking an intricate measure of her and her family; it takes more than an unusual sister to throw off the calculation. James Foot had decided that the Philpots had neither the money nor the social standing for him to pursue Margaret. My brandishing stained gloves and a suggestively shaped fossil only confirmed what he had already determined.

I was upset for Margaret, but I did not regret James Foot's withdrawal. I suspected he would always have looked at me as if my gloves were soiled. And if he judged me, how would he judge my sister? Would he suck the liveliness right out of her? I could not have borne it if my sister married such a man.

Years later I ran into James Foot at Colway Manor. Margaret always had a headache coming on when we were invited to their parties and suppers, and out of loyalty Louise and I wouldn't attend without her. But once when I had gone to discuss some fossil business for the Annings with Lord Henley, I came upon James Foot and his wife arriving as I was leaving. She was small and pale and trembled like a pansy; she would never wear a turban to a ball. I knew then that it was just as well Margaret had been kept from that fate.

The summer of James Foot had been the height of Margaret's potential. The following season she was treated as a fine gown that has dated in storage, the neckline now too high or low, the cloth a touch faded, the cut no longer so flattering. We were surprised that this could happen as easily in Lyme as London, yet there was little we could do to change it. Margaret kept her friends and made new ones from the seasonal visitors. But she no longer returned at night with a sparkle and a dance around the kitchen. In time the turbans she persisted in wearing seemed less daring and more a Philpot peculiarity. She did not manage to escape into marriage like Frances, but sank into spinsterhood beside Louise and me.

There are worse fates.

3

Like looking for a four-leaf clover

I don't remember there ever being a time when I weren't out upon beach. Mam used to say the window was open when I was born, and the first thing I saw when they held me up was the sea. Our house in Cockmoile Square backed onto it next to Gun Cliff, so as soon as I could walk I'd be out there upon the rocks, with my brother Joe but a few years older to look after me and keep me from drowning. Depending on the time of year, there'd be plenty of others about, walking to the Cobb, looking at the boats, or going out in the bathing machines, which looked like privies on wheels to me. Some even went in the water in November. Joe and me laughed at them, for the swimmers would come out wet and cold and miserable, like dunked cats, but pretending it was good for them.

I had my share of tussles with the sea over the years. Even I, with the tide times as natural in me as the beat of my heart, got caught out from looking for curies and cut off by the sea creeping up, and had to wade through it or climb over the cliffs to get home. I never bathed deliberately, though, not like the London ladies coming to Lyme for their health. I always been one for solid ground, rocks rather than water. I thank the sea for giving me fish to eat, and for releasing fossils from the cliffs, or washing them out of the sea bed. Without the sea the bones stay locked up in their rock tombs forever, and we'd have no money for food and lodging.

I was always looking for curies, for as long as I can recall. Pa took me out and showed me where to look, said what they were – verteberries, Devil's toenails, St Hilda's snakes, bezoars, thunderbolts, sea lilies. Before long I could hunt on my own. Even when you go out with someone hunting, you're not beside them every step. You can't be inside their eyes, you have to use your own, look your own way. Two people can look over the same rocks and see different things. One will see a lump of chert, the other a sea urchin. When I was a girl I'd be out with Pa and he'd find verteberries in the spot I'd already turned over. "Look," he'd say, and reach over to pick one up that was right at my feet. Then he would laugh at me and cry, "You'll have to look harder than that, girl!" It never bothered me, for he was my father and he was meant to find more than me, and teach me what to do. I wouldn't have wanted to be better than him.

To me, looking for curies is like looking for a four-leaf clover: it's not how hard you look, but how something will appear different. My eyes will brush over a patch of clover, and I'll see 3, 3, 3, 3, 4, 3, 3. The four leaves just pop out at me. Same with curies: I'll wander here and there along the beach, letting my eyes drift over stones without thinking, and out will jump the straight lines of a bellie, or the stripy marks and curve of an ammo, or the grain of bone against the smooth flint. Its pattern stands out when everything else is a jumble.

Everyone hunts differently. Miss Elizabeth studies the cliff face and the ledges and the loose stones so hard you think her head will burst. She does find things, but it takes her much more effort. She don't have the eye like me.

When he hunted, my brother Joe had a different method again, and hated my way. He is three years older than me, but when we were young it felt sometimes like he was years and years older. He was like a little grown up, slow and serious and careful. It was our job to find curies and bring them back to Pa, though sometimes we set about cleaning them too, if Pa were busy with his cabinets. Joe never liked to be outside when it were blowy. He found curies, though. He was good at it even if he didn't want to do it. He had the eye. His way was to take a patch of beach, divide it into squares, and search each square equally, going back and forth at an even pace, slow and steady. He found more than me, but I found the unusual bits, the crocodile ribs and teeth, the bezoar stones and sea urchins, the things you didn't expect.

Pa hunted by using a long pole to poke amongst the rocks so he wouldn't have to bend over. He learned this from Mr Crookshanks, the friend who first taught Pa about curies. He jumped off Gun Cliff behind our house when I was only three. Pa said he'd had too much debt and even curies couldn't keep him from the workhouse. Not that Pa learned from Mr Crookshanks' mistake. Pa was always looking to find what he called the monster that would pay all our debts. Over the years we'd found teeth and verteberries and what looked like ribs, as well as funny little cubes like kernels of corn, and other bones we couldn't make out but thought must come from a big animal like a crocodile. Miss Elizabeth showed one to me once when I was cleaning curies for her. She had a book full of drawings of all sorts of animals and their skeletons, by a Frenchman called Cuvier.

Pa didn't hunt as much as we did, for he had his cabinet making, though he'd come out when he could. He preferred curies to woodwork, which upset Mam, for the money was unpredictable, and hunting took him away from Cockmoile Square and the family. She probably suspected he preferred being alone upon beach to a house full of squally babies – for she did have some squallers. All of them cried but Joe and me. Mam never come upon beach, except to shout at Pa if he went hunting on a Sunday and shamed her at Chapel. Though it didn't stop him, he agreed not to take Joe and me out on Sundays.

Other than us there were but one other who sold curies: an ancient hostler called William Lock, who worked at the Queen's Arms at Charmouth, where coaches between London and Exeter changed horses. William Lock found he could sell fossils to the travellers as they stretched their legs and looked about. As fossils were known as curiosities, or curies, he come to be called Captain Cury. Though he'd been finding and selling fossils for years – longer even than Pa had – he didn't carry a hammer, but picked up whatever was lying easily to hand, or dug things up with the spade he kept with him. He was a mean old man who looked at me funny. I stayed away from him.

We would see Captain Cury from time to time upon beach, but until Miss Elizabeth come to Lyme, the shore were deserted of other cury hunters apart from us. Mostly I went looking with Joe or with Pa. Sometimes, though,

I went down upon beach with Fanny Miller. She was the same age as me and lived just up the river from Lyme, past the cloth factory, in what we called Jericho. Her father was a wood cutter who sold wood to Pa, her mam worked at the factory, and the Millers were members of the Congregationalist Chapel in Coombe Street like us. Lyme was full of Dissenters, though it had a proper church too, St Michael's, that was always trying to lure us back. We Annings wouldn't go, though – we were proud to think differently from the traditional Church of England, even if I couldn't really say what those differences were.

Fanny was a pretty thing, small and fair-haired and delicate, with blue eyes I envied. We used to play finger games during Sunday services when it got dull, and would run up and down the river chasing sticks and leaves we'd made into boats, or picking watercress. Though Fanny always preferred the river, sometimes she would go with me upon beach between Lyme and Charmouth, though she would never go as far as Black Ven, for she thought the cliff there looked evil and stones would tumble down on her head. We would build villages from pebbles, or fill in the holes tiny clams called piddocks made in the rock ledges. At the same time I would keep an eye out for curies, so it was never just play for me.

Fanny had the eye but hated to use it. She loved pretty things: chunks of milky quartz, striped pebbles, knobs of fool's good. Her jewels, she called them. She would find these treasures, yet wouldn't touch good ammos and bellies even when she knew I wanted them. They scared her. "I don't like them," she would say with a shiver, but could never explain why, other than to say "They're ugly," if I pressed her, or "Mam says they're from the fairies." She said a sea urchin was a fairy loaf, which was their bread, and if you kept it on a shelf your milk wouldn't go sour. I told her what Pa taught me: that ammos were snakes that had lost their heads, that bellies were thunderbolts God had thrown down, that gryphies were the Devil's own toenails. That scared her even more. I knew they were just stories. If the Devil really shed that many toenails, he would have to have had thousands of feet. And if lightning was to create that many bellies, it would be striking all day long. But Fanny couldn't think like that, and would hold on to her fear. I've met plenty of others the same – frightened of what they don't understand.

But I loved Fanny, she being my one true friend then. Our family weren't popular in Lyme, for people thought Pa's interest in fossils odd. Even Mam did, though she would defend him if she heard talk about him at the Shambles or outside Chapel.

Fanny did not remain my friend, though, no matter how many jewels I brought back for her from the beach. It weren't just that the Millers were suspicious of fossils; they were suspicious of me too, especially once I started helping the Philpots, who people in town made fun of as the London ladies too peculiar even to get a Lyme man. Fanny would never come if I was going upon beach with Miss Elizabeth. She got more and more funny with me, making comments about Miss Elizabeth's bony face and Miss Margaret's silly turbans, and pointing out holes in my boots and clay under my nails. I begun to wonder if she were my friend after all.

Then when we did go along the shore one day, Fanny were so sullen that I let us get cut off by the tide, as a punishment for her mood. When she saw the last strip of sand next to the cliff disappear under a foamy wave, Fanny begun to cry. "What we going to do?" she kept sobbing.

I watched, with no desire to comfort her. "We can wade through the water or climb up to the cliff path," I said. "You choose." Myself, I did not want to wade a quarter of a mile along the cliff to the point where the town begun on higher ground. The water was freezing and the sea rough, and I could not swim, but I did not tell her that.

Fanny gazed equally fearfully at the churning sea and the steep climb we faced. "I cannot choose," she squealed. "I cannot!"

I let her cry a little more, then led her up the rough path, pulling and pushing her to the top where the cliff path goes between Charmouth and Lyme. Once she'd recovered, Fanny would not look at me, and when we neared the town she run off, and I did not try to catch her up. I had never been cruel to anyone, and did not like myself for it. But it was the start of the feeling I had ever after that I did not entirely belong to the people I ought to in Lyme. Whenever I run into Fanny Miller – at Chapel, on Broad Street, along the river – her big blue eyes turned hard like ice covering a puddle, and she talked about me behind her hand with her new friends. I felt even more like an outsider.

Our troubles truly begun when I was eleven and we lost Pa. Some say it were his own fault for taking a bad tumble one night coming back to Lyme along the cliff path. He swore he'd had no drink, but of course we could all smell it. He was lucky he weren't killed going over, but he was laid up for months. He couldn't make cabinets, and the curies Joe and I found only brought in a bit, so the debt he had already got us into become much worse. Mam said the fall weakened him so that he couldn't fight the illness when it come a few months later.

I was sad to lose him, but I had no time to dwell on it, for he left us with such debts and not a shilling in our pockets: me and Joe and Mam, and her carrying a baby born a month after we buried Pa. Joe and I had to hold her up and almost carry her into the Coombe Street Chapel for the funeral. Between us we got her there, but we were a sight, staggering in with Mam to a funeral we couldn't even pay for. They had to take up a collection in the town, and most showed up, to see what it was they had bought.

Afterwards we put Mam to bed and I went out upon beach, as I did most days, funeral or no, though I did wait till Mam were asleep. It would upset her if she knew where I was going. To her, Pa's falling off the cliff when he should have been in his workshop were just proof from God that we shouldn't have spent so much time on curies.

I walked towards Charmouth, an eye on the tide, which was coming in now but slow enough that I wouldn't get caught out yet. I got past Church Cliffs and the narrow bit where the beach curves round and then widens out, with Black Ven hanging above, grey and brown and green stripes of rock and grass like the coat of a tabby cat, slipping down gradual rather than like the sheer face of Church Cliffs. Mud from the Blue Lias oozes onto the beach there and deposits treasures for those willing to dig through it.

I searched the clay, just as I had for so many years with Pa. It were a comfort, hunting by the cliffs. I could forget he was gone, and think that if I just looked round he'd be behind me, bent over stones or poking at a seam of rock in the cliff with his stick, working in his own world while I worked in mine. Of course he weren't there that day, nor any day after, no matter how many times I looked up to catch sight of him.

I found nothing in the Blue Lias but shards of bellies, which I kept even though they were worthless with the tip broke off. Visitors only want to buy long bellies, preferably with the tip intact. But once I've picked something up it's hard to drop it again.

In the rocks, though, I discovered a complete unbroken ammonite. It fitted perfectly in my palm, and I closed my fingers over it and squeezed it. I wanted to show it to someone; you always do want to show your finds, to make them real. But Pa – who would have known how hard it was to find such a perfect ammo – Pa weren't there. I shut my eyes to stop the tears. I wanted to keep that ammo in my hand always, squeezing it and thinking of Pa.

"Hello, Mary." Elizabeth Philpot was standing over me, dark against the grey light of the sky. "I didn't expect to find you out here today."

I couldn't see her expression, and wondered what she thought of me being upon beach rather than at home, comforting Mam.

"What have you found?"

I scrambled to my feet and held out the ammo. Miss Elizabeth took it. "Ah, a lovely one. *Liparoceras*, is it?" Miss Elizabeth liked to use what she called the Linnaean names. Sometimes I thought she did it to show off. "The points on the ribs are all intact, aren't they? Where did you find it?"

I gestured to the rocks at our feet.

"Don't forget to write down where you found it, which layer of rock and the date. It is important to record it." Since I'd learned to read and write at Chapel Sunday school, Miss Elizabeth was always nagging me to make labels. She glanced down the beach. "Will the tide cut us off, do you think?"

"We've a few minutes, ma'am. I'll turn back soon."

Miss Elizabeth nodded, knowing that I would prefer to walk back on my own rather than with her. She took no offence – hunters often like to be alone. "Oh, Mary," she said as she turned to go. "My sisters and I are all very sorry about your father. I will come by tomorrow. Bessy has made a pie, Louise a tonic for your mother, and Margaret has knitted a scarf."

"That be kind," I mumbled. I wanted to ask what use scarves and tonics were to us now, when we needed coal or bread or money. But the Philpots had always been good to me, and I knew better than to complain.

A gust blew the rim of Miss Elizabeth's bonnet so that it turned inside out. She pushed it back and wrapped her shawl close, then frowned. "Where's your coat, girl? It's cold to be out without."

I shrugged. "I'm not cold." In fact, I *was* cold, though I hadn't noticed till she said so. I'd forgot my coat, which was too small for me anyway, for it held my arms back when I need them to be free. I weren't thinking about coats that day.

I waited until Miss Elizabeth had got to the curve in the deserted beach before I made my own way back, still squeezing the ammo. The line of her straight back far ahead kept me company and was a comfort of sorts. Only when

I reached Lyme did I see anyone else. A group of Londoners in town for the last of the season were strolling by Gun Cliff at the back of our house. As I slipped past them, a lady called to me, "Find anything?"

Without thinking I opened my hand. She gasped and caught up the ammo to show the others, who stopped to admire it. "I'll give you half a crown for it, girl." The lady handed the ammo to one of the men and opened a purse. I wanted to say it weren't for sale, that it was mine to help me remember Pa by, but she'd already put the coin in my hand and turned away. I stared at the money and thought, "Here is a week's bread. It'll keep us from the workhouse." Pa would've wanted that.

I hurried home, squeezing that coin tight. It was proof that we could still make a business out of the curies.

Mam no longer complained about our hunting. She didn't have time to: by the time she recovered from the shock of Pa's death, the baby were born, which she called Richard after Pa. Like all the past babies, this one were a cryer. He was never very well, and nor was Mam; she was cold and tired, with baby not sleeping well and feeding badly. It were baby's crying – that and the debt – that sent Joe out into the bitter cold he hated, one day a few months after Pa's death. We needed fossils. I wanted to go out too, even with the cold, but I was stuck indoors, jiggling baby about to stop his crying. He was such a squally little thing it was hard to like him. The only thing that shut him up was when I held him tight and jiggled him and sang "Don't Let Me Die an Old Maid" over and over.

I was just singing the last lines for the sixth time – "Come old or come young, come foolish or witty/ Don't let me die an old maid, but take me for pity" – when Joe come in, banging the door back so I jumped. A bank of cold air hit me and started baby crying again. "Look what you done!" I shouted. "He was just quieting and you gone and woke him."

Joe shut the door and turned back to me. That's when I saw that he was excited. Usually nothing stirs my brother – he has a face like a rock, with little expression or change. Now, though, his brown eyes were lit like the sun shone through them, his cheeks were red, his mouth was open. He snatched his cap off and rumpled his hair so that it stood straight up.

"What is it, Joe?" I said. "Oh, hush, baby, hush!" I put baby over my shoulder. "What is it?"

"I found something."

"What? Show me." I looked to see what he was holding.

"You have to come out. It's in the cliff. It's big."

"Where?"

"The end of Church Cliffs."

"What is it?"

"Don't know. Something – different. Long jaw, lots of teeth." Joe looked almost scared.

"It's a crocodile," I declared. "It must be."

"Come and see."

"Can't – what would I do with baby?"

"Bring him with."

"Can't do that – it's too cold."

"What about leaving him next door?"

I shook my head. "They done too much for us already – we can't ask them again, not for something like this." Our neighbours in Cockmoile Square were wary of curies. They envied us the little money we made from them, while also asking why anyone would want to part with even a penny for a bit of stone. I knew we had to ask for their help only when we really needed them.

"Take him a minute." I handed the baby to Joe and went to look at Mam in the next room. She was flat out asleep, looking so peaceful for a change that I hadn't the heart to lay screaming baby next to her. So we took him with us, wrapped in as many shawls as would stay on the little thing.

As we picked our way along the beach – slower than usual, for I was clutching baby and couldn't use my hands for balance over the stones – Joe described how he was looking for curies in the new rubble that had come down during the storms. He told me he weren't searching the cliffs themselves, but when he stood up after scrabbling round in the loose rocks, a row of teeth embedded in a seam of the cliff face caught his eye.

"Here." Joe stopped where he'd left four stones piled up, three as a base and one on top, the marker we Annings used to keep track of our finds if we had to leave them. I set down baby, who was barely whimpering by now, he were that cold, and stared hard at the layers of rock where Joe pointed. I didn't feel the cold at all, I was so excited.

Straightaway I saw the teeth, just below eye level. They weren't in even rows, but all a jumble between two long dark pieces that must have been the creature's mouth and jaw. These bones met together in a tip, making a long, pointy snout. I ran my finger over it all. It give me a lightning jolt to see that snout. Here was the monster Pa had been looking for all these years, but now would never see.

There was a bigger surge of lightning to come, though. Joe put his finger on a large bump above where the jaw was hinged. Rock covered some of it, but it looked to be circular, like a bread roll sitting on a saucer. From the curve you might think it were part of an ammonite, but there were no spiral with spines going round. Instead there were plates of bone overlaid round a big empty socket. I stared at that socket and got the feeling it was staring back.

"Is that its eye?" I asked.

"Think so."

I shuddered, one of them shivers that come over you when you're not even cold but you can't stop yourself. I didn't know crocodile eyes could be so big. In the picture Miss Elizabeth showed me the croc had little piggy eyes, not huge owly ones. It made me feel odd looking at that eye, like there was a world of curiosities I didn't know about: crocodiles with huge eyes and snakes with no heads and thunderbolts God threw down that turned to stone. Sometimes I got that hollowed-out feeling too when looking at a sky full of stars or into the deep water the few times I went out in a boat, and I didn't like it: it was as if the world were too strange for me ever to understand it. Then I would have to go and sit in Chapel until I felt I could let God take care of all the mysteries and the worry went away.

"How long is it?" I said, trying to make sense of the monster by asking questions.

"Dunno – three or four feet, just the skull." Joe ran his hand over the rock to the right of the jaw and eye. "Don't see the body."

Bits of loose shale tumbled down the cliff and fell near us. We looked up and stepped back, but nothing further come down.

I glanced at baby, wrapped up in his cocoon so he looked like a caterpillar. He'd stopped whimpering and was squinting into the grey sky. I couldn't tell if he were following the clouds that scudded across.

Far down the beach at Charmouth two men were pulling a row boat down to the shore, out to check lobster pots. Joe and I quick stepped back from the cliff, like children caught eyeing a plate of cakes. The men were too far away to see where we were or what we were doing, but we were still cautious. Though few hunted the way we did, people were sure to be interested in such a thing as the croc. And now I could see it, it was so obvious in the cliff, with its forest of teeth and saucer eye, that I was sure someone else would soon spot it.

"We got to dig out the croc," I said.

"We never dug anything this big," Joe said. "Could we even lift four feet of rock?"

He was right. I had used my hammer to get ammos out of rocks on the beach, and out of the cliff, but most of the time we let the wind and the rain wear away the cliff and release the curies for us.

"We need help," I said, though I did not like to admit it. We had already had so much help from the village since Pa's death, and it were hard to ask for more without paying, especially when it was to do with curies. Fanny Miller weren't the only one who hated fossils. "Let's ask Miss Elizabeth what to do."

Joe frowned. Like Mam and Pa, he had always been suspicious of Elizabeth Philpot. He couldn't understand what

73

a lady like her would want with curies, nor why she was willing to have anything to do with me. Joe didn't get the same feeling when he found a cury as Miss Elizabeth and I did, like we were discovering a new world. Even now, with something as amazing as the crocodile, he was quick losing his excitement, and only seeing the problems. I wanted to go to Miss Elizabeth not only because she could help us, but because she would be as thrilled as I was.

We stayed a long time, chipping at the croc with my hammer and talking about what to do. We spent so long there that the tide cut us off and we had to climb over the cliffs back to Lyme – not easy with baby in my arms. Poor mite. He died the following summer. I always wondered if it weakened him, being taken upon beach in the cold. Of course, so many of Mam's babies died that it were no surprise he didn't last. But I could have stayed inside with him, and gone the next day to see the croc. That's how fossil hunting is: it takes over, like a hunger, and nothing else matters but what you find. And even when you find it, you still start looking again the next minute, because there might be something even better waiting.

I hadn't ever seen anything better than what Joe found that day, though. That brought the lightning straight through me, as if waking me from a long sleep. I was glad to see it. I just wished I had discovered it rather than Joe. It was a surprise to everyone that Joe found such an unusual specimen, for it weren't in his nature to look out for something new. That was what I was good at. I tried not to be jealous, but it was hard. Soon enough, people forgot it was Joe who found the croc, and made it my croc. I didn't stop them, and Joe didn't seem to mind. He was happy to step back from it and just be plain Joe Anning rather than a hunter who could find a monster. It was hard for him, being part of a family so talked about and judged. If he could have stopped being an Anning, I think he would have. Since he couldn't, he kept his thoughts to himself.

Next morning we took Miss Elizabeth to see the skull. It were one of those clear cold days that makes all the rocks look crisp, though it didn't last long, the winter sun just skimming the horizon past Lyme Bay. Despite the cold, Miss Elizabeth needed no convincing, but come out straightaway, though their servant Bessy muttered and Miss Margaret twittered that they had guests coming soon. Now I was getting older I'd begun to find Miss Margaret a little silly, preferring the quietness of Miss Louise or the tartness of Miss Elizabeth. Miss Elizabeth didn't care about guests, but wanted to see the monster.

When we reached the end of Church Cliffs, I almost gasped at how clear its peculiar outline was in the cliff face. Miss Elizabeth was silent. She took off her nice gloves and put on the work gloves with the tips cut off so that she could run her fingers along its long, pointy snout and its great jumble of teeth. At the end where the jaws were hinged, she prised off a flake of stone. "Look," she said, "there is a slight upturn of its mouth where it seems to be smiling. Do you recall that in the drawing I showed you of the crocodile in Cuvier's book?"

"Yes, ma'am. But look at its eye!" I used my hammer to tap carefully and reveal more of the ring of bones that overlapped like giant fish scales round an empty centre where the eyeball must have been once.

Miss Elizabeth stared. "Are you sure that is the eye?" She seemed disturbed by it.

"Don't know what else it could be," Joe said.

"That is not how the eye looked in Cuvier's drawing."

"Maybe this one had a problem with its eye," I suggested. "Like a disease. Or maybe the Frenchman drew it wrong."

Miss Elizabeth snorted. "Only a girl like you would dare question the work of the world's finest zoological anatomist."

I frowned. I didn't like this Cuvier.

Thankfully Miss Elizabeth didn't dwell on my stupidity, nor on the croc's eye. She was more concerned with practical matters. "How are you going to get this out of the cliff? It must be four feet long at least."

"It'll take digging like we've never done before, won't it, Joe?"

Joe shrugged.

"But four feet of rock – won't that be too heavy for you? What you need are men to help you. Strong men." Miss Elizabeth thought for a moment. "What about the men building the walkway along the beach to the Cobb? They know how to cut rock, and they're strong. Perhaps they could do it for you."

"Perhaps they could, ma'am," I said, "but we haven't the money to pay 'em."

"I will advance you the money, and you can pay me back when you have sold the specimen."

I brightened. "Oh, could you, Miss Elizabeth? We would be so grateful, wouldn't we, Joe?"

But Joe weren't listening. "Mary, Miss Philpot, step away from it!" he hissed. "It's Captain Cury!"

I looked back. Clambering round the bend that hid

Lyme from us was the only other fossil hunter who might consider trying to get at our croc. While most respected other's finds, Captain Cury didn't care who had spotted something first. Once he took a giant ammonite Joe and me had begun digging out from a cliff on Monmouth Beach, and laughed in our faces when we told him it was ours. "Shouldn't have left it, then, should you? It were me finished the digging, so it's me as gets it," he'd said. Even when Pa went to talk to him about it, he swore he'd already seen it and marked it out, and that it were Joe and me that was wrong to do the digging when it was his.

Captain Cury mustn't see the croc. If he did, we would have to guard it all the time. I stepped back from the skull, picked up a likely nodule and moved down towards the water's edge where there was a flat stone good for hammering on. Joe headed in the Charmouth direction, then stopped fifty feet away to scrabble amongst small chunks of fool's gold, looking for a pyritised ammo. Golden serpents, we called them. Miss Philpot took several steps and begun studying the ground, then kneeled to pick up a stone. From under my bonnet rim I watched as Captain Cury approached the croc in the cliff face, his spade over one shoulder. Now that I had exposed its eye more clearly, the skull seemed to be staring and grinning to attract attention. Captain Cury's eyes skimmed the cliff, and he paused right where we had been standing. Joe's feet on the stones went quiet, and I stopped hammering.

Captain Cury bent over and picked up something. When he straightened, his face was just inches from the monster's eye. My heart begun to pound. Then he held out a glove. "Miss Philpot, is this yours? It's too fine for Mary."

"I expect it is mine, Mr Lock," Miss Elizabeth answered. She never called him Captain Cury, but used his real name, the way she called Joe Joseph, and ammos ammonites, and not snakestones, and bellies belemnites rather than thunderbolts. She was formal like that. "Bring it here, please."

He went over and handed it to her. I could breathe again, now he were away from the croc. "Found anything?" he asked when she'd thanked him.

"Just a gryphaea. Devil's toenail to you."

"Let's see it." Captain Cury squatted next to her. Fossil hunting does that to people – it breaks down the rules. On the beach a hostler can speak to a lady in a way he wouldn't dream of doing anywhere else.

I hurried over to rescue her. "What are you doing here, Captain Cury?" I demanded.

He chuckled. "Same as you, Mary – looking out for curies to bring in a few pennies. Mind you, you need 'em more'n I do now, don't you, the way your father left you fixed. Here." He tossed something to me. It was a golden serpent.

"This is what I think of your curies, Captain Cury." I turned and threw it as hard as I could. Though the tide was out, I got it to land in the water.

"Hey, now!" Captain Cury glared at me. No one likes to have their curies wasted like that. It's like throwing coins in the sea. "What a nasty girl you become," he said. "Must've been that lightning shook you up and made you that way. You should've carried a thunderbolt to keep from getting hit. Instead you're so mean you'll grow up into a sour old spinster no man will look at."

I opened my mouth to respond, but Miss Elizabeth got there before me. "It's time you moved on, Mr Lock," she said.

Captain Cury's glittery eyes shifted from me to her. "Next time I won't bother to pick up your glove, ma'am," he sneered. By now Joe had come back, so he said no more, but swung his spade onto his shoulder and carried on down the beach towards Charmouth, glancing back now and then.

"Mary, you were very rude to him," Miss Elizabeth said. "I'm ashamed of you."

"He was ruder to me! And to you!"

"Nevertheless, you should show respect to your elders, else they will think the worse of you."

"Sorry, Miss Philpot." I didn't feel at all sorry.

"You two stay here until the tide comes in," Miss Elizabeth commanded, "in sight of the creature, to make sure William Lock doesn't come back and discover it. I will go to the Cobb to see about engaging the men to dig out the crocodile tomorrow – if it is a crocodile. Though what else could it be?"

I shrugged. Her question made me uneasy, though I couldn't say why.

"It be one of God's creatures, of course," Joe said.

"Sometimes I wonder. . ."

"Wonder what, ma'am?" I asked.

Miss Elizabeth looked at me and Joe and seemed to come to her senses, like she just realised it was us she was with. She shook her head. "Nothing. It is just an odd-looking crocodile." She glanced at the skull once more before she left.

Twin brothers, Davy and Billy Day, come the next after-noon to dig. It was a shame the tide was lowest in the early afternoon, for it was a busier time upon the beach than the early morning or evening. We would rather have done the digging when no one was about, at least until we knew what we had, and had it secure.

The Days were quarrymen who built roads and did repairs on the Cobb. They had block-like chests and massive arms and short stocky legs, and they walked with their chests thrust forward and their arses pinched. They didn't say much, nor show any surprise when they come to the crocodile staring at them from the cliff face with its saucer eye. They treated it as the work it was, for all the world like they were cutting a block of stone to be used as paving, or for a wall, and didn't have a monster locked in it.

They ran their hands over the stone round the skull, feeling for natural fissures they could hammer wedges into. I kept quiet, for they had more experience than me with cutting rock. I would learn much from them over the years, once my hunting begun to include cutting large specimens from the cliff face or stone ledges that were uncovered at low tide. The Days were to cut many monsters for me when I couldn't do it myself.

They took their time, despite the short afternoon light and the tide creeping up and them only given half a day off for the work. Before each blow, they studied the rock surface. Once deciding on where to place the iron wedge, they then talked about the angle and force needed before at last using the hammer. At times, each tap was delicate and seemed to have no effect on the rock. Then Billy or Davy – I could never tell which was which – used all his might to strike the blow that brought out another chunk of cliff.

As they worked, a crowd gathered, both people who had been out upon beach already and children who seemed to know we were there almost before we arrived – including Fanny Miller, who would not look at me, but hung back with her friends. It's impossible to keep secrets in Lyme – the place is too small and the need for amusement too great. Even a freezing winter day won't stop people coming out to watch something new. The children ran along the shore, skimming stones and scrabbling about in the mud and sand. Some of the grown ups searched for fossils, though few knew what they were doing. Others stood and chatted, and a few men gave advice to Davy and Billy about how to cut the rock. Not everyone remained the four hours it took to get the skull out, for once the sun went behind the cliffs it got even colder. But quite a number did stay.

In the crowd was Captain Cury, come up the beach from Charmouth. When the Days finally managed to prise loose the skull, in three sections – two of the snout and eye, one with part of the head behind the eye socket – and laid it out on a stretcher made from cloth hung between two poles, Captain Cury stood over it with the others and examined the monster. He was paying special attention to the jumble of verteberries at the back of the skull. Their presence hinted at a body that must have been left behind in the cliff. It was too dark now to see back into the hole where the skull had been. We would have to come back when it was light again to look for the body.

I hated Captain Cury being so nosy but didn't dare be rude again, for he frightened me. "Don't like him here," I whispered to Miss Elizabeth. "Don't trust him. Can't you get the Days to bring it home now, ma'am?"

Billy and Davy were sitting on a rock, passing a jug and a loaf of bread between them. They looked as if they would not budge, though it was twilight, and frost was already covering the rocks and sand. "They deserve their rest," Miss Elizabeth said. "The tide will move them along soon enough."

At last the brothers wiped their mouths and stood. Once they'd picked up the stretcher, Captain Cury vanished into the gloom towards Charmouth. We headed in the opposite direction, back to Lyme, following the Days as if they were carrying a coffin to its grave. Indeed, we took the path that led into town through St Michael's graveyard, and then down Butter Market to Cockmoile Square. Along the way people stopped to peer at the slabs of stone on the stretcher, and there were murmurs of "crocodile" all along the street.

The day after we got the skull out, I run back to Church Cliffs as soon as the tide let me, but Captain Cury had already got there. He was willing to wade through water and freeze his feet so he would be first. I couldn't challenge him, for I was on my own – Joseph had been hired to do a day's work at Lyme's mill, where one of the workers had taken ill, and couldn't give up the chance to earn us a day's bread. I hid and watched Captain Cury poking into the great hole the skull had left in the cliff. Cursing him, I hoped a rock would fall from above and hit his head.

Then I had a wicked, wicked idea, and I'm ashamed to say I followed it. I never told anyone how bad I was that day. I run back along the beach, then climbed the path above Church Cliffs, creeping along it to where I was just above the crocodile hole. "God damn you, Captain Cury,"

I whispered, and pushed a loose rock the size of my fist over the edge. I heard him give a shout, and smiled as I lay flat on the ground to be sure he wouldn't see me. Though I did not mean to hurt him, I did want to scare him off.

He would be standing away from the cliff now, watching to see what more would come down. I chose a larger rock and shoved it over, along with a handful of dirt and pebbles to make it seem like an avalanche. This time I heard nothing, but kept low. If he knew what I was doing he would punish me, I was sure.

Then it occurred to me he might come looking. Though it was common for rocks to fall, Captain Cury was the suspicious sort. I crept back from the cliff and hurried back down the path. Just in time I darted behind a clump of tall grass as he come past with a face full of fury. Somehow he'd worked out the stones weren't naturally falling. I hid till he was out of sight, then nipped down the path to the beach and run along the cliff to the crocodile hole. With luck I could have a quick look before he come back, just to see if we would need to get the Day brothers digging again.

In the clear daylight it was easier to see back into the hole Billy and Davy had made. The skull had come out at an angle, and the body, depending how long it was, could extend far into the stone. With a head four foot long it could easily be ten to fifteen feet into the cliff. I crawled into the space and felt near the spot where I remembered the skull's verteberries ended. I touched a long ridge of knobbly rock and begun to scrape at it to get the dirt and clay off.

Then Captain Cury rushed up behind me in a rage. "You! Not surprised to find you here, you nasty little bitch."

I shrieked and jumped out of the hole, then flattened myself against the cliff, terrified to be caught alone with him. "Get away from me – it's my croc!" I cried.

Captain Cury grabbed my arm and twisted it behind me. He were strong for an old man. "Trying to kill me, was you, girl? I'll teach you a lesson!" He reached behind him for his spade.

I never found out what he would have taught me, for at that moment the cliff come to my aid. In the years since I've many times felt it my enemy. That day, though, the cliff sent down a shower of rocks near by, some of them as large as those I'd rolled over, accompanied by a slide of pebbles. Captain Cury, who'd been about to hurt me, suddenly become my saviour, jerking me away from the cliff as a rock smashed down where I'd just been standing. "Quick!" he cried, and we clung onto each other as we stumbled towards the water to a safe distance. Then we looked back to see that the whole section of cliff I'd been standing on top of not long before had crumbled, turning from solid ground into a river of stones raining down. The roar of it was like the thunder I'd heard as a baby, but it lasted longer and rushed through me like darkness rather than the bright buzz of lightning. It took at least a minute for the rocks and scree to finish falling to the bottom of the cliff. Captain Cury and I remained frozen, watching and waiting.

When at last the cliff stopped moving and it grew quiet, I begun to cry. It weren't just that I'd almost died. The landslip was now completely blocking the hole where the crocodile's body was. We couldn't get to it without years of digging. Captain Cury took a pewter flask from his pocket, unscrewed the top, took a swig and handed it to me.

I wiped my eyes and nose on my sleeve, then drank. I'd never had strong spirits. It burned a road down my throat and made me cough, but I did stop crying.

"Thanks, Captain Cury," I said, handing back the flask.

"All that hammering yesterday must have weakened the cliff and brought it down. There were a bit of it earlier, but I thought—" Captain Cury didn't finish. "You'll have the damnedest work ahead of you, getting anything out of there." He nodded at the landslip. "My spade's in there too. Looks like I'll have to get another."

It were almost comical how quickly hard work put him off looking for anything. Now it was my crocodile again – buried behind a pile of rubble.

4

That is an abomination

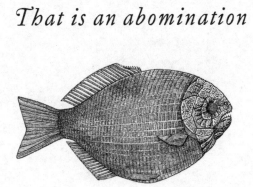

There are several people I have met throughout my life whom I have regarded with disdain, but none has angered me more than Henry Hoste Henley.

Lord Henley came to see me the day after the Days dug out the skull. He did not use the boot scraper, but trailed mud into our parlour. When Bessy announced him, Louise was out, Margaret was sewing and I was writing to our brother to tell him about the events on the beach the previous day. Margaret gave a little cry, bobbed at Lord Henley and excused herself, stumbling upstairs to her room. Although she often saw the Henleys at services at St Michael's, she did not expect ever to find him breaching the safety of her own home, where she did not have to wear her brave, light-hearted public face.

Lord Henley looked so surprised at Margaret's abrupt exit that it was clear he'd known nothing about what had gone on between her and his friend James Foot. Granted, that had taken place a few years before, and he might have expected Margaret to have got over it. Or he may have forgotten: he was not the sort of man to remember what women cared about.

Not Margaret, however. A spinster does not forget.

Nor, it appeared, had he noted our shunning of invitations to Colway Manor, or he would not have come to Morley Cottage. Lord Henley was a man of little imagination, who found it impossible to see the world through another's eyes. It made his interest in fossils preposterous: truly to appreciate what fossils are requires a leap of imagination he was not capable of making.

"You must pardon my sister, sir," I said now. "Just before you arrived she had been complaining of a cough. She would not want to inflict her illness on a visitor."

Lord Henley nodded with an attempt at patience. Margaret's health was clearly not why he was paying a visit. At my insistence he sat in the armchair by the fire, but on the edge, as if he would jump up at any moment. "Miss Philpot," he said, "I have heard you discovered something extraordinary on the beach yesterday. A crocodile, is it? I should very much like to see it." He looked about as if expecting it already to be on display in the room.

I wasn't surprised that he knew about the Annings' find. Though Lord Henley was rather grand to be included in Lyme's circle of wagging tongues, he did often employ stone cutters, as he had land abutting the sea cliffs where he extracted stone for building. Indeed, he had obtained most of his best specimens from the quarrymen, who set aside finds for him from the stone they cut, knowing they would be paid extra. The Days must have told him of what they'd dug out for the Annings.

"Your information is almost accurate, Lord Henley," I replied. "It was young Mary Anning who found it. I merely oversaw the extraction. The skull is at her house in

Cockmoile Square." Already I was leaving Joseph out of the story, as would happen for generations. Perhaps it was inevitable given his retiring nature, the very nature that would stop him correcting people when they spoke of the creature as solely Mary's discovery.

Lord Henley knew of the Annings, for Richard Anning had sold him a few specimens. He was not the sort of man to go to their workshop, however, and he was clearly disappointed that the skull was not at Morley Cottage, which was a more acceptable house for him to visit. "Have them bring it to me so I can look at it," he said, jumping to his feet, as if he suddenly realised he was wasting time with inconsequential people.

I stood as well. "It is rather heavy, sir. Did the Days tell you the skull is four feet long? They had enough to do to get it to Cockmoile Square from Church Cliffs. Certainly the Annings couldn't manage the hill to Colway Manor."

"Four feet? Splendid! I will send my coach for it tomorrow morning."

"I am not sure—" I stopped myself. I did not know what Mary and Joseph planned to do with the skull, and decided it was best not to speak for them until I did know.

Lord Henley seemed to think the specimen was his to claim. Perhaps it was – the cliffs where it was found were on Henley's land. Yet he should pay the hunters for their work and their skill at finding and extracting the fossil. I did not appreciate this proprietary attitude of the collector, who pays for others to find specimens for him to display. As I noted the greedy glitter in Lord Henley's eyes, I vowed to get Mary and Joseph a good price for the crocodile – for I knew he would want to deal with me rather than the

Annings. "I will speak to the family and see what I can arrange, Lord Henley. You may be sure of it."

When he had gone and Bessy was sweeping up the mud he'd left behind, Margaret came downstairs, her eyes red. She sat at the piano and began to play a melancholy song. I patted her shoulder and tried to comfort her. "You would not have been happy with that set."

Margaret shrugged off my hand. "You don't know how I would have felt. Just because it suits you not to marry doesn't mean the rest of us feel the same way!"

"I never said I didn't want to marry. It just didn't happen – I am not the sort of lady a man chooses to marry, for I am too plain and too serious. Now I am reconciled to being on my own. I thought you were too."

Margaret was crying again. I could not bear it, for she would make me cry as well, and I do not cry. I left her to take refuge in the dining room with my fossils. Let Louise comfort her when she returned.

Later that day I used Lord Henley's visit as an excuse to go down to Cockmoile Square. I wanted to discuss with the Annings his interest in the skull, and also to hear about what Mary had found back on the beach, for she'd told me she was going to look for the crocodile's body. When I arrived, I went first to the kitchen to speak to Mary's mother. Molly Anning was a tall, gaunt woman wearing a mop cap and a grubby white apron. She stood at the range, stirring what smelled like oxtail broth, while a baby squalled without conviction in a drawer in the corner.

I set down a bundle. "Bessy made too many rock cakes and thought you might like some, Mrs Anning. There's a round of cheese in there too, and part of a pork pie." The kitchen was cold, with the fire in the range feeble. I should have brought coal as well. I did not tell her that Bessy had made the rock cakes only because I ordered her to. Whatever their hardships, Bessy did not like the Annings, feeling – like other good families in Lyme, I expect – that our association with them demeaned us.

Molly Anning murmured thanks but did not look up. I knew she did not think much of me, for I was the embodiment of what she did not want Mary to become: unmarried and obsessed with fossils. I understood her fears. My mother would not have wished my life on me either – nor would I, a few years back. Now I was living it, though, it was not so bad. In some ways I had more freedom than ladies who married.

The baby continued to wail. Of the ten children Molly Anning had borne, only three survived, and this one did not sound as if he would last his infancy. I looked around for a nurse or maid, but of course there was none. Forcing myself to go over to him, I gave the swaddled body a pat, which only made him cry harder. I have never known what to do with babies.

"Leave him, ma'am," Molly Anning called. "Attention will only make him worse. He'll settle in a bit."

I stepped away from the drawer and looked about, trying not to reveal my dismay at the shabbiness of the room. Kitchens are normally the most welcoming part of a house, but the Annings' lacked the basic warmth and well-stocked feeling that encourages lingering. There was a battered table with three chairs pulled up to it and a shelf holding a few chipped plates. No bread or pies or jugs of milk sat out as they did in our kitchen, and I felt a sudden fondness for

Bessy. However much she grumbled, she kept the kitchen full of food, and that abundance was a comfort that spread through Morley Cottage. The security she created was what saw us Philpot sisters through the day. Not to have it must gnaw at the gut as much as real hunger did.

Poor Mary, I thought. To be on the cold beach all day and come back to this. "I'm here to see Mary and Joseph, Mrs Anning," I said aloud. "Are they about?"

"Joe's got work at the mill today. Mary's downstairs."

"Did you see the skull they brought back from the beach yesterday?" I couldn't help asking. "It is quite exceptional."

"Haven't had the time." Molly picked up a head of cabbage from a basket and began to chop at it savagely. She led with her hands, though not as Margaret did with frivolous gestures. Molly's were always busy with work: stirring, wiping, clearing.

"It is just downstairs, though," I persisted, "and well worth a look. It would only take a moment. You could do it now – I'll look after the soup and the baby while you go."

Molly Anning grunted. "You look after the baby, eh? I'd like to see that." Her chuckle made me turn red.

"They'll get a good price for the crocodile once they've cleaned it up." I spoke of the skull in the one way I knew would interest her.

Indeed, Molly Anning looked up, but didn't have a chance to reply before Mary came clattering up the stairs. "You here to see the croc, Miss Philpot?"

"And you as well, Mary."

"Come down, then, ma'am."

I had been in the Annings' workshop a handful of times during the years we'd lived in Lyme, to order cabinets from

Richard Anning, or to pick up or drop off specimens for Mary to clean, though most often she came to me. While Richard Anning worked as a cabinet maker, the room had been a battleground between the elements representing two parts of his life: the wood he made a living from and the stone that fed his interest in the natural world. Still stacked against the wall on one side of the room were sheets of wood planed fine, as well as smaller strips of veneer. Buckets of old varnish and tools littered the floor, which was strewn with wood shavings. Little had been touched on this side of the room in the months since Richard Anning's death, though I suspected the Annings had sold some of the wood in order to eat, and would soon sell off the rest, as well as the tools.

On the other side of the room were long shelves crammed with chunks of rock containing specimens as yet unlocked by Mary's hammer. Also on the shelves and on the floor, in no order that I could discern in the dim light, were crates of various sizes containing a jumble of broken bits of belemnites and ammonites, slivers of fossilised wood, stones carrying traces of fish scales, and many other examples of half-realised, incomplete, or inferior fossils that could never be sold.

Over all of the room, uniting wood and stone, there lay the finest coat of dust. Crumbled limestone and shale creates sticky clay and, when dry, a ubiquitous dust that is almost as soft and fine as talcum powder, gritty underfoot and drying to one's skin. I knew this dust well, as did Bessy, who complained bitterly about having to clean up after me when I brought back specimens from the cliffs.

I shivered, partly from the cold of the cellar, where there was no fire, but also because the room's disorder upset me. When out collecting I had learned to discipline myself and not pick up every bit of fossil I found, but look instead for whole specimens. Both Bessy and my sisters would rebel against the insistent creep of partial fossils over all available space. Morley Cottage was meant to be our refuge from the harsh outdoor world. If allowed indoors at all, fossils had to be tamed – cleaned, catalogued, labelled and placed in cabinets, where they could be looked at safely without threat to the order of our daily lives.

The chaos in the Annings' workshop signalled to me something worse than poor housekeeping. Here was muddled thinking and moral disorder. I knew Richard Anning had been politically rebellious, with admiring stories still circulating years later about a riot he had led protesting over the price of bread. The family were Dissenters – not unusual in Lyme, perhaps, which because of its isolation seemed to be a haven for independent Christians. I had no ill feelings towards Dissenters. I wondered, though, if now her father was gone, Mary might benefit from a little more order in her life – physical if not spiritual.

However, I would put up with a great deal of dirt and confusion in order to see what had been laid out on a table in the middle of the room and surrounded by candles, like a pagan offering. There were not enough candles to light it properly, though. I vowed to have Bessy drop off some the next time she came down the hill.

On the beach with so many others about, I'd not had much chance to study the skull. Now, seen in full rather than in silhouette, it looked like a craggy, knobbly model of a mountainous landscape, with two hillocks bulging out like Bronze Age tumuli. The crocodile's grin, now that I could see all of it, seemed otherworldly, especially in the flickering candlelight. It made me feel I was peering through a window into a deep past where such alien creatures lurked.

I looked for a long time in silence, circling the table to inspect the skull from every angle. It was still entrapped in stone, and would need much attention from Mary's blades, needles and brushes – and a good bit of hammering too. "Take care you don't break it when you clean it, Mary," I said, to remind myself that this was work, not a scene from one of the gothic novels Margaret enjoyed scaring herself with.

Mary twisted her face up in indignation. "Course I won't, ma'am." Her confidence was just for show, however, for she hesitated. "It'll be a long job, though, and I don't know how best to go about it. I wish Pa were here to tell me what to do." The importance of the task seemed to overwhelm her.

"I've brought you Cuvier as a guide, though I am not sure how much it will help." I opened the book to the page with the drawing of a crocodile. I had studied it earlier, but now, standing next to the skull with the picture in hand, it was clear to me that this could be no crocodile – or not a species we were aware of. A crocodile's snout is blunt, its jaw line bumpy, its teeth many different sizes, its eye a mere bead. This skull had a long, smooth jaw and uniform teeth. The eye sockets reminded me of pineapple rings I was served at the dinner at Lord Henley's when I discovered how little he knew about fossils. The Henleys grew pineapples in their glass house, and it was a rare treat for me, which even my host's ignorance could not sour.

If it was not a crocodile, what was it? I did not share my concern about the animal with Mary, however, as I had begun to on the beach, before thinking the better of it. She was too young for such uneasy questions. I had discovered from conversations I'd had about fossils with the people of Lyme that few wanted to delve into unknown territory, preferring to hold on to their super-stitions and leave unanswerable questions to God's will rather than find a reasonable explanation that might challenge previous thinking. Hence they would rather call this animal a crocodile than consider the alternative: that it was the body of a creature that no longer existed in the world.

This idea was too radical for most to contemplate. Even I, who considered myself open-minded, was a little shocked to be thinking it, for it implied that God did not plan out what He would do with all of the animals He created. If He was willing to sit back and let creatures die out, what did that mean for us? Were we going to die out too? Looking at that skull with its huge, ringed eyes, I felt as if I were standing on the edge of a cliff. It was not fair to bring Mary there with me.

I laid the book down next to the skull. "Did you have a look for the body this morning? Did you find anything?"

Mary shook her head. "Captain Cury was nosing about. Not for long, though – there was a landslip!" She shivered, and I noted that her hands were trembling. She picked up her hammer as if to give them something to do.

"Is he all right?" Although I did not care for William Lock, I would not have him killed, especially by the falling rocks that terrified me and other hunters.

Mary grunted. "Nothing wrong with him, but the croc's body's buried under a pile of rubble. We'll be a time waiting for it."

"That is a shame." Behind this understatement I hid my disappointment. I had wanted to see the body of such a creature. It might provide some answers.

Mary tapped at the edge of the rock with her hammer, knocking off a sliver attached to the jaw. She seemed less bothered about this delay, perhaps because she was more used to having to wait to get even the most basic things: food, warmth, light.

"Mary, Lord Henley has paid me a visit and enquired after the skull," I said. "He would like to see it, with a view to paying you for it."

She looked up, her eyes bright. "He would? What will he pay?"

"I expect you could get five pounds for it. I can agree the terms for you. I think he rather expects me to. But. . ."

"What, Miss Elizabeth?"

"I know you need the money now. But if you wait until you find the body, and unite it with the head, I think you'll be able to sell the whole specimen for more than if it's in two parts. The skull is unusual as it is, but it would be spectacular if united with its body." Even as I said it I knew this was too difficult a decision for Mary to make. What child can look beyond the bread that will fill her stomach now to the fields of wheat that may feed her for years to come? I would have to sit her mother down and discuss the matter.

"Mary, Mr Blackmore wants to see the croc!" Molly Anning shouted down the stairs.

99

"Tell him to come back in half an hour!" Mary called back. "Miss Philpot ain't done yet." She turned to me. "People been stopping by all day to see it," she added proudly.

Molly's feet appeared on the stairs. "Reverend Gleed from Chapel is waiting too. Tell your Miss Whatsit there be other folk wants a look. Anyone would think this were a shop with new frocks just come in," she muttered.

That gave me an idea for a way the crocodile head could bring in a bit of money to the Annings if they were prepared to wait for the body. And they would not have to take the skull up to Colway Manor for Lord Henley to see it.

The next morning Mary and Joseph and two of his stronger friends carried the skull over to the Assembly Rooms in the main square, just around the corner from the Annings. The rooms were used little for much of the winter, to Margaret's lasting despair. The main room had a large bay window that looked south out to sea and let in sufficient light for the specimen to be clearly displayed. A steady stream of visitors paid a penny to look at it. When Lord Henley arrived – I had sent a boy with a message to invite him – Mary wanted to charge him a penny too, but I frowned at her and she lapsed into a sullen silence I fretted might put Lord Henley off an eventual sale.

I need not have worried. Lord Henley cared nothing about what Mary thought. Indeed, he hardly noticed her, instead making a show of examining the skull with a magnifying glass he had brought with him. Mary was so curious to use the glass herself that she came out of her sulk and hovered at Lord Henley's shoulder. She did not dare ask him for the glass, but when he handed it to me to use I let her have a turn. Similarly, he directed questions about where the skull was found and how it was extracted to me, and I answered for Mary.

Only when he asked about the whereabouts of the body did she respond before I could. "We don't know, sir. There were a landslip at the site, and if it's there it's buried. I'll be watching for it. It just needs a good storm to wash it out."

Lord Henley stared at Mary. I suppose he wondered why she was speaking; he had already forgotten she was involved. Then, too, she was not very presentable, to a gentleman or to anyone: her dark hair was matted from all of her time outdoors and the lack of a brush, her nails were ragged and rimmed with clay, and her shoes were caked with mud. She had grown tall in the last year without having a new dress, and the hem of her skirt was too high, and her wrists and hands shot out from her sleeves. At least her face was bright and keen, despite her wind-burned cheeks and the grubbiness of her skin. I was used to her looks, but seeing her from Lord Henley's eyes made me flush with shame for her. If this was who was responsible for the specimen he was already claiming for his own, Lord Henley would indeed be concerned for its well-being.

"It is a splendid specimen, is it not, Lord Henley?" I interjected. "It just needs cleaning and preparing – which I shall oversee, of course. But think how striking it will look when reunited with its body one day!"

"How long will you require for the cleaning?"

I glanced at Mary. "A month at least," I guessed. "Perhaps longer. No one has dealt with such a large creature before."

Lord Henley grunted. He was eyeing the skull as if it

were a haunch of venison dressed in port sauce. It was clear he wanted to take it back to Colway Manor immediately – he was the sort of man who made a decision and did not like to wait for the results. However, even he could see that the specimen needed attention – partly to present it in its best light, but also to preserve it. The skull had been pressed between layers of rock in the cliff, protecting it from exposure to air and keeping it damp. Now that it was free it would soon dry out and begin to crack as it shrank, unless Mary sealed it with the varnish her father had used on his cabinets. "All right, then," he said. "A month to clean it, then bring it to me."

"We ain't giving up the skull till the body turns up," Mary declared.

I frowned and shook my head at her. I was trying to lead Lord Henley gently to the notion of paying for the skull and body together, and Mary was blundering into my delicate negotiations. She ignored me, however, and added, "We're keeping the head at Cockmoile Square."

Lord Henley gazed at me. "Miss Philpot, why should this child have any say over what happens to the specimen?"

I coughed into my handkerchief. "Well, sir, she did find it – she and her brother – so I suppose her family has some claim on it."

"Where is the father, then? I should be talking to him, not to a—" Lord Henley paused, as if saying "woman" or "girl" were too undignified for him.

"He died a few months ago."

"The mother, then. Bring the mother here." Lord Henley spoke as if commanding a groom to bring his horse.

It was hard to picture Molly Anning bargaining with Lord

Henley. The day before she had agreed that I would try to convince Lord Henley to wait for a complete specimen. We had not discussed her doing the business dealings herself. I sighed. "Run and fetch your mother, Mary."

We waited in awkward silence for them to come back, taking refuge in studying the skull. "Its eyes are rather large for a crocodile, do you not think, Lord Henley?" I ventured.

Lord Henley scuffed his boots on the floor. "It's simple, Miss Philpot. This is one of God's early models, and He decided to give the subsequent ones smaller eyes."

I raised my eyebrows. "Do you mean God rejected it?"

"I mean God wanted a better version – the crocodile we know now – and replaced it."

I had never heard of such a thing. I wanted to ask Lord Henley more about this idea, but he always stated things so baldly that there was no room for questions. He made me feel an idiot, even when I knew he was a bigger one than I.

It was just as well that we were interrupted by Molly Anning. Mercifully she did not bring the crying baby, but arrived trailing Mary and the smell of cabbage. "I'm Molly Anning, sir," she said, wiping her hands on her apron and looking around her, for she would never have been inside the Assembly Rooms. "I run our fossil shop. What was it you wanted?" She was the same height as Lord Henley, and her level gaze seemed to subdue him a little. She surprised me too. I had never heard of the workshop being called a shop, or of her having anything to do with it. But then, without a husband, she had to take on new tasks. Running a business appeared to be one of them.

"I want to take this specimen, Mrs Anning. If your daughter will allow it," Lord Henley added with a touch of sarcasm. "But then, your daughter answers to you, does she not?"

"Course." Molly Anning barely glanced at the skull. "How much you want to pay, then?"

"Three pounds."

"That—" I began.

"I expect there be plenty of gentlemen prepared to pay more," Molly Anning talked over me. "But we'll take your money, if you like, as a deposit for the whole creature once Mary finds it."

"And if she doesn't?"

"Oh, she'll find it all right. My Mary always finds things. She's special like that – always has been, since she was struck by lightning. That were in your field, weren't it, Lord Henley, where she was struck?"

Several things astonished me: that Molly Anning was talking so confidently to a member of the gentry; that she had rather cleverly allowed him to name his price, throwing him off balance and getting an idea of the worth of an object whose value she didn't know; that she had the cunning to make the lightning strike seem to be his responsibility. Most surprising, though, she had actually complimented her daughter just when Mary needed it. I'd heard people say that Molly Anning was an original; now I understood what they meant.

Lord Henley hardly knew how to respond. I stepped in to help him out. "Of course, the Annings will give you the head for three pounds if the body isn't found within, shall we say, two years?"

Lord Henley glanced from Molly Anning to me. "All right," he replied at length, placing his hand again on his prize.

After encountering the skull, I found it difficult to sleep, dreaming of the eyes of animals I had looked into: horses, cats, seagulls, dogs. There was a flatness in them, the lack of a God-given spark, that frightened me into wakefulness.

On Sunday I remained behind after the service at St Michael's, waving on Bessy and my sisters. "I will catch you up," I said, and stood at the back of the church, waiting for the vicar to finish his goodbyes to the other parishioners. Reverend Jones was a plain man, with a boxy head and close-cropped hair, whose thin lips twisted and turned even when every other part of him was still. I had not spoken with him except to mouth pleasantries, for he was uninspiring during services, his voice reedy, his sermons lacklustre. However, he was a man of God, and I hoped he might be able to give me guidance.

At last only a girl remained behind, sweeping the floor. Reverend Jones was going up and down the pews, picking up hymn sheets and checking for gloves or prayer books left behind. He did not see me. Indeed, it felt as if he did not want to see me. His pastoral duties over for the day, he was doubtless thinking about the dinner he would soon sit down to and the sleep by the fire afterwards. When I cleared my throat and he looked up, he could not stop his mouth tightening into a brief grimace. "Miss Philpot, is this handkerchief yours?" He held out a ball of white cloth, probably hopeful that I could be easily dismissed.

"I'm afraid not, Reverend Jones."

"Ah. You are looking for something else, perhaps? A purse? A button? A hair pin?"

"No, I wished to discuss a matter with you."

"I see." Reverend Jones pushed out his lips. "My dinner will be ready soon and I need to finish up here. You don't mind. . .?" He continued along the pews, straightening cushions as I trailed behind. All the while I could hear the scratch of the girl's broom on the floor.

"I wanted to ask you what you thought of fossils." In trying to hold his attention, my voice came out louder than I had intended in the empty church. The sweeping stopped, but Reverend Jones continued up the aisle to the oak pulpit, where he picked up his own handkerchief and put it in his pocket.

"What do I think of fossils, Miss Philpot? I do not think of them."

"But do you know what they are?"

"They are skeletons that have been compressed by rock over time to become stone themselves. Most educated people know that."

"But the skeletons – are they of creatures that still exist today?"

Reverend Jones hurried to the altar and gathered up a set of candlesticks and the altar cloth. I felt like an idiot following him about.

"Of course they exist," he said. "All of the creatures God made exist." He opened a door in the aisle to the left of the altar, which led to a small back room where church bits and pieces were stored. Over his shoulder I spied a jug labelled "Holy Water" sitting on a table. I remained in the doorway while Reverend Jones shut the candlesticks and cloth in a cupboard. "I'm afraid I don't understand your question, Miss Philpot," he called over his shoulder.

I opened my purse and poured into my palm a few bits of fossils that had found their way there. Most of my pockets and purses held fossil pieces. Reverend Jones' mouth twisted in disgust as he glanced at the contents: ammonites, belemnite shafts, a chunk of fossilised wood, a length of crinoid stem. He reacted as if I had trailed horse dung into the church on my shoes. "Why on earth are you carrying those about?"

Ignoring his question, I held out an ammonite. "I should like to know where the live versions of these are, Reverend Jones, for I have never seen one." As we gazed at the fossil, I felt for a moment that I was being sucked into its spiral, farther and farther back in time until the past was lost in the centre.

Reverend Jones' response to the ammonite was more prosaic. "Perhaps you haven't seen them because they live out at sea, and their bodies only wash up after they die." He turned away and, pulling the door shut, locked it with the deft turn of a key, a gesture he seemed to enjoy.

I stepped in front of him so that he could not hurry off to his dinner. Indeed, he could not move at all, but was pinned in the corner. Not being able to get away from me and my awkward questions seemed to disturb Reverend Jones even more than my bringing out the ammonite had. He whipped his head from side to side. "Fanny, have you done yet?" he called. There was no response, however. She must have gone outside to dump the sweepings.

"Have you heard about the crocodile head the Annings have found in the cliffs and are showing at the Assembly Rooms?" I asked.

Reverend Jones forced himself to look straight at me. He had narrow eyes that seemed to be seeking out a horizon even when they were set on mine. "I know of it, yes."

"Have you seen it?"

"I have no desire to see it."

I was not surprised. Reverend Jones showed no curiosity about anything other than what would soon be on his plate. "The specimen does not look like any creature that lives now," I said.

"Miss Philpot—"

"Someone – a member of this congregation, in fact – has suggested that it is an animal that God rejected in favour of a better design."

Reverend Jones looked aghast. "Who said that?"

"It is not important who said it. I just wondered if there was any truth in the theory."

Reverend Jones brushed down the sleeves of his coat and pursed his lips. "Miss Philpot, I am surprised. I thought you and your sisters were well versed in the Bible."

"We are—"

"Let me make it clear: you need only look to Scripture for answers to your questions. Come." He led the way back to the pulpit, where the Bible he had read from lay.

As he began flipping through the pages, the girl approached. "Reverend Jones, sir, I done the sweeping."

"Thank you, Fanny." Reverend Jones regarded her for a moment, then said, "There is something else I would like you to do for me, child. Come over to the Bible. I want you to read something out to Miss Philpot. There's another penny in it for you." He turned to me. "Fanny Miller and her family joined St Michael's a few years ago from the

Congregationalists, for they were deeply disturbed by the Annings' fossil hunting. The Church of England is clearer in its biblical interpretation than some of the Dissenters' churches. You have found much comfort here, haven't you, Fanny?"

Fanny nodded. She had wide, crystal blue eyes topped with smooth, dark eyebrows that contrasted with her fair hair. She would never lead with her eyes, though they were her best feature, but with her brow, which was wrinkled with apprehension as she gazed at the Bible.

"Don't be frightened, Fanny," Reverend Jones said to soothe her. "You are a very good reader. I have heard you at Sunday school. Start here." He laid a finger on a passage.

She read in a halting whisper:

"And God said, 'Let the waters bring forth abundantly the moving creature that hath life, and fowl that may fly above the earth in the open firmament of heaven.' And God created great whales, and every living creature that moveth, which the waters brought forth abundantly, after their kind, and every winged fowl after his kind; and God saw that it was good. And God blessed them, saying, 'Be fruitful, and multiply, and fill the waters in the seas, and let fowl multiply in the earth.' And the evening and the morning were the fifth day.

"Excellent, Fanny, you may stop there."

I thought he had finished patronising me by having an ignorant girl read out from Genesis, but Reverend Jones himself continued, "And God said, 'Let the earth bring forth the living creature after his kind, cattle, and creeping thing, and beast of the earth after his kind,' and it was so."

I stopped listening after a few lines. I knew them anyway, and couldn't bear his oboe voice, which lacked the depth one expected of a man in his position. I actually preferred Fanny's unschooled recitation. While he read I let my eye rest on the page. To the left of the Biblical words were annotations in red of Bishop Ussher's chronological calculations of the Bible. According to him, God created Heaven and Earth on the night preceding the 23rd October 4004 BC. I had always wondered at his precision.

". . .And the evening and the morning were the sixth day." When Reverend Jones finished we were silent.

"You see, Miss Philpot, it really is very simple," Reverend Jones said. He seemed much more confident now that he had the Bible with him. "All that you see about you is as God set it out in the beginning. He did not create beasts and then get rid of them. That would suggest He had made a mistake, and of course God is all-knowing and incapable of error, is He not?"

"I suppose not," I conceded.

Reverend Jones' mouth writhed. "You *suppose* not?"

"Of course not," I said quickly. "I'm sorry; it's just that I am confused. You are saying that everything we see around us is exactly as God created it, are you not? The mountains and seas and rocks and hills — the landscape is as it was at the beginning?"

"Of course." Reverend Jones looked around at his church, tidy and quiet. "We are done here, aren't we, Fanny?"

"Yes, Reverend Jones."

But I was not done. "So every rock we see is as God created it at the beginning," I persisted. "And the rocks came first, as it says in Genesis, before the animals."

"Yes, yes." Reverend Jones was becoming impatient, his mouth chewing an imaginary straw.

"If that is the case, then how did the skeletons of animals get inside rocks and become fossils? If the rocks were already created by God before the animals, how is it that there are bodies in the rocks?"

Reverend Jones stared at me, his mouth at last stilled into a tight straight line. Fanny Miller's forehead was a field of furrows. One of the pews creaked in the stillness.

"God placed the fossils there when He created the rocks, to test our faith," he responded at last. "As He is clearly testing yours, Miss Philpot."

It is my faith in *you* that is being tested, I thought.

"Now, I really am very late for my dinner," Reverend Jones continued. He picked up the Bible, a gesture that seemed to suggest he thought I might steal it. "Do not ask me difficult questions," he might as well have said.

I never again mentioned fossils to Reverend Jones.

Lord Henley had to wait almost the agreed two years for the crocodile body to emerge. At first when I saw him at church or the Assembly Rooms or on the street, he would shout each time, "Where's the body? Have you dug it out yet?" I would have to explain that the landslip was still blocking it and could not easily be shifted. He seemed not to understand until Mary and Joseph Anning and I took him one day to see the landslip for himself. He was startled, and also angry. "No one told me there was this much rock blocking it," he claimed, stomping at a bubble of clay. "You've misled me, Miss Philpot, you and the Annings."

"Indeed no, Lord Henley," I replied. "Remember, we said it may take up to two years to clear, and if the body isn't uncovered by then you will get the skull regardless."

He was still angry, and would not listen, but mounted the grey horse he rode everywhere and galloped back up the beach, spraying water.

It was Molly Anning who reined in Lord Henley. She did little but let him rant. When he had run out of words and breath, she said, "You want your three pounds back, I'll give it you now. There be plenty of others lined up to buy that skull, and for a better price too. Here, take your money." She reached into her apron pocket as if she had anything other than air in it, the money being long spent. Of course Lord Henley backed down. I envied Molly her confidence with such a man, though I didn't tell her, for she would have responded with a scornful, "And I envy you your one hundred and fifty pounds per year."

Eventually Lord Henley's pursuit of the crocodile died down. It requires patience to look for fossils. Only Mary and William Lock and I remained attentive, checking the landslip after every storm and spring tide. Mary tried to get there first, but sometimes William Lock slipped in before her.

Mercifully, a fever kept the hostler abed and got Mary and me out early the day she found it. A huge storm had lasted two days, and was too fierce for anyone to venture out during it. On the third morning I woke at dawn to a strange quiet, and knew. I left my warm bed, dressed quickly, threw on my cloak and bonnet and hurried out.

The sun was just a sliver off Portland, and the beach was empty but for a familiar figure in the distance. As I got to the end of Church Cliffs I could see the landslip was gone, the storm having scrubbed clean the beach as if expecting a special guest. Mary had climbed up onto the ledge the hole made and was hammering at the cliff. When I called to her she turned. "It's here, Miss Philpot! I found it!" she cried, jumping from the ledge. We smiled at each other. For this brief moment, before all the fuss began, we savoured the solitude of the dawn, and the purity of finding treasure together.

It took the Day brothers three days to extract the body, working around the tides. As they got out each slab and laid it on the beach, it was like watching a mosaic being put together before us. As when the skull had been dug out, a crowd gathered to watch the Days and inspect the crocodile. A few were fascinated and keen to speculate on its origins. Others enjoyed the spectacle but threw dark looks at it. "It be a monster, is what it be," a man muttered. "Watch the croc'll come and eat you in your bed if you're bad!" a mother called after her children. "Lord, it be ugly," another said. "Let Lord Henley come and lock it away in the Manor!"

Lord Henley also came to see it, though he did not even dismount from his horse. "Excellent," he declared, the horse jogging sideways as if to keep its distance from the stone slabs. "I will send my coach as soon as it's ready." He seemed to have forgotten that cleaning and mounting the specimen would take several weeks. And he still had to agree a price before the Annings would give it up.

I had expected to be involved in this negotiation, but discovered soon after the specimen had been brought back to the workshop that Molly Anning had already done the business, and Lord Henley paid them twenty-three pounds for it. Moreover, she shrewdly got him to waive any rights to other fossils they found on his property. She had even written it out in a note he signed, when I had assumed she couldn't write. I could not have done better myself.

It was only when the body had been cleaned and placed next to the skull that we could at last see the creature for what it was: an impressive, eighteen-foot stone monster unlike anything we had ever heard of. It was not a crocodile. It was not just the huge eyes, the long smooth snout and the even teeth. It also had paddles rather than legs, and its torso was an elongated barrel woven of ribs along a strong spine. It ended in a long tail, with a kink partway along the vertebrae. It made me think a bit of a dolphin, of a turtle, or a lizard, and yet none of these was quite right.

I couldn't help thinking of what Lord Henley had said about the creature being one of God's rejected models, and of Reverend Jones' response. I did not know what to make of it. Most who came to look at the specimen called it a crocodile, as did the Annings themselves. It was easier to think that was what it was, perhaps an unusual species that lived somewhere else in the world – Africa, perhaps. But I knew it was something different, and after I saw it complete, I stopped referring to it as a crocodile, instead calling it simply Mary's creature.

Joseph Anning built a wooden frame, and once Mary had cleaned and varnished the bones, they cemented into the frame the limestone slabs that held the creatures. Then she added a skim of lime plaster around the specimen to set off the bones and give the whole thing a smooth, finished appearance. She was pleased with her handiwork, but once it disappeared to Colway Manor she heard nothing from Lord Henley, who seemed to have lost interest in the specimen, like a hunter not bothering to eat the deer he has slain. Though of course, Lord Henley was no hunter, but a collector.

Collectors have a list of items to be obtained, a cabinet of curiosities to be filled by others' work. They might go out onto the beach sometimes and walk along, frowning at the cliffs as if looking at an exhibition of dull paintings. They cannot concentrate, for the rocks all look the same to them: quartz looks like flint, beef like bones. They find little more than a few bits of broken ammonite and belemnite and call themselves experts. Then they buy from the hunters what they need to make up their list. They have little true understanding of what they collect, or even that much interest. They know it is fashionable, and that is enough for them.

Hunters spend hour after hour, day after day out in all weather, our faces sunburned, our hair tangled by the wind, our eyes in a permanent squint, our nails ragged and our fingertips torn, our hands chapped. Our boots are trimmed with mud and stained with sea water. Our clothes are filthy by the end of the day. Often we find nothing, but we are patient and hard-working and not put off by coming back empty-handed. We may have our special interest – an intact brittle star, a belemnite with its sac attached, a fossil fish with every scale in place – but we pick up other things too, and are open to what the cliffs and beach offer us. Some, like Mary, sell what they find. Others, like me, keep our finds. We label the specimens, recording where and when we found them, and display them in cases with glass tops. We study and compare specimens, and we draw conclusions. The men write up their theories and publish them in journals, which I read but may not contribute to myself.

Lord Henley stopped collecting other fossils once he had Mary's creature. Perhaps he considered it the pinnacle of his collecting achievement. Those more serious about fossils know their search is never over. There will always be more specimens to discover and study, for, as with people, each fossil is unique. There can never be too many.

Unfortunately, that would not be the last of my dealings with Lord Henley. Though we occasionally nodded at each other on the street or across church pews, I had little real contact with him for some time. When I next did, it was vehement.

It began in London. We visited annually, each spring, once the roads were clear enough to travel. It was our treat for getting through another winter in Lyme. I didn't mind so much the storms and the isolation, for these were good conditions in which to find fossils. Louise, however, could not garden, and became frustrated and silent. Worse, though, was watching Margaret grow grey and melancholic. She was a summer person, needing warmth and light and variety to stimulate her. She hated the cold, and Morley Cottage was a prison she felt trapped in, with the Assembly Rooms quiet now the season was finished and no new visitors were arriving to be entertained. Winter months gave

116

her too much time to think about the years passing and the loss of her prospects and, bit by bit, her looks. She no longer had the fresh roundness of youth, but was becoming lined and thin. By March Margaret had always faded like a threadbare nightgown worn for too long.

London was her tonic. It gave all of us a dose of old friends and new fashions, of parties and fine food, of new novels for Margaret and natural history journals for me, and of the joy of having a child in the house, our young nephew Johnny providing welcome distraction from the onset of middle age. We went at the end of March, and generally stayed a month to six weeks, depending upon how irritated we became with our sister-in-law, and she with us. While too timid to show it outright, our brother's wife grew more and more brittle as the weeks went on, and found excuses to remain in her bedroom, or in the nursery with Johnny. I believe she thought we had grown coarse from living in Lyme, while we found her too concerned with how things might look to others. Lyme had fostered an independent spirit in us that surprised more conservative Londoners.

We went out a good deal – to visit friends, to plays, to the Royal Academy, and of course to the British Museum, which was so close to our brother's house that it could be seen from the drawing room windows on the first floor. I was always keen to lean over the cases containing the museum's fossil collection, fogging the glass with my breath till the guards frowned. I even donated a fine complete specimen of a dapedium, a fossil fish I was particularly fond of. In thanks, Charles Konig, the Keeper of the Natural History Department, waived the museum's entrance fee for the month I was visiting. On the label the collector was called simply Philpot, neatly sidestepping the question of my sex.

One spring during our stay in London, we began to hear excellent reports of William Bullock's Museum in the newly built Egyptian Hall on Piccadilly. His expanding collection contained art, antiquities, artefacts from all over the world, and a natural history collection. My brother took all of us there one day. The exterior was in the Egyptian style, with huge windows and doors with slanted sides, like the entrance to a tomb, fluted columns topped with papyrus scrolls, and statues of Isis and Osiris looking out over Piccadilly from their perches on the cornice above the door. The building's façade was painted a startling yellow, with MUSEUM trumpeted from a large sign. I thought it overly dramatic in amongst the otherwise sober brick buildings; but then, that was the point.

Perhaps it was just that, having become used to the simple whitewashed houses of Lyme, I found such novelty jarring. The collection in the Egyptian Hall was even more startling. Displayed in the oval entrance hall were a variety of curious pieces from all over the world. There were African masks and feathered totems from Pacific islands; tiny warrior figures in clay and decorated with beads; stone weapons and fur-lined cloaks from northern climates; a long, thin boat called a kayak, that could hold just one person, with carved paddles decorated with designs burnt into the wood. An Egyptian mummy was displayed in an open sarcophagus painted with gold leaf.

The next room was much larger and housed a collection of unconvincing paintings "by the Old Masters", we were told, though they looked to me to be copies done by indifferent Royal Academy students. More interesting were the cases of stuffed and mounted birds, from the plain English blue tit to the exotic red-footed booby brought back by Captain Cook from the Maldives. Margaret, Louise and I were content to study them, as from living in Lyme we had all become more aware of birds than we had been in London.

Bored with birds, however, little Johnny had gone on with his mother to the Pantherion, the museum's biggest room. He was gone but a moment before he came running back. "Auntie Margaret, come, you must see the enormous elephant!" He grabbed his aunt's hand and pulled her into the next room. The rest of us followed, bemused.

Indeed, the elephant was enormous. I had never seen one before, nor a hippopotamus, an ostrich, a zebra, a hyena or a camel. All were stuffed and grouped under a domed skylight in the centre of the room, in a grassy enclosure dotted with palm trees, depicting their habitat. We stood and stared, for these were rare sights indeed.

Being young and not appreciating rarity, Johnny did not look for long, but raced around the room. He ran up as I was inspecting a boa constrictor that had been wound around a palm tree above my head. "It's your crocodilly, Auntie Elizabeth! Come and see it!" He tugged my arm and gestured at an exhibit at the far end of the room. My nephew knew about the Lyme beast which he, like others, persisted in calling a crocodile. For his birthday I had done two watercolours of it for him, one of the fossil itself, the other of how I imagined the creature to have looked when it was alive. I went with Johnny now, curious to see a real crocodile and compare it to what Mary had found.

Johnny was not wrong, however: it was indeed "my" crocodile. I gaped at the display. Mary's creature lay on a gravel beach next to a pool of water with reeds poking out along the edges. When Mary first uncovered it, it had been flattened, its bones jumbled, but she had felt that she should leave it as she found it, rather than try to reconstruct it. Apparently William Bullock felt no such constraint, having prised the whole body away from the slabs that held it, rearranged the bones so the paddles had clear forms, stacked the vertebrae in a straight line, and even added what were probably plaster of Paris ribs added where some had gone missing. Worse, they'd put a waistcoat around its chest, with the paddles sticking out of the arm holes, and perched an oversize monocle by one of its prominent eyes. Near its snout was spread a tempting array of animals a crocodile might feed on: rabbits, frogs, fish. At least they had not managed to prise open the mouth and stuff prey into its craw.

The label read:

STONE CROCODILE
Found by Henry Hoste Henley
In the wilds of Dorsetshire

I had always assumed the specimen was still in one of the many rooms at Colway Manor, mounted on a wall or set on a table. To see it in an exhibition in London, laid out in a dramatic tableau so alien to what I knew of it, and claimed by Lord Henley as his own discovery, was a shock that froze me.

It was Louise who spoke for me when the rest of the family joined Johnny and me. "That is an abomination," she said.

"Why did Lord Henley buy it if he was just going to pass it on to this – circus?" I looked around and shuddered.

"I expect he made a pretty profit," my brother said.

"How could he do that to Mary's specimen? Look, Louise, they've straightened out its tail she worked so hard to preserve as she found it." I gestured to the tail, which no longer had a kink three-quarters of the way along.

Perhaps the most upsetting thing about Mary's creature being presented in this vulgar way was how much it cheapened the experience of seeing it. In Lyme people were impressed by its strangeness, and gave it hushed respect. At Bullock's Museum it was just another display amongst many, and not even the most awe-inspiring. Though I hated seeing it laid out and dressed so ludicrously, I grew angry at visitors who gave it just a quick glance before hurrying back to the flashier elephant or hippo.

John had a word with one of the attendants and discovered that the specimen had been on display since the previous autumn, meaning Lord Henley had only owned it for a few months before selling it on.

I was so angry that I could not enjoy the rest of the museum. Johnny grew bored with my mood, as indeed did everyone but Louise, who took me off to Fortnum's for a cup of tea so that I could rant without disturbing the rest of the family. "How could he sell it?" I repeated, stirring my tea violently with a tiny spoon. "How could he take something so unusual, so remarkable, so linked to Lyme and to Mary, and sell it to a man who dresses it up like a doll and shows it off as if it is something to be laughed at! How dare he?"

Louise laid her hand over mine to stop me doing damage to one of Fortnum's cups. I dropped the spoon and leaned forward. "Do you know, Louise," I began, "I think – I think it's not a crocodile at all. It doesn't have the anatomy of a crocodile, but no one wants to say so publicly."

Louise's grey eyes remained clear and steady. "What is it, if not a crocodile?"

"A creature that no longer exists." I waited for a moment, to see if God would bring the ceiling crashing down on me. Nothing happened, however, except for the waiter arriving to refill our cups.

"How can that be?"

"Do you know of the concept of extinction?"

"You mentioned it when you were reading Cuvier, but Margaret made you stop, for it upset her."

I nodded. "Cuvier has suggested that animal species sometimes die out when they are no longer suited to survive in the world. The idea is troubling to people because it suggests that God does not have a hand in it, that He created animals and then sat back and let them die. Then there are those like Lord Henley, who say the creature is an early model for a crocodile, that God made it and rejected it. Some think God used the Flood to rid the world of animals He didn't want. But these theories imply God could make mistakes and need to correct Himself. Do you see? All of these ideas upset someone. Many people, like our Reverend Jones at St Michael's, find it easiest to accept the Bible literally and say God created the world and all its creatures in six days, and it is still exactly as it was then, with all of the animals still existing somewhere. And they find Bishop Ussher's calculation of the world's age as six thousand years comforting rather than limiting and a little absurd." I picked up a langue de chat from the plate of biscuits between us and snapped it in two, thinking of my conversation with Reverend Jones.

"How does he explain Mary's creature, then?"

"He thinks they are swimming about off the coast of South America, and we haven't yet discovered them."

"Could that be true?"

I shook my head. "Sailors would have seen them. We have been sailing around the world for hundreds of years and never had a sighting of such a creature."

"And so you believe that what we were looking at in Bullock's Museum is a fossilised body of an animal that no longer exists. It died out, for reasons that may or may not be God's intention." Louise said this carefully, as if to make it crystal clear to herself and to me.

"Yes."

Louise chuckled and took a biscuit. "That would certainly surprise some members of the congregation at St Michael's. Reverend Jones might have to ask you to leave and join a Dissenting church!"

I finished the langue de chat. "I don't know that Dissenters are any different, really. They may differ doctrinally from the Church of England, but the Dissenters I know in Lyme interpret the Bible just as literally as Reverend Jones does. They would never accept the idea of extinction." I sighed. "Mary's creature needs studying, by anatomists, like Cuvier in Paris, or geologists from Oxford or Cambridge. They might be able to provide persuasive answers. But that will never happen while it is masquerading as an exotic Dorset croc at Bullock's!"

"It could be worse, tucked away in Colway Manor," Louise countered. "At least here more people will see it. And if the right people – your learned geologists – see it and recognise its worth, they may think it worth studying."

I had not thought of that. Louise was always more sensible than I. It was a relief to talk to her, and gave me a little comfort, but not enough to stem my fury at Lord Henley.

When we returned to Lyme the following month, I went to confront him, even before I saw Mary Anning. I did not announce my visit, nor tell my sisters where I was going, but strode across the fields between Morley Cottage and Colway Manor, ignoring the wildflowers and blooming hedgerows I'd missed while in London. Lord Henley was not at home, but I was directed to one of the boundaries of his property, where he was overseeing the digging of a drainage ditch. It had been a rainy spring while we were away, and my shoes and the hem of my dress were sodden and muddy by the time I reached him.

Lord Henley was sitting on his grey horse, watching his men work. It annoyed me that he did not get down and stand amongst them. By then, anything he did would have made me cross, for I'd had a whole month during which to fuel my anger. He did dismount for me, however, bowing and welcoming me back to Lyme. "How was your stay in London?" As he spoke, Lord Henley eyed my muddy skirt, probably thinking his wife would never be seen publicly in such dirty clothes.

"It was very good, thank you, Lord Henley. I was astonished, however, by something I saw at Bullock's Museum. I thought the specimen you bought from the Annings was still at Colway Manor, but I discovered you sold it on to Mr Bullock."

Lord Henley's face lit up. "Ah, the crocodile is on display, then? How does it look? I trust they spelled my name correctly."

"Your name was there, yes. I was rather surprised not to see Mary Anning named, however, nor even Lyme Regis."

Lord Henley looked blank. "Why would Mary Anning be named? She didn't own it."

"Mary found it, sir. Have you forgotten that?"

Lord Henley snorted. "Mary Anning is a worker. She found the crocodile on my land – Church Cliffs are part of my property, you know. Do you think these men – " he nodded at the men shifting mud " – do they own what is on this land simply because they dig it up? Of course not! It belongs to me. Besides which, Mary Anning is a female. She is a spare part. I have to represent her, as indeed I do many Lyme residents who cannot represent themselves."

For a moment the air seemed to crackle and buzz, and Lord Henley's piggish face bulged at me. It was my anger distorting everything. "Why did you make such a fuss to obtain the specimen if you were only going to sell it on?" I demanded when I had finally mastered my emotions.

Lord Henley's horse was becoming restless, and he stroked its neck to calm it. "It was cluttering up my library. It's much better where it is."

"Indeed it is, if that is the casual attitude you took towards it. I did not expect such fickle behaviour from you, Lord Henley. It demeans you. Good day, sir." I turned before I could see the effect of my feeble words on him, but as I stumbled away across the field I heard his bark of laughter. He did not call out to me, as other men might have. Doubtless he was glad to see the back of me, a bedraggled spinster scattering mud and bile.

As I walked I cursed under my breath, and then began to out loud, for there was no one about to hear me. "God damn you, you bloody idiot" I had never said such words aloud, nor even thought them, but I was so angry that I had to do something out of the ordinary. I was furious at Lord Henley for riding roughshod over scientific discovery; for turning a mystery of the world into something banal and foolish; for throwing my sex back at me as something to be ashamed of. A spare part, indeed.

But I was angrier at myself. I had lived nine years in Lyme Regis by then, and had come to value my independence and forthrightness. However, I had not learned to stand up to the Lord Henleys of the world. I could not tell him what I thought of his selling Mary's creature in a way that he understood. Instead he ridiculed me and made me feel it was I who had done something wrong. "Idiot. Bloody idiot!" I repeated.

"Oh!"

I looked up. I was crossing a small bridge over the river just as Fanny Miller was coming along the path that led down to the centre of town. She had clearly heard me, for her cheeks were bright red and her brow wrinkled, and her girlish eyes were wide, like shallow puddles with no depth.

I glared at her, and did not apologise. Fanny hurried away, glancing back now and then as if she feared I might follow her and swear some more. Though horrified, she was doubtless also keen to tell family and friends what the queer Miss Philpot had said.

Although I dreaded having to tell Mary about her creature, I have never been one to put off bad news – the wait only makes it worse. I went that afternoon to Cockmoile Square. Molly Anning directed me to Pinhay Bay, to the west of Monmouth Beach, where Mary had been commissioned by a visitor to extract a giant ammonite. "They want it for a garden feature," Molly Anning added with a chuckle. "Daft."

I flinched. In the Morley Cottage garden there was a giant ammonite with a one-foot diameter that Mary had helped me to dig out; I had given it to Louise for Christmas. Molly Anning probably didn't know that, as she had never come up Silver Street to see us. "Why climb a hill if there's no need to?" she often said.

Molly Anning would be glad for the money from that ammonite, however. Since selling the monster to Lord Henley, Mary had been hunting without success for another complete specimen. She had only found tantalising pieces – jawbones, fused vertebrae, a fan of small paddle bones – which brought in a little money, but far less than if she had discovered them all together.

I found her near the Snakes' Graveyard – I now called it the Ammonite Graveyard – which had attracted me to Lyme years before. She had managed to cut out the ammonite from a ledge, and was wrapping it in a sack to drag back along the beach – hard work for a girl, even one used to it.

Mary greeted me with joy, for she often said she missed me when I was making my London visit. She told me about all that she had found while I was away, and what they had managed to sell, and who else had been out hunting. "And how was London, Miss Elizabeth?" she asked finally. "Did you buy any new gowns? I see you've a new bonnet."

"Yes, I have. How observant you are, Mary. Now, I have to tell you about something I saw in London." I took a deep breath and told her about going to Bullock's and discovering her creature, describing in frank terms the state of it, down to its waistcoat and monocle. "Lord Henley should not have sold it to someone who would treat it so irresponsibly, no matter how many people got to see it," I finished. "I hope you won't be approaching him with any future finds." I did not tell her I had just been to see Lord Henley and been laughed at.

Mary listened, her brown eyes widening only when I mentioned that the creature's tail had been straightened. Apart from that her reaction was not what I had expected. I thought she would be angry that Lord Henley had profited from her find, but for the moment she was more interested in the attention being given to it.

"Was lots of people looking at it?" she asked.

"A fair number." I didn't add that other exhibits were more popular.

"Lots and lots? More even than the number of people living in Lyme?"

"Far more. It has been on show for several months, so I expect thousands have seen it."

"All them people seeing my croc." Mary smiled, her eyes bright as she looked out to sea, as if spying a queue of spectators on the horizon, waiting to see what she would find next.

5

We will become fossils,
trapped upon beach forever

Finding that crocodile changed everything. Sometimes I try to imagine my life without those big, bold beasts hidden in the cliffs and ledges. If all I ever found were ammos and bellies and lilies and gryphies, my life would have turned out as piddling as those curies, with no lightning jolts to turn me inside out and give me joy and pain at the same time.

It weren't just the money from selling the croc that changed things. It was knowing there was something to hunt for, and that I was better at finding it than most – this was what were different. I could look ahead now and see – not random rocks thrown together, but a pattern forming of what my life could be.

When Lord Henley paid us twenty-three pounds for the whole crocodile, I wanted lots of things. I wanted to buy so many sacks of potatoes they'd reach the ceiling if you stacked them. I wanted to buy lengths of wool and have new dresses made for Mam and me. I wanted to eat a whole dough cake every day, and burn so much coal the coalman would have to come every week to refill the coal bin. That was what I wanted. I thought my family wanted those things too.

One day Miss Elizabeth come to see Mam after the deal had been done with Lord Henley, and sat with her and Joe at the kitchen table. She didn't talk of wool or coal or dough cakes, but of jobs. "I think it will benefit the family most if Joseph is apprenticed," she said. "Now you have the money to pay the apprentice fee, you should do so. Whatever he chooses will be a steadier income than selling fossils."

"But Joe and me are looking for more crocs," I interrupted. "We can make money enough off them. There's plenty of rich folk like Lord Henley who'll want crocs of their own now he's got one. Think of all them London gentlemen, ready with good money for our finds!" By the end I was shouting, for I had to defend my great plan, which was for Joe and me to get rich finding crocs.

"Quiet, girl," Mam said. "Let Miss Philpot talk sense."

"Mary," Miss Elizabeth begun, "you don't know if there are more creatures—"

"Yes, I do, ma'am. Think of all them bits we found before – the verteberries and teeth and pieces of rib and jaw that we didn't know what they were. Now we know! We got the whole body now and can see where those parts come from, how the body's meant to be. I've made a drawing of it so we can match what goes where. I'm sure there's crocs everywhere in them cliffs and ledges!"

"Why didn't you find any other whole specimens until now, then, if there are as many as you say?"

I glared at Miss Elizabeth. She had always been good to me, giving me work cleaning curies, bringing us extra bits of food and candles and old clothes, encouraging me to go to Sunday school to learn to read and write, sharing her finds with me and showing interest in what I found too. We couldn't have got the croc out of the cliff without her paying the Day brothers to do it, and she handled Lord Henley, her and Mam.

Why, then, was she being so contrary with me, just when my hunting had got exciting? I knew the monsters were there, whatever Elizabeth Philpot said. "We didn't know what we was looking for till now," I repeated. "How big it was, what it looked like. Now we know, Joe and I can find 'em easy, can't we, Joe?"

Joe didn't answer straightaway. He fiddled with a bit of string, twirling it between his fingers.

"Joe?"

"I don't want to look for crocodiles," he said in a low voice. "I want to be an upholsterer. Mr Reader has offered to take me on."

I was so surprised I couldn't say a word.

"Upholstering?" Miss Philpot was quick to get in. "That is a useful trade, but why choose it over others?"

"I can do it indoors rather than out."

I found my voice. "But, Joe, don't you want to find crocs with me? Weren't it a thrill to dig it out?"

"It was cold."

"Don't be stupid! Cold don't matter!"

"It do to me."

"How can you care about cold when these creatures are out there just waiting for us to find 'em? It's like treasure scattered all over the beach. We could get rich off them crocs! And you say it's too cold?"

Joe turned to Mam. "I do want to work for Mr Reader, Mam. What do you think?"

Mam and Miss Elizabeth had kept quiet while Joe and I argued. I expect they didn't need to butt in, as Joe had clearly made up his mind the way they wanted. I didn't wait to hear what they said, but jumped up and ran downstairs to the workshop. I'd rather work on the croc than listen to them, with their plan to take Joe off the beach. I had work to do.

With head and body together again, the monster was almost eighteen feet long. Getting it out of the cliff had been an ordeal that took three days, the Days and me working flat out whenever the tide let us. The whole thing was too big to lay on the table, so we'd spread the croc out along the floor. In the dim light it was a jumble of stony bones. I'd already spent a month cleaning it, but I still had some way to go to release it from the rock. My eyes were inflamed with squinting at it so much and rubbing dust into them.

At the time I was too young to understand Joe's choice, but later on I come to see that he had decided he wanted an ordinary life. He didn't want to be talked about the way I was, sneered at for wearing odd clothes and spending so much time alone upon beach with just rocks for company. He wanted what others in Lyme had – security and the chance to be respectable – and he jumped at an apprenticeship. There was nothing I could do about it. If I were offered the chance like Joe – if a girl could be apprenticed to a trade – would I have chosen the same and become a tailor or a butcher or a baker?

No. Curies were in my bones. For all the misery that come to my life from being upon those beaches, I wouldn't have abandoned curies for a needle or a knife or an oven.

"Mary." Miss Philpot was standing over me. I didn't answer; I was still angry at her for siding with Joe. Picking up a blade, I begun to scrape at a verteberry. It were one of a long line, stacked one against the other like a row of tiny saucers.

"Joseph has made a sensible choice," she said. "It will be better for you and your mother. That doesn't mean you can't continue to look for creatures. You don't need Joseph to help you find them, do you, now that you know what you're looking for? You can do that yourself, and then hire the Days to extract them, just as we did with this one. I can help you with that until you are old enough to manage the men yourself. I offered to help your mother with the business side as well, but she says she will do it herself. And she was rather good with Lord Henley." Miss Philpot kneeled by the croc and ran a hand over its ribs, which were all flattened out and crisscrossed like a willow basket. "How beautiful this is," she murmured, her tone softer and less sensible than before. "I am still amazed at its size, and its strangeness."

I agreed with her. The croc made me feel funny. While working on it I'd begun going to Chapel more regularly, for there were times sitting alone in the workshop with it that I got that hollowed-out feeling of the world holding things I didn't understand, and I needed comfort.

I may have lost Joe, but that didn't mean I was alone upon beach. One day as I went along the shore to Black Ven I saw two strangers hunting by the cliffs. They barely looked up, they were so excited to be swinging their hammers and grubbing about in the mud. The next day there were five men, and two days after that, ten. None was known to me. From overhearing their talk I learned they were looking for their own crocodiles. It seemed my crocodile had brought them to Lyme beaches, attracted by the promise of treasure.

Over the next few years Lyme grew crowded with hunters. I had been used to a deserted beach and my own company, or that of Miss Elizabeth or Joe, and being with them had often felt like being by myself, they were so solitary in their hunting. Now there was the tinking of hammer against stone all along the shore between Lyme and Charmouth, as well as on Monmouth Beach, and men were measuring, peering through magnifying glasses, taking notes, and making sketches. It was comical. For all the fuss made, not one found a complete croc. A cry would go up from someone, and the others would hurry over to look, and it would be nothing, or just a tooth or a bit of jaw or a verteberry – if they were lucky.

I was passing a man searching amongst the stones one day when he picked up a bit of round, dark rock. "A verte-bra, I think," he called to his companion.

I couldn't help it – I had to correct his mistake, even though he hadn't asked me. "That'll be beef, sir," I said.

"Beef?" The man frowned. "What is 'beef'?"

"It's what we call shale that's been calcified. Bits of it often look like verteberries, but it's got vertical lines in the layers, a bit like rope fibres, that you don't see in verteber-ries. And verteberries are darker in colour. All the bits of the croc are. See?" I dug out a verteberry from my basket that I'd found earlier and showed him. "Look, sir, verteberries have six sides, like this, though they're not always clear till you clean them. And they're concave, like someone's pinched them in the middle."

The man and his companion handled the verteberry as if it were a precious coin – which, in a way, it was. "Where did you find this?" one asked.

"Over there. I got others too." I showed them what I'd found and they were astonished. When they showed me theirs, most of it was beef we had to throw out. All day they come up with would-be curies for me to judge. Soon others caught on, and I was called here and there to tell the men what they had or hadn't found. Then they would ask me where they should look, and before long I was leading them on fossil hunts along the beach.

That was how I come to be in the company of the geologists and other interested gentlemen, looking over their mistakes and finding curies for them. A few were from Lyme or Charmouth: Henry De La Beche, for instance, who had just moved to Broad Street with his mother and was but a few years older than me. But most were from farther away, Bristol or Oxford or London.

I had never been in the company of educated gentlemen. Sometimes Miss Elizabeth come with us, and that made it easier for me, for she was older and of their class, and could go between as needed. When I was alone with them I was nervous at first, wondering how I was meant to act and what I could say. But they treated me as a servant, and that was a part I could play easily enough – though I was a servant who spoke her mind sometimes, and surprised them.

It was always a little awkward with the gentlemen, though, and become more so as I grew older and my chest and hips rounder. Then people begun to talk.

Maybe they would have talked less if I had been more sensible. But something took hold of me when I begun to grow up, and I become a bit silly, as girls do when they're leaving their childhoods behind. I started to think about the gentlemen, and looked at their legs and the way they moved. I begun to cry without knowing why, and shout at Mam when there was no reason to. I begun to prefer Miss Margaret to the other Philpots, as she was more sympathetic to my moods. She told me stories from the novels she read, and helped me try to make my hair prettier, and taught me to dance in the parlour at Morley Cottage – not that I would ever get to with a man. Sometimes I stood outside the Assembly Rooms and watched them through the bay window, dancing under the glass chandeliers, and imagined it was me floating round in a silk gown. I would get so upset I'd have to run along the Walk, which is the path the Day brothers built along the beach to link the two parts of the town. It took me to the Cobb, where I could walk up and down and let the wind blow away my tears, with no one to follow and tut at my silliness.

Mam and Miss Elizabeth despaired over me, but they couldn't fix me, for I didn't think I was broke. I was growing up, and it was hard. It took two brushes with death, with a lady and a gentleman, before Miss Elizabeth pulled me out of the mud and I truly joined the adult world.

Both happened along the same stretch of beach, just at the end of Church Cliffs, before the shore curves towards Black Ven. It was early spring, and I was walking along the beach at low tide, scanning for curies, thinking about one of the gentleman I had helped the day before who smiled at me with teeth as white as quartz. I was so blinded by

140

rocks and my thoughts that I didn't see the lady till I almost stepped on her. I stopped short, feeling a jolt in my stomach like when you're carrying a kicking child away from something they want and their foot catches you.

She were lying where the tide had left her, face down, seaweed all tangled in her dark hair. Her fine dress was sodden and dragged down with sand and mud. Even in that state I could see it cost more than all of our Anning clothes together. I stood over her a long time, watching to see if she might take a breath and spare me from seeing death in her face. It come to me that I would have to touch her, turn her over to see if she was dead and if I knew her.

I didn't want to touch her. I spent most of the days of my life picking up dead things off the shore. If she had been stone like a croc or an ammo I would have turned her over quick as you like. But I weren't used to touching dead flesh that had been a real person. I knew I had to do it, though, so I took a deep breath, quickly grabbed a shoulder and rolled her over.

I knew she were a lady the moment I saw her beautiful face. Others laughed at me when I said so, but I could see it in her noble brow and fine, sweet features. I called her the Lady, and I was right.

I kneeled by her head, closed my eyes, and said a prayer to God to take her into His bosom and comfort her. Then I pulled her up towards the cliff so the sea wouldn't take her back while I went for help. I couldn't leave her all unkempt, though: it would be disrespectful. Now I weren't afraid to touch her, though her flesh was cold and hard like a fish. I untangled the seaweed from her hair and combed it out. I straightened her limbs and dress, and folded her hands over her breast as I'd seen others laid out. I even begun to enjoy the ritual of it – that's how odd I were at that time in my life.

Then I saw a fine chain round her neck and pulled at it. Out from under her dress come a locket, small and round and gold, with MJ engraved in fancy lettering. There was nothing inside – any pictures or locks of hair had been scrubbed away by the sea. I didn't dare take it with me for safe keeping. Anyone finding me with it could accuse me of being a thief. I tucked the locket away, and hoped no one found her and stole it off her while I was gone.

When I was satisfied the Lady looked presentable, I said another little prayer, blew her a kiss, and run back to Lyme to tell them I'd found a drowned lady.

They laid her out in St Michael's and put a notice in the *Western Flying Post* to see if someone could identify her. I went to see her every day. I couldn't stop myself. I brought flowers gathered from the wayside – daffs and narcissi and primroses – and set them round her, and tore up some of the petals to scatter over her dress. I liked to sit in the church, though it weren't where we normally worshipped. It was quiet, with the Lady lying there so peaceful and beautiful. Sometimes I had a little cry for her or for myself.

It was like an illness come over me those days with the Lady, though I had no fever or chills. I'd never felt so strongly about anything before, though I wasn't sure what it was I felt. I just knew that the Lady's story was tragic, and maybe my story, if I had one, would be tragic too. She had died, and if I hadn't found her, she might have become a fossil, her bones turned to stone, like all the other things I hunted upon beach.

One day I arrived and the lid on the Lady's coffin was nailed shut. I cried because I couldn't see her beautiful face. Everything made me cry. I lay down on a pew and cried myself to sleep. I don't know how long I was asleep for, but when I woke Elizabeth Philpot was sitting beside me. "Mary, get up and go home, and don't come here again," she said quietly. "This has gone on long enough."

"But— "

"For one thing, it's unwholesome." She was referring to the smell, which never bothered me, as I'd smelled worse upon beach, and in the workshop, when I brought back slabs of limestone and the piddocks in their holes died after a few days out of the water.

"That don't matter to me."

"It is sentimental behaviour that should remain in the gothic novels Margaret reads. It doesn't suit you. Besides that, she has been identified and her family is coming to fetch her. There was a shipwreck off Portland of a ship arriving from India. She was on board with her children. Imagine sailing all that long way, only to be lost at the very end."

"They know who she is? What's her name?"

"Lady Jackson."

I clapped my hands, so pleased I were right about her being a Lady. "What's her Christian name? The M on the locket?"

Miss Elizabeth hesitated. I think she knew her answer would feed my obsession. But she does not lie easily. "It's Mary.

I nodded, and begun to cry. Somehow I knew it.

Miss Elizabeth sighed hard, like she was trying to keep

from shouting. "Don't be silly, Mary. Of course it is a sad story, but you don't know her, and sharing a name doesn't mean you are anything alike."

I covered my face with my hands and kept on crying, out of embarrassment now as much as anything else, for not being able to control myself in front of Miss Elizabeth. She sat with me for a little bit, then gave up and left me to my tears. I didn't tell her, but I was crying because Lady Jackson and I *were* alike. We were both Marys and we would both die. However beautiful or plain a person was, God would take you in the end.

For a week after they took Lady Jackson away, I couldn't touch curies on the beach for thinking of what they had been – poor creatures that had died. For that little while I allowed myself to be as timid and superstitious as my old playmate Fanny Miller. I avoided the gentlemen out hunting, and hid on Monmouth Beach, where it was quieter.

But no curies means no food on the table. Mam ordered me back upon beach and said she wouldn't let me inside if I returned with an empty basket. Soon enough I pushed death away, till the next time when he come to stand much closer.

Later that spring I at last found a second crocodile. Perhaps all the gentlemen I was attending was what made it take so long to find one. Elizabeth Philpot must have been pleased she were right that the cliffs and ledges don't give up their monsters so easily as I'd thought. When I found it at last, I was out at Gun Cliff one May afternoon, not even thinking of crocs, but of my empty stomach, for I'd had nothing to eat all day. The tide was coming in, and I'd almost got back home when I slipped on a ledge covered with seaweed. I come down hard on my hands and knees, and as I pushed myself up I felt a ridge of knobs under my hand. Just like that, I was touching a long line of verteberries. It was so simple I wasn't even surprised. I was relieved to find that croc, for it proved there were more than one, and that I could make a living from them. That second croc brought money, respect, and a new gentleman.

It was a week or two after we'd removed the croc to the workshop. I was meant to be cleaning it, but there'd been a storm the night before, and a small landslip had appeared under Black Ven that I wanted to look over. There were no men about, and Miss Elizabeth had a cold, and Joe was counting tacks or blacking wood or whatever it is upholsterers are meant to do, so it was just me upon beach. I was scrabbling about in the landslip, the lias mud pushing under my nails and lining my shoes, when the sound of clacking stones made me look up. Along the beach from Charmouth a man come, riding on a black horse. He was silhouetted against the bright sunlight, so it was hard to make him out, but when he got closer I saw the horse was a mare, a plodder, and the man wore a cloak over sloped shoulders, and a top hat, and carried a sack at his side. Once I saw the sack was blue I knew it was William Buckland.

I doubted he recognised me, though I knew him: he used to buy curies from Pa when I was younger. I remembered him best for that blue sack he always carried with him to put specimens in. It was made of heavy material – just as well, since it was always bulging with rocks Mr Buckland had picked up. He would show them to Pa, who could see no use in them as they held no fossils. But Mr Buckland remained enthusiastic about his rocks, as he was about everything.

He had grown up just a few miles away in Axminster, and knew Lyme well, though now he lived in Oxford, where he taught geology. He had also taken his orders, though I doubted any church would have him. William Buckland was too unpredictable to be a vicar.

He had been along to look at the crocodile skull back when we'd showed it in the Assembly Rooms, but though he'd smiled at me, he'd spoken only to Miss Philpot. Two years later, when the croc was united, head and body, and cleaned and sold to Lord Henley, I heard Mr Buckland went to see it at Colway Manor. And since the gentlemen had come to hunt upon beach, I saw him occasionally amongst them. He had never paid much attention to me, though, so I was astonished now to hear him shout, "Mary Anning! Just the girl I wanted to see!"

No one had ever called out my name that enthusiastically. I stood up, confused, then quickly tugged at the hem of my skirt, which I'd tucked into my waist to keep it out of the mud. I often did that when the beach was empty. It wouldn't do for Mr Buckland to see my knobby ankles and muddy calves.

"Sir?" I bobbed a sort of curtsy, though it weren't very graceful. There weren't many I curtsied to in Lyme – just Lord Henley, and him I didn't want to now I understood that he'd sold on my croc and made such a lot more money than he'd ever paid us for it. Him I would scarcely bend my knee for now, even if Miss Philpot hissed at me to be polite.

Mr Buckland got down from his horse and stumbled across the pebbles. The mare must have been so used to his constant stopping that she just stood there without having to be tied up. "I heard you found another monster, and I've come all the way from Oxford to see it," he declared, his eyes already scanning the landslip. "I cancelled my last lectures just to come early." As he talked he never stopped moving about and peering at things. He picked up a clod of mud, studied it, dropped it, and picked up another. Each time he stooped I got a glimpse of the bald spot on top of his head. He had a round face like a baby's, with big lips and sparkling eyes, and sloping shoulders and a little belly. He made me want to laugh, even when he hadn't made a joke.

He was looking eager and expectant, gazing here and there, and I realised he thought the croc was still on the beach. "It ain't here, sir. We got it back at the workshop. I'm cleaning it," I added with pride.

"Are you, now? Well done, well done." Mr Buckland looked disappointed for a moment that he wouldn't see the croc right there, but he soon recovered. "Let us go to your workshop, then, Mary, and on the way you can show me where you dug up the creature."

As we started along the beach towards Lyme, I noted all the hammers and bags hanging off his poor, patient horse. There was also, tied to the bridle and flopping against the horse's side, a dead seagull. "Sir," I said, "what you doing with that gull?"

"Ah, I'm going to have the kitchen at the Three Cups roast it for my dinner! I am eating my way through the animal kingdom, you see, and have had such things as hedgehogs and field mice and snakes, yet in all this time I haven't had a common gull."

"You've eaten mice!"

"Oh, yes. They are rather good on toast."

I wrinkled my nose at the thought, and at the smell of the bird. "But – the gull stinks, sir!"

Mr Buckland sniffed. "Does it?" For such a keen observer of the world, he often overlooked the obvious. "Never mind, I'll have them boil it up, and use the skeleton for my lectures. Now, what have you found today?"

Mr Buckland got very excited by the things I showed him – some golden ammos, a fish's scaly tail I would give to Miss Elizabeth, and a verteberry the size of a guinea. He asked so many questions, mixing in his own thoughts as he did, that I begun to feel like a pebble rolled back and forth in the tide. Then he insisted we turn round and go back to the landslip to look for more. The mare and I followed him until he stopped suddenly, just a stone's throw from the slip, and said, "No, no, I won't have time – I'm to meet Doctor Carpenter at the Three Cups shortly. Let's come back this afternoon."

"Can't, sir – the tide'll be in."

Mr Buckland looked puzzled, as if a high tide were nothing to consider.

"We can't reach the landslip along this side of the beach when the tide's high," I explained. "Because of the cliffs bulging out there. The beach gets cut off."

"What about coming from the Charmouth end?"

I shrugged. "We could – but we'd have to go all the way round along the road to get to Charmouth first. Or take the

148

cliff path – but that's not stable now, as you can see, sir." I nodded towards the landslip.

"We can ride my mare to Charmouth – that's what she's here for. She'll take us quick as you like."

I hesitated. Though I had accompanied gentlemen upon beach, I had never ridden on a horse with one. The townsfolk would certainly have things to say about that. Though Mr Buckland's high spirits seemed innocent to me, they might not to others. Besides, I didn't like being upon beach at high tide, hemmed in between cliff and sea. If there were another slip there was nowhere to escape to.

It was hard arguing with Mr Buckland, for his enthusiasm ran roughshod over everything. However, I soon discovered he changed his mind so often that by the time he reached Lyme he'd had about a dozen other ideas of how to spend the afternoon, and we didn't return to the landslip at all that day.

Mr Buckland didn't get to see where I'd dug up the second croc, as the tide had covered the ledge by the time we passed it. I did show him the cliff where the first one had come from, though, and he made a little sketch. He kept stopping to look at things – silly, some of them, like ammo impressions in the rock ledges that he had surely seen many times before – so I had to remind him of Doctor Carpenter waiting for him at the Three Cups, as well as the much more interesting specimen sitting in the workshop. "Did you know, sir," I added, "that Doctor Carpenter saved my life when I were a baby?"

"Did he, now? That is what doctors often do – dose babies when they have fevers."

"Oh, it was more than that, sir. I'd been struck by lightning, see, and Doctor Carpenter told my parents to put me in a bath of lukewarm water—"

Mr Buckland halted on the rock he was about to jump from. "You were struck by lightning?" he cried, his eyes wide and delighted.

I stopped as well, embarrassed now that I had brought it up. I did not normally talk about the lightning to anyone, but had wanted to show off to this clever Oxford gentleman. This was the only thing I could think of that would impress him. It was silly, really, for it turned out later I were more than a match for him when it come to finding and identifying fossils, and his feeble grasp of anatomy sometimes made me laugh. I didn't know that at the time, though, and so I spent an uncomfortable time being questioned by him about what had happened to me in that field when I were a baby.

It did have its effect, though, for Mr Buckland clearly respected me for my experience. "That is truly remarkable, Mary," he said at last. "God spared you, and gave you an experience almost unique in the world. Your body housed the lightning and clearly benefited from it." He looked me up and down, and I blushed with the attention.

At last we got back, and I left Mr Buckland in the workshop, hopping round the crocodile and calling out questions to me even as I went up to the kitchen. Mam was at the range, boiling another family's linens. Doing laundry brought her just enough money for coal to keep the fire going so that she could wash another set of linens. She never liked it when I pointed out this circle to her.

"Who's that downstairs?" she demanded now, hearing Mr Buckland's voice. "You get tuppence off him to see it?"

I shook my head. "Mr Buckland's not the tuppence type."

"Course he is. You don't let anyone see that thing without paying. Penny for the poor, tuppence for the rich."

"You ask him, then."

Mam frowned. "I will." Handing me the paddle she used to stir the linens, she wiped her hands on her apron and headed downstairs. I poked at the washing, happy enough for a little break from Mr Buckland's questions – though it would have been funny to see Mam try to cope with him. She was fine with some of the other gentlemen. Henry De La Beche, for instance, she bossed about like another son. But William Buckland defeated even my mam. She come up a time later, exhausted from his constant chatter, and without tuppence. She shook her head. "Your pa used to tell me when that man come to the workshop, he'd give up getting any work done and settle back for a sleep while Mr Buckland went on. Now, he wants you back down to tell him about the cleaning and what we're going to do with it. Tell him we want a good price, and don't want being cheated by a gentleman again!"

When I come in Mr Buckland was leaving by the door that led onto Cockmoile Square. "Oh, Mary, I'll just be a moment. I'm fetching Doctor Carpenter here to see this. And a few others this afternoon who I'm sure will be most interested in it."

"Just as long as it's not Lord Henley!" I called after him.

"Why not Lord Henley?"

I explained about the first croc, with its monocle, waist-coat and straightened tail as Miss Philpot had described it. "That idiot!" Mr Buckland cried. "He should have sold it to Oxford or the British Museum rather than to Bullock's.

I'm sure I could have convinced either to take it. I shall do so with this one."

Without asking, Mr Buckland took over the selling of the croc from Mam and Miss Elizabeth. Before Mam could stop him he'd written enthusiastic letters to possible buyers. She were cross at first, but not once he'd found us a rich gentleman in Bristol who paid us forty pounds for it – the museums having said no. That made up for all that Mam and me had to put up with from Mr Buckland. For he was about all summer, fired with the idea of crocodiles entombed in the cliffs and ledges, waiting to be freed. While we had ours in the workshop, he was in and out all day as if the room were his, bringing with him gentlemen who poked about, measuring and sketching and discussing my croc. I noticed during all the talk, Mr Buckland never once called it a crocodile. He was like Miss Elizabeth that way. It made me begin to accept it were something else – though until we knew what that was, I would still call it a crocodile.

One day when it were just Mr Buckland and me in the workshop, he asked if he could clean a bit of the croc himself. He was always keen to try out new things. I surrendered my brushes and blade, for I couldn't say no to him, but I feared he would do real damage. He didn't, but that was because he kept stopping and examining and talking about the croc till I wanted to scream. We needed to eat; we needed to pay the rent. We still had debts of Pa's to pay, and the thought of ending up in the workhouse never left us. We couldn't spend the time talking. We needed to sell the croc.

Finally I managed to interrupt him. "Sir," I said, "let me do the work and you do the talking, or this creature will never be ready."

"You're quite right, Mary, of course you are." Mr Buckland handed me the blade, then sat back to watch me scrape along one of the ribs, freeing and brushing away the limestone that clung to it. Slowly a clear line emerged, and because I went at it carefully, the rib weren't nicked or scored, but smooth and whole. For once he was quiet, and that made me ask the question I'd been wanting to for several days now. "Sir," I said, "is this one of the creatures Noah brought on his ark?"

Mr Buckland looked startled. "Well, now, Mary, why do you ask that?"

He didn't go chatting on as he normally would, and his waiting for me to speak made me shy. I concentrated on the rib. "Dunno, sir, I just thought. . ."

"What did you think?"

Maybe he had forgotten I weren't one of his students, but just a girl working to live. Still, for a moment I acted the student. "Miss Philpot showed me pictures of crocodiles drawn by Cruver – Cuver – the Frenchman who does all those studies of animals."

"Georges Cuvier?"

"Yes, him. So we compared his drawings to this and found it were different in so many ways. Its snout is long and pointed like a dolphin's, while a croc's is blunt. And it's got paddles instead of claws, and they're turned outward rather than forward the way a croc's legs are. And of course, that big eye. No crocodile has eyes like that. So Miss Philpot and I wondered what it could be if it's not a croc. Then I heard you and a gentleman you brought here the other day, Reverend Conybeare. You was talking about the Flood –" actually they'd used the words "deluge" and "diluvian", and I'd had to ask Miss Elizabeth what they meant "– and it made me wonder: if this ain't a crocodile, which Noah would've had on the ark, then what is it? Did God make something that was on the ark we don't know about? So that's why I'm asking, sir."

Mr Buckland was silent for longer than I thought he could ever manage. I begun to worry he didn't understand what I meant, that I was too uneducated to make sense to an Oxford scholar. So I asked again, a slightly different question. "Why would God make creatures that don't exist any more?"

Mr Buckland looked at me with his big eyes, and I saw there a flickering worry.

"You are not the only person to ask this question, Mary," he said. "Many learned men are discussing it. Cuvier himself believes there is such a thing as the extinction of certain animals, in which they die away completely. I am not so sure of that, however. I cannot see why God would want to kill off what He has created." Then he brightened, and the worry left his eyes. "My friend the Reverend Conybeare says that while the Scriptures tell us that God created Heaven and Earth, they don't describe how He did it. That is open to interpretation. And that is why I'm here – to study this remarkable creature, and find more of them to study, and through careful contemplation arrive at an answer. Geology is always to be used in the service of religion, to study the wonders of God's creation and marvel at His genius." He ran a hand over the croc's spine. "God in His infinite wisdom has peppered this world with mysteries for men to solve. This is one of them, and I am honoured to take on the task."

His words sounded fine, but he had given no answer. Perhaps there was no answer. I thought for a moment. "Sir, do you think the world was created in six days, the way the Bible says?"

Mr Buckland waggled his head – not a yes or a no. "It has been suggested that 'day' is a word that should not be interpreted literally. If one thinks instead of each day as an epoch during which God created and perfected different parts of Heaven and Earth, then some of the tensions between geology and the Bible disappear. After five epochs, during which all of the layering of rock and the fossilisation of animals occurred, then man was created. That is why there are no human fossils, you see. And once there were people, on the sixth 'day', the Flood came, and when it subsided, it left the world as we see it today, in all its grandeur."

"Where did all the water go?"

Mr Buckland paused, and I saw again that flicker of uncertainty in his eyes. "Back into the clouds from whence the rain came," he replied.

I knew I should believe him, as he taught at Oxford, but his answers did not feel complete. It was like having a meal and not getting quite enough to eat. I went back to cleaning the croc and did not ask more questions. It seemed I was always going to feel a little hollowed out round my monsters.

Mr Buckland stayed at the Three Cups in Lyme for much of the summer, long after the second crocodile had been cleaned, packed and sent to Bristol. He often called for me at Cockmoile Square, or asked me to meet him upon beach. He assumed I would accompany him and attend him, showing him where fossils could be found, sometimes finding them for him. He was particularly keen to find another monster, which he would take back to Oxford for his collection. While I wanted to find one too, I were never sure what would happen if we did discover one while out together. I had the eye and was more likely to spot it first. Would that mean Mr Buckland should pay me for it? It were never clear, as we didn't talk about money, though he was quick to thank me when I found curies for him. Even Mam didn't mention it. Mr Buckland seemed to be above money, as a scholar ought to be, living in a world where it didn't matter.

By then Joe was well into his apprenticeship and never come out with me unless there was heavy lifting or hammering to do. Sometimes Mam come with us, and sat knitting while we ranged round her. But Mr Buckland wanted to go farther than she did, and she had laundry to do and the house to look after, and the shop – for we still set out a table of curies in front of the workshop, the way Pa used to, and Mam sold 'em to visitors.

Other times Miss Elizabeth went hunting with us. It weren't as it had been with the other gentlemen, though, where she and I had laughed at the men behind their backs when they kept making beginner's mistakes, picking up beef or thinking a bit of fossilised wood was a bone. Mr Buckland was smarter, and kinder too, and I could see Miss Elizabeth liked him. I felt sometimes that she and I were two women competing for his attention, for I weren't a child any more. I would look up from my hunting and see her eyes lingering on him, and want to tease her about it, but knew it would hurt her. Miss Elizabeth was clever, which Mr Buckland appreciated. She could talk to him about fossils and geology, and read some of the scientific papers he lent her. But she was five years older than him, too old to start a family, and without the money or the looks to tempt him anyway. Besides, he was in love with rocks, and would fondle a pretty bit of quartz more likely than flirt with a lady. Miss Elizabeth hadn't a chance. Not that I did, either.

When we were together she become quieter, and sharper when she did speak. Then she made excuses, leaving us to walk farther down the beach, and I would see her in the distance, her back very straight, even when she stooped to examine something. Or she would say she preferred to hunt at Pinhay Bay or Monmouth Beach rather than by Black Ven, and disappear altogether.

Mostly, then, Mr Buckland and me were alone. Though we were fixed only on finding curies, our being together so often was too much even for Lyme folk. Eventually town gossip caught up with us – fuelled, I was sure, by Captain Cury. In the years since the landslip that almost killed him and me and buried the first crocodile, he had let me be. But he had never managed to find himself a complete croc, and still liked to spy on what I was doing. Once I begun hunting with Mr Buckland, Captain Cury got jealous. He would make sly comments as he passed us upon beach, clanging his spade against the rock ledge. "Having fun here on your own, you two?" he'd say. "Enjoy being alone?"

Mr Buckland mistook Captain Cury's attention as inter-est, and hurried over to show him the fossils we'd found, and baffle him with scientific terms and theories. Captain Cury stood there uncomfortable, then made an excuse to get away. He loped down the beach, sneering at me over his shoulder, ready to tell everyone that he'd seen us together.

I ignored the talk, but one day Mam overheard someone in the Shambles calling me a gentleman's whore. She marched straight down to Church Cliffs where Mr Buckland and I were prising out the jaw of a crocodile. "Get your things and come back with me," she ordered, ignoring Mr Buckland's greeting.

"But, Mam, we've only an hour left to dig till the tide's in. Look, you can see all the teeth here."

"Come away, you. Do as I say." Mam made me feel guilty when I hadn't even done anything. I stood up quick and brushed the mud off my skirt. Mam glared at Mr Buckland. "I don't want you out here alone with my daughter." I had never heard her be so rude to a gentleman.

Luckily Mr Buckland was not easily offended. Perhaps it was because he misunderstood her, for he was not the sort of man to think as the town did. "Mrs Anning, we have found a most splendid jaw!" he cried. "Here, feel the teeth, they are as even as a comb's. I promise you, I'm not wasting Mary's time. She and I are engaged in tremendous scientific discovery."

"I don't care nothing for your scientific so-and-so," Mam muttered. "I've my daughter's reputation to think of. This family's been through enough already – we don't need Mary's prospects ruined by a gentleman with no concern other than what he can get out of her."

Mr Buckland turned to look at me as if he'd never thought of me in that way before. I flushed and hunched my shoulders to hide my breasts. Then he looked down at his own chest, as if suddenly reconsidering himself. It would be comical, if it weren't already tragical.

Mam begun picking her way back across the beach, skirting pools of water. "Come along, Mary," she said over her shoulder.

"Wait, ma'am," Mr Buckland called. "Please. I have the greatest respect for your daughter. I would never want to compromise her reputation. Is it our being alone that is the problem? For that is easily solved. I shall find us a chaperone. If I ask at the Three Cups I'm sure they can spare us someone."

Mam stopped but didn't look round. She was thinking. So was I. Mam's words had given me an idea about myself I had never really considered. I had prospects. A gentleman could be interested in me. I might not always be so poor and needy.

"All right," Mam said at last. "If Miss Elizabeth or me ain't with you, you take someone else. Come, Mary."

I picked up my basket and hammer.

"But what about this jaw? Mary?" Mr Buckland looked a little frantic.

I walked backwards so I could look at him. "You have a go at it, sir. You been collecting fossils all these years, you don't need me."

"But I do, Mary, I do!"

I smiled. Swinging my basket, I turned and followed Mam.

That was how Fanny Miller come back into my life. When Mr Buckland collected me from home the next morning, Fanny was hovering behind him, looking about as miserable as a coachman in the rain. She kept her eyes on her boots, scuffing them on the cobblestones of Cockmoile Square to get the mud off. Like me, she were growing into a young woman, her curves a little softer than mine, her face the shape of an egg, framed by a battered bonnet trimmed with a blue ribbon to match her eyes. Though poor, she was so pretty I wanted to slap her.

Mr Buckland didn't seem to notice that, though, nor the frosty look that passed between her and me. "There, you see," he said, "I've brought us a chaperone. She works in the Three Cups' kitchen, but they said they could spare her for a few hours while the tide is out." He beamed, clearly pleased with himself. "What is your name, my girl?"

"Fanny," she said, so soft I weren't sure Mr Buckland even heard.

I sighed, but there was nothing I could do. After all the fuss Mam made about him getting someone to come out with us, I couldn't complain about his choice. I would just have to put up with her – and she with me. Fanny were sure to be just as unhappy as I was that she had to come upon beach with us, but she needed the work, and would do as she was told.

We went back to the jaw in Church Cliffs, Fanny trailing behind us. As we worked she sat some way away, sifting through the stones at her feet. Maybe she still liked shiny pebbles. She looked so bored and frightened I almost pitied her.

So did Mr Buckland. Perhaps he felt idleness was an evil anyone would want to avoid. When he saw her playing with the stones he went over to talk "undergroundology", as he liked to call geology. "Here – Fanny, is it?" he said. "Would you like me to tell you what those stones are you're arranging? Most of what you've got there is limestone and flint, but that pretty white bit is quartz, and the brown with

160

the stripe is sandstone. There are several different layers of rock along this beach, you see, like this." He took up a stick and drew in the sand the different layers of granite, limestone, slate, sandstone and chalk. "All over Great Britain, and indeed on the Continent as well, we are discovering these layers of rock, always in the same order. Isn't that surprising?"

When Fanny did not respond, he said, "Perhaps you would like to come and see what we're digging out."

Fanny approached reluctantly, glancing up at the cliff face. She seemed not to have overcome her fear of falling rocks.

"Do you see this jaw?" Mr Buckland ran his finger along it. "Beautiful, isn't it? The snout is broken off, but the rest is intact. It will make an excellent model to use during my lectures on fossil discoveries." He peered at Fanny as if to savour her response, and looked puzzled when she screwed up her face with disgust. Mr Buckland found it hard to understand that others didn't feel as he did about fossils and rocks.

"You saw the creatures Mary discovered when they were on display in town, did you not?" he persisted.

Fanny shook her head.

He tried once more to draw her in. "Perhaps you would like to help? You may hold the hammers. Or Mary can show you how to look for other fossils."

"No, thank you, sir. I've my own work." As she turned to go back to her safe seat away from the cliff, Fanny's face was full of spite. If I were younger I would have pinched her. But she had punishment enough, being out upon beach with us, her presence allowing for the discovery of the very

161

things she despised most. She must have hated that, and would have preferred to scrub any number of pots in the kitchen of the Three Cups.

Later Miss Elizabeth come along, hunting on her own. She frowned at Fanny, who now had out some lace she was making – though how she could keep it clean with so much mud about I didn't know. "What is she doing here?" Miss Elizabeth demanded.

"Chaperone," I said.

"Oh!" Miss Elizabeth watched her for a moment, then shook her head. "Poor girl," she murmured, before passing on.

It's your fault she's here, I thought. If you weren't so funny about Mr Buckland you could stay with us and release Fanny from her torment. And my torment too that she's sitting there reminding me of the sort of woman I'll never be.

Fanny was with us all summer. Usually she sat on rocks away from us, or followed at a distance when we were wandering. Though she didn't complain, I knew she hated it when we went farther, to Charmouth or beyond. She preferred remaining close to Lyme, by Gun Cliff or Church Cliffs. Then a friend might come out to see her, and Fanny cheered up and become more confident. The two would sit and peek round their bonnets at us and whisper and giggle.

Mr Buckland tried to interest Fanny in what we found, or to show her what to look for, but she always said she had other things to do, and brought out lace or sewing or knitting. "She thinks they're the Devil's works," I finally explained in a low voice, when Fanny had once again rebuffed him and gone to sit with her lace. "They scare her."

"But that's absurd!" Mr Buckland said. "They are God's creatures from the past, and there is nothing to be frightened of."

He got up from his knees as if he would go to her, but I caught his arm. "Please, sir, leave her be. It's better that way."

When I looked over at Fanny she was staring at my hand on Mr Buckland's sleeve. She always seemed to notice when his hand touched mine as he passed me a fossil, or when I grabbed his elbow when he stumbled. She gasped outright when Mr Buckland hugged me the afternoon we managed to get the croc jaw out of the cliff. In that way her accompanying us made things worse, for I suspect Fanny spread plenty of gossip. We might have been better off alone, without a witness to report back everything she saw that she didn't understand. I still had funny looks from townspeople, and laughter behind my back.

Poor Fanny. I should be kinder to her, for she paid a price, going out with us.

My trade is best done in bad weather. Rain flushes fossils out of the cliffs, and storms scrub the ledges clean of seaweed and sand so more can be seen. Joe may have left fossils for upholstery because of the weather, but I was like Pa – I never minded the cold or the wet, as long as I was finding curies.

Mr Buckland also wanted to go out even when it was raining. Fanny had to come with us, and would huddle wretched in her shawl, curling up amongst the boulders to shelter against the wind. We were often the only folk upon beach then, for in poor weather visitors preferred to go to the bath houses, which had heated water, or to play cards and read the papers at the Assembly Rooms, or to drink at the Three Cups. Only serious hunters went out in the rain.

One rainy day towards the end of the summer, I was upon beach with Mr Buckland and Fanny. There was no one else on that stretch of shore, though Captain Cury passed by at one point, nosing about to see what we were doing. Mr Buckland had discovered a ridge of bumps not far from where we'd dug out the jaw in Church Cliffs, and thought they might be a row of verteberries from the same animal.

I was chiselling away at it to try and uncover the bones when Mr Buckland left my side. After a minute Fanny come to stand close by, and I knew Mr Buckland must be pissing in the water. He was always careful not to embarrass me, and slipped off to do his business far enough away that I didn't have to see. I was used to him doing that, but it always bothered Fanny, and it were the one time she come up to the cliff by me. Even after several weeks in his company, she was still a little scared of Mr Buckland. His friendliness and constant questions were too demanding for someone like Fanny.

I felt sorry for her. The rain was coming down hard, and dripping on her face from her bonnet rim. It was too wet for her to sew or knit, and there's nothing worse than having nothing to do in the rain. "Why don't you just turn away when he's down there?" I said, trying to be helpful. "He's not going to wave it in your face. He's too much of a gentleman for that."

Fanny shrugged. "You ever seen one?" she said after a moment. I think it was the first question she'd asked me in ten years. Maybe the rain had wore her down.

I thought of the belemnite Miss Elizabeth showed James Foot on this beach years before and smiled. "No. Just Joe's, when he were little. You?"

I didn't think she would answer, but then she said, "Once, at the Three Cups, a man got so drunk he dropped his trousers in the kitchen, thinking it were the privy!"

We both laughed. For a second I wondered if we might be starting to get on better.

We'd no chance for that. There were no warning, no pebbles raining down or the groan of stone splitting from stone. It were that sudden that one moment Fanny and I were laughing about men's parts by the cliff, and the next the cliff just dropped, and I was knocked down and buried in the thick, rocky clay.

Though I don't remember doing it, I'd thrown my hand up to my mouth as the cliff come down on me, and that made a little space for me to breathe in. I couldn't see anything, and though I struggled I couldn't move at all, for the clay was cold and wet and heavy, and it held me fast. I couldn't even call out. All I could do was think that I was going to die and wonder what God would say to me when He met me.

There was a long, long time when nothing happened. Then I heard a scrabbling and felt hands clawing at me and wiping my eyes, and I opened them and saw Mr Buckland's terrified face, and I thought maybe I would not meet God yet.

"Oh, Mary!" he cried.

"Sir. Get me out, sir!"

"I— I—" Mr Buckland pulled at the rocks and mud but could not move them. "It's too heavy, Mary. I can't get you with no tools." He was in a kind of daze, as if he couldn't think straight.

We heard a cry then. We had forgot about Fanny. She was just a few feet from us, and weren't so heavily buried as me, but there was blood on her face. She begun to scream, and Mr Buckland jumped up and went to her. The clay was looser round her and he managed to shift it enough that he could pull her out. He wiped the blood from her face, and in doing so knocked the bonnet from her head, for he was scared and clumsy. It got caught up in a gust of wind and rolled away down the beach. Losing her bonnet seemed to upset Fanny more than anything else. "My bonnet!" she cried. "I need my bonnet. Mam will kill me if I lose it!" Then she screamed again as Mr Buckland tried to move her.

"Her leg is broken," Mr Buckland panted. "I'm going to have to leave you to get help."

At that moment part of the cliff further along crumbled and crashed to the ground. Fanny screamed again. "Don't leave me, sir, please don't leave me in this godforsaken place!"

I did not want to be left either, but I did not cry out. "Best to carry her, sir, if you can. At least you can save one of us."

Mr Buckland looked horrified. "Oh, I don't think I should do that. It wouldn't be proper." It seemed even he, who ate field mice and carried a bright blue sack and pissed in the sea, was uneasy about holding a girl in his arms. But now was not the time for worrying about what was proper.

"Put an arm round her shoulders and one under her knees and lift, sir," I coached. "She's a little thing – you should be able to carry her, even a scholar like you."

Mr Buckland did what I said and heaved Fanny into his arms. She screamed again, in pain and shame. Letting her arms flop wide, she turned her head away from him.

"For God's sake, Fanny, put your arms round him!" I cried. "Help the man or he'll never get you back."

Fanny obeyed me, throwing her arms round his neck and burying her head against his chest.

"Take her to the bath house – that's the closest place – and send people straight back with spades." I wouldn't normally direct a gentleman so, but Mr Buckland seemed to have lost his wits. "Hurry, please, sir. I can't bear being alone like this."

As he nodded, another section of cliff fell away with a crash. Mr Buckland flinched, terror written all over his face. I fastened my eyes on his. "Sir, pray for me. And if I die, tell Mam and Joe—"

"D– d– don't say such a thing, Mary. I'll be back shortly." Mr Buckland would not listen, but staggered away, Fanny gazing at me with glazed eyes over his shoulder. Now that she had surrendered to his arms she was beyond care. Later Doctor Carpenter would set her leg, but the break was awkward and never healed properly, and left her with one leg shorter than the other. She could never walk far or stand for long, and could never again come out upon beach – not that she would want to. Whenever I saw her hobbling down Broad Street to the Three Cups, I ducked my head to avoid that fearful blue gaze.

Course I didn't know any of that then, held fast in the landslip. I watched Mr Buckland weaving down the beach with his burden, not going fast enough for me, and wondered why it was that the pretty ones were always rescued before the plain. That was how the world worked: with her big eyes and dainty features, Fanny did not get stuck, whereas I was caught in the mud, the cliff threatening to crumble on top of me.

There was a lot of time to think. I thought of Mr Buckland, and how odd it were that for an ordained man so interested in what God had been up to in the past, he hadn't been much comfort with prayers, but run away from them. I closed my eyes and said a long prayer myself, for God to spare me, to let me live on to help Mam and Joe, to find more crocs, to have enough to eat and coal to burn, even to have a husband and children one day. "And please, God, make Mr Buckland a runner rather than a walker today. Make him find someone quick, and come back." Although Mr Buckland was happy wandering miles along the cliff, and regularly walked to Axminster and back while in Lyme, he did not hurry. He had a scholar's belly on him, and I worried that with Fanny in his arms he would not get back quick enough to save me.

It was quiet now. The wind had died down, and a fine misty rain sprayed my face. Now and then I heard the faint skitter of more debris tumbling down the cliff to the ground. I couldn't see it because it were behind me and I couldn't turn my head all the way round. That was the worst, hearing it and not knowing how close it was, or if it would bury me.

The mud that held me was cold and heavy and pressing on my chest, making it hard to breathe. I closed my eyes for a bit, thinking that sleep might make the time go faster. But I couldn't sleep, so instead I followed Mr Buckland in my mind as he went back to Lyme. Now he's passing where we found the first croc, I thought. Now he's passing the ledge with the ammo impressions. Now he's reached the bend where the path starts. Now he's in sight of Jefferd's Baths. Maybe Mr Jefferd is there and will come running, faster than Mr Buckland. I traced the path there and back again – and it was not so far back to Lyme – but no one come.

I opened my eyes. Mr Buckland was a dot along Church Cliffs. I couldn't believe he hadn't got farther. But then, it was hard to say how much time had passed – it could have been ten minutes or hours. I looked the other way, down the beach towards Charmouth. There were no boats out, or fishermen checking crab pots, for it was too rough. There was no one at all. And the tide had turned, and was slowly creeping up.

I gave up looking for help, and begun to notice things closer to me. The landslip had caused a churning up of rocks caught in an ooze of blue-grey clay. My eyes flicked over the stones near to me and come to rest on a familiar shape about four feet from me: a ring of overlapping bony scales the size of my fist. A croc's eye. It were like it was staring straight at me. I cried out with the surprise of seeing it. Then, several feet past the eye, there was a movement. It was only tiny, but I cried out again, and it moved again. It was just a little pink spot sticking out of the clay, and with the rain in my eyes it was hard to see what it was. I wondered if it were a crab, scrabbling about in the mud.

"Hey!" I called, and it moved. It was not a crab, but a finger. I felt so relieved and sick at the same time that I think I fainted. When I come to I looked at the spot again, and it wasn't moving. I cleared my throat.

"Who's that?" I said, but not loud enough. "Who's that?" I repeated, as loud as I could. The finger moved. I was so happy not to be alone that I laughed aloud.

"Joe? Is it Joe?" The finger didn't move.

"Mam? Miss Philpot?"

No movement. I knew it couldn't have been any of them, for I would have known they were upon beach. But who else would be out in such weather? I supposed it could have been one of the children from Lyme, come to spy on Mary Anning and the man she attended, hoping to see something scandalous that they could report back on. But it seemed unlikely. We would have spotted them if they were upon beach. Unless they'd been up on the cliff – which meant they'd come down with the slip. It was a miracle they was alive.

It was thinking of the cliff and landslips that made me realise who it must be. "Captain Cury?" I remembered now that I had seen him earlier.

Even as the finger wriggled, I saw the handle of his spade, poking out of the clay that had buried him. I was so glad he was there that any spite I felt towards him vanished. "Captain Cury! Mr Buckland's gone to get help. They'll be back to dig us out."

The finger moved, but less than before.

"Was you up on the cliff and come down with the slip?"

The finger didn't move.

"Captain Cury, can you hear me? Are your bones broke? Fanny's leg is broke, I think. Mr Buckland's taken her with him. He'll come back soon." I was chattering on to mask my terror.

The finger stayed stiff, pointing up at the sky. I knew what that meant, and begun to cry. "Don't go! Stay with me! Please stay, Captain Cury!"

Between me and Captain Cury the croc eye watched us both. Captain Cury and I are going to be like the croc, I thought. We will become fossils, trapped upon beach forever.

After a while I stopped looking at Captain Cury's finger, now as still as any rock caught in the clay. I couldn't bear to watch the tide steadily rising. Instead I gazed up into the flat white sky, a few pewter clouds swimming about in it. After spending so much of my life looking down at stones, it was strange to look up into emptiness. I spotted a gull circling high above. It seemed it would never get closer, but would always be a dot hovering far away. I kept my eyes fixed on it, and did not look at the finger or the croc again.

It was so quiet I wanted to make a noise to break the spell. I wanted the lightning to pass through me and jolt me into life, for I was feeling the opposite of that sensation – a slow darkness was creeping through my body.

There had been plenty of deaths in our family – Pa and all the children. I spent most of my time collecting what were dead bodies of animals. But I had not thought much of my own death before. Even when I had been visiting Lady Jackson I'd really thought more of her passing than mine, and treating death as a drama to revel in. But dying was no drama. Dying was cold and hard and painful, and dull. It went on too long. I was exhausted and growing bored with it. Now I had too much time to think about whether I was going to die from the tide coming in and drowning me like Lady Jackson, or the mud pressing the air out of me as it had Captain Cury, or a falling rock striking me. I couldn't think for long or it hurt too much, like touching a piece of ice. I tried to think of God instead, and how He would help me through it.

I never told anyone this, but thinking of Him then didn't make me less scared.

It was hard to breathe now with the mud so heavy. My breathing got slower, and so did the beat of my heart, and I closed my eyes.

When I come to, someone was digging at the clay round me. I opened my eyes and smiled. "Thank you. I knew you would come. Oh, thank you for coming to me."

6

A little in love with him myself

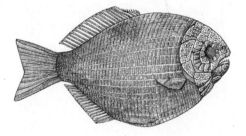

You might think saving someone's life would bind you ever after. That is not what happened with Mary and me. I am not blaming her, but digging her out of the landslip that day, using Captain Cury's spade and racing against the tide and the rocks that rained down on either side of us, seemed to drive us apart rather than bring us closer.

It was a miracle Mary survived, and intact as well, especially given Captain Cury's terrible suffocating death just a few feet from her. She had bad bruising up and down her body, but only a few broken bones – some ribs and her collarbone. This kept her in bed a few weeks – not long enough to satisfy Doctor Carpenter, but she refused to convalesce any longer, and soon reappeared on the beach, bound up tightly to keep the bones in place.

I was amazed she was willing to go out hunting again after what she'd been through. Not only that – she did not change her habits, but went back to pacing along the base of the cliffs, where landslips could come down. When I suggested that Molly and Joseph Anning would understand if she did not want to go back to hunting, Mary declared, "I been struck by lightning and buried in a landslip and survived both. God must have other plans for me. Besides," she added, "I can't afford to stop."

On top of her father's debts, which years later the family was still struggling to clear, they now owed Doctor Carpenter. He was fond of Mary because of their shared interest in fossils, as well as for the pleasure he took from knowing his advice had saved her from the lightning strike. However, he still had to be paid for his care of Mary, and of Fanny Miller as well, as insisted on by her family. The Annings did not challenge this demand. More surprising, they did not expect William Buckland to pay for Fanny's care; nor would Molly Anning let me write to him about it on their behalf. "He can afford it more than you," I reasoned when I was visiting Mary to lend her a Bible she wanted to read while she was still in bed. "And it is because of him that Fanny was out on the beach at all."

Molly Anning did not pause while she counted a pile of pennies from the fossil table sales. "If Mr Buckland felt he ought to pay, he would have offered to before he went back to Oxford. I ain't going to chase after him for his money."

"I don't think he has thought about it one way or the other," I said. "He is a scholar, not a practical man. If put to him, though, I am sure he would honour the debt and pay Doctor Carpenter – for Mary's treatment as well as Fanny's."

"No." Molly Anning's stubbornness revealed a certain pride I had not realised she possessed. She measured most things by the coins they represented and the distance they put between the Annings and the workhouse, but in this instance I believe she understood that money was not the issue. Whether or not William Buckland was involved, the Annings had placed an innocent girl in danger, and effectively crippled her. Fanny could not now expect to marry well, or at all. Her fair looks might make up for a great deal, but most husbands at that working level of society would need a wife who was able to walk a mile. No amount of money could make up for what Fanny had lost. Molly Anning took on the debt as a sort of punishment.

Mary never talked about the half hour she was buried before I found her. But the experience changed her. I often caught in her eyes a faraway expression, as if she were listening to someone calling from the top of Black Ven, or a gull crying out at sea. Death had come and camped next to her on the beach, taking Captain Cury while sparing her, and reminding her of its presence and of her own limits. All of us begin to feel deeply our mortality at some time in our lives, but it is usually when we are older than Mary was then.

Mary's contact with death also came at a time when she was maturing. One day I helped Molly Anning remove the bandages that had bound Mary's broken bones, and discovered that under her ill-fitting dress she had a womanly figure, with her waist and breasts and hips all in good proportion. Her shoulders were perhaps a little hunched from her fascination with the ground, and her knuckles were raw, her fingers rough and cracked from use. She was not graceful, as Margaret had been at that age. But she had a fresh, bold presence that could attract men.

She had begun to sense it as well. She took more care to wash her face and hands, and asked Margaret for some of the salve she had concocted to try to save my own hands from the drying force of Blue Lias clay. Made of beeswax, turpentine, lavender and yarrow, it was useful for dressing wounds as well as chapped skin, but Mary wore it on her hands, elbows and cheeks, and I began to associate her with that scent, a curious mixture of the medicinal and the floral.

Mary's hair was always going to be a dull brown, and scrubby from the wind rather than the curled ringlets that were the fashion. But she did at least comb her fringe daily, and pull the rest into a bun which she covered with a cap and bonnet. I am not sure how much good making an effort with her looks did, for her reputation was already much compromised by her time with Mr Buckland, even with the ill-fated Fanny as companion. The landslip accident might normally have brought Mary some sympathy, but Fanny's injuries caused much indignation amongst working people, creating sides that cast Mary as the villain. If she was trying to soften her elbows and tame her hair, it could not be for any Lyme man she fancied she could snare. She had too openly flouted the rules of what was expected from a girl in her position. Now that it had tangible consequences in the form of Fanny's broken gait, vague impressions hardened into harsh opinions.

Mary paid little attention to what others said about her, a trait in her I both admired and despaired of. Perhaps I was a little jealous that she could be so free with her contempt for society's workings in a way that a woman of my class could not. Even in a place as independent-minded as Lyme, I was all too aware of the judgements made if one stepped too far out of place.

Perhaps Mary did not care for the sort of life Lyme had decided for her. She had spent a great deal of time with people above her station – me most of all, but also William Buckland, and various gentlemen who made their way to

Lyme, having heard of or seen the creatures Mary had found. It rather turned her head, and raised her hopes that she might be able to move up in the world. I do not think she ever seriously considered any of the men as potential suitors: most gentlemen viewed her as little more than a knowledgeable servant. William Buckland was more appreciative of her talent, but was too caught up in his own head to notice her as a woman. Such a man would be deeply frustrating, as I briefly allowed myself to discover.

For Mary's interest in men piqued my own, which I had thought dead but discovered was merely dormant, a rose-bush that needed but a little attention to attempt to flower. Once I invited William Buckland to dine with us at Morley Cottage so that he might look at my specimen collection. He accepted with an enthusiasm I suspected was for my fossils, yet I allowed myself to think might be directed towards me as well. For a match between him and me was not such a mad idea. Granted I was several years older than him, and too old to have many children. But it was not impossible. Molly Anning had borne her last child at the age of forty-six. William Buckland and I were of similar social standing, and intellectually suited. Of course I was not educated to his degree, but I read widely. I knew enough about geology and fossils to be a supportive wife to him in his profession.

Margaret, always quick to spot romantic potential even for an aging spinster, encouraged these thoughts by going on about Mr Buckland's vivid eyes, and nagging me about what I would wear to dinner. What began as genial interest grew to such a pitch of quiet excitement that by the appointed day my stomach was fizzing with nerves.

We waited for him for two hours, Bessy harrumphing and tossing pots about in the kitchen, before we gave in and sat down to a ruined meal that I forced myself to eat. If nothing else, I was obliged to Bessy for making the special effort. She was already on the verge of giving notice once more, and certainly would if I refused to eat. I would also not display disappointment to my sisters, though every bite was lead in my mouth.

The next day I did not seek him out, but nonetheless came upon William Buckland on the beach, for once without Mary. He greeted me heartily, but when I mentioned being disappointed that we had not seen him the day before, he looked surprised. "Was I meant to dine with you, Miss Philpot? Are you sure? Because, you see, yesterday I heard a man had found part of a long sequence of vertebrae down at Seatown, and I had to go and see for myself. And do you know, I'm glad I did, for they are well preserved and yet quite different from Mary's creature's vertebrae. I am wondering if they might be from a different animal altogether."

Unrepentant at his social error, he also did not sense that I was upset. To him it was perfectly normal that going to see a set of unusual vertebrae would take precedence over dining with ladies.

I said nothing but "Good day, sir," and turned away. It was then I understood that only a woman beautiful enough to distract him or patient enough to put up with him would manage to marry William Buckland.

I thought that was the end of my new regard for men. I had never imagined there would be a Colonel Birch.

*   *   *

The summer Colonel Birch arrived in Lyme, Mary was in a peculiar state, pulled this way and that. On the one hand, the creature she and Joseph had discovered had become quite famous. Charles König bought the original specimen from Bullock's and put it on display at the British Museum. He named it an ichthyosaurus, which means "fish lizard", for its anatomy falls somewhere between the two. He and others studied it and published articles in which they speculated that the ichthyosaurus was a marine reptile, for it breathed in air like a mammal but swam like a fish. I read these papers, lent to me by William Buckland, with great curiosity, noting that none of them discussed the thorny questions of extinction or God's hand in the creature's disappearance. Indeed, they did not bring up religious issues at all. Perhaps they were copying Cuvier, who never mentioned God's intentions in his writings. It was a relief to me to accept the ichthyosaurus as what it was – an ancient marine reptile with its own name.

Mary found it harder, and often still called it a crocodile, as did most of the local residents, though eventually she settled on ichie. To her the new scientific name took her creature away from her even more effectively than its physical removal. Learned men were discussing it at meetings and writing about it, and Mary was excluded from their activity. She was relied upon to find the specimens, but not to take part in studying them. And even that hunting was proving difficult – she had not found a complete ichthyosaurus in over a year, though she combed Church Cliffs and Black Ven every day.

One day I suggested we look for brittle stars and crinoids on the beach towards Seatown, several miles east of Charmouth.

We did not usually go so far afield, but I thought a change of scene would do Mary good, and suggested Seatown to get her away from her endless tramping up and down the same beach in search of an elusive monster. We chose a sunny day when the tides favoured an early start. She left behind Church Cliffs and Black Ven willingly enough, but at Gabriel's Ledge, just beyond Charmouth, she kept turning and looking behind us, as if the cliffs were calling her back. "There was a flash back there," she insisted. "Didn't you see it?"

I shook my head and continued along the beach, hoping she would follow.

"There it is again," Mary said. "Oh, look, Miss Philpot, do you think he's coming for us?"

A man was striding up the beach. Although there were other people out, taking advantage of the mild weather and the glorious morning light, he cut through them as if he knew exactly what his goal was, and it was us. He was tall and erect, and wore the high boots and long red coat of a soldier. The uniform's brass buttons winked in the sun. I am not often moved by the sight of a man, but having this one make it his clear purpose to reach us was a thrill I will long remember.

He smiled as he approached. He was a striking figure of fifty or so, with the straight military bearing so pleasing in a man, trim and upright and confident. His face was weathered, his eyes slits against the sun and wind, but he was handsome with it. When he removed his cocked hat and bowed, I could see the parting in his bushy black hair, which was threaded with grey.

"Ladies," he announced, "I have been searching all morning for you, and am delighted to have found you at last." He put his hat back on, making the white plumes it was trimmed with waggle. His hair was so thick and wavy the hat was in danger of springing off.

I have never trusted a man who leads with his hair. Only a vain, overconfident man does that.

"I am Colonel Birch, late of the 1st Regiment of the Life Guards." He paused, looking back and forth between us, then settled his attention on Mary. "And you must be the remarkable Mary Anning who has found several ichthyosaurus specimens, is that right?"

Mary nodded, unable to stop staring at him.

Of course, anyone who knew of Mary would also know that she was young and of a low background, and there could be no mistaking me for her, with my twenty extra years etched onto my face and my finer clothes and bearing. Yet I felt the sharp dart of jealousy pierce me, that a handsome man was not striding along the beach for me.

It made me more prickly than I'd intended. "I suppose you'll be wanting her to find you one, rather like commissioning a print dealer to find you a print to hang on a particular wall."

Mary shot me an annoyed look, for such rudeness was unlike me, but Colonel Birch laughed. "As it happens, I *do* want Mary to help me find an ichthyosaurus, if she is willing."

"Of course, sir!"

"You will have to ask her mother and brother for permission," I said. "It wouldn't be appropriate otherwise." I couldn't hold back barbed comments.

"Oh, that don't matter – they'll say yes," Mary put in.

"Of course I will speak to your family," Colonel Birch said. "You have nothing to fear from me, Mary – nor you, Miss—"

"Philpot." Of course he assumed I was a spinster. Would a married lady be out on the beach, far from home, hunting for fossils? I stooped to pick up something from the sand. It was just a bit of beef shaped like one of the paddle bones of an ichthyosaurus, but I paid it more attention than it was due so that I wouldn't have to look at Colonel Birch.

"Let's go back and ask Mam now," Mary suggested.

"Mary, we were going to Seatown, don't you remember?" I reminded her. "To look for brittle stars and sea lilies. If you go back to Lyme we'll have to give up the day."

Colonel Birch cut in. "I could accompany you to Seatown. That's rather a long way for ladies to go on their own, isn't it?"

"Seven miles," I snapped. "We're certainly capable of walking that far. We do it all the time. We'll get the coach back at the end."

"I shall see you to the coach," Colonel Birch declared. "I would not want it on my conscience to leave you two ladies undefended."

"We don't need—"

"Oh, thank you, Colonel Birch, sir!" Mary interrupted.

'Sea lilies, did you say?" Colonel Birch said. "I have some lovely specimens of pentacrinites myself. I'll show you sometime, if you like. They're back at my hotel in Charmouth."

I frowned at the impropriety of his suggestion. Mary's judgement, however, had fallen away. "I'd like to see them," she said. "And I've other crinoids back home you be welcome to look at, sir. Crinoids and ammos, and bits of croc– ichthyosaurus, and all sorts." The girl was enamoured with him already. I shook my head and stalked off down the beach, my head lowered, pretending to hunt, though I was walking too fast to find anything. After a moment they followed.

"What is a brittle star?" Colonel Birch asked. "I have not heard of such a thing."

"It's shaped like a star, sir," Mary explained. "The centre is marked with the outline of a flower with five petals, and a long, wavy leg extends off each petal. It's hard to find one with all five legs intact. I've had a collector ask specially for one that's not broken. That's why we've come this far. Normally I stay between Lyme and Charmouth, by Black Ven and off the ledges by town."

"Is that where you have found the ichthyosauri?"

"There, and one along Monmouth Beach, just to the west of Lyme. But there might be some along here. I just haven't looked here for them. Have you seen an ichthyosaurus, sir?"

"No, but I've read about them, and seen drawings."

I snorted.

"I am here for the summer to expand my fossil collection, Mary, and I hope you will be able to help – There!" Colonel Birch stopped. I turned to look. He reached down and picked up a bit of crinoid.

"Very good, sir," Mary said. "I was just going to have a look at that, but you beat me to it."

He held it out to her. "It is for you, Mary. I would not deprive you of such a lovely specimen. It is my gift to you."

It was indeed a fine specimen, fanning out like the lily it was named for. "Oh no, sir, it's yours," Mary said. "You found it. I could never take it from you."

Colonel Birch took her hand, laid the crinoid in it and

closed her fingers around it. "I insist, Mary." He held his hand over her fist and looked at her. "Did you know crinoids are not plants as they appear, but creatures?"

"Really, sir?" Mary was staring into his eyes. Of course she knew about crinoids. I had taught her.

I stepped forward. "Colonel Birch, I must ask you to show proper respect or I shall require that you leave us."

Colonel Birch dropped his hand. "My apologies, Miss Philpot. The discovery of fossils excites me in ways I find hard to control."

"Control it you must, sir, or you will lose the privileges you seek."

He nodded and fell back to a respectful distance. We walked in silence for a time. But Colonel Birch could not be quiet for long, and soon he and Mary were lagging behind while he asked her about the fossils she preferred, her method of hunting, even her thoughts on what the ichthyosaurus was. "I don't know, sir," she said of her most spectacular find. "It seems the ichie's got a bit of crocodile in it, some lizard, some fish. And a bit of something all its own. That's what's difficult, that bit. How it fits in."

"Oh, I expect your ichthyosaurus has a place in Aristotle's Great Chain of Being," Colonel Birch said.

"What's that, sir?"

I tutted. She didn't need him to explain it, for I had described the theory to Mary myself. She was flirting with him. Of course he loved telling her what he knew. Men do.

"The Greek philosopher Aristotle suggested that all creatures could be placed along a scale, from the lowest plants up to the perfection that is man, in a chain of creation. So

186

your ichthyosaurus may fall between a lizard and a crocodile in the chain, for instance."

"That is very interesting, sir." Mary paused. "But that
don't explain about the bit of the ichie that's like nothing
else, that don't fit in with the categories. Where does that fit
in the chain, if it's different from everything else?"

Colonel Birch suddenly stopped, squatted and picked up
a stone. "Is this – Oh, no, it's not. My mistake." He threw
the stone into the water.

I smiled. He might dazzle with his handsome head of
hair, but his grasp of knowledge was superficial, and Mary
had picked it apart.

"What about you, Miss Philpot? What do you like to
collect?" In two lively steps Colonel Birch had caught up
with me, escaping Mary's awkward question. I did not want
his attention, for I was not sure I could bear it, but I could
not be impolite.

"Fish," I answered as briefly as I could.

"Fish?"

Though I did not want to converse with him, I could
not help showing off a bit of my knowledge. "Primarily
Eugnathus, Pholidophorus, Dapedius, and *Hybodus* – the last is
an ancient shark," I added as his face went blank at the
Latin. "Those are the genus names, of course. The different
species have not yet been identified."

"Miss Philpot has a big collection of fossil fish at her
home," Mary put in. "People come and look all the time,
don't they, Miss Elizabeth?"

"Really? Fascinating," Colonel Birch murmured. "I shall
be sure to visit as well and see your fish."

He was careful, so I could never accuse him of rudeness,

187

but his tone bore a trace of sarcasm. He preferred the bold ichthyosaurus to the quiet fish. But then, most do. They do not understand that the clear shape and texture of a fish, with its overlapping scales, its dimpled skin, and its shapely fins, all make up a specimen of great beauty – beautiful because it is plain and definite. With his gleaming buttons and thrusting hair, Colonel Birch could never comprehend such subtlety.

"You'd best move along," I snapped, "else the tide will catch us out before we reach Seatown. Mary, if you don't stop talking you'll never find a brittle star for your collector."

Mary scowled, but I was done tolerating Colonel Birch. I turned and strode towards Seatown, blind to any fossils underfoot.

Colonel Birch was to stay for several weeks to build up his collection, taking rooms in Charmouth but coming to Lyme daily. His claim on Mary's time was sudden and absolute. She went out with him every day. To start with I accompanied them, for even if Mary didn't, I worried what the town would think. When we three were together I tried to find the comfortable rhythm I had when I was out only with Mary, where we each concentrated on our own hunting and yet felt the reassuring presence of a companion close by. That rhythm was ruined by Colonel Birch, who liked to remain with Mary and talk. It is a testament to her hunting skills that she was able to find anything at all that summer with him babbling at her side. Yet she tolerated him. More than tolerated – she doted on him. There was no place for me on the beach with them. I might as well have been an empty crab shell. I went out three times with them, and that was enough.

For Colonel Birch was a fraud. To be accurate, I should say, *Lieutenant* Colonel Birch was a fraud. That was one of his many petty ruses – leaving off the "Lieutenant" to promote himself higher than he was. Nor did he offer up that he was long retired from the Life Guards, though anyone who knew a bit about them could see he wore the old uniform of long coat and leather breeches rather than the shorter coat and blue-grey pantaloons of the current soldiers. He was happy to bask in the Life Guards' glory at Waterloo, without having taken part.

Worse, I discovered from those three days on the beach with him that he did not find fossils himself. He did not keep his eyes on the ground as Mary and I did, but searched our faces and followed our gazes so that as we stopped and leaned over, he reached out and picked up what we were looking at before we had time to do so ourselves. He only tried this method with me once before my glare stopped him. Mary was more tolerant, or blinded by her feelings, and let him rob her of many specimens and call them his own finds.

Colonel Birch's amateurism appalled me. For all his professed interest in fossils, and his supposedly robust military constitution ready for all hardships, he was not a scrabbler in the mud in search of specimens. He found his through his wallet, or his charm, or by picking them off others. He had a fine collection by the end of the summer, but Mary had found and given them to him, or nudged him towards those she had spotted. Like Lord Henley and other men who came to Lyme, he was a collector rather than a hunter, buying his knowledge rather than seeking it with his own eyes and hands. I could not understand how Mary would find him appealing.

Yes, I could. I was a little in love with him myself. For all my complaints, I found him very attractive: not only physically, though there was that, but because his interest in fossils seemed genuine and penetrating. When he was not flirting with Mary, he was capable – and keen – to discuss the origins of the ichthyosaurus, and what it meant to be extinct. He was also clear about God's role, without seeming disrespectful or blasphemous. "I am sure God has better things to do than watch over every living creature on this earth," he said once when we were walking back to Lyme along the cliff path, the tide having cut us off. "He has done such amazing work to create what He has; surely now He needn't follow the progress of every worm and shark. His concern is with us, and He showed that by making us in His image and sending us His son." Colonel Birch made it sound so clear and sensible that I wished Reverend Jones could hear him.

Here, then, was a man who thought and talked about fossils, who encouraged us women to look for them, who would not mind that I regularly ruined my gloves. My anger at him stemmed not so much from irritation at his inability to be a hunter rather than a collector, but from indignation that he never for a moment considered me – closer to his age and of a similar class – as a lady he might court.

Whatever I thought of him, it was not for me to decide what Mary did or did not do with Colonel Birch. That was for Molly Anning to sort out. Over the years Molly and I had grown to understand each other, so that she was less suspicious and I less intimidated. While she had little education, and saw neither poetry nor philosophy in our discoveries, she accepted their importance to me and to others. That importance may have been measured in coins that kept her family fed, clothed and sheltered, but she did not ridicule their value. Fossils became an item to be sold, as significant as buttons or carrots or barrels or nails. If she thought it peculiar that I did not sell the specimens I found, she did not show it. After all, in her eyes I did not need to. Louise, Margaret and I could not be extravagant, but we were never fearful of the bailiff or the workhouse. The Annings, however, lived on the edge of starvation, and that can sharpen a mind. Molly Anning became quite a shrewd saleswoman, squeezing out extra shillings and pennies here and there.

She envied me my income and my position in society – what society there was in Lyme – but she pitied me too, for I had never known a man, never felt the security of marriage or the love of a baby in my arms. That rather balanced out the envy, and left her neutral and reasonably tolerant towards me. As for me, I admired her business sense and her ability to find her way through difficult circumstances. She did not complain much even though she had a right to, given her hard life.

Unfortunately, Molly Anning allowed herself to be carried away by Colonel Birch's charm almost as much as her daughter was. I had always thought she was a good judge of character, and would have thought she'd see Birch as the greedy schemer he was. Perhaps like Mary she sensed he was the first real – and possibly the only – opportunity her daughter had to be lifted from the hard life of her own class into a kinder, more prosperous world.

I do not think Colonel Birch originally intended to court Mary. He was drawn to Lyme by a fever many have felt for finding treasure on the beach, where old bones with their hints of earlier worlds become as precious as silver. It is hard to stop looking once you have become infected. However, Colonel Birch was also presented with the unusual opportunity of passing whole days with an unaccompanied woman, and could not resist.

First, though, he had to win over her mother. He did so by flirting shamelessly with her, and for perhaps the only time in her life, Molly Anning lost her head. Ground down by poverty and loss, Molly had enjoyed little happiness in the years since Richard Anning's death, but suffered constant worry over money and fear of the prospect of being sent to the workhouse. Now a handsome retired soldier in a smart uniform was kissing her hand and complimenting her housekeeping and asking her leave to go along the beach with her daughter. She who had been so indignant at William Buckland innocently taking Mary out now threw away her caution for the price of a kiss on the hand and a kind word or two. Perhaps she was simply tired of saying no.

The shop where Molly Anning sold fossils to visitors began to run low on even basic specimens such as ammonites and belemnites, for Mary had stopped picking up other fossils, leaving nodules for others to break open, ignoring requests by other collectors for sea urchins or gryphaea or brittle stars. The good specimens she found she gave to Colonel Birch, or encouraged him to pick up himself. Molly did not complain to her daughter, however. I helped as best I could by donating what I found, for I primarily hunted for fossil fish and left other specimens to others. But the Annings were low on funds and running debts with the baker and the butcher, and would soon with the coal merchant once it grew cold. Still Molly Anning said nothing – perhaps seeing Mary's time with Colonel Birch as a future investment.

Since her mother wouldn't, I tried to talk to Mary about Colonel Birch. When the tide was high they could not go out, and he would stop in at the Three Cups, or attend the Assembly Rooms, where of course Mary did not go. Then she would help her mother, or clean Colonel Birch's specimens for him, or simply wander about Lyme in a daze. One day I met her as I was coming up Sherborne Lane, a small passage that led to Silver Street from the centre of town. I used it when I was not feeling sociable enough to greet everyone walking along Broad Street. Mary was drifting down the lane, her eyes on Golden Cap, a smile on her face, which shone with an appealing inner joy. For a moment I could almost believe Colonel Birch might seriously court her.

Seeing her so happy twisted my jealous heart, so that when she greeted me I did not restrain myself. "Mary," I said abruptly, without the small talk that eases such conversation, "is Colonel Birch paying you for your time?"

Mary gave her head a shake, as if trying to rouse herself, and met my eyes with all of her attention. "What do you mean?"

I shifted the basket I was carrying from one arm to the other. "He is taking up all of your hunting time. Is he paying you for it, or at least for the fossils you find him?"

Mary narrowed her eyes. "You never asked me that about Mr Buckland, or Henry De La Beche, or any of the other gentlemen I've taken out. Is Colonel Birch any different?"

"You know he is. For one thing, the others found their own fossils, or paid you for those you found for them. Is Colonel Birch paying you?"

Mary's eyes registered a flicker of doubt, which she covered up with scorn. "He finds his own curies. He don't need to pay me."

"Oh? And what have you found to sell, then?" When Mary didn't answer, I added, "I've seen your mother's cury table in Cockmoile Square, Mary. There is little on it. She's selling broken ammonites you would have thrown back into the sea once."

Mary's elation had entirely disappeared. If that was my intention, I had been successful. "I'm helping Colonel Birch," she declared. "There's nothing wrong with that."

"And he should be paying you for it. Otherwise he is using you for his own gain and leaving you and your family the poorer." I should have left it there, where my words might have had a positive effect. But I could not resist pressing harder. "His behaviour does not speak well of his character, Mary. You would do better not to associate with such a man, for it will hurt you in the end. Already the town is talking, and it is worse than when you attended William Buckland."

Mary glared at me. "That's nonsense. You don't know him at all, not like I do. You'd do better to stop listening to gossip, or you'll become a gossip yourself!" Pushing past me, she hurried down Sherborne Lane. Mary had never before been so rude to me. It was as if she had taken a great leap from deferring to me as a working girl to acting as my equal.

Afterwards I felt bad about what I had said and how I had said it, and decided as penance I would force myself to go out with Mary and Colonel Birch again, to blunt the sharp tongues of Lyme. Mary accepted my gesture easily, for love made her forgiving.

That was why I was with them out by Black Ven when they at last found the ichthyosaurus Colonel Birch was so keen to add to his collection. I was finding very little that day, for I was distracted by the behaviour of Mary and Colonel Birch, who were more openly affectionate than they had been weeks before: touching an arm to get the other's attention, whispering together, smiling at each other. For an awful moment I wondered if Mary had succumbed completely to him. But then I reasoned that if she had, she would not go to such lengths to seem accidentally to touch his arm. I did not know of married couples who caressed each other so eagerly. They did not need to.

I was pondering this when I saw Mary pause on a ledge and look down, the way I'd seen her do hundreds of times. It was the quality of her stillness that told me she'd found something.

Colonel Birch went on a few paces, then stopped himself and came back. "What is it, Mary? Have you seen something?"

Mary hesitated. Perhaps if she'd realised I was watching she wouldn't have done what she did next. "No, sir," she said. "Nothing. I just—" She let slip her hammer, which fell with a clang to rest. "Sorry, sir, I've come over a little dizzy. It must be the sun. Could you fetch my hammer for me?"

"Of course." Colonel Birch bent to pick it up, froze, then dropped to his knees. He glanced up at Mary, as if trying to read her face.

"Have you found something, sir?"

"Do you know, I think I have, Mary!"

"That's a dorsal vertebra, isn't it? See, sir, if you measure it you can tell how long your creature is. For every inch in diameter the ichie is five feet in length. This is about an inch and a half in diameter, so the creature would be about eight feet long. Look round and see if you can uncover other parts of it in the ledge. Here, use my hammer."

She was giving the ichthyosaurus to him, and he knew it. I turned away, disgusted. While they excitedly traced the outline of the creature in the ledge, I busied myself knocking open random rocks, just to keep myself busy, until they called to me to come and see Colonel Birch's find. I could barely look at it, which was a shame, for it was perhaps the finest ichthyosaurus Mary ever found, and it is always an impressive sight to see one embedded in its natural environment before it is cut out of the stone. However, I had to put on a civil face and congratulate him. "Well done, Colonel Birch," I said. "It will make a fascinating addition to your collection." I allowed the slightest hint of sarcasm into my voice, but it was lost on them both, for Colonel Birch had taken Mary into his arms and was swinging her about as if they were at an Assembly Rooms ball.

They spent the next two weeks having the Day brothers dig out the ichthyosaurus, and cleaning it back at the workshop, with Mary doing the delicate work to make it presentable. She worked so hard on it her eyes went red. I did not visit while she prepared it, for I did not want to be caught in the close quarters of the workshop with Colonel Birch. Indeed, I avoided him as best I could. Not well enough, however.

One afternoon Margaret convinced me to play cards at the Assembly Rooms. I did not go often, for it was full of young ladies and men courting, and mothers watching the proceedings. The select friends I had made in Lyme were of a more cerebral nature, like young Henry De La Beche or Doctor Carpenter and his wife. We usually met at one another's houses rather than at the Assembly Rooms. But Margaret wanted a partner, and insisted.

In the middle of a game Colonel Birch walked in. Of course I noticed him immediately, and he me – he caught my eye before I could look away, and came straight over. Trapped by my cards, I responded to his greeting with as little expression as possible, though that did not stop him from standing over me and chatting with onlookers. The other players looked at me with amused surprise, and I began to play badly. As soon as I was able I feigned a headache and got up from the table. I had hoped Colonel Birch would take my place, but instead he followed me to the bay window, where we both looked out to sea. A ship was sailing past, about to dock at the Cobb.

"That is the *Unity*," Colonel Birch said. "I am having the ichthyosaurus shipped on it to London when it leaves tomorrow."

Despite not wanting to engage in conversation, I could not help myself. "Has Mary done with her work on the specimen, then?"

"It's set in its frame, and just this afternoon she put a plaster skim around it to finish it. It should be dry later, and she'll pack it up."

"But you are not going on the *Unity* yourself?" I was not sure if I wanted him to stay or go, but I had to know.

"I will go up by coach, stopping first at Bath and Oxford to see friends."

"Now that you have what you came for, I suppose there is no reason to stay on." Hard as I tried to keep it steady, my voice wavered. I did not add that his haste to depart after securing his treasure was in poor taste. Instead I kept my eyes on the waves that chopped and swayed under the window, for the tide was high. I could feel Colonel Birch's eyes on me, but I did not turn to face him. My cheeks were flushed.

"I have very much enjoyed our conversations, Miss Philpot," he said. "I shall miss them."

I turned then and looked at him direct.

"Your eyes are very dark today," he added. "Dark and honest."

"I am going to go home now," I replied, as if he had asked. "No, don't accompany me, Colonel Birch. I do not want you to." I turned. It seemed the entire room was watching us. I went over to fetch my sister, and was truly relieved that he did not follow.

I believe the months after Colonel Birch's departure were the hardest ever for the Annings – even harder than after Richard Anning died, for at least then they had the sympathy of the town. Now people simply thought they had brought on their misery.

I first truly understood how much damage Colonel Birch had done to Mary's reputation when, not long after, I heard for myself what people were saying. I went into the baker's one day – Bessy had forgotten to, but refused to go down the hill once more. As I entered I overheard the wife of the baker – who was an Anning himself, and a distant cousin of Mary's – say to a customer, "She spent every day on the beach with that gentleman. Let him take care of her." She chuckled crudely, but stopped when she saw me. Even though no names had been mentioned, I knew whom she was referring to: It was clear from the defiant tilt of her chin, as if she were daring me to chide her for being so judgemental and ungenerous.

I didn't rise to the challenge. It would have been like trying to damn a flood. Instead I fingered a loaf of bread, raised my eyebrows, and said in a ringing voice, "I don't really *need* stale bread today. I'll come another day when I do." It gave me only momentary satisfaction, though – for Simeon Anning was the only baker in Lyme, and we would have to continue to buy from his wife if we wanted bread we could actually eat, as opposed to Bessy's brick-like attempts. Besides, my words were weak and petty, and did little to help Mary. I left the shop red-faced, and it was made worse by the laughter that followed me. I wondered if I would ever be able to speak up for myself without feeling an idiot.

While Molly and Joseph Anning suffered materially that winter, with many days of weak soup and weaker fires, Mary barely noticed how little she was eating or the chilblains on her hands and feet. She was suffering inside.

She still came to Morley Cottage, but preferred to visit Margaret, for my sister could provide her with the empathy that Louise and I lacked. We had not lost a man the way Mary and Margaret had, and it was not in our natures to dissemble. Not that Mary felt she had lost Colonel Birch at that point. For a long time she was hopeful, and simply missed him and the constant presence he had been in her life all summer. She wanted to talk about him with someone who knew him and approved of him, or at least didn't express the sour criticism of his character that I had. Margaret had met Colonel Birch several times at the Assembly Rooms, had played cards with him and even danced with him twice. While I worked on my fossils at the dining room table, I could hear Mary with Margaret next door, making her describe again and again the dances, what Colonel Birch had worn, what his gait and touch had been like, what they had chatted about as they went through their motions. Then she wanted to know about the cards, what they had played and whether he won or lost, and what he had said. Margaret had not noticed such details, for Colonel Birch had not been a memorable companion to her. His vanity and confidence were too much even for Margaret. However, for Mary she made up details to add to the little she did remember, until a fulsome picture emerged of Colonel Birch in his leisure moments. Mary drank in every detail, to store and pore over later.

I wanted to order Margaret to stop, for the pathos of a girl feeding on another's scraps of polite dances and indifferent card games upset me, bringing to mind an image of Mary standing outside the Assembly Rooms and pressing her face to the cold glass to watch the dancers. Though I had never seen her do so, I would not have been surprised to learn that she had. I held my tongue, however, for I knew Margaret meant well, and was providing the little comfort Mary had in her life at the time. I was grateful too that Margaret never told Mary I had briefly been with Colonel

Birch at the Assembly Rooms, for Mary would have wanted me to recall every detail of that afternoon.

Though it would not be proper to initiate correspondence herself, Mary hoped and expected to hear from Colonel Birch. She and Molly Anning occasionally received letters, from William Buckland asking after a specimen, or Henry De La Beche telling them where he was, or other collectors they'd met and who wanted something from them. Molly Anning was even corresponding with Charles Konig at the British Museum, who had bought Mary's first ichthyosaurus from William Bullock and was interested in buying others. All of these letters continued to arrive, but in amongst them there was never the flash of Colonel Birch's bold, scrawling hand. For I knew his hand.

I could not tell Mary that it was I who heard from Colonel Birch, a month after he'd left Lyme. Of course it was not a letter declaring himself, though as I opened it my hands trembled. Instead he asked if I would kindly look out for a dapedium specimen, of the sort I had donated to the British Museum, as he was hoping to add choice fossil fish to his collection. I read it out to Margaret and Louise. "The cheek of it!" I cried. "After his scorn of my fish, to go and ask me for one, and one so difficult to find!" As angry as I sounded, I was also secretly pleased that Colonel Birch had discovered the value of my fish enough to want one for himself.

Still, I made to throw the letter on the fire. Margaret stopped me. "Don't," she pleaded, reaching for it. "Are you sure there's nothing about Mary? No postscript, or a coded message to her or about her?" She looked over the letter but could find nothing. "At least keep it so that you'll know where he lives." As she said this Margaret was reading the address – a street in Chelsea – doubtless memorising it in case I burned the letter later.

"All right, I will put it away," I promised. "But I will not answer it. He doesn't deserve an answer. And he will never get his hands on any of my fish!"

We did not tell Mary Colonel Birch had written to me. It would have devastated her. I had never expected such a strong character as Mary's to be so fragile. But we are all vulnerable at times. So she continued to wait, and talk, and ask Margaret to describe Colonel Birch's conduct at the Assembly Rooms, and Margaret did it, though it pained her to lie. And slowly the bloom left Mary's cheeks, the bright light in her eyes dimmed, her shoulders took on their habitual hunch, and her jaw hardened. It made me want to weep, to see her joining the ranks of us spinsters at such a young age.

One sunny winter day I had a surprise visitor to Silver Street. I was out in the garden with Louise, who missed working during the cold months and was looking for something she could do: spreading mulch around sleeping plants, checking on the bulbs she had planted, raking stray leaves that had blown into the garden, pruning back the rose bushes that persisted in growing. The cold did not bother us as it would have once, and in the sun it was surprisingly warm. I was finishing a watercolour of the view towards Golden Cap, which I had begun months before, but brought out again with the hope that the oblique winter sunlight might give the painting the magic quality it yet lacked.

I was adding a yellow wash to the clouds when Bessy appeared. "Someone to see you," she muttered. She stepped aside to reveal Molly Anning, who in the many years we'd lived there had never ventured up Silver Street.

Bessy's scorn vexed me. Despite my friendship with the Annings, Bessy all too readily took on the views of the rest of Lyme about the family, even when she had seen enough of Mary to form her own judgement. I punished her by standing and saying, "Bessy, bring out a chair for Mrs Anning, and one for Louise, and tea for all of us, please. You don't mind sitting outside, Molly? In the sun it's quite mild."

Molly Anning shrugged. She was not the sort to take pleasure in sitting in the sun, but she would not stop others doing it.

I raised my eyebrows at Bessy, who was lingering in the doorway, clearly livid at the thought of having to wait on someone she considered lower than herself. "Go on, Bessy. Do as I ask, please."

Bessy grunted. As she disappeared inside, I heard Louise chuckle. Bessy's moods were greatly entertaining to my sisters, though I still fretted that she might walk out on us, as her slumped shoulders often threatened. After all this time she persisted in making clear that our move to Lyme had been a disaster. For Bessy my relations with the Annings represented all that was jumbled and wrong about Lyme. Bessy's a social barometer was still set to London standards.

I didn't care, except that it might mean losing a servant. Nor did Louise. Margaret I suppose lived the most conventional life here, still occasionally attending the Assembly Rooms, visiting other good Lyme families and doing charitable work for the poor. The salve she had created to soothe my chapped hands she took with her everywhere, distributing it to whoever needed it.

I gestured to my chair. "Do take a seat, Molly. Bessy will bring another."

Molly Anning shook her head, uneasy about sitting while I stood. "I'll wait." She seemed to understand Bessy's judgement that we should not have Annings as visitors; indeed, perhaps she agreed with her, and it was that rather than the climb up the hill that had kept her from Morley Cottage all this time. Now her eyes rested on my water-colour, and I found myself embarrassed – not for the quality of the painting, which I already knew was not good, but because what had been a pleasure to me now seemed a frivolity. Molly Anning's day began early and ended late, and consisted of many hours of backbreaking work. She barely had time even to look at a view, much less to sit and paint it. Whether or not she felt that way, she showed nothing, but moved on to inspect Louise's pruning. This at least was less frivolous – though not much less so, for roses serve little purpose other than to dress a garden, and feed no one other than bees. Perhaps Louise felt similar to me, for she hurried to finish the bush she was trimming and laid down her pruning knife. "I'll help Bessy with the tray," she said.

As more chairs were brought out, and a small table on which to place the tray, and finally the tray itself – all accompanied by huffs and sighs from Bessy – I began to regret my suggestion to take tea outside. It too seemed frivolous, and I had not meant to cause such a fuss. Then as we sat, the sun went behind a cloud and it instantly grew chilly. I felt an idiot, but would have even more so if I then said we ought to troop back inside, reversing the move of furniture and tea. I clung to my shawl and cup of tea to warm me.

Molly sat passively, allowing the bustle of cups and saucers and chairs and shawls to take place around her without comment. I rattled on about the unusually clement weather, and the letter I'd had from William Buckland saying he'd be down in a few weeks, and how Margaret couldn't join us because she was taking some of her salve to a new mother sore from nursing. "Useful, that salve," was Molly's only comment.

When I asked how they fared, she revealed why she had come to see us. "Mary ain't right," she said. "She ain't been right since the Colonel left. I want you to help me fix it."

"What do you mean?"

"I made a mistake with the Colonel. I knew I were making it, and I done it anyway."

"Oh, I'm sure you didn't—"

"Mary worked with the Colonel all summer, found him a good croc and all sorts of curies for his collection, and never had any money off him. I didn't ask him for any neither, for I thought he'd give her something at the end."

I had suspected no money changed hands between Colonel Birch and the Annings, but only now was it confirmed. I twisted the ends of my shawl, enraged that he could be so callous.

"But he didn't," Molly Anning continued. "He just went off with his croc and his curies and all he give her were a locket." I knew only too well about the locket: Mary wore it under her clothes, but pulled it out to show Margaret whenever they discussed Colonel Birch. It contained a lock of his thick hair.

Molly Anning sucked at her tea as if she were drinking beer. "And he hasn't written since he left. So I wrote him. That's where I need your help." She reached into the pocket of an old coat she wore – it had probably been Richard Anning's – and pulled out a letter, folded and sealed. "I already wrote it, but I don't know if it'll reach him like this. It would if it were going to a place like Lyme, but London be that much bigger. Do you know where he lives?" Molly Anning thrust the letter at me. "Colonel Thomas Birch, London" was written on the outside.

"What have you said in the letter?"

"Asked him for money for Mary's services."

"You didn't mention – marriage?"

Molly Anning frowned. "Why would I do that? I'm no fool. Besides, that be for him to say, not me. I did wonder about the locket, but then there's no letter, so…" She shook her head as if to rid it of a silly notion like marriage, and returned to the safer topic of payment for services rendered. "He owes us not only for all the time he took Mary away from hunting curies, but for the loss now. That be the other thing I wanted to say to you, Miss Philpot. Mary's not finding curies. It were bad enough this summer that she give everything she found to the Colonel. But since he went she ain't found anything. Oh, she goes upon beach every day, but she don't bring back curies. When I ask her why not she says there's nothing to find. Times I go with her, just to see, and what I see is that something's changed about her."

I had noticed it too when I was out with Mary. She seemed less able to concentrate. I would look up and catch her eyes wandering over the horizon or across the outline of Golden Cap or the distant hump of Portland, and knew her mind was on Colonel Birch rather than on fossils. When I questioned her she simply said, "I haven't got the eye today." I knew what it was: Mary had found something to care about other than the bones on the beach.

"What can we do to get her finding curies again, Miss Philpot?" Molly Anning said, running her hands over her lap to smooth out her worn skirt. "That's what I come to ask – that and how to get the letter to Colonel Birch. I thought if I wrote and he sent money, that would make Mary happy and she would do better upon beach." She paused. "I've wrote plenty of begging letters these last years — they take their time paying up at the British Museum – but I never thought I would have to write one to a gentleman like Colonel Birch." She took up her cup and gulped the rest of her tea. I suspect she was thinking about him kissing her hand, and cursing herself for being taken in.

"Why don't you leave the letter to us and we'll have it sent to London?" Louise suggested.

Molly Anning and I both looked at her gratefully for this neat solution: Molly because responsibility for the letter reaching its destination was taken out of her hands, I because I could decide what to do without having to reveal to her that Colonel Birch had written to me. "And I shall take Mary out hunting," I added. "I'll keep an eye on her and encourage her." And put what fossils I find in her basket, until she has recovered her senses, I added to myself.

"Don't tell Mary about the letter," Molly ordered, pulling at her coat.

"Of course not."

Molly looked at me, her dark eyes moving back and forth over my face. "I weren't always sure of you Philpots," she said. "Now I am."

When she'd gone – seeming spryer now that she was no longer weighed down with the letter – I turned to Louise. "What shall we do?"

"Wait for Margaret," was her reply.

On our sister's return in the evening, we three sat by the fire and discussed Molly Anning's letter. Margaret was in her element. This was the sort of situation that she read about in the novels she favoured by authors such as Miss Jane Austen, whom Margaret was sure she'd met long ago at the Assembly Rooms the first time we visited Lyme. One of Miss Austen's books had even featured Lyme Regis, but I did not read fiction and could not be persuaded to try it. Life itself was far messier, and didn't end so tidily, with the heroine making the right match. We Philpot sisters were the very embodiment of that frayed life. I did not need novels to remind me of what I had missed.

Margaret held the letter in both hands. "What does it say? Is it really only about money?" She turned it over and over, as if it might magically open and reveal its contents.

"Molly Anning wouldn't waste the time to write about anything else," I said, knowing my sister was thinking about marriage. "And she wouldn't lie to us."

Margaret ran her fingers over Colonel Birch's name. "Still, Colonel Birch must see it. It may remind him of what he has left behind."

"He'll be reminded that I received his letter and never responded. For if I add to the address he'll know it's I who has been meddling – no one else in Lyme would have his address."

Margaret frowned. "This is not about you, Elizabeth, but about Mary. Don't you want him to get this letter? Or would you prefer he live in perfect ignorance of Mary's circumstances? Don't you want the best for both parties?"

"You sound like one of your lady author's novels," I snapped, then stopped. I was gripping a copy of the *Geological Society Journal* Mr Buckland had sent me. To calm myself I took a breath. "I believe Colonel Birch is not an honourable man. Sending the letter will just raise Molly Anning's hopes for the outcome."

"You and Louise have already done that very thing by taking the letter off her and promising to post it!"

"That is true, and I am beginning to regret saying we would. I don't want to play a part in a fruitless, humiliating plea." I knew my arguments were swinging all about.

Margaret waved the letter at me. "You're jealous of Mary gaining his attention."

"I am not!" I said this so sharply that Margaret ducked her head. "That is ridiculous," I added, trying to soften my tone.

There was a long silence. Margaret set the letter down, then reached over and took my hand. "Elizabeth, you mustn't stand in Mary's way of getting something you were never able to."

I pulled my hand from her grasp. "That is not why I'm objecting."

"Why, then?" I sighed.

"Mary is a young working girl, uneducated apart from what little we and her church have taught her, and from a poor family. Colonel Birch is from a well-established Yorkshire family with an estate and a coat of arms. He would never seriously consider marrying Mary. Surely you know that. Molly Anning knows it – that is why she has only written about the money. Even Mary knows it, though she won't say it. You are only encouraging her. He has used her to enhance his collection – for free. That is all. She's lucky he didn't do worse. To ask him for money, or to re-establish the connection, just prolongs the Annings' agony. We mustn't do so just to please your and Mary's romantic notions."

Margaret glared at me.

"Your Miss Austen would never allow such a marriage to take place in her novels you so love," I went on. "If it can't happen in fiction, surely it won't happen in life."

At last I made myself understood. Margaret's face crumpled and she began to cry, great shuddering sobs that shook her entire body. Louise put her arms around her sister but said nothing, for she knew I was right. Margaret grasped on to the magic of novels because they held out hope that Mary – and she herself – might yet have a chance at marriage. While my own experience of life was limited, I knew such a thing would not happen. It hurt, but the truth often does.

"It's not fair," Margaret gasped as her sobs finally subsided. "He shouldn't have paid her the attention he did. Spending so much time with her and complimenting her, giving her the locket and kissing her—"

"He kissed her?" A dart of the jealousy I was trying so hard to hide even from myself shot through me.

Margaret looked chastened. "I wasn't meant to tell you! I wasn't meant to tell anyone! Please don't say anything.

Mary only told me because – well, it's just so delicious to talk it over with someone. It's as if you relive the moment." She fell silent, doubtless thinking about her own past kisses.

"I wouldn't know about that," I said, trying to limit the acid in my voice.

I did not sleep well that night. I was not used to having the power to affect someone's life so, and did not easily carry its weight, as a man might have done.

The next day, before taking the letter to Coombe Street to be posted, I added Colonel Birch's address to it. For all my arguments with Margaret against encouraging a continued link between Colonel Birch and Mary, I could not in the end act as if I were God, but had to let Molly Anning write what she would to him.

The postmistress glanced at the letter, then at me, her eyebrows raised, and I had to turn away before she could say anything. I am sure by the afternoon the gossip had gone all around town that desperate Miss Philpot had written to that cad Colonel Birch.

The Annings waited for an answer, but they received no letter.

I hoped that would be the end of our dealings with Colonel Birch, and that we would never see him again. He had his fossils – apart from the dapedium I would not send him – and could move on to another collecting fashion, such as insects or minerals. That is what gentlemen like Colonel Birch do.

It had never occurred to me that I might run into him in London. As Molly Anning had said, it is not Lyme. One million people lived in London compared to the 2000 in Lyme, and I rarely went to Chelsea, where I knew he lived, except to accompany Louise on her annual pilgrimage to the Physic Garden there. I never expected the tide would turn up two such different pebbles side by side.

We took our annual trip to London in the spring, eager to escape Lyme for a time, to see our family and make the usual rounds of visits to friends, shops, galleries and theatres. When the weather was not good we often went to the British Museum, housed in Montague Mansion close to our brother's house. Having regularly visited since we were children, we knew the collection intimately.

One particularly rainy day we had separated and were each in different rooms, with our own favourite exhibits. Margaret was in the Gallery, hovering over a collection of cameos and sealstones, while Louise was in the Upper Floor with Mary Delany's exquisite florilegium, a collection of pictures of plants made of cut paper. I was in the Saloon, where the Natural History collection ranged over several rooms – mostly displays of rocks and minerals, but now with four rooms of fossils that had recently been rearranged and added to. There were a fair number of specimens from the Lyme area, including a few more fish that I had donated.

Mary's first ichthyosaurus was also there, displayed in a long glass case of its own, thankfully without waistcoat or monocle, though there were still traces of plaster of Paris here and there on the specimen, the tail was still straight, and Lord Henley's name was still attached. I had already visited it several times, and written to the Annings to describe its new position.

It was quiet in the room, with just one other party of visitors wandering amongst the cases. I was studying the skull identified by Cuvier as a mammoth when I heard a familiar voice ringing out across the room. "Dear lady, once you have seen this ichthyosaurus you will understand just how superior my own specimen is." I closed my eyes for a moment to still my heart.

Colonel Birch had entered by the far door, dressed as usual in his outdated red soldier's coat, while a lady a bit older than I held his arm and walked alongside. From her sombre dress it seemed she was a widow. She wore a fixed, pleasant expression, and was one of those rare people who lead with no feature whatsoever.

I froze as the two went over to Mary's ichthyosaurus. Though close to them, my back was turned, and Colonel Birch did not notice me. I heard all of their conversation – or rather, all that Colonel Birch said, for his companion added little except to agree with him.

"Do you see what a jumble of bones this is compared to mine?" he declared. "How the vertebrae and ribs have been squeezed into a mass? And how incomplete it is? Look, do you see the discoloured plaster of Paris, in the ribs there, and along the spine? That is where Mr Bullock filled it in. Mine, however, needs no filling in. It may be smaller than this one, but I found it intact, not a bone out of place."

"How fascinating," the widow murmured.

"And to think they thought this was a crocodile. I never did, of course. I always knew it was something different, and that I must find one myself."

"Of course you did."

"These ichthyosauri are some of the most important scientific finds ever."

"Are they?"

"As far as we know, no ichthyosaurus exists now, and has not done for some time. This means, dear lady, that learned men are charged with discovering how these creatures died out."

"What do they think?"

"Some have suggested they died in Noah's Flood; others that some other sort of catastrophe killed them, like a volcano or an earthquake. Whatever the cause, their existence affects our knowledge of the age of the world. We think it may be older than the 6000 years Bishop Ussher allotted it."

"I see. How interesting." The widow's voice trembled a little, as if Colonel Birch's suggestions disturbed her ordered thoughts, which were clearly slight and not used to being challenged.

"I have been reading about Cuvier's Doctrine of Catastrophes," Colonel Birch continued, showing off his knowledge. "Cuvier suggests that the world has been shaped over time by a series of terrible disasters, violence on such a great scale that it has created mountains and blasted seas and killed off species. Cuvier himself did not mention God's hand in this, though others have interpreted these catastrophes as systematic – God's regulation over His creation. The Flood would be simply the most recent of these events – which does make one wonder if another is on its way!"

"One does wonder," the widow said in a small voice, her uncertainty making me grit my teeth. For all he annoyed me, Colonel Birch was curious about the world. If I were at his side I would have said more than "One does wonder."

I might have kept my back to them and let Colonel Birch pass forever from our lives, but for what he said next. He couldn't resist boasting. "Seeing all of these specimens reminds me of last summer in Lyme Regis. I grew rather good at hunting fossils, you see. Not just the complete ichthyosaurus, but fragments of many others, and a large collection of pentacrinites – the sea lilies I showed you, do you remember?"

"I'm not sure."

Colonel Birch chuckled. "Of course not, dear lady. Ladies are not equipped to look at such things so carefully as men."

I turned around. "I should like Mary Anning to hear you say that, Colonel Birch! She would not so easily agree, I think."

Colonel Birch started, though his military bearing prevented him from revealing too much astonishment. He bowed. "Miss Philpot! What a surprise – and a pleasure, of course – to find you here. When we last met we discussed my ichthyosaurus, did we not? Now, may I present to you Mrs Taylor. Mrs Taylor, this is Miss Philpot, whom I met when I was staying in Lyme. We share an interest in fossils."

Mrs Taylor and I nodded to each other, and though her face didn't lose its pleasant expression, her features seemed to snap into place so that I noticed her lips were thin, with pursed lines along them like a drawstring bag.

"And how fares lovely Lyme?" Colonel Birch asked. "Do its residents still comb the shores daily in search of ancient treasure, of evidence of denizens of previous eras?"

I presumed this was an elaborate way of asking after Mary, couched in bad poetry. I did not have to respond with poetry, however. I preferred straightforward prose. "Mary Anning still hunts for fossils, if that's what you're asking, sir. And her brother helps when he can. But in truth the family is doing poorly, for they have found little of value for many months."

As I spoke, Colonel Birch's eyes followed the other party of visitors heading into the next room. Perhaps he wished he could disappear with them.

"Nor have they been paid for their services to others, as you will be aware from correspondence," I added, raising my voice and allowing a needle into it that made Mrs Taylor's mouth pucker as if its strings were being pulled tight.

Just then Margaret and Louise entered from the far end of the room, in search of me, for we were expected home shortly. They stopped when they saw Colonel Birch, and Margaret turned pale.

"I should very much like to speak with you further about the Annings, Colonel Birch," I declared. It was bad enough to come face to face with him in all his smugness, showing off to his widow friend about fossils he had not found. But it was his dismissal of women's power of observation – thus denying Mary and me any credit for all that we had found over the years – which made me completely reverse my decision about keeping him out of the Annings' lives. He owed them a great deal, and I would tell him so. I had to speak up.

Before I could continue, however, Margaret hurried forward, pulling Louise with her. Introductions between my sisters and Mrs Taylor, as well as banal words to and from Colonel Birch, interrupted me – which is what Margaret intended, I am sure. I waited until the polite conversation was dying down before I repeated, "I should like to speak with you, sir."

"I am sure there is much to say," Colonel Birch replied with an uneasy smile, "and I would dearly love to call on all of you – " he nodded at my sisters – "but sadly I am shortly to travel to Yorkshire."

"Then it will have to be now. Shall we?" I gestured to another corner of the room, away from the others.

"Oh, I don't think Colonel Birch—" Margaret began, but was interrupted by Louise, who tucked her arm through Mrs Taylor's and said, "Do you like gardens, Mrs Taylor? If you do you must see Mrs Delany's florilegium – you will be enchanted. Come, both of you." It took all of Louise's good will to drag Mrs Taylor through the Saloon towards the exit, Margaret trailing behind them and throwing me warning looks. Her face was still white, but with two red spots in her cheeks.

When they were gone Colonel Birch and I faced each other alone in the long room, the high windows throwing a rainy grey light over us. He was no longer looking neutral, but concerned and a little annoyed. "Well, Miss Philpot."

"Well, Colonel Birch."

"Did you receive my letter about providing a dapedium for my collection?"

"Your letter?" I was thrown off guard, for I had not been thinking about that letter. "Yes, I did receive it."

"And you did not answer?"

I frowned. Colonel Birch was already steering the conversation away from where I had intended it to go, making

217

it a criticism of my own behaviour rather than his. His tactics were low, and angered me, so that my response was direct as a dagger. "No, I didn't answer it. I do not respect you, and I will never let you have any of my fossil fish. I did not feel the need to put such sentiments in writing."

"I see." Colonel Birch reddened as if he had been slapped. I expect no one had ever told him to his face that they did not respect him. Indeed, it was a new experience for us both: unpleasant for him, frightening and thrilling for me. Over the years, living in Lyme had made me bolder in my thoughts and words, but I had never before been quite so reckless and rude. I lowered my eyes and unbuttoned and rebuttoned my gloves, to give my trembling hands something to do. They were new, from a haberdasher's in Soho. By the end of the year they too would be ruined by Lyme clay and sea water.

Colonel Birch laid his hand on the glass case nearest him, as if to steady himself. It contained a variety of bivalves, which in other circumstances he might have studied. Now he looked at them as if he had never seen one before.

"Since you left," I began, "Mary has not found one specimen of value, and the family has little stock on hand to sell, for she gave everything she found last summer to you."

Colonel Birch looked up. "That is unjust, Miss Philpot. I found my specimens."

"You did not, sir. You did not." I held up my hand to stop him as he tried to interrupt. "You may think you found all of those jaw fragments and ribs and shark teeth and sea lilies, but it was Mary who directed you to them. She located them and then led you to find them. You are no hunter. You are a gatherer, a collector. There is a difference."

"I—"

"I have seen you on the beach, sir, and that is what you do. You did not find the ichthyosaurus. Mary did, and dropped her hammer by it so that you would pick it up and see the specimen. I was there. I saw you. It is her ichthyosaurus, and you have taken it from her. I am ashamed of you."

Colonel Birch stopped trying to interrupt me, but remained still, his head bowed, his lips in a pout.

"Perhaps you did not realise she was doing this," I continued more gently. "Mary is a generous soul. She is always giving away when she cannot afford to. Did you pay her for any of the specimens?"

For the first time Colonel Birch looked contrite. "She insisted they were already mine, not hers."

"Did you pay for her time, as her mother requested in a letter a few months back? I know of the letter because I added your address for her. I am surprised, sir, that you chide me for not answering your letter when you have not answered one that is about far more important matters than collecting a fossil fish."

Colonel Birch was silent.

"Do you know, Colonel Birch, this winter I discovered the Annings about to sell their table and chairs to pay the rent? Their table and chairs! They would have had to sit on the floor to eat."

"I – I had no idea they were suffering so much."

"I only convinced them not to sell their furniture by advancing them the money against future fossil fish Mary finds for me. I would have preferred just to give them the money – in general I find specimens myself rather than pay for them. But the Annings will not take charity from me."

"I do not have the money to pay them."

His words were so stark that I could not think of a reply. We were both silent then. Two women wandered arm in arm into the room, caught sight of us, glanced at each other, and hurried out again. It must have looked to them as if we were having a lovers' quarrel.

Colonel Birch ran a hand over the glass of the case. "Why did you write to me, Miss Philpot?"

I frowned. "I did not. We have already established that."

"You wrote to me about Mary. The letter was anonymous, but the writer was articulate, and said she knew Mary well, so I thought it must be from you. It was signed 'a well wisher who only wants the best for both parties', and it encouraged me to consider – marrying Mary."

I stared at him, the words he had quoted reminding me of something Margaret had said about "both parties". I thought of her bright cheeks as she left the room, of her memorising Colonel Birch's address on the letter, and of her discussing Colonel Birch with Mary. She had taken it upon herself to write to him on Mary's behalf. Molly's letter about money was not enough; Margaret wanted marriage to be part of the discussion as well. Damn her meddling, I thought. Damn her novel reading.

I sighed. "I did not write that letter, though I know now who did. Let us leave aside the thought of marriage. Of course that is an impossibility." I tried now to be clear, as this was my chance to help Mary. "But, sir, you must understand that you have robbed the Annings of their livelihood, and Mary of her reputation. It is because of you that they are selling their furniture."

Colonel Birch frowned. "What would you have me do, Miss Philpot?"

"Give her back what she found – at least the ichthyosaurus, which will bring them in enough money to pay their debts. It is the least you can do, whatever your own financial difficulties."

"I do not – I am very fond of Mary, you know. I think of her a great deal."

I snorted. "Don't be ridiculous." I could not bear his foolishness. "Such sentiments are completely inappropriate."

"That may be. But she is a remarkable young woman."

It was hard to say it, but I forced myself. "You would do better to consider someone closer to your age, and of your class. Someone…" We stared at each other.

At that moment Mrs Taylor entered at the far end of the room, pursued by my sisters and looking as if she hoped Colonel Birch would rescue her. As she hurried over to take his arm, I could only finish in a whisper, "You must do what is honourable, Colonel Birch."

"I believe we are expected elsewhere," Mrs Taylor announced, firm at last and leading with her mouth. They left us then, with promises to visit us in Montague Street another time. I knew that would not happen, but I simply nodded and waved goodbye.

The moment they were gone, Margaret burst into tears. "I'm sorry, I'm sorry, I should never have written that letter! I regretted it the moment I posted it!" Louise looked at me, bewildered. I did not take Margaret in my arms in a sisterly embrace of forgiveness, however. That would take several days, for meddling deserves punishment.

Leaving the British Museum I felt lighter, as if I had transferred a burden I'd been carrying over to Colonel Birch. At least I had spoken out for the Annings, if not completely for myself. I had no idea if it would make a difference.

I found out soon enough.

It was my brother who saw the notice of the auction. John came home from his chambers one evening and joined us in the drawing room – an over-decorated room on the first floor with large windows looking out onto the street. A crowd was there to greet him: apart from us Lyme sisters and our sister-in-law, our other sister, Frances, was visiting from Essex with her two children, eight-year-old Elizabeth, named after me, and three-year-old Francis. They were running after Johnny, now a proud eleven year old who suffered the adoration of his cousins. The children were toasting tea cakes over the fire, which had been lit only for that purpose since it was a warm May evening. Johnny relished dangling the cakes so close that they caught fire, with the younger ones following suit, and in the chaos of putting out the flames and scolding the children about the danger and the waste, I didn't notice the peculiar look on my brother's face until the children had settled down.

"I saw something in the newspaper today that I know will interest you," John said to me, his brow furrowed. He handed me the paper, folded so that a boxed advertisement was in view. As I scanned it, my face went red. I looked up, and the eyes of all my siblings rested on me. Even Johnny was gazing intently. It can be unnerving to have so many Philpots give you their attention.

I cleared my throat. "It appears Colonel Birch is selling his fossil collection," I announced. "At Bullock's, next week."

Margaret gasped, while Louise gave me a sympathetic look and reached for the newspaper to study the notice.

I turned the news over in my mind. Had Colonel Birch known when we met at the British Museum that he was selling his collection? I doubted it, given the possessive pride with which he spoke of his ichthyosaurus to Mrs Taylor. Moreover, surely he would have told me? On other hand, I had made so plain my dissatisfaction with his conduct that perhaps he was unlikely to have told me he was planning to turn his fossils into cash. All of the specimens Mary had given him would now go towards lining his empty pockets. My words to him had had no effect at all. This stark evidence of my impotence brought tears of anger to my eyes.

Louise handed back the paper. "There are previews of the sale," she said.

"I'm not going anywhere near Bullock's," I snapped, taking out a handkerchief and blowing my nose. "I know exactly what is in that collection. I don't need to inspect it."

But later, when John and I were on our own in his study, discussing the Lyme sisters' finances, I interrupted his dry discourse on numbers. "Will you accompany me to Bullock's?" I did not look at him as I asked, but kept my eyes on the smooth nautilus I had found on Monmouth Beach and given him to use as a paperweight. "Just you and I, not a large party to make an outing of it. I only want to slip in and have a quick look, that's all. The others needn't know. I don't want them to fuss."

I thought I saw a look of pity cross his face, but he quickly hid it with the bland expression he often used as a solicitor. "Leave it with me," he said.

John made no mention of a visit for several days, but I knew my brother, and had faith that he would arrange things. One evening at supper he announced that he would need the Lyme sisters to come to his chambers later in the week to look over certain documents he had drawn up for us.

Margaret made a face. "Can't you bring the papers home?"

"It needs to be at chambers, as a colleague must be present to witness it," John explained.

Margaret groaned, and Louise pushed a bit of haddock around her plate. All of us found the law chambers dull. Indeed, though I loved and respected him, I found my brother dull too at times – perhaps more so since we'd lived in Lyme, for there people were many things, but rarely dull.

"Of course," John added, with a glance towards me, "you needn't all come. One could represent the others."

Margaret and Louise looked at each other and at me, each hoping for a volunteer. I waited a suitable interval, then sighed. "I will do it."

John nodded. "To sweeten the pill, we shall dine at my club after. Would Thursday suit?"

Thursday was the first day of the preview, and John's club was in the Mall, not far from Bullock's.

By Thursday John had managed to have some sort of paper drawn up that I could sign, so that his ruse was not a lie. And we did dine at his club, but briefly, just one course, so that we arrived at the Egyptian Hall in good time.

I shuddered as we entered the yellow building, still with its statues of Isis and Osiris keeping watch over the entrance. After seeing Mary's ichthyosaurus there several years before, I had vowed never to go back, no matter how tempting the exhibits. Now I was choking on that vow.

Colonel Birch's fossils were displayed in one of the Hall's smaller rooms. Although set out like a museum collection, and divided into sets of similar specimens – pentacrinites, fragments of ichthyosauri, ammonites and so on – the fossils were not behind glass, but laid out on tables. The complete ichthyosaurus was on show in the middle of the room, and it was just as breath-taking as it had been in the Annings' workshop.

What surprised me more than Lyme fossils transplanted to London – for I had already witnessed that phenomenon at the British Museum -- was seeing just how crowded the room was. Everywhere men were picking up fossils, studying them, and discussing them with others. The room with vibrant with interest, and I picked up the thrum. There were no other women there, however, and I clutched my brother's arm, feeling awkward and conspicuous.

After a few minutes I began to recognise people, mainly men who had made fossil trips to Lyme and stopped in at Morley Cottage to see my displays. The British Museum Keeper, Charles Konig, was with the complete ichthyosaurus; perhaps comparing it to the specimen he had bought the year before from Bullock. He gazed about the room, perplexed. I am sure he would have been thrilled to have so many visitors to the Museum's fossil rooms. But his collection was not for sale, and it was the possibility of ownership that made the room buzz.

I noted Henry De La Beche across the room, and was just making my way to him when I heard my name called. I started, fearing it was Colonel Birch come to justify himself. When I turned, however, I was relieved to see a friendly face. "Mr Buckland, how very good to see you, sir," I said. "I believe you have not met my brother: may I present John Philpot. This is the Reverend William Buckland, who is often at Lyme and shares my passion for fossils."

My brother bowed. "I have certainly heard a great deal about you, sir. You lecture at Oxford, I believe?"

William Buckland beamed. "I do, indeed. It is a pleasure to meet the brother of a lady I hold in such high regard. Did you know, sir, that your sister knows more about fossil fish than just about anyone? What a clever creature she is. Even Cuvier could learn from her!"

I flushed with the rare praise, coming from such a man. My brother too seemed surprised, and glanced at me sideways, as if looking for evidence of the special quality William Buckland spoke of that I had hidden from him. Like many, John thought my fascination with fossil fish peculiar and indulgent, and so I had never discussed in any depth the knowledge I had gained over the years. John wasn't expecting support of me from so lofty a quarter. Nor was I. It reminded me that I had once briefly considered William Buckland as a potential suitor. While Colonel Birch brought pain, the thought of William Buckland as a husband now made me want to chuckle.

"It seems the whole of the scientific world is gathering for this auction," Mr Buckland continued. "Cumberland is here, and Sowerby, and Greenough, and your own Henry De la Beche. And did you ever meet Reverend Conybeare when he visited Lyme?" He indicated a man standing at his elbow. "He wants to make a study of the ichthyosaurus and present his findings to the Geological Society."

Reverend Conybeare bowed. He had a severe, knowing face, with a long nose that seemed to point like a finger at me.

William Buckland lowered his voice. "I myself have been commissioned by Baron Cuvier to bid on a number of specimens. In particular, he wants an ichthyosaurus skull for his museum in Paris. I have my eye on one. Shall I show you?"

As he spoke I spied Colonel Birch across the room, holding up a jawbone for a group of men gathered around him. I shuddered with the pain of seeing him.

"Elizabeth, are you all right?" my brother asked.

"Fine." Before I could step sideways to escape Colonel Birch's eyes, he looked past the jawbone he held and saw me. "Miss Philpot!" he called. Setting down the jawbone, he began to push his way through the crowd.

"Do you know, John," I said, "I am feeling faint. There are so many people here and it is warm. Could we step outside for some air?" Without awaiting an answer I hurried towards the door. Luckily a wall of visitors separated me from Colonel Birch, and I was able to escape before he could get to me. On the street I turned down a rubbish-strewn passage that would normally have terrified me, preferring it to having to speak civilly to the man who both repelled and attracted me.

When we emerged onto Jermyn Street next to a shop where John usually bought his shirts, he took my hand and threaded it through his elbow. "You are a funny little thing, Elizabeth."

227

"I expect I am."

John said no more, but found a cab to take us back to Montague Street, discussing business and not mentioning where we had been. For once I was pleased my brother took little interest in the drama of human emotion.

At breakfast the next morning, however, I was looking at a paper William Buckland had sent over to me called "The Connection between Geology and Religion Explained" when John casually tucked inside it a catalogue for the auction listing all the specimens Colonel Birch intended to sell. I pored over it while pretending to read Mr Buckland's article.

Going to Bullock's that once should have been enough to satisfy my curiosity about the auction. I did not need to see the fossils again, or the excited buyers. I certainly did not need to see Colonel Birch and have to hear his justification for his actions. I did not want to hear it.

On the morning of the auction I woke early. If we had been in Lyme I would have got up and sat at the window with the view towards Golden Cap, but in London I did not feel comfortable prowling about early in my brother's house. And so I lay in bed, staring at the ceiling and trying not to wake Louise with my fidgeting.

Later I sat in the drawing room with my sisters, going over a list of purchases we had made and what was still needed, for we were returning home later that week. We always shopped in London for things we couldn't get in Lyme: good gloves and hats, well-made boots, books, art supplies, quality paper. I was twitchy and nervous, as if waiting for guests to arrive. My niece and nephews were with us, and their childish games grated on my nerves, until

I snapped at Francis for laughing loudly. Everyone looked at me. "Are you feeling unwell?" my sister-in-law asked.

"I have a headache. I think I will go and rest." I stood up, ignoring concerned murmurs. "I'll be fine with a bit of sleep. Please don't wake me for dinner or if you go out. I will come down later."

Upstairs in my room I sat for a few minutes, allowing my head to catch up with what my heart had already decided. Then I drew the curtains to dim the room, and arranged cushions under my bedclothes so that anyone peeking in would think they were seeing my sleeping form. I doubted sharp-eyed Louise would be fooled, but she might take pity on me and say nothing.

I fastened my bonnet and cloak, then crept downstairs to the ground floor. I could hear the banging of pots and the cook's voice from the kitchen below, and the children's laughter above, and felt guilty – as well as a little silly – for stealing away. I had never done such a thing in my life, and it seemed ludicrous to do so now, at the age of forty-one. I should have simply announced that I was going to the auction, arranging for an appropriate chaperone such as Henry De La Beche. But I could not face the questions, the explanations and justifications I would have to give. I was not sure I could explain why I had to attend the auction. I was not planning to bid on any specimens – the few fossil fish Colonel Birch had managed to collect were inferior to mine – and it was sure to upset me to see Mary's hard work callously distributed. Yet I felt I had to witness this momentous event. After all, it seemed even the great Cuvier might soon own one of Mary's specimens, even if he did not know she found it. For Mary's sake, I had to be there.

As I pulled open the heavy front door, I heard a sound behind me and froze. Having created such a clear excuse as a headache, what could I say to the servants or my sisters if they caught me now?

My nephew Johnny was staring at me from the stairs. After a moment I raised a finger to my lips. Johnny's eyes widened, but he nodded. He crept down the rest of the stairs. "Where are you going, Auntie Elizabeth?" he whispered.

"I have an errand to run. A secret one. I will tell you about it later, Johnny. I promise to, as long as you promise not to tell the others I have gone out. Will you keep our secret?"

Johnny nodded.

"Good. Now, what are you doing down here?"

"I'm to give cook a message about the soup."

"Go, then, and I'll see you later."

Johnny went to the stairs leading down to the kitchen, then stopped and watched as I slipped through the front door. I was not sure if he could keep the secret, but I would have to trust him.

I clicked the door shut behind me, tapped down the steps, and hurried away without looking back to see if anyone was at one of the windows. I did not slow down until I had turned the corner and my brother's house was out of sight. Then I stopped, pressed my handkerchief to my mouth and took a deep breath. I was free.

Or so I thought. As I started along Great Russell Street past the British Museum, I became aware of other women walking in clumps, in couples or groups, with maids or husbands or fathers or friends. Except for the occasional servant, only men walked on their own. While I did so often enough in Lyme, I had never actually walked down a London street alone; I had always been with my sisters or brother or friends or a servant. In Lyme there was less concern over such conventions, but here a lady of my station was expected to be accompanied. I found myself being stared at by men and women alike, as the odd one out. Suddenly I felt exposed, the air around me cold and still and empty, as if I were walking with my eyes shut and might bump into something. I passed a man who looked at me with glittering black eyes, and another who appeared eager to bid me good day until he saw my plain, middle-aged face and backed away.

I had intended to walk to Bullock's, but it became clear from the reception I received on a reasonably tame, familiar road such as Great Russell Street that I could not walk through Soho to Piccadilly on my own. I looked around for a passing cab, but there were none, or none stopped when I raised my hand. Perhaps they were not looking out for a lady to do such a thing.

I considered asking a man for help, but they all stared so much that I was put off. Finally I stopped a boy running along behind horses to pick up the dung, and promised him a penny to find me a cab. Waiting for him was almost worse than walking, though, for I drew even more attention by standing still. Men sidled past, eyeing me and whispering. One man asked if I were lost; another offered to share a carriage with me. Both may have genuinely meant to help, but by then they all seemed sinister. I have never hated being a lady and yet at the same time hated men as much as I did during those minutes alone on the London streets.

The boy returned at last with a cab, and I was so relieved I gave him two pennies. Inside it was stuffy and smelly, but it was also dark and quiet and empty; I sat back and closed my eyes. Now I really did have a headache.

What with my late decision to go out and the delay in finding a cab, when I arrived at Bullock's the auction was well under way. The room was packed, with all the seats taken and people standing two deep at the back. Now I benefitted from my sex, for no man would sit and leave a lady standing. I was offered several seats, and took one in the back row. The man I sat next to nodded at me congenially, acknowledging a shared interest. Though alone this time rather than accompanied by my brother, I felt less conspicuous, for everyone was intent on the front of the room, where the sale was taking place.

Mr Bullock, a stocky man with a broad neck, stood at a lectern. He played the part of auctioneer as if it were a role on a stage, drawing out his words and accompanying them with theatrical flourishes of his arms. He stoked up the excitement in the room, even for Colonel Birch's endless supply of pentacrinites. I had been surprised to see so many of them listed in the catalogue, for I knew Colonel Birch was keen on them. He must truly be deep in debt to part with them, as well as with the ichthyosaurus.

"You thought the last specimen was fine?" Mr Bullock cried, holding up another pentacrinite. "Well, then, have a look at this beauty. See? Not a crack or chip anywhere, the form in all its mysterious perfection. Who can resist its feminine charms? Not I, ladies and gentlemen, not I. Indeed, I am going to do something highly unusual and start the bidding myself, at two guineas. For what is two guineas if I can give my wife and myself such a fine example of the beauty of nature? Will anyone deprive me of my beauty? What? You will, sir? How dare you! It will have to be for two pounds ten shillings, sir. It is? And yours is three pounds, sir? So be it. I cannot compete for such beauty as these gentlemen can. I can only hope my wife forgives me. At least we know it is for a worthy cause. Let us not forget why we are here."

His auctioning approach was irregular – I was used to the smoother, quieter, understated tone of the auctioneers who came to sell the contents of Lyme houses. But then, they were auctioning off china plates and mahogany side tables, not the bones of ancient animals. Perhaps a different tone was necessary. And his style worked. Mr Bullock sold every pentacrinite, every shark's tooth, every ammonite, for more than I expected. Indeed, bidders were surprisingly generous, especially when ichthyosaurus parts began to be sold – jaws, snouts, vertebrae. It was then that men I knew joined the bidding. Reverend Conybeare bought four large fused vertebrae. Charles Konig bought a jaw for the British Museum. William Buckland fulfilled his mission and bought part of an ichthyosaurus skull for Baron Cuvier's collection at the Natural History Museum in Paris, as well as a femur. And the prices were quite high – two guineas, five guineas, ten pounds.

Twice more Mr Bullock drew attention to the worthiness of the auction, making me shift in my seat. To call Colonel Birch's pocket a worthy cause infuriated me, and the high regard in which he was held made me want to flee. However, standing up and pushing through the wall of

233

men behind would have brought more attention than I could withstand, and it had taken so much effort to get here that I remained seated, and fumed.

"Quite remarkable what Colonel Birch has done," the man next to me whispered when there was a pause in the proceedings.

I nodded. Though I did not share his admiration, I did not want to argue with a stranger over Colonel Birch's character.

"So generous of him," the man continued.

"What do you mean, sir?" I asked, but my words were lost as Mr Bullock bellowed like a circus ringmaster, "And now, the finest and most unusual specimen in all of Colonel Birch's collection. A most mysterious animal has arrived at Bullock's. Indeed, its brother graced Bullock's Museum for several years to an enormous admiring audience. Then we called it a crocodile, but some of the finest British minds have studied it carefully and confirmed it is a different animal, not yet found in the world. You have already seen parts of it sold today – vertebrae, ribs, jaws, skulls. Now you will see how all of those parts fit together, in one complete, perfect, glorious specimen. Ladies and gentlemen, I present to you: the Birch ichthyosaurus!"

The crowd rose to its feet as the mounted specimen was carried in. Even I stood and craned my neck to look, though I had already thoroughly studied it in the Anning workshop. Such was the power of Mr Bullock's flagrant, effective showmanship. It was not just me. William Buckland craned his neck too, as did Charles Konig and Henry De La Beche and Reverend Conybeare. We were all drawn in by the spell the beast cast.

It did look very fine. As with the other specimens sold, the artificial London setting, in a brightly painted, finely furnished room so different from Lyme's raw sea air and natural rough tones, made the ichthyosaurus look even odder and more out of place, as if from another world altogether – older and harsher and more alien. It was difficult to imagine such a creature ever having lived in the world of people, or taking a place in Aristotle's Great Chain of Being.

Bidding was brisk, and resulted in the Royal College of Surgeons buying it for one hundred pounds. Mary would be pleased, I thought, if she weren't more likely to be furious at being robbed of such a fee.

The ichthyosaurus was the final lot of the sale. I had been missing from Montague Street for an hour and a half; if I got a cab quickly I might yet manage to get back to my bedroom without anyone noticing my absence. I stood, preparing to slip out so that the men I knew in the room wouldn't see me. It was at that moment, however, that Colonel Birch chose also to detach himself from the front row. He moved to the lectern and called out over the hubbub, "Gentlemen! Gentlemen – and ladies," for he had spied me. I froze.

"I am overwhelmed by your interest and by your generosity. As I announced earlier," he continued, his eyes reaching out and pinning me to my place so that I would at last listen to what he had to say, "I have auctioned off my collection to raise money for a very worthy Lyme family – the Annings."

I shied like a nervous horse, but managed not to gasp.

"You have kindly responded in a most generous fashion." Colonel Birch kept his eyes on my face, as if to calm me. "What I did not tell you before, ladies and gentlemen, is that it was the daughter of this family – Mary Anning – who discovered the majority of the specimens that make up my collection, including the fine ichthyosaurus just sold. She is – " he paused " – possibly the most remarkable young woman I have had the privilege to meet in the fossil world. She has helped me, and she may well help you in future. When you admire the specimens you have bought today, remember it was she who found them. Thank you."

As a wave of murmurs swept the room, Colonel Birch nodded at me, then stepped aside and was engulfed by a mob of coats and top hats. I began to push my way towards the exit. All about me men were looking me over – not as they had done on the street, but with a more cerebral curiosity. "Pardon me, are you Miss Anning?" asked one.

"Oh no, no." I shook my head vigorously. "I'm not." He looked disappointed, and I felt a thread of anger tug at me. "I am Elizabeth Philpot," I declared, "and I collect fossil fish."

Not everyone heard my answer, for there were murmurs of "Mary Anning" all around me. Feeling a hand on my shoulder, I did not turn, but shoved my way between the men in front of me until I reached the street. I managed to control myself until I was safe inside a cab heading up Piccadilly and no one could see me. Then I – who never cry – began to weep. Not for Mary, but for myself.

7

Like the tide making its highest mark on the beach and then retreating

I still remember the date his letter arrived: the 12th of May, 1820. Joe wrote it in the catalogue, but I would have remembered anyway.

By then I weren't expecting a letter any more. It had been months since he'd left. I had begun to forget what he looked like, how his voice sounded, the way he walked, the things he said. I no longer talked to Margaret Philpot about him, nor asked Miss Elizabeth if she had heard of him from the other fossil gentlemen. I didn't wear the locket, but put it away and didn't take it out to look at and finger the lock of his thick hair.

I didn't go upon beach either. Something had happened to me. I couldn't find curies. I went out and it was like I was blind. Nothing glittered; there were no tiny jolts of lightning, no pattern popping out from the random shapes.

They tried to help – Mam, Miss Philpot. Even Joe left his upholstering to come out hunting with me when I knew he'd rather be inside covering chairs. And when he come to Lyme, Mr Buckland, who never noticed anything about other people, was gentle with me, guiding me to specimens he found, showing me where he thought we should look, staying at my side more than usual – in fact, doing all the things I normally done for him upon beach. He also entertained me with stories of his travels to the Continent with Reverend Conybeare, and with his antics at Oxford, how he kept a tame bear as a pet, and dressed it up and introduced it to the other Oxford dons. And how a friend brought back a crocodile in brine from a voyage, and Mr Buckland got to add a new member of the animal kingdom to his tasting list. I couldn't help smiling at his stories.

He was the only one who got through the fog even briefly. He begun talking to me about things we'd found over the years that didn't seem to belong to the ichie: verteberries wider and chunkier, paddle bones flatter than they should be. One day he showed me a verteberry with a piece of rib that was attached lower than on an ichie's verteberry. "Do you know, Mary, I think there may be another creature out there," he said. "Something with a spine and ribs and paddles like the ichthyosaurus, but with anatomy rather more like a crocodile's. Wouldn't that be something, to find another of God's creatures?"

For a moment my mind went clear. I studied Mr Buckland's kindly face, even rounder and pudgier than when I first knew him, his eyes bright and his brow bulging with ideas, and I almost said, "Yes, I think so too. I been wondering about a new monster for years." I didn't say it. Before I could, my mind sank down again like a leaf settling to the bottom of a pond.

Mam and Joe went hunting while I stayed back and minded the shop. It was a surprise the first time Mam went out with Joe to Black Ven. She give me a funny look as they left, but she said nothing. She had been out with me now and then, but always as company, not to hunt herself. She was good at the business side – writing letters to collectors, chasing up what we was owed and describing specimens for sale, convincing visitors to buy more than they'd meant to at the shop. She never went looking for curies. She didn't have the eye, or the patience. Or so I'd thought. I was amazed when they come back hours later and Mam, all smug, handed me a basket heavy with finds. It was mostly ammos and bellies – the easiest curies for a beginner to see since their even lines stand out from the rocks. But she'd also managed to find some pentacrinites, a damaged sea urchin, and, most surprising of all, part of the shoulder bone of an ichie. We could get three shillings for that bone alone, and eat for a week.

When she was in the privy I accused Joe of putting what he found in her basket and saying it were hers. He shook his head. "She did it herself. I don't know how she manages it, she's so haphazard in her hunting. But she finds things."

Mam later told me she'd made a bargain with God: if He showed her where the curies were, she would never again question His judgment, which she had done many times over the years with all the death and debt she had to suffer. "He must have listened," Mam said, "for I didn't have to look hard to find 'em. They were just there upon beach, waiting for me to pick up. I don't know why you fussed so much when you went out looking, needing all that time day after day. It ain't so hard to find curies."

I wanted to argue with her but was in no position to since I weren't going hunting any more. And it was true that when Mam went out she always filled her basket. She had the eye all right, she just didn't want to admit it.

All of that changed on the 12th of May, 1820. I was behind our table in Cockmoile Square, showing sea lilies to a Bristol couple, when a boy come by with a packet for Joe. He wanted a shilling to pay for it, as it was bigger than your average letter. I didn't have a shilling, and was about to send the boy away again when I saw the handwriting I had been waiting for these months. I knew his hand because, just as Miss Elizabeth had taught me, I'd shown him how to write labels of each specimen he found – a description of it, the Linnaean name if known, where and when found, in which layer of rock, and any other information that might be useful.

I snatched the packet from the boy and stared at it. Why were it addressed to Joe? They weren't ever over friendly together. Why wouldn't he write to me?

"You can't have that unless you pay, Mary." The boy pulled at the packet.

"I haven't the shilling yet, but I'll get it somehow. Can't you let me have it and I'll owe you?"

In answer he pulled at the packet again. I hugged it to my chest. "I'm not giving it up. I been waiting for this letter for months."

The boy sneered. "That be from your sweetheart, eh? The old man you went round with who left you, didn't he?"

"You shut your gob, boy!" I turned to the gentleman, knowing such a fuss in front of customers would sell no curies. "Sorry, sir. Have you decided what you want?"

"Indeed," the lady answered for her husband. "We shall take a *shilling's* worth of crinoids." She smiled as she held out a coin.

"Oh, thank you, ma'am, thank you!" I handed the shilling to the boy. "You get out now, you!"

He made a rude gesture as he left, and I apologised again to the couple. Though the lady had been so understanding about the letter, she took her time about choosing her crinoids, and I had to swallow my impatience. Then I had to wrap them up in paper, and the man wanted extra string, and I got it all in knots, and thought I would go mad with fixing it. At last it was done and they left, the lady whispering, "I hope there is good news in your letter."

I went inside then and sat in the dusty workshop, the packet in my lap. I read the address again: "Joseph Anning, Esq., The Fossil Shop, Cockmoile Square, Lyme Regis, Dorsetshire." Why had he written to my brother? And why was it a packet wrapped in brown paper rather than a letter? What could Colonel Birch want to send to my brother?

Why hadn't he sent it to me?

I knew from the incoming tide that Joe and Mam would be back in half an hour. I didn't know how I could sit there with the letter and wait even that little while for them to return. I couldn't bear it.

I looked at the packet. Then I turned it over, counted to three, and broke the seal. Joe would be angry, but I couldn't help it. I was sure it was really meant for me.

Along with a folded letter there was a pamphlet the size of the exercise books I used to practise my letters in at Sunday school. On the front page it read:

A Catalogue of
a small but very fine Collection of
Organised Fossils,
from the Blue Lias Formation
at Lyme and Charmouth, in Dorsetshire
consisting principally of Bones,
illustrating the
Osteology of the Ichthio-Saurus, or Proteo-Saurus,
and of Specimens of
the Zoophyte, called Pentacrinite,
the Genuine Property of Colonel Birch,
collected at a considerable Expense,
which will be sold at Auction,
by Mr Bullock,
at his Egyptian Hall in Piccadilly
on Monday, the 15th Day of May, 1820
Punctually at one o'clock

I studied this page without really taking it in. Only when I turned the pages of the catalogue and read the list of specimens, each of which I could picture and name where it had been found, did I begin to understand. He was selling it, every last cury I had worked so hard to add to his collection just for the satisfaction of knowing he would be handling it. All the pentacrinites he loved so, the ammos and parts of lobsters, the fish I should really have given to Elizabeth Philpot, the strange crustaceous insect I had never seen before and would have studied more carefully with the Philpots' magnifying glass, but that he wanted it. All the fragments of ichies, jaws and teeth and eye sockets and verteberries, all about to be scattered.

And of course the ichie, the most perfect specimen I'd ever seen, that I'd stayed up night after night to finish cleaning and mounting the very best I could. I did it all for him, and now he was going to sell it, just like Lord Henley sold my first ichie. And Mr Bullock was in the middle of it again. My head buzzed so that I thought it would explode. I held the catalogue tight in my hands, wanting to rip it apart. I would have done so if it had been sent to me rather than Joe. I would have torn it all apart and thrown it in the fire, catalogue and letter alike.

The letter. I had not read it yet. I had such an ache behind my eyes I weren't sure I could read anything now. But I unfolded it, smoothed it out, rubbed my eyes, and let them rest on his words. Then I begun to read.

When I finished, my throat was that tight I couldn't swallow, and I'd gone hot in the face like I'd run all the way up Broad Street. By the time Mam and Joe come in, I was sobbing so hard my heart was sure to come out of my mouth.

There were three coaches a week from London, and each one brought me another piece of the puzzle of what had gone on there.

The newspaper account arrived first. Normally there was no money for newspapers, but Mam come home with one. "We has to find out if we can afford this newspaper," was her logic. I could hardly turn the pages, my hands were trembling so. On page three I found the following notice and read it out to Mam and Joe:

An auction yesterday by Mr. Bullock at his Egyptian Hall on Piccadilly of the fossil collection of Lt.-Col. Thomas Birch, late of the Life Guards, has raised in excess of £400. The collection included a fine and rare specimen of the ichthyosaurus, which was sold to the Royal College of Surgeons for £100. Lt.-Col. Birch announced that the funds raised would be given to the Anning family of Lyme Regis, who helped him to assemble the collection.

It was brief, but it was enough. To see it in print like that made my hands go cold.

Mam was usually cautious with money, making no plans for it until she held it in her hands. Seeing word of it in the newspaper, though, was as good as proof to her that it was coming, and she begun discussing with Joe what to do with it. "We'll pay off our debts," Joe said. "Then we'll think about buying a house further uphill, away from the floods." Cockmoile Square was regularly flooded, by the river or the sea.

"I'm in no hurry to move," Mam replied, "but we do need new furniture. And then you'll need money to set up a proper upholstery business." They talked on and on, with plans they'd never dared to dream of a week ago, relaxing in the luxury of being able to fart in the face of the work-house, as Mam put it. It was comical how quick they went from being poor to thinking rich. I didn't say anything as they talked, nor did they expect me to. We all knew we were getting the money because of me. I had done my part, and it were like I was a queen and could sit back and let my courtiers arrange things.

I didn't want to talk anyway, for I could not put my head to plans. All I wanted was to run off to the cliffs to be alone and think of Colonel Birch and what his actions meant. I wanted to relive the kiss he gave me, and go over every feature of his face, and recall his voice, and all the things he said to me, and all the ways he looked at me, and all the days we spent together. That is what I wanted to do, sitting at our only table. Not for long, it seemed – if Mam had her way we'd be buying a mahogany dining set to rival Lord Henley's.

I got out the locket and begun to wear it again, under my clothes. I didn't want to talk about Colonel Birch to Mam or Joe, for I didn't know his intentions towards me. He'd not said in the letter, which was after all addressed to Joe as man of the family, and so was formal rather than loving. He wanted to do things proper. But what man would give a family four hundred pounds and not have real intentions?

When the next coach come from London I was at Charmouth, waiting for it. I'd begun to go upon beach again, to hunt curies. When the coach were due I went up the lane to meet it, even though I'd said nothing to Mam or Joe about going, and hadn't even thought through what I would do when I saw Colonel Birch. I just went, and sat outside the Queen's Arms, where others were waiting as well, to meet passengers or take the coach on to Exeter. I got funny looks, which was nothing new, except instead of sneers there was wonder and respect, which I hadn't felt since first discovering the ichthyosaurus. The news of our fortune had spread.

When the coach appeared, my stomach flip-flopped like a fish in the bottom of a boat. It seemed to take a year to drive up the long hill through the village. When at last it stopped and the door opened, I closed my eyes and tried to calm my heart, which had joined my stomach – two fish now flopping.

Then Margaret Philpot stepped down, and then Miss Louise, and finally Miss Elizabeth. I had not expected the Philpots. Normally Miss Elizabeth wrote to tell me which coach they would be on, but I'd had no letter. I did wonder if Colonel Birch might come out as well, but I knew Miss Elizabeth would never ride in the same coach as him.

I was never so disappointed as at that moment.

But they were my friends, and I went up to greet them. "Oh, Mary," Miss Margaret cried, hanging on my neck, "what news we have for you! It is so overwhelming I almost can't speak!" She clutched a handkerchief to her mouth.

Laughing, I freed myself from her embrace. "I know, Miss Margaret. I know about the auction. Colonel Birch wrote to Joe. And we saw the newspaper account."

Miss Margaret's face fell, and I felt a little bad to have robbed her of the pleasure of giving me such dramatic good news. But she soon recovered. "Oh, Mary," she said, "how your fortunes have changed. I am so glad for you!"

Miss Louise too beamed at me, but Miss Elizabeth merely said, "It is good to see you, Mary," and pecked at the air near my cheek. As usual she smelled of rosemary, even after two days in a coach.

When the Philpots and their things had been transferred to a cart to go on to Lyme, Miss Margaret called out, "Won't you come with us, Mary?"

"Can't." I gestured towards the beach. "I've curies to pick up."

"Come and see us tomorrow, then!" With a wave they left me alone at Charmouth. It was then the disappointment that Colonel Birch had not been on the coach struck me, and I went back upon beach feeling low and not at all like a girl whose family was coming into four hundred pounds. "He'll be on the next one," I said aloud to comfort myself. "He'll come and I'll have him to myself."

Normally when the Philpots suggested I visit them, I went straightaway. I always liked Morley Cottage, for it was warm and clean and full of food and the good smells from Bessy's baking – even if she liked to scowl at me. There were views of Golden Cap and the coast to lift the heart, and Miss Elizabeth's fish to look at. Miss Margaret played the piano to entertain us and Miss Louise gave me flowers to bring home. Best of all, Miss Elizabeth and I talked about fossils, and looked over books and articles together.

Now, though, I didn't want to see Miss Elizabeth. She had kept an eye on me for most of my life, and had become my friend even when others wouldn't, but when she stepped off the coach in Charmouth I sensed disapproval from her rather than any happiness at seeing me again. Maybe she was not thinking of me, though. Maybe she was ashamed of herself. And she should be – her judgement of Colonel Birch had been completely wrong, and she must feel bad about it, though she wouldn't say so. I could afford to be generous and ignore her foul mood, for I loved a man who would pull me from my poverty and make me happy, while she had no one. But I would not seek her out to sour my happiness.

I found reasons why I couldn't go up Silver Street. I needed to hunt curies to make up for the months when I hadn't. Or I insisted on cleaning the house to prepare for Colonel Birch coming to see us. Or I went out to Pinhay Bay to find him a pentacrinite since he had sold all of his. Then I went to meet each coach from London, though three came and went without him stepping off.

I was on my way back from the third coach, cutting through St Michael's from the cliff path, when I met Miss Elizabeth coming the other way. Both of us jumped a little, startled, like we wished we'd seen the other first and had held back so we wouldn't have to stop and greet each other.

Miss Elizabeth asked if I had been upon beach, and I had to admit I'd gone to Charmouth without hunting. She knew it were the day the coach arrived – I could see it in her face, working out why I had been there, and trying to hide her displeasure. She changed the subject, and we talked a little of Lyme and its doings while she had been gone. It was awkward, though, not the way we usually were with each other, and after a time we fell silent. I felt stiff, as if I'd sat too long on a leg and it had gone to sleep. It made me stand funny. Miss Elizabeth too held her head at an angle, like her neck still had a crick in it from all that riding in the London coach.

I was about to make an excuse and set off for Cockmoile Square when Miss Elizabeth seemed to reach a decision. When she is going to say something important she sticks out her chin and tightens her jaw. "I want to tell you about what happened in London, Mary. You are not to tell anyone I told you. Not your mother or brother, nor particularly my sisters, for they do not know what I witnessed." Then she told me all about the auction, describing in detail what was sold and who was there and what they bought, how even the Frenchman Cuvier wanted a specimen for Paris. She said how Colonel Birch made his announcement about me at the end, naming me as the hunter. All the time she was talking I felt I were listening to a lecture about someone else, a Mary Anning who lived in another town, in another country, on the other side of the world, who collected something other than fossils – butterflies or old coins.

Miss Elizabeth frowned. "Are you listening, Mary?"

"I am, ma'am, but I'm not sure I'm hearing right."

Miss Elizabeth gazed at me, her grey eyes pinched and serious. "Colonel Birch has named you in public, Mary. He has told some of the most interested fossil collectors in the country to seek you out. They will be coming here to ask you to take them out as you have done Colonel Birch. You must prepare yourself, and take care that you don't. . . . compromise your character further." She said the last with such a pursed mouth it were a marvel any words come out at all.

I fingered some lichen on the gravestone I stood next to. "I am not worried for my character, ma'am, nor what others think of me. I love Colonel Birch, and am waiting for him to come back."

"Oh, Mary." A whole set of emotions crossed Miss Elizabeth's face – it was like watching playing cards being dealt one after the other – but mostly there was anger and sadness. Those two combined make jealousy, and it come over me then that Elizabeth Philpot was jealous of the attention Colonel Birch paid me. She shouldn't be. She never had to sell or burn her furniture to keep a roof over her head and stay warm. She had plenty of tables rather than just the one. She didn't go out every day no matter the weather or her health and stay out for hours hunting curies till her head swam. She didn't have chilblains on her hands and feet, and fingertips cut and torn and grey with embedded clay. She didn't have neighbours talking about her behind her back. She should pity me, and yet she envied me.

I shut my eyes for a moment, steadying myself with the gravestone. "Why can't you be glad for me?" I said. "Why can't you say, 'I hope you will be very happy'?"

"I—" Miss Elizabeth gulped as if words were choking her. "I do hope that," she finally managed to say, though it come out all strangled. "But I don't want you to make a fool of yourself. I want you to think sensibly about what is possible for your life."

I ripped the lichen off the stone. "You're jealous of me."

"I'm not!"

"Yes, you are. You're jealous of Colonel Birch because he courted me. You loved him and he paid no attention to you."

Miss Elizabeth looked stricken, like I'd hit her. "Stop, please."

But it was as if a river had risen in me and broken its banks. "He never even looked at you. It was me he wanted! And why shouldn't he? I'm young, and I've got the eye! All your education and your one hundred and fifty pounds a year and your elderflower champagne and your silly tonics, and your silly sisters with their turbans and roses. And your fish! Who cares about fish when there are monsters in the cliffs to be found? But you won't find them because you haven't got the eye. You're a dried up old spinster who will never get a man or a monster. And I will." It felt so good and so horrible to say these things aloud that I thought I might be sick.

Miss Elizabeth stood very still. It were like she was waiting for a gust of wind to blow itself out. When it had and I was finished, she took a deep breath, though what come out were almost a whisper, with no force behind it. "I saved your life once. I dug you out of the clay. And this is how you repay me, with the unkindest thoughts."

The wind come back like a gale. I cried out in such rage Miss Elizabeth stepped back. "Yes, you saved my life! And I'll feel the burden of being grateful to you for always. I'll never be equal to you, no matter what I do. Whatever monsters I find, however much money I earn, it will never equal your place. So why can't you leave Colonel Birch to me? Please." I was crying now.

Miss Elizabeth watched me with her level grey eyes until I had used up my tears. "I release you of the burden of your gratitude, Mary," she said. "I can at least do that. I dug you out that day as I would have done for anyone, and as anyone else passing would have done for you too." She paused, and I could see her deciding what to say next. "But I must tell you something," she continued, "not to hurt you, but to warn you. If you are expecting anything from Colonel Birch you will be disappointed. I had occasion to meet him before the auction. We ran into each other at the British Museum." She paused. "He was accompanying a lady. A widow. They seemed to have an understanding. I'm telling you this so that you will not have your expectations raised. You are a working girl, and you cannot expect more than you have. Mary, don't go."

But I had already turned and begun to run, as fast and far from her words as I could.

*   *   *

253

I was not there to meet the next London coach when it come to Charmouth. It was a soft afternoon, with plenty of visitors out, and I was behind the table outside our house, selling curies to passersby.

I am not a superstitious person, but I knew he would come, for though he did not know it, it was my birthday. I had never had a birthday present, and was due one. Mam would say his auction money was the present, but to me he was the gift.

When the clock on the Shambles bell-tower struck five I begun to follow Colonel Birch's progress in my mind even as I was selling. I saw him alight from the coach and hire a horse from the stables, then ride along the road till he could cut across one of Lord Henley's fields above Black Ven to Charmouth Lane. He would follow that to Church Street, then down past St Michael's and into Butter Market. There all he had to do was to go right round the corner and he'd come into Cockmoile Square.

When I looked up, he appeared just as I knew he would, riding up on his borrowed chestnut horse and looking down at me. "Mary," he said.

"Colonel Birch," I replied, and curtseyed very low, as if I were a lady.

Colonel Birch dismounted, reached for my hand and kissed it in front of all the visitors rummaging through the curies and the villagers walking past. I didn't care. When he looked up at me, still bent over my hand, I spied behind his gladness uncertainty, and I knew then that Elizabeth Philpot had not been lying about the widow lady. As much as I had wanted to disbelieve her, she was not the sort to lie. As gently as I could I pulled my hand from Colonel Birch's grasp. Then the shadow of uncertainty become a true flame of sorrow, and we stood looking at each other without speaking.

Over Colonel Birch's shoulder there was a movement that distracted me from his sad eyes, and I saw a couple come arm in arm along Bridge Street, he stocky and strong, she bobbing up and down at his side like a boat in rough water. It was Fanny Miller, who had lately married Billy Day, one of the quarrymen who helped me dig out monsters. Even the quarrymen were taken, then. Fanny stared at us. When she met my eye she clutched her husband's arm and hurried away along the street as fast as her game leg would let her.

Then I knew what I would do with Colonel Birch, widow lady or no. It would be my present to myself, for I was not likely to have another chance. I nodded at him. "Go and see Mam, sir. She's been expecting you. I'll find you after."

I did not want to watch him hand over the money. Though I was grateful for it, I did not want to see it. I only wanted to see him. When he had tied up the horse and gone inside, I packed away the curies, then went quick up Butter Market and followed Colonel Birch's path in reverse. I knew he would lodge as he always did at the Queen's Arms in Charmouth, and so would pass this way again. When I got to Lord Henley's field off Charmouth Lane I crossed to a stile and sat on it to wait.

Colonel Birch held his back so straight as he rode he looked like a tin soldier. With the sun low behind him and casting a long shadow before, I could not see his face until he pulled up alongside me. As I climbed to the top rung of the stile and balanced there, he took my hand so that I would not fall.

"Mary, I cannot marry you," he said.

"I know, sir. It don't matter."

"You are sure?"

"I am. It is my birthday today. I am twenty-one years old and this is what I want."

I was not a horse rider, but that day I had no fear as I reached over and swung into the space between his arms.

He took me inland. Colonel Birch knew the surrounding countryside better than I did, for I never normally went into the fields, but spent all of my time on the shore. We rode through dusk's shadows lit here and there with panes of sunlight, up to the main road to Exeter. Once across we headed down darkening fields. Along the way we did not murmur sweet words to each other like courting couples, for we were not courting. Nor did I relax in his arms, for the horse swayed and the saddle pushed hard against me and I had to concentrate so I wouldn't fall off. But I was where I wanted to be and did not mind.

An orchard at the bottom of the field waited for us. When I lay down with Colonel Birch it was on a sheet of apple blossom petals covering the ground like snow. There I found out that lightning can come from deep inside the body. I have no regret discovering that.

I learned something else that evening, which come to me afterwards. I was lying in his arms looking up at the sky, where I counted four stars, when he asked, "What will you do with the money I have given your family, Mary?"

"Pay off our debts and buy a new table."

Colonel Birch chuckled. "That is very practical of you. Will you not do something for yourself?"

"I suppose I could buy a new bonnet." Mine had just been crushed under our coupling.

"What about something more ambitious?"

I was silent.

"For example," Colonel Birch continued, "you could move to a house with a bigger shop. Up Broad Street, for example, to where there's a good shop front, with a big window and more light in which to display your fossils. That way you would get more trade."

"So you're expecting me to keep on finding and selling curies, are you, sir? That I'll never marry, but run a shop."

"I did not say that."

"It's all right, sir. I know I won't marry. No one wants someone like me for a wife."

"That is not what I meant, Mary. You misunderstand me."

"Do I, sir?" I rolled off his shoulder and lay flat on the ground. Even since we had been talking it seemed the sky had got darker, and more and more stars had joined the first scattering.

Colonel Birch sat up stiffly, for he was old, and lying on the ground must hurt him. He looked down at me. It was too dark to see his expression. "I was thinking about your future as a fossil hunter, not as a wife. There are many women – most women, in fact – who can be perfectly good wives. But there is only one of you. Do you know, when I set up the auction in London I met many people who professed to know a great deal about fossils: what they are, how they came to be here, what they mean. But none of them knows even half of what you understand."

"Mr Buckland does. And Henry De La Beche. And what about Cuvier? They say that Frenchman knows more than any of us."

"That may be. But the others don't have the instinct for it that you do, Mary. Your knowledge may be self-taught and come from experience rather than from books, but it is no less valuable for that. You have spent a great deal of time with specimens; you have studied their anatomies and seen their variations and subtleties. You recognise the uniqueness of the ichthyosaurus, for example, that it is not like anything we have ever imagined."

But I didn't want to talk about me, or about curies. There were so many stars now that I couldn't count them. I felt very small, pinned to the ground under the knowledge of them all. They were beginning to hollow me out. "How far away do you think those stars are?"

Colonel Birch turned his face upward. "Very far. Farther than we can even imagine."

Perhaps it was because of what had just happened to me, of the lightning that come from inside, which made me open up to larger, stranger thoughts. Looking up at the stars so far away, I begun to feel there was a thread running between the earth and them. Another thread was strung out too, connecting the past to the future, with the ichie at one end, dying all that long time ago and waiting for me to find it. I didn't know what was at the other end of the thread. These two threads were so long I couldn't even begin to measure them, and where one met the other, there was me. My life led up to that moment, then led away again, like the tide making its highest mark on the beach and then retreating.

"Everything is so big and old and far away," I said, sitting up with the force of it. "God help me, for it does scare me."

Colonel Birch put his hand on my head and stroked my hair, which was all matted from my lying on the ground. "There is no need to fear," he said, "for you are here with me."

"Only now," I said. "Just for this moment, and then I will be alone again in the world. It is hard when there's no one to hold on to."

He had no answer to that, and I knew he never would. I lay back down and looked at the stars until I had to close my eyes.

8

An adventure in an unadventurous life

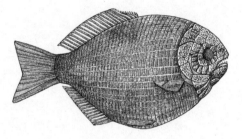

It is rare for anything reported in the *Western Flying Post* to surprise me. Most are predictable stories: a description of a livestock auction in Bridport, or an account of a public meeting on the widening of a Weymouth road, or warnings of pickpockets at the Frome Fair. Even the stories of more unusual events where lives are changed – a man transported for stealing a silver watch, a fire burning down half a village – I still read with a sense of distance, for they have little effect on me. Of course if the man had stolen my watch, or half of Lyme burned down, I would be more interested. Still, I read the paper dutifully, for it makes me at least aware of the wider region, rather than trapped in an inward-looking town.

Bessy brought me the paper as I rested by the fire one mid-December afternoon. I did not often fall ill, and my weakness irritated me so that I had become as grumpy as Bessy normally was. I sighed as she set it on a small table next to me along with a cup of tea. Still, it was some diversion, for my sisters were busy in the kitchen, making up a batch of Margaret's salve to go in Christmas baskets, along with jars of rosehip jelly. I had wanted to include an ammonite in each basket, but Margaret felt they did not invoke a festive spirit and insisted on pretty shells instead. I forget sometimes that people see fossils as the bones of the dead. Indeed, they are, though I tend to view them more as works of art reminding us of what the world was once like.

I paid little attention to what I read until I came across a short notice, wedged between news of two fires, one burning down a barn, the other the premises of a pastry cook. It read:

On Wednesday evening Mary Anning, the well-known fossilist, whose labours have enriched the British and Bristol Museums, as well as the private collections of many geologists, found, east of town, and immediately under the celebrated Black Ven Cliff, some remains, which were removed on that night and the succeeding morning, to undergo an examination, the result of which is, that this specimen appears to differ widely from any which have before been discovered at Lyme, either of the Ichthyosaurus or Plesiosaurus, while it approaches nearly to the structure of the Turtle. The whole osteology has not yet been satisfactorily disclosed, owing to its very recent removal.

It will be for the great geologists to determine by what term this creature is to be known. The great Cuvier will be informed when the bones are completely disclosed, but probably it will be christened at Oxford or London, after an account has been accurately furnished. No doubt the Directors of the British or Bristol Museums will be anxious to possess this relic of the "great Herculaneum".

Mary had found it at last. She had found the new monster that she and William Buckland had speculated must exist, and I had to find out about her discovery in the newspaper, as if I were just anyone and had no claim on her. Even the men producing the *Western Flying Post* knew about it before me.

It is difficult to have a falling-out in a town the size of Lyme Regis. I had first learned that when we Philpots stopped seeing Lord Henley: we then managed to run into him everywhere, so that it became almost a game dodging him on Broad Street, along the path by the river, at St Michael's. We provided the town with years of gossip and amusement, for which we ought to have been thanked.

With Mary the severing was far more painful, because she was so close to my heart. After our fight in the churchyard, I regretted what I'd said to her almost immediately, wishing I had let her find out from Colonel Birch himself about the widow he might marry. I shall never forget the look of betrayal and despair on her face. On the other hand, I felt the sting of her comments about my jealousy and my sisters and my fish like a whipping that lingered.

I was too proud to go and apologise, though, and I expect she was too. I longed to have Bessy come into the parlour with a telltale grimace and announce that I had a visitor. But it didn't happen, and once the time for such a rapprochement had passed, it became impossible to regain our old standing.

It is not easy to let someone go, even when they have said unforgivable things to you. For at least a year it cut me deeply to see her, out on the beach, or on Broad Street, or by the Cobb. I began to avoid Cockmoile Square, taking back-lanes to St Michael's, and the path by the church to the beach. I no longer went to Black Ven, where Mary usually hunted, instead heading in the opposite direction, past the Cobb and onto Monmouth Beach. There were not so many fossil fish there, and so I collected less, but at least I was not so likely to run into her.

It was lonely, though. Over the years Mary and I had spent a great deal of time together out hunting. Some days we wouldn't speak for hours, but her presence near by, bent over the ground, scrabbling in the mud or splitting open rocks, was a familiar comfort. Now I would glance around and still be surprised to find there was only me on the deserted beach. Such solitude brought on a self-indulgent melancholy that I detested, and I would make cutting remarks to jolt myself out of it. Margaret began to complain that I had grown more prickly, and Bessy threatened to give notice when I was sharp with her.

It wasn't only on the beach that I missed Mary. I also longed for the company of her sitting at my dining table while I unpacked my basket and showed off what I had found. I could only do so the rare times when Henry De La Beche or William Buckland or Doctor Carpenter was about, or when someone occasionally came to see my collection and showed more than simply a fashionable interest in fossils. Without Mary's knowledge and encouragement, I felt my own studies slacken.

At the same time I had to watch her become more popular with outsiders. They actively sought her out, and she began taking visitors on fossil walks to Black Ven. With Colonel Birch's auction money and Mary's growing fame, the Annings were at last freeing themselves from the debt

266

Richard Anning had put them into many years before. Mary and Molly Anning had new dresses, and they bought proper furniture again, and coal to warm themselves. Molly Anning stopped taking in laundry and began running the fossil shop properly, and it became a busy place. I should have been glad for them. Instead I was envious.

For a short time I even considered leaving Lyme and going to live with my sister Frances and her family, who had recently moved to Brighton. When I casually mentioned the possibility to Louise and Margaret, they both reacted with horror. "How can you think of leaving us?" Margaret cried, and Louise was pale and silent. I even found Bessy sniffling into her pastry dough, and had to reassure them all that Morley Cottage would always remain my home.

It took a long time, but eventually I did grow used to not having Mary's company or her friendship. It became as if she lived in Charmouth or Seatown or Eype. It was surprising that in such a small town she and I were able to avoid each other so well. But then, she was so busy with new collectors that I would have seen less of her even if I hadn't been trying to. While I accommodated her absence, a dull ache in my heart remained, like a fracture that, though healed, ever after flares up during damp weather.

I did run into her once where I couldn't get away. I was with my sisters, heading along the Walk, when Mary came from the opposite direction, a small black and white dog at her heels. It happened too quickly for me to duck aside. Mary started when she saw us, but continued towards us, as if determined not to be deterred. Margaret and Louise said hello to her, and she to them. She and I carefully avoided meeting each other's eyes.

"What a lovely little dog!" Margaret cried, kneeling to pet it. "What is his name?"

"Tray."

"Where did you get him?"

"A friend give him to me, to keep me company upon beach." Mary turned red, which told us who the friend was. "If he likes you, he lets you pet him. If he don't, he growls."

Tray sniffed at Louise's dress, then mine. I stiffened, expecting him to growl, but he looked up at me and panted. I had always assumed pets did not like those their owners did not like.

Other than that meeting, I was able to avoid her, though I sometimes saw her in the distance, Tray following, on the beach or in town.

There was one moment when I was briefly tempted to try to restore our friendship. A few months after our fight, I heard that Mary had discovered a loose jumble of bones, which she pieced together in a speculative fashion, though the specimen was without a skull. I wanted to see it, but the Annings sold it to Colonel Birch and shipped it to him before I got up the courage to visit Cockmoile Square. I was only able to read about it in papers Henry De La Beche and Reverend Conybeare published, in which they named this notional creature a plesiosaurus, a "near lizard". It had a very long neck and huge paddles, and William Buckland likened it to a serpent threaded through the shell of a turtle.

Now, according to the newspaper, she had found another specimen, and I was once again being tempted to visit Cockmoile Square. After reading the brief notice, questions popped into my head that I wanted to ask Mary. What did she find first? How big was the specimen, and in what sort of condition? How complete? Did this one have a skull? Why did she stay out all night to work on it? Whom did they expect to sell it to: the British or Bristol Museums, or to Colonel Birch once more?

My desire to see it was so strong that I went so far as to get up to fetch my cloak. At that moment, however, Bessy appeared with another cup of tea for me. "What are you doing, Miss Elizabeth? Surely you're not going out in the cold?"

"I—" As I looked into Bessy's broad face, her cheeks red and accusing, I knew I couldn't tell her where I wanted to go. Bessy had been pleased that Mary and I were no longer friends, and would now have plenty of opinions about my desire to visit Cockmoile Square which I didn't have the energy to fight. Nor could I explain to Margaret and Louise, who had both encouraged me to make amends with Mary and then, when I wouldn't, let the matter drop and never mentioned her.

"I was just going to the door to see if I could see the post coming," I said. "But do you know, I'm feeling a little dizzy. I think I'll go to bed."

"You do that, Miss Elizabeth. You don't want to go any-where."

It is rare that I feel Bessy's caution is sound.

William Buckland arrived two days later. Margaret and Louise had gone to deliver the Christmas baskets to various deserving persons, but I was still ill enough to stay behind. Louise had looked envious as they left; such visits were tedious for her – as they were for me. Only Margaret enjoyed social calls.

It seemed I had only just allowed my eyes to close when Bessy came in to announce that a gentleman had arrived to see me. I sat up, rubbed my face and smoothed my hair.

William Buckland bounded in. "Miss Philpot!" he cried. "Don't get up – you look so comfortable there by the fire. I didn't mean to disturb you. I can come back." He looked about him with every intention of remaining, however, and I got to my feet and gave him my hand. "Mr Buckland, what a pleasure to see you. It has been such a long time." I waved at the chair opposite. "Please sit and tell me all of your news. Bessy, some tea for Mr Buckland, please. Have you just come from Oxford?"

"I arrived a few hours ago." William Buckland sat. "Thankfully the term has just ended, and I was able to set out almost as soon as I received Mary's letter." He jumped up again – he was never good at sitting for long – and paced up and down. His forehead was growing larger as his hairline receded, and it gleamed in the firelight. "It really is remarkable, isn't it? Bless Mary, she has found the most spectacular specimen! We have now incontrovertible evidence of another new creature without having to guess at its anatomy as we did before. How many more ancient animals might we find?" Mr Buckland picked up a sea urchin from the mantelpiece. "You are very quiet, Miss Philpot," he said as he examined it. "What do you think? Is it not magnificent?"

"I have not seen the specimen," I confessed. "I've only read about it – though there is little enough in the newspaper account."

Mr Buckland stared at me. "What? You've not been to see it? Why ever not? I've just come like lightning all the way from Oxford, and yet you can simply stroll down the hill.

Would you like to go now? I am going back again and can accompany you." He set down the sea urchin and held out his elbow for me to take.

I sighed. It had been impossible to get Mr Buckland to understand that Mary and I no longer had anything to do with each other. Though I counted him as a friend, he was not the sort of man who was sensitive to others' feelings. To Mr Buckland life was about the pursuit of knowledge rather than the expression of emotions. Almost forty years old, he showed no sign of marrying, to no one's surprise, for what lady could put up with his erratic behaviour and profound interest in the dead rather than the living?

"I'm afraid I cannot go with you, Mr Buckland," I said now. "I have a chesty cough and have been ordered by my sisters to stay by the fire." This much at least was true.

"A pity!" Mr Buckland sat down again.

"The newspaper says Mary's find is unlike either the ichthyosaurus or the plesiosaurus – what has been guessed at about the latter, anyway."

"Oh no, it is a plesiosaurus," Mr Buckland declared. "This one has a head, and it is just as we'd imagined – so small compared to the rest of the body. And the paddles! I have made Mary promise to clean them first. But I have not told you why I have come to see you, Miss Philpot. It is this: I want you to convince the Annings not to sell this specimen to Colonel Birch as they did the last one. He sold that on to the Royal College of Surgeons, and we would rather this one not go there as well."

"He sold it on? Why would he do that?" I gripped the arms of my chair. Any mention of Colonel Birch made me tense with nerves.

Mr Buckland shrugged. "Perhaps he needed the money. It is no bad thing for it to be on public display, but the College is full of men keen to exploit plesiosauri without the intelligence behind it. Conybeare is much more reliable in studying the specimen. He may want it brought to the Geological Society so that he can lecture on it as he did previously. I should think such a meeting would be very well attended. Did you know, Miss Philpot, that I am to become the Society's President in February? Perhaps I can combine his lecture with my inauguration."

"According to the *Post* the Annings are considering the Bristol or the British Museums." I was a little humiliated to be quoting the newspaper account to someone who had seen the specimen for himself. It was like describing London from a guidebook to someone who has lived there.

"That is an indication of the newspaper's inclination rather than the Annings'," William Buckland said. "No, Molly Anning mentioned Colonel Birch to me just now, and wouldn't consider my suggestions."

"Did you tell her that Colonel Birch sold on the first specimen, and probably for a pretty profit?"

"She wouldn't listen to me. That is why I have come to you."

I studied my hands. Despite my wearing fingerless gloves and applying Margaret's salve daily, they were rough and scarred, with puckered fingers and a rim of blue clay under each nail. "I have little influence over the Annings and whom they choose to sell to. They run their own business now, and would not welcome my interference."

"But will you try, Miss Philpot? Talk to her. She is certain to respect your judgement – as do we all."

I sighed. "Really, Mr Buckland, if you want Molly Anning to sit up and take note, you must speak in the language she understands. Not museums and scientific papers, but money. Find her a collector who will pay her substantially more than Colonel Birch and she will gladly sell to them."

Mr Buckland looked startled, as if the thought of money had not occurred to him.

"Now," I continued, determined to change the subject, "I've a case of fish on the landing you haven't seen before, including the dorsal fin of a *Hybodus* that will amaze you, for the ridges along the spine truly resemble teeth! Come, I'll show you."

When he was gone, I sat again by the fire and thought. Now William Buckland had enthused about the plesiosaurus, I wanted more than ever to see it. If I didn't while it was still in Lyme, I might never get another chance, especially if he found a private buyer who would keep it in his house, inaccessible to someone like me.

Mary would be cleaning and preparing the specimen for the next several weeks, rarely leaving it, and not at predictable moments. I did not know how I could get to it without seeing her. However, I could not face her. I had grown used to not facing her, to not thinking about the superiority she felt to me. I did not want to open that wound again.

On Sunday, however, I got an unexpected chance. We were walking along Coombe Street towards St Michael's when I saw ahead of us all three Annings enter the Congregationalist Chapel. I was used to seeing Mary in the distance. It no longer made me want to bolt, for she was doing her best to ignore me too.

Once inside St Michael's, I sat with my sisters and Bessy,

and while Reverend Jones led us in prayer, I thought about the Annings' empty house just around the corner.

I began to cough, first a stray one here and there, then building up so that it sounded as if I had a persistent tickle in my throat I could not get rid of. Neighbours shifted in their seats and glanced around, and Margaret and Louise looked at me with concern.

"The cold is bothering my throat," I whispered to Louise. "I'd best go home. But you stay – I'll be fine." I slipped into the aisle before she could argue. Reverend Jones gazed at me as I hurried away, and I swear he knew that I was putting fossils before church.

Outside, I discovered that Bessy had followed me. "Oh Bessy, you needn't come with me," I said. "Go back inside." Bessy shook her head stubbornly. "No, ma'am, I has to relight the fire for you."

"I am perfectly capable of lighting the fire myself. Some days I do, when I get up before you, as you well know."

Bessy frowned, displeased to be reminded that I sometimes caught her out. "Miss Margaret told me to come with you," she muttered.

"Well, go back in and tell Margaret I sent you back. Surely you'd rather stay so that you can say hello to your friends after?" Post-church gossip amongst servants was lively, I had noticed.

I could see Bessy was tempted, but her natural suspicion made her study me with narrowed eyes. "You ain't going out on the beach, are you, Miss Elizabeth? I won't allow it, not after your cold. And it's Sunday!"

"Of course not. The tide is high." I had no idea what the tide was doing.

"Oh." Although she had now lived in Lyme almost twenty years, Bessy still had little sense of the tides. With a few more words of encouragement, I convinced her to return to the church.

Cockmoile Square and Bridge Street were deserted, as most of the town was at church or asleep. I could not hesitate or I would be caught or lose my nerve. Hurrying down the steps to Mary's workshop, I got out the spare key I had seen Molly Anning hide under a loose stone, unlocked the door and let myself in. I knew I should not do it, that it was far worse than my sneaking out to the auction at Bullock's in London. But I could not help it.

There was a whining, and Tray came up to me, sniffing my feet and wagging his tail. I hesitated, then reached down and petted him. His fur was coarse like coir, and he was covered in Blue Lias dust, a true Anning dog.

I stepped around him to look at the plesiosaurus laid out in slabs on the floor. It was about nine feet long, and half that width, which accommodated the span of its massive diamond-shaped paddles. Much of its length was made up of its swan-like neck, and at the end was a surprisingly small skull perhaps five inches long. The neck was so very long it didn't make sense. Could an animal have a neck longer than the rest of its body? I wished I had my Cuvier volume on anatomy with me. The body was a barrel-shaped mass of ribs, completed by a tail far shorter than the neck. All in all it was as unlikely looking as the ichthyosaurus with its enormous eye had been. It made me shiver and smile all at once. It also made me enormously proud of Mary. Whatever anger there was between us, I was delighted that she had found something no one ever had before.

I walked around it, looking and looking, getting my fill, for I was unlikely to see it again. Then I looked around the workshop, which I had once spent so much time in and now hadn't seen in a few years. It hadn't changed. There was still little furniture, a great deal of dust, and crates overflowing with fossils that awaited attention. On top of one such pile there was a sheaf of papers in Mary's hand. I glanced at the top sheet, then picked up the bundle and leafed through it. It was a copy of an article Reverend Conybeare had written for the Geological Society about Mary's beasts. There were twenty-nine pages of text, as well as eight pages of illustrations, all of which Mary had painstakingly copied out. She must have spent weeks doing this, night after night. I myself had not seen the article, and found myself drawn in to reading parts of it and wishing I could borrow the copy from her.

I could not stand in the workshop all day reading it, however. I flipped to the end to read the conclusion, and there discovered a note in small writing at the bottom of the last page. It read: "When I write a paper there shall not be but one preface."

It appeared Mary felt confident enough to criticise Reverend Conybeare's wordiness. Moreover, she had plans to write her own scientific paper. Her boldness made me smile.

Then Tray yipped, and the door opened, and Joseph Anning stood in the entrance. It could have been worse. It could have been Molly Anning, whose initial suspicion of me would have been revived. Of course it could have been Mary, and I would never have been able to justify such an intrusion to her.

It was still terrible, however. People do not enter others' homes unless they are thieves. Not even a harmless spinster can do such a thing. "Joseph, I – I – I am so sorry," I stammered. "I wanted to see what Mary found. I knew I could not come when she was here – it would be too awkward for us both. But I should never have let myself in. It is unforgivable, and I am sorry." I would have rushed out, but he was blocking the doorway, the light behind him throwing his face in shadow so that I could not see his expression – if he had one. Joseph Anning was not known for showing emotion.

He stood very still for a time. When he finally stepped forward he was not frowning or scowling, as one might have expected. Nor was he smiling. However, he was polite. "I've come back for another shawl for Mam. 'Tis cold at Chapel." How strange that Joseph should feel he owed me an explanation for being there. "What do you think of it, then, Miss Philpot?" he added, nodding at the plesiosaurus.

I had not expected him to be so reasonable. "It is truly extraordinary."

"I hate it. It's not natural. I'll be glad when it's gone." That was Joseph through and through.

"Mr Buckland told me he has been in touch with the Duke of Buckingham, who wants to buy it."

"Maybe. Mary has other ideas."

I cleared my throat. "Not – Colonel Birch?" I couldn't bear the answer.

But Joseph surprised me. "No, not him. Mary's let that go– she knows he'll never marry her."

"Oh." I was so relieved I almost laughed. "Who, then?"

"She won't say, not even to Mam. Mary's got a swollen head these days." Joseph shook his head, clearly disapproving. "She sent off a letter and said we've to wait for the answer before we tell Mr Buckland."

"How odd."

Joseph shifted from one foot to the other. "I have to get back to Chapel, Miss Philpot. Mam'll want her shawl."

"Of course." I glanced at the plesiosaurus once more, then set the paper Mary had copied back down on the pile of rocks in the crate. As I did so my eyes spied the tail of a fish. Then I saw a fin, and another tail, and realised the entire crate was full of fish fossils. A scrap of paper was stuck amongst them with "EP" in Mary's hand. She was saving them for me. She must think that one day we would be friends again, that she would forgive me and want me to forgive her. The thought made my eyes brim.

Joseph stood aside so that I could go. I paused as I passed him. "Joseph, I should be very grateful if you didn't tell Mary or your mother that I have been here. There is no need to upset them, is there?"

Joseph nodded. "I guess I owe you a favour anyway."

"Why?"

"It were you suggested I become an apprentice after we sold the croc. That were the best thing ever happened to me. I thought once I started I wouldn't never have to hunt curies again, but always something pulls me back into it. After this is sold –" he nodded at the plesiosaurus " – I'm done with curies for good. It'll be upholstering and nothing else. I'll be glad if I never have to go down upon beach again. So I will keep your secret for you, Miss Philpot." Joseph smiled briefly – the only smile I had ever seen on his face. It brought out a touch of his father's handsomeness.

"I hope you will be very happy," I said, using the words I hadn't been able to say to his sister.

The rapping on our front door interrupted us as we were eating. It was so sudden and loud that we all three jumped, and Margaret upset her watercress soup.

Normally we let Bessy go to the door in her own ponderous fashion, but the knocks were so urgent that Louise sprang up and hurried down the passage to answer it. Margaret and I could not see whom she let in, but we heard low voices in the passage. Then Louise put her head around the door. "Molly Anning is here to see us," she said. "She has said she will wait until we have finished eating. I've left her to warm by the fire and will get Bessy to build it up."

Margaret jumped up. "I'll just get Mrs Anning some soup."

I looked down at my own soup. I could not sit and eat it while an Anning waited in the other room. I got up as well, but stood uncertain in the doorway of the parlour.

Louise saved me, as she often does. "Brandy, perhaps," she said as she brushed past with a grumbling Bessy in tow.

"Yes, yes." I went and fetched the bottle and a glass.

Molly Anning was sitting motionless by the fire, the centre of all the activity around her, much as she had been when she came to see us with her letter to Colonel Birch. Bessy was poking the fire and glaring at our visitor's legs, which she perceived to be in the way. Margaret was setting up a small table at her side for the soup, while Louise

279

moved the coal scuttle. I hovered with the brandy bottle, but Molly Anning shook her head when I offered it. She said nothing while she ate her soup, sucking at it as if she didn't like watercress and was eating it only to please us.

As she mopped her bowl with a chunk of bread, I felt my sisters' eyes on me. They had played their parts with the visitor, and were now expecting me to play mine. My mouth felt glued shut, however. It had been a very long time since I had spoken either to Mary or to her mother.

I cleared my throat. "Is something wrong, Molly?" I managed at last. "Are Joseph and Mary all right?"

Molly Anning swallowed the last of her bread and ran her tongue around her mouth. "Mary's taken to her bed," she declared.

"Oh dear, is she ill?" Margaret asked.

"No, she's just a fool, is all. Here." Pulling a crumpled letter from her pocket, Molly Anning handed it to me. I opened it and smoothed it out. A glance told me it was from Paris. The words "plesiosaurus" and "Cuvier" popped out at me, but I hesitated to read the contents. However, as Molly seemed to expect me to, I had no choice.

Jardin du Roi
Musée National d'Histoire Naturelle
Paris

Dear Miss Anning,
Thank you for your letter to Baron Cuvier concerning a possible sale to the museum of the specimen you have discovered at Lyme Regis, and believe to be an almost compete skeleton of a plesiosaurus. Baron Cuvier has studied with interest the sketch you enclosed, and is of

the opinon that you have joined together two separate individuals, perhaps that of the head of a sea serpent with the body of an ichthyosaurus. The jumbled state of the vertebrae just below the head seems to indicate the disjuncture between the two specimens.

Baron Cuvier holds the view that the structure of the reported plesiosaurus deviates from some of the anatomical laws he has established. In particular, the number of cervical vertebrae is too great for such an individual. Most reptiles have between three and eight neck vertebrae; yet in your
sketch the creature appears to have at least thirty.

Given Baron Cuvier's concerns over the specimen, we will not consider purchasing it. In future, Mademoiselle, perhaps your family might take more care when collecting and presenting specimens.

Yours faithfully,
Joseph Pentland Esq.
Assistant to Baron Cuvier

I threw down the letter. "That is outrageous!"

"What is?" Margaret cried, caught up in the drama.

"Georges Cuvier has seen a drawing of Mary's plesiosaurus and has accused the Annings of forgery. He thinks the anatomy of the animal is impossible, and says that Mary may have put together two different specimens."

"The silly girl's taken it as an insult to her," Molly Anning said. "Says the Frenchman has ruined her reputation as a hunter. She's gone to bed over it, says there's no reason to get up and hunt curies now, as no one'll buy them. She's as

bad as when she were waiting for Colonel Birch to write."
Molly Anning glanced sideways at me, gauging my reaction.
"I come to ask you to help me get her out of bed."

"But—" Why ask me, I wanted to say. Why not someone
else? On the other hand, perhaps Mary had no other friends
Molly could ask. I had never seen her with other Lyme people
of her age and class. "The trouble is," I began, "Mary may well
be right. If Baron Cuvier believes the plesiosaurus is a fake,
and makes public his view, it could cause people to question
other specimens." Molly Anning did not seem to respond to
this idea, so I made it plainer. "You may find your sales will
fall as people wonder whether Anning fossils are authentic."

At last I got through to her, for Molly Anning glared
at me as if I had suggested such a thing myself. "How dare
that Frenchman threaten our business! You'll have to sort
him out."

"Me?"

"You speak French, don't you? You've had learning. I
haven't, you see, so you'll have to write to him."

"But it's nothing to do with me."

Molly Anning just looked at me, as did my sisters.

"Molly," I said, "Mary and I have not had a great deal to
do with each other these last few years—"

"What is all that about, then? Mary would never say."

I looked around. Margaret was sitting forward, and
Louise was giving me the Philpot gaze, both also waiting
for me to explain, for I had never provided a sufficient
reason for our break. "Mary and I... we did not see eye to
eye on some things."

"Well, you can make it up to her by sorting out this
Frenchman," Molly Anning declared.

"I am not sure I can do anything. Cuvier is a powerful, well-respected scientist, whilst you are just—" a poor, working family, I wanted to finish, but didn't. I didn't need to, for Molly Anning understood what I meant. "Anyway, he won't listen to me either, whether I write in French or English. He doesn't know who I am. Indeed, I am nobody to him." To most people, I thought.

"One of the men could write to Cuvier," Margaret suggested. "Mr Buckland, perhaps? He has met Cuvier, hasn't he?"

"Maybe I should write to Colonel Birch and ask him to write," Molly Anning said. "I'm sure he would do it."

"Not Colonel Birch." My tone was so sharp that all three women looked at me. "Does anyone else know that Mary wrote to Cuvier?"

Molly Anning shook her head.

"And so no one else knows of this response?"

"Only Joe, but he won't say anything."

"Well, that is something."

"But people will find out. Eventually Mr Buckland and Reverend Conybeare and Mr Konig and all those men we sell to will know that the Frenchman thinks the Annings are frauds. The Duke of Buckingham might hear and not pay us!" Molly Anning's mouth started to tremble, and I feared she might actually cry – a sight I didn't think I could bear.

To stop her I said, "Molly, I am going to help you. Don't cry, now. We will manage."

I had no idea what I would do. But I was thinking of the crate full of fossil fish in Mary's workshop, waiting for me to thaw, and knew I had to do something. I thought for a moment. "Where is the plesiosaurus now?"

"On board the *Dispatch*, heading for London, if it ain't already arrived. Mr Buckland saw her off. And Reverend Conybeare is meeting it at the other end. He's addressing the Geological Society later this month at their annual dinner."

"Ah." So it was gone already. The men had charge of it now. I would have to go to them.

Margaret and Louise thought I was mad. It was bad enough that I wanted to travel to London rather than simply write a forceful letter. But to go in winter, and by ship, was folly. However, the weather was so foul, the roads so muddy, that only mail coaches were getting through to London, and even they were being delayed, and were full besides. A ship might be quicker, and the weekly one was leaving when I needed it.

I knew too that the men I wanted to see would be blinded by their interest in the plesiosaurus and would not attend to my letter, no matter how eloquent or urgent. I must see them in person to convince them to help Mary immediately.

What I did not tell my sisters was that I was excited to go. Yes, I was fearful of the ship and of what the sea might do. It would be cold and rough, and I might feel sick much of the time, despite a tonic for seasickness that Margaret had concocted for me. As the only lady on board, I could not be sure of sympathy or comfort from the crew or other passengers.

I also had no idea if I could make any difference to Mary's predicament. I only knew that when I read Joseph Pentland's letter, I was consumed with anger. Mary had been so generous for so long, to so little gain – apart from

Colonel Birch's sudden, madcap auction – while others took what she found and made their names from it as natural philosophers. William Buckland lectured on the creatures at Oxford, Charles Konig brought them into the British Museum to acclaim, Reverend Conybeare and even our dear Henry De La Beche addressed the Geological Society and published papers about them. Konig had had the privilege of naming the ichthyosaurus, and Conybeare the plesiosaurus. Neither would have had anything to name without Mary. I could not stand by and watch suspicions grow about her skills when the men knew she outstripped them all in her abilities.

I was also making amends to Mary. I was at last asking her to forgive me my jealousy and disdain.

There was something else, though. This was also my chance for an adventure in an unadventurous life. I had never travelled alone, but was always with my sisters or brother or other relatives, or with friends. As secure as that had felt, it was a bind as well that sometimes threatened to smother me. I was rather proud now as I stood on the deck of the *Unity* – the same ship that had taken Colonel Birch's ichthyosaurus to London – and watched Lyme and my sisters grow smaller until they disappeared and I was alone.

We sailed straight out to sea rather than hug the coast, for we had to clear the tricky isle of Portland. So I did not get to see up close the places I knew well – Golden Cap, Bridport, Chesil Beach, Weymouth. Once past Portland we remained out at sea until we had gone around the Isle of Wight, before finally coming closer to shore.

A sea voyage is very different from a coach trip to London, where Margaret, Louise and I were packed with several strangers into a stuffy, rattling, jolting box that stopped constantly to change horses. That was a communal event, uncomfortable in ways that as I grew older took days to recover from.

Being on board the *Unity* was much more solitary. I would sit on deck, tucked out of the way on a small keg, and watch the crew at work with their ropes and sails. I had no idea what they were doing, but their shouts to one another and their confident routines soothed my fears of being at sea. Moreover, the cares of daily life were taken out of my hands, and nothing was expected of me but to stay out of the men's way. Not only did I not feel ill on board, even when it was rough; I was actually enjoying myself.

I had been anxious about being the only lady on the ship – the three other passengers were all men with business in London – but I was mostly ignored, though the Captain was kind enough, if taciturn, when I joined him to dine each night. No one seemed at all curious about me, though one of the passengers – a man from Honiton – was happy to talk about fossils when he heard of my interest. I did not tell him about the plesiosaurus, however, or of my intended visit to the Geological Society. He knew only about the obvious – ammonites, belemnites, crinoids, gryphaea – and had little of use to say, though he made sure to say every word of it. Luckily he could not bear the cold, and most often stayed belowdecks.

Until I boarded the *Unity*, I had always thought of the sea as a boundary keeping me in my place on land. Now, though, it became an opening. As I sat I occasionally saw another vessel, but most of the time there was nothing but sky and moving water. I often looked to the horizon, lulled into a wordless calm by the rhythm of the sea and by ship life. It was oddly satisfying to study that far-off line, reminding me that I spent much of my life in Lyme with my eyes fixed to the ground in search of fossils. Such hunting can limit a person's perspective. On board the *Unity* I had no choice but to see the greater world, and my place in it. Sometimes I imagined being on shore and looking out at the ship, and seeing on deck a small, mauve figure caught between the light grey sky and dark grey sea, watching the world pass before her, alone and sturdy. I did not expect it, but I had never been so happy.

The winds were light, but we made steady if slow progress. The first I saw of land was on the second day when the chalk cliffs to the east of Brighton came blinking into view. When we made a brief stop there to unload cloth from Lyme's factory, I considered asking Captain Pearce if I might go ashore to see my sister Frances. However, rather to my surprise, I felt no real urge to do so, or to send her a note saying I was there, but was content to remain on board and watch the residents of Brighton on land walking back and forth along the promenade. Even if Frances herself had appeared, I am not sure I would have called out to her. I preferred not to disturb the delicious anonymity of standing on deck with no one looking for me.

On the third day we had passed Dover with its stark white cliffs, and were coming around the headland by Ramsgate when we saw a ship off our port side run aground on a sandbar. As we drew nearer I heard one of the crew name it as the *Dispatch*, the ship carrying Mary's plesiosaurus.

I sought out the Captain. "Oh yes, that be the *Dispatch*," he confirmed, "run aground on Goodwin Sands. They'll have tried to turn too sharp." He sounded disgusted and entirely without sympathy, even as he called for the men to cast anchor. Soon two sailors set out in a boat to cross over to the listing vessel, where they met with a few men who had by now appeared on deck. The sailors talked to them for just a few minutes before rowing back. I leaned forward and strained to hear what they shouted to the Captain. "Cargo was taken to shore yesterday!" one called. "They're taking it overland to London."

At this the crew jeered, for they had little respect for travel by land, I had learned during the trip. They saw it as slow, rough and muddy. Others – coachmen, for instance – might retort that the sea was slow, rough and wet.

Whoever was right, Mary's plesiosaurus was now some-where in a long, slow train of carts grinding through Kent towards London. Having left a week before me, the speci-men would now probably arrive in London after me, too late for the Geological Society meeting.

We reached London in the early hours of the fourth day, docking at a wharf on Tooley Street. After the relative calm on board, all now became a chaos of unloading by torch-light, of shouts and whistles, of coaches and carts clattering away full of people and cargo. It was a shock to the senses after four days of Nature providing her own constant rhythms. The people and the noise and the lights reminded me too that I had come to London for a reason, not to enjoy anonymity and solitude whilst eyeing the wider horizon.

I stood on deck and looked out for my brother at the quayside, but he was not there. The letter I had posted at the same time as I left must have got stuck in the mud *en route* and lost its race with me. Though I had never been before, I had heard about London's docks, how crowded and dirty and dangerous they were, especially for a lady on her own with no one expecting her. Perhaps it was because the darkness made everything more mysterious, but the men unloading the *Unity*, even the sailors I had got to know on board, now appeared much rougher and harder.

I hesitated to disembark. There was no one to turn to for help, though: the other passengers – even the cocksure man from Honiton – had hurried away in ungentleman-like haste. I could have panicked. Before the journey I might have. But something had shifted in me while I spent all that time on deck watching the horizon: I was responsible for myself. I was Elizabeth Philpot, and I collected fossil fish. Fish are not always beautiful, but they have pleasing shapes, they are practical, and they lead with their eyes. There is nothing shamful about them

I picked up my bag and stepped off the boat amidst a score of bustling men, many of whom whistled and shouted at me. Before anyone could do more than call out, I walked quickly to the Customs House, despite swaying with the shock of being on land again. "I would like a cab, please," I said to a surprised clerk, interrupting him as he ticked items on a list. He had a moustache that fluttered like a moth over his mouth. "I shall wait here until you fetch me one," I added, setting down my bag. I did not stick out my chin and sharpen my jaw, but gazed steadily at him with my Philpot eyes.

He found me a cab.

*   *   *

The Geological Society's offices in Covent Garden were not far from my brother's house, but to get there one had to pass through St Giles and Seven Dials, with its beggars and thieves, and I was not keen to do so on foot. Thus on the evening of the 20th February, 1824, I waited in a cab across from 20 Bedford Street, my nephew Johnny beside me. There was snow on the street, and we huddled under our cloaks against the cold.

My brother was horrified that I had come all the way to London on a ship because of Mary. When he was woken in the middle of the night to find me at the door, he looked so ill with surprise that I almost regretted I had come. Being quietly tucked away in Lyme, my sisters and I had rarely given him cause to worry, and I did not like to do so now.

John did everything he could to persuade me not to go to the Geological Society, bar expressly forbidding me. It seemed he was only willing to indulge me in unusual behaviour just the once, when he had escorted me to Bullock's to view Colonel Birch's auction preview. Mercifully he had never found out I attended the auction itself. He would not help me with something so odd and risky again. "They will not let you in, for you are a lady, and their charter does not allow it," he began, using first the legal argument. We were in his study, the door closed, as if John were trying to protect his family from me, his erratic sister. "Even if they let you in they would not listen to you, for you are not a member. Then," he added, holding up a hand as I tried to interrupt, "you have no business discussing and defending Mary. It is not your place to."

"She is my friend," I replied, "and no one else will take her part if I don't."

John looked at me as if I were a small child trying to convince my nurse I could have another helping of pudding. "You have been very foolish, Elizabeth. You have come all this way, making yourself ill *en route* –"

"It is just a cold, nothing more."

" – ill *en route*, and worrying us unnecessarily." Now he was using guilt. "And to no purpose, for you will gain no audience."

"I can at least try. It is truly foolish to come all this way and then not even try."

"What exactly do you want from these men?"

"I want to remind them of Mary's careful methods of finding and preserving fossils, and to convince them to agree to defend her publicly against Cuvier's attack on her character."

"They will never do that," John said, running his finger along the spiral of his nautilus paperweight. "Though they may defend the plesiosaurus, they will not discuss Mary. She is only the hunter."

"Only the hunter!" I stopped myself. John was a London solicitor, with a certain way of thinking. I was a stubborn Lyme spinster, with my own mind. We were not going to agree, nor either of us convince the other. And he was not my target anyway; I must save my words for more important men.

John would not agree to accompany me to the meeting, and so I did not ask, but turned to an alternative – my nephew. Johnny was now a tall, lanky youth who led with his feet, had a residual fondness for his aunt and an active fondness for mischief. He had never told his parents about discovering me sneaking out of the house to go to the auction at Bullock's, and this shared secret bound us. It was this closeness I now relied on to help me.

I was lucky, for John and my sister-in-law were dining out on the Friday evening of the Geological Society meeting. I had not told him when the meeting was to take place, but allowed him to believe it was the following week. The afternoon of the supper I took to bed, saying my cold was worse. My sister-in-law pursed her lips in clear disapproval of my folly. She did not like unexpected visitors, or the sort of problems that, for all my quiet life at Lyme, I seemed to trail behind me. She hated fossils, and disorder, and unanswered questions. Whenever I brought up topics like the possible age of the earth, she twisted her hands in her lap and changed the subject as soon as it was polite to.

When she and my brother had gone out for the evening, I crept from my room and went to find Johnny and explain what I needed from him. He rose to the occasion admirably, coming up with an excuse for his departure to satisfy the servants, fetching a cab and hurrying me into it without anyone in the house discovering. It was absurd that I had to go to such lengths to take any sort of action out of the ordinary.

However, it was also a relief to have company. Now we sat in the cab on Bedford Street across from the Geological Society house, Johnny having gone in to check and found that the members were still dining in rooms on the first floor. Through the front windows we could see lights there and the occasional head bobbing about. The formal meeting would begin in half an hour or so.

"What shall we do, Aunt Elizabeth?" he demanded. "Storm the citadel?"

"No, we wait. They will all stand so that the meal can be cleared away. At that moment I will go in and seek out Mr Buckland. He is about to become President of the Society, and I am sure he will listen to me."

Johnny sat back and propped his feet up on the seat across from him. If I had been his mother I would have told him to put his feet down, but the pleasure of being an aunt is that you can enjoy your nephew's company without having to concern yourself with his behaviour. "Aunt Elizabeth, you haven't said why this plesiosaur is so important," he began. "That is, I understand that you want to defend Miss Anning. But why is everyone so excited about the creature itself?"

I straightened my gloves and rearranged my cloak around me. "Do you remember when you were a small boy and we took you to the Egyptian Hall to see all the animals?"

"Yes, I recall the elephant and the hippo."

"Do you remember the stone crocodile you found, and I was so upset by? The one that is now in the British Museum and they call an ichthyosaurus?"

"I've seen it at the British Museum, of course, and you've told me about it," Johnny answered. "But I confess I remember the elephant better. Why?"

"Well, when Mary discovered that ichthyosaurus, she did not know it at the time, but she was contributing to a new way of thinking about the world. Here was a creature that had never been seen before, that did not seem to exist any longer, but was extinct – the species had died out. Such a phenomenon made people think that perhaps the world is changing, however slowly, rather than being a constant, as had been previously thought.

293

"At the same time, geologists were studying the different layers of rock, and thinking about how the world was formed, and wondering about its age. For some time now men have wondered if the world isn't older than the 6000 years calculated by Bishop Ussher. A learned Scotsman called James Hutton even suggested that the world is so old it has 'neither a beginning nor an end,' and that it is impossible for us to measure it." I paused. "Perhaps it would be best if you didn't mention any of what I'm saying to your mother. She doesn't like to hear me talk of such things."

"I won't. Carry on."

"Hutton thought the world is being sculpted by volcanic action. Others have suggested it has been formed by water. Lately some geologists have taken elements of both and said a series of catastrophes has shaped the world, with Noah's Flood being the latest."

"What does this have to do with the plesiosaurus?"

"It is concrete evidence that the ichthyosaurus was not a unique instance of extinction, but that there are others – maybe many extinct creatures. That in turn supports the argument that the earth is in flux." I looked at my nephew. Johnny was frowning at the light snowflakes swirling about outside. Perhaps he was more like his mother than I realised. "I'm sorry – I didn't mean to upset you with such talk."

He shook his head. "No, it's fascinating. I was just wondering why none of my tutors discuss this in lessons."

"It is too frightening for many, for it challenges our belief in an all-knowing, all-powerful God, and raises questions about His intentions."

"What do *you* believe, Aunt Elizabeth?"

"I believe…" Few had ever asked me what I believed. It was refreshing. "I am comfortable with reading the Bible figuratively rather than literally. For instance, I think the six days in Genesis are not literal days, but different periods of creation, so that it took many thousands – or hundreds of thousands of years – to create. It does not demean God; it simply gives Him more time to build this extraordinary world."

"And the ichthyosaurus and plesiosaurus?"

"They are creatures from long, long ago. They remind us that the world is changing. Of course it is. I can see it change when there are landslips at Lyme that alter the shoreline. It changes when there are earthquakes and volcanic eruptions and floods. And why shouldn't it?"

Johnny nodded. It was a relief to say such things to a sympathetic ear and not be judged either ignorant or blasphemous. Perhaps he could be so open-minded because he was young.

"Look." He pointed at the windows of the Geological Society house. Figures were blocking the light as the men got up from their tables. It was time for me to lead with my eyes. I took a deep breath and opened the cab door. Johnny leaped out and helped me down, excited to be acting at last. He strode to the door and knocked boldly. The same man answered as had the first time, but Johnny treated him as if he had never spoken to him before. "Miss Philpot here to see Professor Buckland," he announced. Perhaps he thought such confidence would open all doors.

The doorman, however, was not taken in by youthful assuredness. "Women are not allowed in the Society," he replied, not even glancing at me. It was as if I did not exist.

He began to shut the door, but Johnny stuck his foot on the jamb so that it wouldn't close. "Well, then, John Philpot Esquire here to see Professor Buckland."

The doorman looked him up and down. "What business?"

"It's to do with the plesiosaurus."

The doorman frowned. The word meant nothing to him, but it sounded complicated and possibly important. "I'll take up a message."

"I can only speak to Professor Buckland," Johnny replied in a haughty tone, enjoying every moment.

The doorman appeared unmoved. I had to step forward, forcing him at last to look at me and acknowledge my presence. "As it is to do with the very subject of the meeting that is about to start, it would be wise of you to inform Professor Buckland that we are waiting to speak to him." I looked him straight in the eye, with all of the steadiness and resolve I had discovered in myself on board the *Unity*.

It had its effect: after a moment the doorman dropped his eyes and gave me the briefest of nods. "Wait here," he said, and shut the door in our faces. Clearly my success was limited, for it did not overcome the rule that women were not allowed inside, but must stand out in the cold. As we waited, snowflakes dusted my hat and cloak.

A few minutes later we heard footsteps clattering down the stairs, and the door opened to reveal the excited faces of Mr Buckland and Reverend Conybeare. I was disappointed to see the latter; Reverend Conybeare was not nearly as easy and welcoming as Mr Buckland.

I think they were a little disappointed to see us as well. "Miss Philpot!" Mr Buckland cried. "What a surprise. I did not know you were in town."

"I only arrived two days ago, Mr Buckland. Reverend Conybeare." I nodded at them both. "This is my nephew, John. May we come in? It is very cold outside."

"Of course, of course!" As Mr Buckland ushered us in, Reverend Conybeare pursed his lips, clearly unhappy that a lady was being allowed across the threshold of the Geological Society. But he was not President – Mr Buckland would become so in a moment – and so he said nothing, but bowed to us both. His long narrow nose was red, whether from wine, a seat close to the fire, or temper, I couldn't guess.

The entrance to the house was simple, with an elegant black-and-white tiled floor and solemn portraits hanging of George Greenough, John MacCulloch, and other Society Presidents. Soon a portrait of William Babington, the retiring President, would join the others. I expected to see something displayed that would indicate the Society's interest: fossils, of course, or rocks. But there was nothing. The interesting things were hidden away.

"Tell me, Miss Philpot, do you have news of the plesiosaurus?" Reverend Conybeare asked. "The doorman said you might. Will its presence yet grace our meeting?"

Now I understood their excitement: it was not the Philpot name but mention of the missing specimen that had brought them racing down the stairs.

"I passed the grounded *Dispatch* three days ago." I tried to sound knowledgeable. "Its cargo is now being brought by land, and will arrive as quickly as the roads allow."

Both men looked discouraged at hearing what was not news to them. "Why, then, Miss Philpot, are you here?" Reverend Conybeare said. For a vicar he was quite tart.

I drew myself up straight and tried to look them in the eye as confidently as I had the clerk at the wharf and the Geological Society's doorman. It was more difficult, however, as there were two of them gazing at me – and Johnny too. Then, too, they were more learned, and confident. I might hold some power over a clerk and a doorman, but not over one of my own class. Instead of fixing my attention on Mr Buckland – who as future President of the Society was the more important of the two – I stupidly looked at my nephew as I said, "I wanted to discuss Miss Anning with you."

"Has something happened to Mary?" William Buckland asked.

"No, no, she is well."

Reverend Conybeare frowned, and even Mr Buckland, who was not a frowner, wrinkled his brow. "Miss Philpot," Reverend Conybeare began, "we are about to hold our meeting at which both Mr Buckland and I will be giving important – nay, even history-making – addresses to the Society. Surely your query about Miss Anning can wait until another day while we concentrate on these more pressing matters. Now, if you will excuse me, I am just going to review my notes." Without waiting to hear my response, he turned and padded up the carpeted stairs.

Mr Buckland looked as if he might do the same, but he was slower and kinder, and he took a moment to say, "I should be delighted to talk with you another time, Miss Philpot. Perhaps I could call around one day next week?"

"But sir," Johnny broke in, "Monsieur Cuvier thinks the plesiosaurus is a fake!"

That stopped Reverend Conybeare's retreating back. He turned on the stairs. "What did you say?"

Johnny, the clever boy, had said just the right thing. Of course the men did not want to hear about Mary. It was Cuvier's opinion of the plesiosaurus that would concern them.

"Baron Cuvier believes that the plesiosaurus Mary found cannot be real," I explained as Reverend Conybeare descended the stairs and rejoined us, his face grim. "The neck has too many vertebrae, and he believes it violates the fundamental laws that govern the anatomy of vertebrates."

Reverend Conybeare and Mr Buckland exchanged glances.

"Cuvier has suggested the Annings created a false animal by adding a sea serpent's skull to the body of an ichthyosaurus. He claims they are forgers," I added, bringing the discussion to what concerned me most.

Then I wished I hadn't, for seeing the expressions my words ignited on the men's faces. Both registered surprise, giving way to a degree of suspicion, more prominent in Reverend Conybeare's case, but also apparent even in Mr Buckland's benign features.

"Of course you know that Mary would never do such a thing," I reminded them. "She is an honest soul, and trained – by your good selves, I might add – in the importance of preserving specimens as they are found. She knows they are of little use if tampered with."

"Of course," Mr Buckland agreed, his face clearing, as if all he needed was a prompt from a sensible mind.

Reverend Conybeare was still frowning, however. Clearly my reminder had tapped into a seam of doubt. "Who told Cuvier about the specimen?" he demanded.

I hesitated, but there was no way around revealing the truth. "Mary herself wrote to him. I believe she sent along a drawing."

Reverend Conybeare snorted. "*Mary* wrote? I dread to think what such a letter would be like. The girl is practically illiterate! It would have been much better if Cuvier had learned of it after tonight's lecture. Buckland, we must present our case to him ourselves, with drawings and a detailed description. You and I should write, and perhaps someone else as well, so Cuvier will hear about it from several angles. Johnson in Bristol, perhaps. He was very keen when I mentioned the plesiosaurus at the Institution at the beginning of the month, and I know he has corresponded with Cuvier in the past." As he spoke, Reverend Conybeare ran his hand up and down the mahogany banister, still rattled by the news. If he hadn't irritated me with his suspicion of Mary, I might have felt sorry for him.

Mr Buckland also noted his friend's nerves. "Conybeare, you are not going to withdraw your address now, are you? Many guests have come expressly to hear you: Babbage, Gordon, Drummond, Rudge, even McDownell. You've seen the room: it's packed, the best attendance I've ever seen. Of course I can entertain them with my musings on the megalosaurus, but how much more powerful if we both speak of these creatures of the past. Together we will give them an evening they will never forget!"

I tutted. "This is not the theatre, Mr Buckland."

"Ah, but in a way it is, Miss Philpot. And what wonderful entertainment we have prepared for them! We are in the midst of opening their eyes to incontrovertible evidence of a wondrous past world, to the most magnificent creatures God has created – apart from man, of course." Mr Buckland was warming to his theme.

"Perhaps you should save your thoughts for the meeting," I suggested.

"Of course, of course. Now, Conybeare, are you with me?"

"Yes." Reverend Conybeare visibly donned a more confident air. "In my paper I have already addressed some of Cuvier's concerns about the number of vertebrae. Besides, you have seen the creature, Buckland. You believe in it."

Mr Buckland nodded.

"Then you believe in Mary Anning as well," I interjected. "And you will defend her from Cuvier's unjust charges."

"I do not see what that has to do with this meeting," Reverend Conybeare countered. "I mentioned Mary when I spoke about the plesiosaurus at the Bristol Institution. Buckland and I will write to Cuvier. Is that not enough?"

"Every geologist of note as well as other interested parties are upstairs in that room right now. One announcement from you, that you have complete confidence in Mary's abilities as a fossil hunter, will counter any comments from Baron Cuvier that they might hear of later."

"Why should I want to cast doubt in public on Miss Anning's abilities, and indeed – and more importantly, I might add – doubt on the very specimen I am just preparing to speak about?"

"A woman's good name is at stake, as well as her livelihood – a livelihood that provides you with the specimens you need to further your theories and your own good name. Surely that must matter to you enough to speak out?"

Reverend Conybeare and I glared at each other, our eyes locked. We might have remained like that all evening if it weren't for Johnny, who had become impatient with all of the talk and wanted more action. He ducked behind Reverend Conybeare and leapt onto the stairs above him. "If you don't agree to clear Miss Anning's name, I shall go and tell the roomful of gentlemen upstairs what Cuvier has said," he called down to us. "How would you like that?"

Reverend Conybeare made a move to grab him, but Johnny leaped up several more steps to remain out of reach. I should have scolded my nephew for his bad behaviour, but instead found myself snorting to hide laughter. I turned to Mr Buckland, the more reasonable of the two. "Mr Buckland, I know how fond you are of Mary, and that you recognise how much in debt we all are to her for her immense skill in finding fossils. I understand too that this evening is very important to you, and I would not want to ruin that. But surely somewhere in the meeting there is room for you to express your support of Mary? Perhaps you could simply acknowledge her efforts without mentioning Baron Cuvier specifically. And when his remarks are at last made public, the men upstairs will understand the deeper meaning of your declaration of confidence. That way we will all be satisfied. Would that be acceptable?"

Mr Buckland pondered this suggestion. "It could not be recorded in the Society's minutes," he said at last, "but I am certainly willing to say something off the record if that will please you, Miss Philpot."

"It will, thank you."

He and Reverend Conybeare looked up at Johnny. "That will do, lad," Reverend Conybeare muttered. "Come down, now."

"Is that all, Aunt Elizabeth? Shall I come down?" Johnny seemed disappointed that he could not carry out his threat.

"There is one more thing," I said. Reverend Conybeare groaned. "I should like to hear what you have to say at the meeting about the plesiosaurus."

"I'm afraid women are not allowed in to the Society meetings." Mr Buckland sounded almost sorry.

"Perhaps I could sit out in the corridor to listen? No one but you need know I am there."

Mr Buckland thought for a moment. "There is a staircase at the back of the room leading down to one of the kitchens. The servants use it to bring dishes and food and such up and down. You might sit out on the landing. From there you should be able to hear us without being seen."

"That would be very kind, thank you."

Mr Buckland gestured to the doorman, who had been listening impassively. "Would you show this lady and young man up to the landing at the back, please. Come, Conybeare, we have kept them waiting long enough. They'll think we've gone to Lyme and back!"

The two men hurried up the stairs, leaving Johnny and me with the doorman. I will not forget the venomous look Reverend Conybeare threw me over his shoulder as he reached the top and turned to go into the meeting room.

Johnny chuckled. "You have not made a friend there, Aunt Elizabeth!"

"It doesn't matter to me, but I fear I have put him off his stride. Well, we shall hear in a moment."

I did not put off Reverend Conybeare. As a vicar he was used to speaking in public, and he was able to draw on that well of experience to recover his equanimity. By the time William Buckland had got through the procedural parts of the meeting – approving the minutes of the previous meeting, proposing new members, enumerating the various journals and specimens donated to the Society since the last meeting – Reverend Conybeare would have looked over his notes and reassured himself about the particulars of his claims, and when he began speaking his voice was steady and grounded in authority.

I could only judge his delivery by his voice. Johnny and I were tucked away on chairs on the landing, which led off of the back of the room. Although we kept the door ajar so that we could hear, we could not see beyond the gentlemen standing in front of the door in the crowded room. I felt trapped behind a wall of men that separated me from the main event.

Luckily Reverend Conybeare's public speaking voice penetrated even to us. "I am highly gratified," he began, "in being able to lay before the Society an account of an almost perfect skeleton of *Plesiosaurus*, a new fossil genus, which, from the consideration of several fragments found only in a disjointed state, I felt myself authorised to propound in the year 1821. It is through the kind liberality of its possessor, the Duke of Buckingham, that this new specimen has been placed for a time at the disposal of my friend Professor Buckland for the purpose of scientific investigation. The magnificent specimen recently discovered at Lyme has confirmed the justice of my former conclusions in every essential point connected with the organisation of the skeleton."

While the men were warmed by two coal fires and the collective bodily heat of sixty souls, Johnny and I sat frozen on the landing. I pulled my woollen cloak close about me, but I knew sitting back there was doing my weakened chest no good. Still, I could not leave at such an important moment.

Reverend Conybeare immediately addressed the plesiosaurus' most surprising feature – its extremely long neck. "The neck is fully equal in length to the body and tail united," he explained. "Surpassing in the number of its vertebrae that of the longest necked birds, even the swan, it deviates from the laws which were heretofore regarded as universal in quadrupedal animals. I mention this circumstance thus early, as forming the most prominent and interesting feature of the recent discovery, and that which in effect renders this animal one of the most curious and important additions which geology has yet made to comparative anatomy."

He then went on to describe the beast in detail. By this point I was stifling coughs, and Johnny went down to the kitchen to fetch me some wine. He must have liked what he saw down there better than what he could hear on the landing, for after handing me a glass of claret he disappeared down the back staircase again, probably to sit by the fire and practise flirting with the serving girls brought in for the evening.

Reverend Conybeare delineated the head and the vertebrae, dwelling for a time on the number in different sorts of animals, just as Monsieur Cuvier had done in his criticism of Mary. Indeed, he mentioned Cuvier in passing a few times; the great anatomist's influence was emphasised throughout the talk. No wonder that Reverend Conybeare had been so horrified by Cuvier's response to Mary's letter. However, whatever its impossible anatomy, the plesiosaurus *had* existed. If Conybeare believed in the creature, he must believe in what Mary found too, and the best way to convince Cuvier was to support her. It seemed obvious to me.

It didn't to him, however. Indeed, he did just the opposite. In the middle of a description of the plesiosaurus' paddles, Reverend Conybeare added, "I must acknowledge that originally I wrongly depicted the edges of the paddles as being formed of rounded bones, when they are not. However, when the first specimen was found in 1821, the bones in question were loose, and had been subsequently glued into their present situation, in consequence of a conjecture of the proprietor."

It took me a moment to realise he was referring to Mary as proprietor, and suggesting she had made mistakes in putting together the bones of the first plesiosaurus. Reverend Conybeare only bothered to refer to her – still unnamed – when there was criticism to lay at her feet. "How ungentlemanly!" I muttered, more loudly than I had intended, for a number of the row of heads in front of me shifted and turned, as if trying to locate the source of this outburst.

I shrank back in my seat, then listened numbly as Reverend Conybeare compared the plesiosaurus to a turtle without its shell and speculated on its awkwardness both on land and in the sea. "May it not therefore be concluded that it swam upon or near the surface, arching back its long neck like the swan, and occasionally darting it down at the fish which happened to float within its reach? It may perhaps have lurked in shoal water along the coast, concealed among the sea-weed and, raising its nostrils to a level with the surface from a considerable depth, may have found a secure retreat from the assaults of dangerous enemies."

He finished with a strategic flourish I suspected he'd thought up during the earlier part of the meeting. "I cannot but congratulate the scientific public that the discovery of this animal has been made at the very moment when the illustrious Cuvier is engaged in, and on the eve of publishing, his researches on the fossil ovipara: from him the subject will derive all that lucid order which he never has yet failed to introduce into the most obscure and intricate departments of comparative anatomy. Thank you."

In so saying, Reverend Conybeare linked himself favourably with Baron Cuvier, so that whatever criticism arose from the Frenchman would not seem to be directed at him. I did not join in with the clapping. My chest had become so heavy that I was having difficulty breathing.

An animated discussion began, of which I did not follow every point, for I was feeling dizzy. However, I did hear Mr Buckland at last clear his throat. "I should just like to express my thanks to Miss Anning," he said, "who discovered and extracted this magnificent specimen. It is a shame it did not arrive in time for this most illustrious and enlightening talk by Reverend Conybeare, but once it is installed here, Members and friends are welcome to inspect it. You will be amazed and delighted by this ground-breaking discovery."

That is all she will get, I thought: a scrap of thanks crowded out by far more talk of glory for beast and man. Her name will never be recorded in scientific journals or books, but will be forgotten. So be it. A woman's life is always a compromise.

I did not have to listen any longer. Instead, I fainted.

9

The lightning that signalled my greatest happiness

It was only by luck that I saw her go.

Joe got me up. He come to stand over me one morning when Mam was out. Tray was lying next to me on the bed. "Mary," he said.

I rolled over. "What?"

He didn't say anything for a minute, just looked down at me. Anyone else would think Joe's face was blank, but I could see he was bothered by me staying in bed when I weren't ill. He was biting the inside of his cheek, little bites that tightened his jaw if you knew to look for it.

"You can get up now," he said. "Miss – Mam is fixing it."

"Fixing what?"

"Your problem with the Frenchman."

I sat up, clutching the blanket to me, for it was freezing, even with Tray's warmth beside me. "How's she doing that?"

"She didn't say. But you should get up. I don't want to have to go back upon beach again."

I felt so guilty then that I got up, Tray barking his joy. And I was relieved too. After a day in bed it had got dull, but I felt like I needed someone to tell me to get up before I would do it.

I got dressed and took my hammer and basket and called to Tray, who had stayed with me while I was abed and was eager to get outside. When Colonel Birch give him to me, just before he left Lyme forever, he promised that Tray would be faithful to me. He'd been right.

I stepped outside, my breath turning to fog round my face, it was so cold. The grey sky threatened snow. The tide was in, and Black Ven and Charmouth cut off, so I went the other way, where a narrow strip of land would still be uncovered by the cliffs at Monmouth Beach. Though I had rarely found monsters in those cliffs, sometimes I carted back giant ammonites, like them that were embedded in the Ammo Graveyard, but prised loose from the cliff layers. Tray run ahead of me along the Walk, his claws clicking on the frozen ice. Sometimes he come back to sniff at me and make sure I was following and not going back home. It felt good to be outside, no matter the cold. It was as if I had emerged from a fuzzy fever into a hard, crisp world.

When I drew opposite the end of the Cobb, I saw the *Unity* docked there, being loaded for a journey. This weren't unusual, but what caught my eye amongst all the men rushing about were the silhouettes of three women – two wearing bonnets, the third an unmistakable turban stuck with feathers.

Tray come running back, barking at me. "Shh, Tray, hush now." I grabbed him, fearful they would look over and see me, and I ducked behind an overturned rowboat used to ferry people out to anchored ships.

I was too far away to make out the Philpot sisters' faces, but I could see Miss Margaret handing something to Miss Elizabeth, which she put in her pocket. Then there were hugs and kisses, and Miss Elizabeth took a step away from her sisters, and there was a break in the men running up and down the plank that led on board, and then she was walking up it, and then she was standing on deck.

I couldn't recall Miss Elizabeth ever going on a ship or even a little boat, despite living by the sea and hunting so often on its beaches. Nor had I but once or twice, for that matter. Though they could go by ship to London, the Philpots always chose to go by coach. Some people are meant for water, others land. We were land people.

I wanted to run along the Cobb and call out to them, but I didn't. I stayed behind the rowboat, Tray whining at my feet, and watched as the crew of the *Unity* unfurled the huge sails and cast off. Miss Elizabeth stood on deck, a brave, straight figure in a grey cloak and purple bonnet. I had seen ships leave Lyme many times, but not with someone on board who meant so much to me. Suddenly the sea seemed a treacherous place. I recalled Lady Jackson's body washed up from a shipwreck years before, and wanted to call out for Miss Elizabeth to come back, but it was too late.

I tried not to fret, but to go about my business. I did not look in the papers for news of shipwrecks, nor word of the plesiosaurus' arrival in London, nor of Monsieur Cuvier's doubts about it. This last I knew was not likely to be in the papers, as not being important to most. There were times I wished the *Western Flying Post* would reflect what mattered to me. I wanted to see announcements like "Miss Elizabeth Philpot Safely Arrived in London"; "Geological Society Celebrates Lyme Plesiosaurus"; "Monsieur Cuvier Confirms Miss Anning Has Discovered a New Animal."

One afternoon I run into Miss Margaret outside the Assembly Rooms, going in to play whist, for even in winter they played cards there once a week. Despite the cold she wore one of her outdated feathered turbans, which made her look the part of an aging eccentric spinster with a strange hat. Even I thought that, who had admired Miss Margaret all my life.

When I wished her good day, she started like a dog when its tail is trodden on. "Have you – have you heard from Miss Elizabeth?" I asked.

Miss Margaret give me a funny look. "How did you know she was away?"

I did not say I had seen her ship embark. "Everybody knows. Lyme's small for secrets."

Miss Margaret sighed. "We've not had a letter, but the post has not got through for three days, the roads are so bad. No one has had letters. However, a neighbour has just ridden from Yeovil and brought a new *Post*. There is news that the *Dispatch* ran aground near Ramsgate. That is the ship before Elizabeth's." She shivered, the ostrich feathers in her turban quivering.

"The *Dispatch*?" I cried. "But the plesiosaurus is on it! What happened to it?" I had a horrible vision of my beast sinking to the seabed and being lost to us forever – all of my hard work, as well as the one hundred pounds from the Duke of Buckingham, gone.

Miss Margaret frowned. "The paper said both passengers and cargo are safe and are being transported to London by land. There's no need to fret – though you might have a thought for those on board first rather than the cargo, however precious it is to you."

"Of course, Miss Margaret. Of course I'm thinking of the people. God bless them all. But I do wonder where my – the Duke's – plesie is."

"And I wonder where Elizabeth is," Miss Margaret added, tears welling. "I still feel we should never have let her onto that ship. If it is so easy to run aground as the *Dispatch* did, what might have happened to the *Unity*?" Now she was weeping, and I patted her shoulder. She did not want comfort from me, though, and pulled away, glaring. "Elizabeth would never have gone if it hadn't been for you!" she cried, before turning on her heel and hurrying into the Assembly Rooms.

"What do you mean?" I called after her. "I don't understand, Miss Margaret!" I couldn't follow her into the rooms, however. They were not for the likes of me, and the men standing in the doorway gave me unfriendly looks. I lingered near by, hoping to catch a glimpse of Miss Margaret in the bay window, but she did not appear.

That was the first I knew that Miss Elizabeth went to London on account of me. But I didn't know why until Miss Louise come to explain. She rarely visited to our house, preferring living plants to fossils. But two days after I met Miss Margaret she appeared at the workshop door, ducking her head because she was so tall. I was cleaning a small ichthyosaurus I'd found just before discovering the plesie. It weren't complete – the skull was in fragments and there were no paddles – but the spine and ribs were in a good state. "Don't get up," Miss Louise said, but I insisted on clearing a stool of bits of rock and wiping it clean before she sat down. Tray come then and lay on her feet. She did not speak right away – Miss Louise never were a talker – but studied the heaps of rocks ranged round her on the floor, all containing fossils waiting to be cleaned. Though I always had specimens all round me, now there were even more from waiting while I had been getting the plesie ready. She said nothing about the mess, or the film of blue dust covering everything. Others might have, but I suppose she was used to dirt from her gardening, and from Miss Elizabeth's fossils.

"Margaret told me she saw you and you wanted to know about our sister. We had a letter from her today, and she has arrived safe at our brother's in London."

"Oh, I'm so glad! But – Miss Margaret said Miss Elizabeth went to London for me. Why?"

"She was planning to go to the Geological Society meeting and ask the men there to support you against Baron Cuvier's claim that you fabricated the plesiosaurus."

I frowned. "How did she know about that?"

Miss Louise hesitated.

"Did the men tell her? Did Cuvier write to one of them – Buckland or Conybeare – and they wrote to Miss Elizabeth? And now they're all talking about it in London, about – about us Annings and what we do to specimens." My mouth trembled so much I had to stop.

"Hush, Mary. Your mother came to see us."

"Mam?" Though relieved it was not from the men, I was shocked Mam went behind my back.

"She was worried about you," Miss Louise continued, "and Elizabeth decided she would try to help. Margaret and I could not understand why she felt she had to go in person rather than write to them, but she insisted it was better."

I nodded. "She's right. Them men don't always respond quick to letters. That's what Mam and I found. Sometimes

I can wait over a year for a reply. When they want something they're quick, but they soon forget me. When I want something…" I shrugged, then shook my head. "I can't believe Miss Elizabeth would go all the way to London – on a ship – for me."

Miss Louise said nothing, but looked at me with her grey eyes so direct it made me drop mine.

I decided to visit Morley Cottage a few days later, to say sorry to Miss Margaret for taking her sister away. I brought with me a crate full of fossil fish I had been saving for Miss Elizabeth. It would be my gift to her for when she come back from London. That wouldn't be for some time, as she was likely to stay there for her spring visit, but it were a comfort to know the fish would be there waiting for her return.

I lugged the crate along Coombe Street, up Sherborne Lane, and all the way up Silver Street, cursing myself for being so generous, as it was heavy. When I reached Morley Cottage, however, the house was buttoned up tight, doors locked, shutters drawn, and no smoke from the chimney. I knocked on the front and back doors for a long time, but there was no answer. I were just coming round to the front again to try and peer through the crack in the shutters when one of their neighbours come out. "No point looking," she said. "They're not there. Gone to London yesterday."

"London! Why?"

"It were sudden. They got word Miss Elizabeth is taken ill and dropped everything to go."

"No!" I clenched my fists and leaned against the door. It seemed whenever I found something, I lost something else.

I found an ichthyosaurus and lost Fanny. I found Colonel Birch and lost Miss Elizabeth. I found fame and lost Colonel Birch. Now I thought I'd found Miss Elizabeth again, only to lose her, perhaps forever.

I could not accept it. My life's work was finding the bones of creatures that had been lost. I could not believe that I would not find Miss Elizabeth again too.

I did not take the crate of fossil fish back to Cockmoile Square, but left it round the back in Miss Louise's garden, by the giant ammonite I'd once helped Miss Elizabeth bring back from Monmouth Beach. I was determined that she would one day sift through them and choose the best for her collection.

I wanted to hop on the next coach to London, but Mam wouldn't let me. "Don't be a fool," she said. "What help could you be to the Philpots? They'd just have to waste their time looking after you rather than their sister."

"I want to see her, and say sorry."

Mam tutted. "You're treating her like she's dying and you want to make your peace with her. Do you think that will help her to get well, with you sitting there with a long face saying sorry? It'll send her to her grave quicker!"

I hadn't thought of it that way. It was peculiar but sensible, like Mam herself.

So I didn't go, though I vowed one day I would get to London, just to prove I could. Instead Mam wrote to the Philpots for news, her hand being less upsetting to the family than mine. I wanted her to ask about Cuvier's accusation and the Geological Society meeting too, but Mam wouldn't, as it weren't polite to be thinking about myself at a time like this. Also, it would remind the Philpots of why Miss Elizabeth had gone to London, and make them angry at me all over again.

Two weeks later we got a brief letter from Miss Louise, saying Miss Elizabeth were over the worst of it. The pneumonia had weakened her lungs, though, and the doctors thought she would not be able to return to live in Lyme because of the damp sea air.

"Nonsense," Mam snorted. "What do we have all those visitors for if not for the sea air and water being good for their health? She'll be back. You couldn't keep Miss Elizabeth away from Lyme." After years of suspicion of the London Philpots, now Mam were their biggest supporter.

As certain as she seemed, I weren't so sure. I was relieved Miss Elizabeth had survived, but it looked like I'd lost her anyway. There was little I could do, though, and once Mam had written again to say how glad we all was, we didn't hear anything more from the Philpots. Nor did I know what had happened with Monsieur Cuvier. I had no choice but to live with the uncertainty.

Mam likes to repeat that old saw that it don't rain but pour. I don't agree with her when it comes to weather. I been out upon beach for years and years in days where it don't pour, but spits now and then, the sky never making up its mind what it wants to do.

With curies, though, she were right. We could go months, years, without finding a monster. We could be brought to our knees with how poor we were, how cold and hungry and desperate. Other times, though, we would find more than we needed or could work on. That was how it was when the Frenchman come.

It were one of those glorious days in late June when you know from the sun and the balmy breeze that summer has come at last and you can begin to let go of the tightness in your chest that's kept you fighting against the cold all winter and spring. I was out on the ledges off Church Cliffs, extracting a very fine specimen of *Ichthyosaurus tenuirostris* – I can say that now, for the men have identified and named four species, and I know each one just from a glance. There were no tail or paddles but it had tightly packed vertebrae, and long, thin jaws reaching a point, with the small, fine teeth intact. Mam had already written to Mr Buckland asking him to tell the Duke of Buckingham, who we knew wanted an ichie as company to the plesie.

Someone come to stand near me as I worked. I was used to visitors looking over my shoulder and seeing what the famous Mary Anning were up to. Sometimes I could hear them talking about me from a distance. "What do you think she's found there?" they'd say. "Is it one of those creatures? A crocodile or, what was it I read, a giant turtle without its shell?"

Though I smiled to myself, I didn't bother to correct them. It was hard for people to understand that there had lived creatures they could not even imagine, and which no longer existed. It had taken me years to accept the idea, even when I had seen the evidence so plainly before me. Though they respected me more now I'd found two kinds of monsters, people were not going to change their minds simply because Mary Anning told them so. I had learned that much from taking out curious visitors. They wanted to find treasure upon beach, they wanted to see monsters, but they did not want to think about how and when those monsters lived. It challenged their idea of the world too much.

Now the spectator moved so that he blocked the sun and his shadow fell on the ichie, and I had to look up. It was one of the burly Day brothers, Davy or Billy, I wasn't sure which. I laid down my hammer, wiped my hands and stood.

"Sorry to bother you, Mary," he said, "but there be something Billy and me need to show you, back by Gun Cliff." As he spoke he glanced down at the ichie, checking my work, I expect. I'd got much better over the years at chiselling out a specimen from the rock, and didn't need the Days to help so much, except sometimes to carry slabs of rock back to the workshop.

Their opinion mattered to me, though, and I was glad to see he looked satisfied with what I'd done so far. "What have you found?"

Davy Day scratched his head. "Don't know. One of them turtles, maybe."

"A plesie?" I said. "Are you sure?"

Davy shifted from one foot to the other. "Well, it could be a crocodilly. I never knowed the difference." Recently the Days had begun sea-quarrying in the Blue Lias, and often found things in the ledges off Lyme. They never wanted to understand what they dug up. They knew it made me and them money, and that was all they cared about. People often come to me to help them with what they found. Usually it was a small bit of ichie – a jaw bone, some teeth, a few verteberries fused together.

I picked up my hammer and basket. "Tray, stay," I commanded, snapping my fingers and pointing. Tray come running up from the water's edge, where he had been chasing the waves. He curled his black and white body into a ball and lay his chin on a rock next to the ichie. He was a gentle little dog, but he growled when anyone come near one of my specimens.

I followed Davy Day round the bend that hid Lyme. The sun lit the houses piling up the hill, and the sea was silvery like a mirror. The boats moored in the harbour were strewn about like sticks, abandoned however the water set them on the sea bed at low tide. My heart brimmed with fondness for these sights. "Mary Anning, you are the most famous person in this town," I said to myself. I knew very well I was too full of pride, and would have to go to Chapel and pray to be forgiven my sin. But I couldn't help it: I had come such a long way since Miss Elizabeth first hired the Days for us so many years before, when I was young and poor and ignorant. Now people come to visit me, and wrote about what I found. It was hard not to get a big head. Even the people of Lyme were nicer to me, if only because I brought in visitors and more trade.

One thing did keep me from swelling too much, though, and were a little needle in my heart. Whatever I found, whatever was said of me, Elizabeth Philpot was no longer in Lyme to share it with.

"It be here." Davy Day gestured to where his brother was sitting, holding a wedge of pork pie in his big paw. Near him was a load of cut stone on a wooden frame they were using to carry it. Billy Day looked up, his mouth full, and nodded.

I always felt a little awkward with Billy, now he was married to Fanny Miller. He never said anything, but I often wondered if Fanny spoke harsh words about me to him. I weren't exactly jealous of her – quarrymen are not considered suitable for any but the most desperate women. But their marriage reminded me that I was at the very bottom of the heap, and would never marry. Fanny was getting all the time what I experienced only the once with Colonel Birch in the orchard. I had my fame to comfort me, and the money it brought in, but that only went so far. I could not hate Fanny, for it were my fault she was crippled. But I could not ever feel friendly towards her, nor comfortable round her.

That was the case with many people in Lyme. I had come unstuck. I would never be a lady like the Philpots – no one would ever call me Miss Mary. I would be plain Mary Anning. Yet I weren't like other working people either. I was caught in between, and always would be. That brought freedom, but it was lonely too.

Luckily the ledges gave me plenty of things to think about other than myself. Davy Day pointed at a ridge of rock, and I leaned over and made out a very clear line of vertebrae about three feet long. It seemed so obvious I chuckled. I had been over these ledges hundreds of times and not seen it. It always surprised me what could be found here. There were hundreds of bodies surrounding us, waiting for a pair of keen eyes to find them.

"We was carrying a load to Charmouth and Billy tripped over the ridge," Davy explained.

"You tripped over it, not me," Billy declared.

"It were you, you dolt."

"Not me — you."

I let the brothers argue and studied the vertebrae with growing excitement. They were longer and fatter than an ichie's. I followed the line to where the paddles would be and saw there enough evidence of long phalanges to convince me. "It's a plesiosaurus," I announced. The Days stopped arguing. "A turtle," I conceded, for they would never learn that long, strange word.

Davy and Billy looked at each other and then at me. "That be the first monster we ever found," Billy said.

"So it is," I agreed. The Days had uncovered giant ammonites, but never an ichie or plesie. "You've become fossil hunters."

In unison the Days took a step back, as if distancing themselves from my words. "Oh no, we be quarrymen," Billy said. "We deal in stone, not monsters." He nodded at the blocks of stone awaiting their delivery to Charmouth.

I was astonished at my own luck. There was probably a whole specimen here, and the Days didn't want it! "Then I'll pay you for your time in digging it out for me, and will take it off your hands," I suggested.

"Don't know. We got the stone to deliver."

"After that, then. I can't get this out myself – as you saw, I am working on an ich – a crocodile." I wondered if I were imagining it, but it seemed that for once the Days weren't in complete agreement. Billy was more uneasy about having anything to do with the plesie. I took a chance then at guessing the matter. "Are you going to let Fanny rule what you do, then, Billy Day? Does she think a turtle or crocodile will turn round and bite you?"

Billy hung his head while Davy laughed. "You got the measure of him!" He turned to his brother. "Now, are we going to dig this out for Mary or are you going to sit with your wife while she holds your balls in her claws?"

Billy bunched up his mouth like a wad of paper. "How much you pay us?"

"A guinea," I answered promptly, feeling generous, and also hoping such a fee would stop Fanny's complaints.

"We got to take this load to Charmouth first," Davy said. That were his way of saying yes.

There were so many people upon beach now looking for fossils, especially on a sunny day like this one, that I had to get Mam to come and sit with the plesie so no one else would claim it as theirs. Summers were like that now, and it was partly my fault, for making Lyme beaches so famous. It was only in winter that the shore cleared of people, driven away by the bitter wind and rain. That was when I could go out all day and not meet another soul.

The Days worked fast, and got the plesie out in two days, about the same time I finished with my ichie. As I was just round the corner from them, I could go back and forth between the two sites and give them instructions. It weren't a bad specimen, though it had no head. Plesies seem to lose their heads easily.

We had just got both specimens back to the workshop when Mam called from her table out in the square, "Two strangers come to see you, Mary!"

"Lord help us, it's too crowded here," I muttered. I thanked the Days and sent them out to be paid by Mam, and called for the visitors to come in. What a sight met them! Two monster specimens laid out in slabs on the floor – indeed, covering so much of it the men couldn't even step inside, but hung in the doorway, their eyes wide. I felt a little jolt of lightning run through me, one I couldn't explain, and knew then that they could not be ordinary visitors.

"My apologies for the mess, gentlemen," I said, "but I've just brung in two animals and not had a chance to sort them out yet. Were there something I can help you with?" I knew I must look a sight, with Blue Lias mud all over my face and my eyes flaming red from working so hard to get the ichie out.

The young one – not much older than me, and handsome, with deep-set blue eyes, a long nose, and a fine chin – recovered himself first. "Miss Anning, I am Charles Lyell," he said with a smile, "and I bring with me Monsieur Constant Prévost, from Paris."

"Paris?" I cried. I could not contain the panic in my voice.

The Frenchman gazed at the riot of stone on the floor, and then at me. "*Enchanté, mademoiselle*," he said, bowing. Though he looked kindly, with curly hair and long sideburns and wrinkles round his eyes, his voice was serious.

"Oh!" He was a spy. A spy for Monsieur Cuvier, come to see what I was up to. I stared at the floor, looking at it as he must see it. Laid out side by side were two specimens – an ichie without a tail and a plesie without a head. The plesie's tail was detached from its pelvis and could easily be moved to complete the ichie. Or, I could take the ichie's head, remove some vertebrae from the neck of the plesie, and attach the head. Those who knew the two creatures well wouldn't be fooled, but idiots might buy them. From the evidence in front of him, it was easy enough for Monsieur Prévost to reach the conclusion I was about to join the two incomplete monsters together to create one whole, third monster.

I wanted to sit down with the suddenness of it all, but I couldn't in front of the men.

"I bring greetings from the Reverends Buckland and Conybeare," Charles Lyell went on, oblivious that he was adding fuel to the fire by mentioning their names. "I was Professor Buckland's student at Oxford, and—"

"Mr Lyell, sir, Monsieur Prévost," I interrupted, "I can tell you now I'm an honest woman. I would never fiddle with a specimen, whatever Baron Cuvier thinks! And I will swear on a Bible to it, sirs, that I will! We don't have a Bible here – we had one once for a bit but had to sell it. But I can take you to the Chapel right now and Reverend Gleed will hear me swear on it, if that will do any good. Or we can go to St Michael's, if you prefer. The vicar there don't know me well, but he'll provide a Bible."

Charles Lyell tried to interrupt me, but I could not stop. "I know these specimens here ain't whole, and I swear to you I will set them as I see them, and never try to swap parts. A plesiosaurus' tail might fit onto an ichthyosaurus, but I would never do that. And of course an ichie's head is far too big to fit onto the end of the plesie's neck. It wouldn't work at all." I was babbling, and the Frenchman in particular was looking perplexed.

Then it all started to come down on me, and I had to sit, gentlemen or no. Truly I was ruined. Right there, in front of strangers, I begun to cry.

This upset the Frenchman more than any words could have done. He begun rattling away in French, with Mr Lyell interrupting him and speaking his own slow French, while all I could think of was that I wanted to call out to Mam to pay the Days just a pound, as I'd been too generous and we would need the extra shillings since I would no longer be able to hunt and sell monsters. I would have to go back to the piddling curies, the ammos and bellies and gryphies of my youth. Even then I wouldn't sell so many, as there were that many more hunters selling such things themselves. We would grow poor again, and Joe would never get to set up his own business, and Mam and I would always be stuck on Cockmoile Square and not move up the hill to a better shop. I let myself cry over my future until my tears were spent and the men were silent.

When they were sure I was done crying, Monsieur Prévost pulled a handkerchief from his pocket. Leaning across the slabs so that he wouldn't step on the specimens, he held out the hankie to me like a white flag over a battlefield of stone. When I hesitated, he gestured with it to encourage me, and gave me a little smile that dug deep dimples in his cheeks. So I took it, and wiped my eyes on the softest, whitest cloth I'd ever touched. It smelled of tobacco and made me shiver and smile, for the lightning struck again, just a little. I made to hand it back, now smeared with Blue Lias clay, but he would not take it, indicating that I should keep it. It was then I begun to think maybe Monsieur Prévost were not a spy after all. I folded the handkerchief and tucked it away under my cap, for that was the only place in the room not filthy.

"Miss Anning, please let me speak," Charles Lyell begun tentatively, perhaps fearful I would burst out crying again. I did not; I was done. I noticed then that he was calling me Miss Anning rather than Mary.

"Perhaps I should explain to you what we are doing here. Monsieur Prévost kindly hosted me last year when I visited Paris, introducing me to Baron Cuvier at the Museum of Natural History and accompanying me on

328

geological expeditions in the area. Thus when he wrote to say he was coming to England, I offered to take him to some of the most important geological sites in the southern parts of the country. We have been to Oxford, Birmingham and Bristol, and down to Cornwall and back, via Exeter and Plymouth. Naturally we were keen to come to Lyme Regis and visit you, to go out on the beaches where you collect fossils and to see your workshop. Indeed, Monsieur Prévost has just said he is most impressed by what he sees here. He would tell you himself, but alas, he speaks no English."

As Mr Lyell was speaking, the Frenchman squatted by the ichthyosaurus and run a finger up and down its ribs, which were almost complete and beautifully spaced like iron rail-ings. I could no longer just sit while he was crouching with his thighs so near to me. I picked up a blade, kneeled by the ichie's jaw and begun to scrape at the shale clinging to it.

"We should like to examine the specimens you have found more closely, if we might, Miss Anning," Mr Lyell said. "We would like also to see where they have come from on the beach – they, and the plesiosaurus you found last December. A most remarkable specimen, with its extraor-dinary neck and head."

I froze. His bringing up the most worrying part of the plesie sounded suspicious. "You seen it?"

"Of course. I was there when it arrived at the Geological Society offices. Did you not hear of the drama of it?"

"I heard nothing. Sometimes I feel I could be the man in the moon, for the little I hear of what's happening in the scientific world. I had someone who was going to keep me informed, but – Mr Lyell, do you know of Elizabeth Philpot?"

"Philpot? No, I have not heard that name, I'm sorry. Should I know her?"

"No, no." Yes, I thought. Yes, you should. "What was it you was saying – about the drama?"

"The plesiosaurus was delayed in its arrival," Mr Lyell explained, "and did not reach London until almost two weeks after the Society meeting at which Reverend Conybeare was speaking of it. You know, Miss Anning, at the meeting Reverend Buckland was very complimentary of your collecting skills."

"He was?"

"Yes, indeed. Now, when the plesiosaurus arrived at last, the men could not get it up the stairs, for it was too wide."

"Six feet wide, the frame round it was. I know, for I built it. We had to turn it sideways to get it out this door."

"Of course. They tried the better part of a day to get it up to the meeting rooms. Finally, though, it had to be left in the entranceway, where many Society members came to look at it."

I watched the Frenchman crawl between the ichie and plesie to get round to the plesie's front paddle. I gestured with my head. "Did *he* see it?"

"Not in London, but when we went to Birmingham from Oxford, we stopped *en route* at Stowe House, where the Duke of Buckingham has taken it." Mr Lyell, though polite as a gentleman ought to be, made a little face. "It is a splendid specimen, but rather swamped by the Duke's extensive collection of glittering objects."

I paused, my hand on the ichie's jaw. So this poor specimen would go to a rich man's house, to be ignored amongst all the silver and gold. I could have wept. "So is he –"

I nodded at Monsieur Prévost " – going to tell Monsieur Cuvier that the plesiosaurus isn't a fake? That it really does have a small head and a long neck and I weren't just putting two animals together?"

Monsieur Prévost glanced up from his study of the plesie with a keen look that made me think he understood more English than he spoke.

Mr Lyell smiled at me. "There is no need, Miss Anning. Baron Cuvier is fully convinced of the specimen, even without Monsieur Prévost having seen it. He has had a great deal of correspondence about the plesiosaurus with various of your champions: Reverend Buckland, Conybeare, Mr Johnson, Mr Cumberland—"

"I wouldn't call them my champions exactly," I muttered. "They like me when they need something."

"They have a great deal of respect for you, Miss Anning," Charles Lyell countered.

"Well." I was not going to argue with him about what the men thought of me. I had work to do. I begun scraping again.

Constant Prévost got to his feet, dusted off his knees and spoke to Mr Lyell. "Monsieur Prévost would like to know if you have a buyer for the plesiosaurus," he explained. "If not, he would like to purchase it for the museum in Paris."

I dropped my blade and sat back on my heels. "For Cuvier? Monsieur Cuvier wants one of my plesies?" I looked so astonished that both men begun to laugh.

It took Mam no time to bring me down from the cloud I was floating on. "What do Frenchmen pay for curies?" she wanted to know the minute the men had left to dine at the Three Cups and she could leave the table outside. "Are they looser with their purse strings or do they want it even cheaper than an Englishman?"

"I don't know, Mam – we didn't talk figures," I lied. I would find a better time to tell her I were so taken with the Frenchman that I'd agreed to sell it to him for just ten pounds. "I don't care how much he pays," I added. "I just know Monsieur Cuvier thinks well enough of my work to want more of it. That be pay enough for me."

Mam leaned in the doorway and give me a sly look. "So you're calling the plesie yours, are you?"

I frowned, but did not answer.

"The Days found it, didn't they?" she continued, relentless as always. "They found it and dug it up, and you bought it off them the way Mr Buckland or Lord Henley or Colonel Birch bought specimens off you and called them theirs. You become a collector like them. Or a dealer, as you're selling it on."

"That's not fair, Mam. I been a hunter all my life. And I do find most of my specimens. It's not my fault the Days found one and didn't know what to do with it. If they had dug it out and cleaned it and sold it, it would be theirs. But they didn't want that, and come to me. I oversaw them and paid them for their work, but the plesie's with me now. I'm responsible for it, and so it's mine."

Mam rolled her tongue over her teeth. "You been saying you ain't had recognition by the men, who call the curies theirs once they bought 'em. Do that mean you'll tell the Frenchman to put the Days' names on the label along with yours when they display it in Paris?"

"Of course I won't. They won't list me on the label anyway. No one else ever has." I said this to try to distract from Mam's argument, for I knew she was right.

"Maybe the difference between hunter and collector ain't so great as you been making out all these years."

"Mam! Why are you going on about such a thing when I've just had good news? Can't you leave be?"

Mam sighed and straightened her cap as she prepared to go back out to customers at the table. "All a mother wants is for her children to settle into their lives. I seen you worried about recognition for your work these many years. But you'd be better off worrying about the pay. That's what really matters, isn't it? Curies is business."

Though I knew she meant it kindly, her words cut. Yes, I needed to be paid for what I did. But fossils were more than money to me now – they had become a kind of life, a whole stone world that I were a part of. Sometimes I even thought about my own body after my death, and it turning to stone thousands of years later. What would someone make of me if they dug me up?

But Mam were right: I had become part not just of the hunting and finding, but of the buying and the selling too, and it was no longer so clear what I did. Maybe that was the true price of my fame.

What I wanted to do more than anything was to go up Silver Street to Morley Cottage and sit at the Philpots' dining room table spread with Miss Elizabeth's fossil fish and talk to her. Bessy would bang a cup of tea in front of me and slump off, and we would watch the light change over Golden Cap. I looked up at a watercolour Miss Elizabeth had made of that view and given me not long before our argument – trees and cottages in the fore-ground, the hills along the coast washed in soft light as they backed into the distance. There were no people visible in the painting, but I often felt as if I were there somewhere, just out of sight, looking for curies on the shore.

The next two days I was busy with Mr Lyell and Monsieur Prévost, taking them upon beach to show them where the beasts had come from and teach them how to find other curies. Neither had the eye, though they found a few bits and pieces. Even then my luck were with me, for in front of them I found yet another ichthyosaurus. We were standing on the ledge near to the other ichie's site when I spotted a length of jaw and teeth almost under the foot of the Frenchman. With my hammer I chipped off slices of rock to expose the eye, the vertebrae and ribs. It was a good specimen, apart from a crushed tail which looked like a cart wheel run over it. I confess it were a pleasure to wield my hammer and bring the creature into sight before their eyes. "Miss Anning, you are truly a conjurer!" Mr Lyell exclaimed. Monsieur Prévost too was impressed, though he could not say so in English. I was just as happy that he could not speak, for it meant I could enjoy being in his company without having to worry about what his pretty words might mean.

The men wanted to see more, so I had to fetch the Days to dig out that ichie while I took them to the Ammonite Graveyard at Monmouth Beach, and on along to Pinhay Bay to hunt crinoids. Only once they'd left to go to Weymouth and to Portland were I finally free to return to the plesie. I would have to clean it fast, for Monsieur

Prévost planned to leave for France in ten days. I would be working day and night to get it ready, but it would be worth it. That was how this trade was: for months every day would be just like the last, but for the changes in weather, with me hunting upon beach. Then along come three monsters and two strangers and suddenly I would have to stay up all hours to finish preparing a specimen.

Maybe it were because I was in the workshop all the time till the plesie was done and the men gone that I didn't find out until everyone else in Lyme already knew. It took Mam shouting at me from her perch at the table one morning to get me outside. "What, Mam?" I grumbled as I wiped my hair from my eyes, leaving clay on my forehead.

"It's Bessy," Mam said, pointing. The Philpots' maid was heading up Coombe Street. I run after her and caught up just as she was about to go into the baker's. "Bessy!" I called.

Bessy turned, and grunted when she saw me. I had to grab her arm to keep her from ducking inside. Bessy rolled her eyes. "What you want?"

"You're back! You're – Are they – Is Miss Elizabeth all right?"

"You listen to me, Mary Anning," Bessy said, facing me fully. "You leave 'em alone, do you hear? The last person they want to see is you. Don't you come anywhere near Silver Street."

Bessy had never liked me, so it were no surprise what she was saying. I just had to work out if it were true. I tried to read her face as she spoke. She looked bothered, and nervous and angry. Nor would she look at me direct, but kept turning her head from side to side, as if hoping someone would come and save her from me.

"I'm not going to hurt you, Bessy."

"Yes, you are!" she hissed. "You stay away from us. You're not welcome at Morley Cottage. You almost killed Miss Elizabeth, you did. We thought we lost her one night at her worst, the pneumonia were that bad. She would never have got it if it hadn't been for you. And she ain't been the same since. So you just leave her alone!" Bessy pushed past me into the baker's.

I went back along Coombe Street, but when I reached Cockmoile Square I didn't go over to Mam behind her table. Instead I turned into Bridge Street, crossed the square past the Assembly Rooms and the Three Cups, and started up Broad Street. If I were going to be kept away, I would hear it direct from the Philpots rather than from Bessy.

It was market day, and the Shambles was busy, with stalls extending halfway up Broad Street. The place was thick with people; pushing through them was like trying to wade through the sea with the tide coming in. I kept going, though, for I knew I had to.

With all of the crowd, it took me a moment to spot her, marching down the hill with her quick little steps and her straight back. It was like seeing a vague shape on the horizon that when it comes closer snaps into the clear outline of a ship. At that moment I felt the bolt of lightning pass through me and stopped dead, letting the market crowd part and push round me.

Elizabeth Philpot was surrounded by people, but she herself was alone, unaccompanied by her sisters. She looked thinner, almost skeletal, the familiar mauve dress hanging from her, her bonnet framing a bony face. Her cheekbones and especially her jaw were more prominent, long and straight and hard like an ichie's. But she was walking smartly, as if she knew just where she was going, and when she got closer I could see that her grey eyes were very bright, like a light shone through them. I let out my breath, which I hadn't even noticed I was holding.

When she saw me, her face lit up like Golden Cap does when the sun touches it. Then I begun to run, shoving people out of the way and yet hardly seeming to move at all. When I reached her I threw my arms round her and begun to cry, in front of the whole town, with Fanny Miller at a veg stall staring, and Mam come to see what had happened to me, and everyone who ever talked about me behind my back now talking about me openly, and I didn't care.

We didn't say a word, just clung to each other, both of us crying, even though Miss Elizabeth never cried. No matter all that had happened to me – finding the ichies and plesies, going with Colonel Birch to the orchard, meeting Monsieur Prévost – this was the lightning that signalled my greatest happiness, in all my life.

"I have given my sisters the slip and was just coming to find you," Miss Elizabeth said, when at last we let go. She wiped her eyes. "I am very glad to be home. I never thought I would miss Lyme so much."

"I thought the doctor said you can't live by the sea, that your lungs are too weak."

In response Miss Elizabeth took a deep breath, held it,

and let it out. "What do London doctors know of sea air? London air is filthy. I am much better off here. Besides, no one can keep me away from my fish. Thank you, by the way, for the crate of fish you left for me. They are a delight. Come, let us go down to the sea. I have seen so little of it, as Margaret and Louise and Bessy won't let me out of the house. They worry over me far too much."

She begun walking down Broad Street again, and I reluctantly followed. "They'll be angry at me for letting you do this," I said. "They're already angry that I got you sick."

Miss Elizabeth snorted. "Nonsense. You didn't make me sit on a draughty landing for an evening, did you? Nor go by ship to London. Those follies I take complete responsibility for." She said it as if she weren't sorry for anything she done.

Then she told me about the meeting at the Geological Society and how Mr Buckland and Reverend Conybeare agreed to write to Cuvier, and Mr Buckland said nice things about me to all the gentlemen gathered, even though they weren't recorded in the minutes. And I told her about Monsieur Prévost and the plesiosaurus that was going to Monsieur Cuvier's collection in the Paris museum. It was wonderful to talk to her again, but underneath our words I felt anxious, for I knew I had to do something difficult. I had to say sorry.

We were strolling along the Walk when I stepped in front of her and stopped so that she could go no further. "Miss Elizabeth, I'm sorry for all the things I said," I blurted out. "For being so proud and full of myself. For making fun of your fish and your sisters. I were awful to you and it was

338

wrong, after all you done for me. I've been missing you these many years. And then you went off to London for me and almost died—"

"Enough." Elizabeth Philpot held up her hand. "First of all, you are to call me Elizabeth."

"I – All right. E– Elizabeth." It felt very odd not saying Miss.

Miss Elizabeth begun walking again. "And you need not apologise for my trip to London. After all, I chose to do it. And indeed, I am grateful to *you*. Going to London on the *Unity* was the finest experience of my life. It changed me for the better, and I don't regret it in the slightest."

There *was* something different about her, though I could not say exactly what it was. It was as if she were more certain. If someone were sketching her they would use clear, strong lines, whereas before they might have used faint marks and more shading. She was like a fossil that's been cleaned and set so everyone can see what it is.

"As for our disagreement, I too said things I regret," she continued. "I was jealous of you, as you said then, not just of Colonel Birch, but of your knowledge of fossils too – your ability to find them and understand what they are. I will never have such skills."

"Oh." I looked away, for it was difficult to return her bright, honest gaze. All of our walking and talking had brought us to the bottom of the Cobb. The waves were bursting over it, sending out a spray that made the seagulls wheel up into the sky.

"Do you know, I should like to see the Ammonite Graveyard," Miss Elizabeth declared. "It has been so long."

"Are you sure you can go that far, Miss Elizabeth? You mustn't tire yourself after your illness."

339

"Stop fussing. Margaret and Bessy fuss enough. Not Louise, though, thank heavens. And call me Elizabeth. I will keep insisting until you have learned."

So we continued, arm in arm along the beach, talking until at last we had no more to say, like a storm that blows itself out, and our eyes dropped to the ground, where the curies were waiting for us to find them.

10

Silent together

Mary Anning and I are hunting fossils on the beach, she her creatures, I my fish. Our eyes are fastened to the sand and rocks as we make our way along the shore at different paces, first one in front, then the other. Mary stops to split open a nodule and find what may be lodged within. I dig through clay, searching for something new and miraculous. We say very little, for we do not need to. We are silent together, each in her own world, knowing the other is just at her back.

Postscript.

The reader's patience

Mary Anning's name was first published in a scientific context in France in 1825, when Georges Cuvier added it to a caption for an illustration of a plesiosaur specimen, in the third edition of his book *Discours sur les révolutions de la surface du globe* (Discourse on the revolutionary upheavals on the surface of the earth). She was first mentioned by name in Great Britain in a paper by William Buckland on coprolites in 1829; by then she and Buckland had worked out that bezoar stones were the faeces of ichthyosaurs and plesiosaurs. She also discovered the first complete pterodactyl (now called a pterosaur) in Great Britain, and the squaloraja, a transition animal between sharks and rays, which became a type specimen.

Mary Anning never married, living with her mother until Molly's death in 1842. They moved from Cockmoile Square to a house with a shop front on Broad Street in 1826. Mary's dog Tray was killed in a landslip in 1833; it missed Mary by a few feet. Mary died of breast cancer in 1847 at the age of forty-seven. She is buried in the church yard of St Michael's, which she joined later in life. Her ichthyosaurs and plesiosaurs are on display at the Natural

History Museum in London, and the headless plesiosaur Cuvier bought from her is on display in the Palaeontology Gallery of the Musée National d'Histoire Naturelle in Paris.

In 1834 the Swiss scientist Louis Agassiz came to Lyme and studied Elizabeth Philpot's fossil fish collection. He thanked both Elizabeth and Mary Anning in his book *Recherches sur les poissons fossils* (Research on Fossil Fish) and named fish species after both of them. Elizabeth outlived both Mary Anning and her sisters, dying in 1857 at the age of seventy-eight. Her nephew John inherited her estate, and in 1880 his wife donated the Philpot fossil collection to the Oxford University Museum of Natural History, where there are still drawers full of her superb specimens. Elizabeth's great nephew Thomas later established the Philpot Museum in Lyme Regis. Rather fittingly, the museum is now housed in a handsome building on the site of the Annings' house in Cockmoile Square, where amongst many treasures concerning the town's history you can see on display the fossil hammer Mary's father made for her.

Joseph Anning became a full-time upholsterer in 1825, married in 1829, and had three children. Apparently Mary Anning did not get on with his wife. Joseph managed to achieve the respectable life he craved, overseeing parish relief and becoming a church warden.

Colonel Thomas James Birch became Thomas James Bosvile in 1824, when he inherited the title and the family estate in Yorkshire. He died in 1829.

William Buckland did find a woman to marry him, in 1825 – she was sitting opposite him in a coach and reading a volume of Cuvier. He continued to eat his way through the animal kingdom, and to try to reconcile geology with his religious beliefs. He later became Dean of Westminster School, but towards the end of his life he suffered from mental illness and had to be placed in an asylum.

Between 1830 and 1833 Charles Lyell published *Principles of Geology*, which became the seminal text on modern geology; Charles Darwin took it with him on his famous voyage on the *Beagle*.

Jane Austen visited Lyme in September 1804, and there is no reason why she and Margaret Philpot could not have been in the Assembly Rooms at the same time. Indeed, she did meet Richard Anning, for she went to his shop to have him give her a quote on fixing the broken lid of a chest. According to a letter she wrote to her sister, he charged far too much, and she took her business elsewhere.

Remarkable Creatures is a work of fiction, but many of the people existed, and events such as Colonel Birch's auction and the Geological Society meeting where Conybeare talked about the plesiosaur did take place. And Mary did indeed write at the bottom of a scientific paper she had copied out: "When I write a paper there shall not be but one preface." Sadly she never did write her own scientific paper.

Twenty-first-century attitudes towards time and our expectations of story are very different from the shape of Mary Anning's life. She spent day after day, year after year, doing the same thing on the beach. I have taken the events of her life and condensed them to fit into a narrative that is not stretched beyond the reader's patience. Hence events, while in order, do not always coincide exactly with actual dates and time spans. Plus, of course, I made up plenty. For instance, while there was gossip about Mary and Buckland

and Mary and Birch, there was no proof. That is where only a novelist can step in.

I would like to thank the following: the staff of the libraries at the Geological Society and the Natural History Museum, London; the staff of the Lyme Regis Philpot Museum, the Dorset County Museum and the Dorset History Centre in Dorchester; the Dinosaur Museum, Dorchester, where I first learned of Mary Anning; Philippe Taquet of the Musée National d'Histoire Naturelle, Paris; Paul Jeffery at the Oxford University Museum of Natural History; Maureen Stollery for her help with Philpot genealogy; Alexandria Lawrence; Jonny Geller; Deborah Schneider; Susan Watt; Carole DeSanti; and Jonathan Drori.

Most of all, I would like to thank three people: Hugh Torrens, who knows more about Mary Anning than anyone and has been very cordial to me. Jo Draper, who is a saint, opening up the files at the Philpot Museum and sending me bits and pieces of information about everything, and who wears her erudition lightly and with great humour. Finally, Paddy Howe, fossil hunter extraordinaire, who gave me many fossils and took me to the beach between Lyme and Charmouth to find more, teaching me with patience, intelligence, and grace.

Further Reading

Deborah Cadbury, *The Dinosaur Hunters: A True Story of Scientific Rivalry and the Discovery of the Prehistoric World*, 2000 (UK); as *Terrible Lizard: The First Dinosaur Hunters and the Birth of a New Science*, 2001 (US)

William Conybeare and Henry De La Beche, papers on the ichthyosaur and plesiosaur for the Geological Society, 1821, 1822, 1824, reprinted in *The Dinosaur Papers, 1676–1906*, edited by David B. Weishampel and Nadine M. White, 2004

Jo Draper, *Mary Anning's Town: Lyme Regis*, 2004

John Fowles, *A Short History of Lyme Regis*, 1991

Charles C. Gillispie, *Genesis and Geology: A Study in the Relations of Scientific Thought, Natural Theology, and Social Opinion in Great Britain, 1790–1850*, 1951

S.R. Howe, T. Sharpe and H.S. Torrens, *Ichthyosaurs: A History of Fossil "Sea-Dragons"*, 1981

W.D. Lang, various papers on Mary Anning in the *Proceedings of the Dorset Natural History and Archaeological Society*, 1936–1963

Christopher McGowan, *The Dragon Seekers: The Discovery of Dinosaurs During the Prelude to Darwin*, 2001

Judith Pascoe, chapter on Mary Anning in *The Hummingbird Cabinet: A Rare and Curious History of Romantic Collectors*, 2005

Patricia Pierce, *Jurassic Mary: Mary Anning and the Primeval Monsters*, 2006

George Roberts, *Roberts' History of Lyme Regis and Charmouth*, 1834

Martin J.S. Rudwick, *Bursting the Limits of Time: The Reconstruction of Geohistory in the Age of Revolution*, 2005; and *Worlds Before Adam: The Reconstruction of Geohistory in the Age of Reform*, 2008

Philippe Taquet, "Quand les Reptiles marins anglais traversaient la Manche: Mary Anning et Georges Cuvier, deux acteurs de la découverte et de l'étude des Ichthyosaures et des Plésiosaures," in *Annales de Paléontologie* 89 (2003): 37–64

Crispin Tickell, *Mary Anning of Lyme Regis*, 1996

Hugh Torrens, "Mary Anning (1799–1847) of Lyme; 'the greatest fossilist the world ever knew'," in *British Journal for the History of Science* 28 (1995): 257–84